D1561846

F
ADL   BC   0000038737
      Adler, Warren
      Target Churchill

Target Churchill

By

Warren Adler and James C. Humes

Inquiries: customerservice@warrenadler.com
STONEHOUSE PRODUCTIONS

Distributed by Stonehouse Productions
For ordering, contact Stonehouse Productions
customerservice@warrenadler.com

Cover design by Andy Carpenter Designs

Praise for Warren Adler

"Warren Adler writes with skill and a sense of scene." — *The New York Times Book Review* on *The War of the Roses*

"Engrossing, gripping, absorbing… written by a superb storyteller. Adler's pen uses brisk, descriptive strokes that are enviable and masterful." — *West Coast Review of Books* on *Trans-Siberian Express*

"A faced-paced suspense story…. Only a seasoned newspaperman could have written with such inside skills." — *The Washington Star* on *The Henderson Equation*

"High tension political intrigue with excellent dramatization of the worlds of good and evil." — *Calgary Herald* on *The Casanova Embrace*

"Poignant…believable, moving." — *New York Daily News* on *Banquet Before Dawn*

"A man who willingly rips the veil from political intrigue." — *Bethesda Tribune* on *Undertow*

Warren Adler's political thrillers are:
"Ingenious." — *Publishers Weekly*
"Diverting, well-written and sexy." — *Houston Chronicle*
"Exciting." — *London Daily Telegraph*

Praise for James C. Humes
"James Humes, a brilliant speechwriter and advisor of Presidents of the United States, has long been conspicuous in the extensive ranks of Churchill's American admirers…." — **LORD LEXDEN**, *The House of Lords Magazine*.

"Humes -- who knew Churchill personally -- brilliantly captures the extraordinary life of this gifted, complex, and often troubled leader." —*A&E Biography*

"In hundreds of studies of Churchill, no one else, remarkably enough, has focused on Churchill's predictions and prophecies. James Humes has produced a book that is unique as well as necessary for an understanding of statesmanship." —**DAVID EISENHOWER**, author and senior fellow at the Foreign Policy Research Institute on *Churchill - The Prophetic Statesman*

"Gives us a stunning but overlooked version of conjectural history. Humes outlines dozens of Churchill's own spectacular prophecies, revealing him to be a Nostradamus of the political and military events of the twentieth century." —**MICHAEL KEANE**, author of *Patton: Blood, Guts, and Prayer* on *Churchill - The Prophetic Statesman*

"Engaging memoir… laced with wickedly funny anecdotes; the politicos, presidents, and British royalty whom Humes fondly remembers receive star billing. —*Library Journal* on *Confessions of a White House Ghostwriter – Five Presidents and Other Political Adventures*

Unlike modern wordsmiths, typically journalists enjoying a political interlude, Humes began as an actual politician….. Humes stocks an immense store of stories that have been enjoyable for those who have listened to him or have read his many books." — *Booklist* on *Confessions of a White House Ghostwriter – Five Presidents and Other Political Adventures*

"Intriguing historic approach to public speaking. Humes creates a valuable and practical guide." — Roger Ailes, CEO, Fox News on *Speak Like Churchill, Stand Like Lincoln: 21 Powerful Secrets of History's Greatest Speakers*

The Witch of Watergate
Washington Masquerade

SHORT STORIES
Jackson Hole, Uneasy Eden
Never Too Late For Love
New York Echoes
New York Echoes 2
The Sunset Gang

PLAYS
The War of the Roses, Knight of the Ocean Sea, The Sunset
Gang (Musical), Libido

* * * *

Select Works by James C. Humes
Churchill: Speaker of the Century (Pulitzer Prize nomination)
Confessions of a White House Ghost Writer
The Wit and Wisdom Of Ronald Reagan, Speak Like
Churchill
Stand Like Lincoln
Winston Churchill (A&E Biography)
Eisenhower and Churchill: The Partnership That Saved the
World
Nixon's Ten Commandments of Statecraft
Which President Killed a Man?
Citizen Shakespeare: A Social and Political Portrait

* * * *

"The poet's eye, in fine frenzy rolling,

Doth glance from heaven to earth, from earth to heaven;

And as imagination bodies forth

The forms of things unknown, the poet's pen

Turns them to shapes and gives to airy nothing

A local habitation and a name.

Such tricks hath strong imagination...." — William Shakespeare

A Midsummer Night's Dream, Act V, Scene 1

Chapter 1

From the shattered window of the German warden's former office, General Ivan Vasilyevich Dimitrov observed the crowded yard; men packed like sardines, freezing in the icy late-February cold, a sorry, stinking lot of traitors awaiting transport to oblivion. He chuckled at the euphemism, rubbing the stubble on his chin, squinting from the smoke of the cigarette hanging from his lips.

Following in the wake of the advancing combat troops, Dimitrov always chose the largest prison in town for his temporary *Narodny Kommisariat Vnutrennikh Del* command post, invariably an annex to a now-abandoned Gestapo headquarters with its underground cells and thick-walled torture chambers, the interior tailor-made for his purposes.

Dimitrov's *NKVD* rifle regiments had trailed the path of General Zhukov's astonishing offensive now heading swiftly towards Berlin. Lavrentiy Pavlovich Beria, NKVD Chief, had directly ordered them to show no mercy, to concentrate on anything with the barest stench of collaboration or disloyalty. As soon as Zhukov's combat troops rolled out, Dimitrov's job began. He had ordered his commanders to not put a fine line on discriminating between the Germans and Russians, men, women or children.

"Find them. Waste no time on guilt or innocence. If there is the slightest suspicion of collaboration, consider them all guilty, especially Germans and deserters. Take what you want. Do what has to be done. We are entitled to the spoils." he told his officers. "Exact revenge. Remember what the Nazi bastards had done to us. Remember

Stalingrad. And don't spare the women. Fill them to overflowing with hot Russian sperm. They need a lesson in humiliation." Beria had told Dimitrov how much he enjoyed his verbal reports.

"They will regret what they did to our country for generations to come." Beria had asserted, adding how pleased Marshal Stalin had been with his reports of Dimitrov's successes. For his work, Dimitrov had received a Hero of the Soviet Union citation from Stalin himself.

A compact man with a long angular face creased deeply on either cheek, dark eyes that turned downward at their edges, thin mobile lips that could curl into a deceptively warm half-smile, and a prominent pointed chin that he used effectively to signal a demand, Dimitrov patted the side pocket of his heavy overcoat where he had put the file. The confidential papers had come by courier directly from Beria's office in Moscow.

Nodding with satisfaction, he knew he had been onto something. The information in the file had confirmed the man's story. Dimitrov marveled at the reach of the NKVD intelligence operatives.

Beria had scrawled a comment on the top of the document: *Mole?*

Dimitrov knew what he meant.

A sharp knock broke his concentration. He looked toward the door.

"Come."

"The transport is ready, Comrade. The excavation of deserters completed." the man said, standing stiffly, wearing the uniform and NKVD insignia of his rank of Major.

Dimitrov nodded, pointing his chin in the direction of the prison yard, a mixed bag of deserters and civilians. Some had even dressed as women to escape detection.

Dimitrov laughed. *Heaven will have to receive them with sore assholes.*

"Nearly one thousand traitors in the group," the officer said, understanding the gesture.

"Names and numbers?"

"Duly recorded, Comrade."

Dimitrov nodded. The relatives of the deserters would receive their colorful "death in action" notices signed by Stalin himself, suitable for framing. It would be displayed for generations like a diploma—another brainstorm by Beria.

The man was a genius, Dimitrov acknowledged.

He had learned from the Katyn event, which liquidated twenty-one thousand bastard Poles. No more shots to the back of the head, the typical NKVD execution method. No more old German bullets—too transparent if discovered, although that was highly unlikely. Since then, they had used only recently captured German mounted machine guns and modern ammunition.

Dimitrov had run the operation to then eliminate the liquidators of Katyn. A thorough job, he remembered, earning Beria's deep respect, and proving his loyalty to the head of the NKVD. They were both Georgian, both from the Sukhumi district, which counted a great deal in matters of trust as far as Beria was concerned.

The Georgians were always given the tough jobs; the deportations and executions. Where the Germans had occupied, traitors were endemic and had to be rooted out. Executions were commonplace and vast populations had to be deported. Dimitrov had done his duty with skill and efficiency and had come to Beria's attention early in his NKVD service. Promotions and decorations had come his way. He was the youngest General in the NKVD.

"Always remember," he was told after he had accomplished his first assignments. "You are Beria's man now. You are responsible only to me. We must be forever on the lookout for traitors in our midst. Intrigues are everywhere, even those who we think are our friends. That is why I must demand total obedience, and absolute loyalty without question. Do you understand, Ivan Vasilyevich? Our goal is to rid our nation of all of its enemies, real and potential, without mercy, without hesitation, without remorse."

Beria's words had been an inspiration. If he believed in God, they would be a Holy Writ.

13

"And the others?" Dimitrov asked the waiting captain.

"In the holding cell below as ordered."

"How many?"

"Forty-two."

Dimitrov had cut them from the pack—randomly selected SS officers—for special treatment. It would be a test of the man's purpose.

"We move in the morning," Dimitrov said, looking at his watch. "They are advancing like lightning. The front is already fifty kilometers ahead. I think Zhukov will be in Berlin in ten days, two weeks at the most." He looked at his watch. "Say 0600 hours."

"We will be ready, Comrade."

They had been busy for three days, rounding up deserters and German prisoners. They had "processed" a decimated division of the SS, and interrogators were working them over in the honeycombs below.

"Be merciless. Think of Stalingrad. Think of the millions slaughtered. Show them what we Russians think of the master race. Save some for show. Pick carefully."

Except for the information garnered for Beria's eyes alone, whatever military intelligence had been gathered was sent to Zhukov's people. Not that it mattered. It was a complete rout, the German army in full retreat, running like frightened rabbits.

"We must look ahead now, Dimitrov," Beria had told him in their last conversation as the troops rolled through Poland in the first days of the new offensive that had begun in January.

For Dimitrov, the occasion had been festive, bonding him and his Chief further. Beria had chosen a villa for his overnight stay, formerly occupied by a captured turncoat Pole who had been recently executed. The Pole's wife and her twin thirteen-year-old daughters still lived in the villa and acted as servants to the Russian brass passing through.

Dimitrov had reported his progress with the deserters and German prisoners. Beria was deeply impressed with the body count.

It had always struck Dimitrov how scholarly Beria looked, with his pince-nez spectacles and small balding head. With his low voice and precise, slow sentences, he seemed more like a university professor than the powerful head of the NKVD.

"The real work will start after the war," Beria had told him, periodically polishing his pince-nez as he spoke over brandy and cigars. "Stalin will soon appoint me to the politburo, putting us further on the inside."

Dimitrov loved the reference to "us."

"A lot is going to happen. We will liberate the workers and destroy the bourgeoisie of every nation on earth: Europe first, then Asia, and the best prize of all, the United States. The day is coming. Westerners are weak and without backbone. They are too soft and sentimental. We must not hesitate to weed out the weak in our midst. Their absurd sense of virtue will destroy them. We are the future. To achieve it, all potential enemies must be destroyed. One must keep one's focus on the greater good."

Beria had flicked the ashes on the floor and dipped the sucking end of his cigar in the brandy.

"Ivan Vasilyevich, my dear comrade, we Georgians are the leaders of the future. Stalin, Beria, Dimitrov. Loyal men like you will rise with me."

He lowered his voice almost to a whisper as he bent close to Dimitrov's ear.

"Stalin will not live forever…"

He put his hand on Dimitrov's knee. For a brief moment, the gesture seemed like a sexual pass.

And if it were? Dimitrov asked himself, knowing the answer.

Beria lifted his snifter and swallowed the remnants. Dimitrov did the same, and Beria poured again, remaining silent for a long stretch.

"You know, Ivan Vasilyevich, we have the greatest intelligence service on the globe, the best spy network in the history of the world. I know. I built it. Others might claim otherwise but

15

Stalin knows it was I who made it happen. We will win, make no mistake about it. The West will boil in its own corruption."

Beria shook his head in contempt.

Two weeks earlier, he had returned from Yalta, where Stalin had met Roosevelt and Churchill to discuss the future course of the war and its aftermath.

"Stalin played them like a violin, but Churchill is the more dangerous of the two, distrustful and suspicious. Roosevelt is a naïve fool. Besides, he seemed weak and not attentive. The days of the Western countries are numbered, Ivan Vasilyevich. There is a world for us to take."

Beria's nostrils flared as he sniffed the brandy. He nodded as if he were answering a question in his mind. He took a deep pull on the cigar and blew the smoke into the air.

"We are moving fast for other reasons," he whispered. "The Americans are making a superbomb, something to do with splitting the atom. Roosevelt has promised Stalin that, if the bomb works, he will share the process with the Russians. Churchill has not been informed. He would be the fly in the ointment. The Germans are working on it as well, and we need whatever secret technology we can capture, not to mention the uranium deposits in Saxony and Czechoslovakia and the lab in Dahlem, hence the speed of this offensive."

He lowered his voice to a barely audible whisper.

"Stalin has given me the mission of building such a bomb."

"Congratulations, Comrade. I salute you."

Dimitrov lifted his glass in tribute. Beria nodded and sipped. For a long moment, he was lost in thought.

"They leak like a sieve," he said, no longer whispering. "Stupid democracies! They have no real insight into espionage; they are amateurs. We are light years ahead of them."

Beria chuckled, showing small teeth in a tight smile.

"In Yalta, we had every room in their residences bugged, heard every conversation that took place privately between

Roosevelt and Churchill. My own son, Sergo, did the translations. I can tell you that Churchill despises us; he is our nemesis. Roosevelt, naïve idiot, believes that we will be allies forever. We will play the game as long as we can, but make no mistake, Ivan Vasilyevich, the big war is ahead, and we have already organized our army. We are placing people in readiness everywhere—agitators, organizers, propagandists, assassins." Beria chuckled. "We are *everywhere;* you cannot imagine how deep we are embedded."

He paused and shook his head.

"But for now, we must be clandestine. We must smile and pet our Western friends. Keep the knife hidden inside the velvet glove, especially in America. Now we are beloved: the brave Russians who sacrificed to get rid of the Nazi scourge! We must keep that love affair going as long as we can after the war. But our people are in place, burrowing below the surface, like moles. We need moles, Ivan Vasilyevich, hidden weapons ready for use, while our people eat away at their diseased entrails."

Beria took a sip of his brandy and looked deeply into Dimitrov's eyes.

"Your command of English will be an asset, Ivan Vasilyevich."

"And French, Spanish, and Italian, Comrade," Dimitrov said with pride, reminding Beria of his other natural skills. He was not averse to blowing his own horn, when and where appropriate.

"We will need all of your many skills in the future, Ivan Vasilyevich. We will be giving orders in all of your languages. And you will come with me however high we climb."

Dimitrov felt his heartbeat accelerate, a thrill rising up from his crotch.

"I will serve you with my life, Comrade."

Beria reached out with his glass and clinked it against Dimitrov's. After a long pause, Beria drank, then roused himself, stood up, threw his still-lighted cigar on the carpet and ground it down with his foot.

"Now, Ivan Vasilyevich," he said smiling. "Let us treat

ourselves to the women of the establishment.

What followed, Dimitrov decided, was an experience that would linger in his memory for years. It was the ultimate bonding experience between the two men. They fucked the mother and her two daughters in each other's sight. The women had been quickly compliant. Beria had simply pointed his pistol at the head of one of the twins.

"Will it be this gun?" Beria snickered. "Or this?" he said, opening his fly.

Chapter 2

An NKVD soldier brought the man into the office. Dimitrov sat behind his desk, the file open. The soldier placed the disheveled and dirty man in SS uniform in a chair in front of the desk. His rank was *Obersturmbannführer*, a comparatively high rank for someone still so young-looking. He was tall, blond, with cerulean blue eyes deeply embedded behind high cheekbones. Despite his condition, the man exuded arrogance. Cleaned up, he would look like the Aryan ideal.

"So you are an American," Dimitrov said in English.

The man nodded and smiled.

Dimitrov noted that his teeth were surprisingly white, his lips moist, and two dimples appeared at either end of his smile.

"Your English is quite good, General," the man said, as if it were the compliment of a superior.

"And yours equally, *Obersturmbannführer*," Dimitrov said, offering a soldier-to-soldier greeting. Normally, he would never address an SS officer by his rank. "But then, you are an American."

"By birth, not by choice, General."

Dimitrov studied the man, glanced again at his file, then lifted his face and grinned. He reached into the side pocket of his overcoat and offered him an American cigarette, a Lucky Strike, which had been taken from a high-ranking Luftwaffe officer.

"Well, well, this one has traveled far," said the American, pulling the cigarette from the pack and smelling it.

Dimitrov lighted it, and the American sucked deep and blew out a cloud of smoke.

"Nobody makes a better cigarette," the American said.

Dimitrov turned back to the file.

"Camp Siegfried, was it? Yaphank, Long Island. A summer camp for American Nazis, the German-American Bund."

"You people are good," the American chuckled. "I'll say that. You've burrowed right into the FBI." He shook his head again. "They confiscated the records, that I knew. So you found my name?"

"Franz Mueller."

"Just as I told you. I'm an American citizen. Born in Hoboken, New Jersey. My father was born in Munich. Came to the States in 1913. I was born in 1918."

Dimitrov made a quick calculation. Twenty-seven.

"A quick rise. You might have been a general. Too bad."

The American shrugged indifferently and took another deep draw on the cigarette.

"And your mother?"

"Why must you know the provenance of potential dead meat?"

"You are a pessimist, Mueller."

Mueller and Dimitrov exchanged glances. Then Mueller shrugged his obvious submission.

"I was five when she died in a car crash . . . some bastard Jew drunk. My father never remarried," Mueller said, blowing out another cloud of smoke, this one in the direction of Dimitrov.

"And now, you are still Franz Mueller. Why did you not change your name?"

Mueller smiled broadly.

"After . . . well, after . . ." Mueller hesitated, scratched his neck, and averted his eyes. "I came to Munich in September 1938. My uncle Karl, my father's brother, took me in. He had a son named Franz, two years younger. We were both named after my grandfather."

"Two Franz Muellers," Dimitrov said, amused by the story. "What happened to the other one?"

"Frail bastard. Died of pneumonia that same winter I arrived. I

20

became him. Simple. So, you see, I was born under a lucky star. Besides, I was running, and I needed an authentic identity."

"Running?"

"Why the hell do you think I left America, General?"

Dimitrov observed him closely, admiring his brass.

"I killed two men." He mimed a pistol with his fingers. "No big deal these days, call it a *vorspeise*. It is now a common gesture."

The man baffled Dimitrov, the way he spoke, so open, so unruffled. He could see why his promotions had been rapid.

"Who were they?"

"Couple of Yids."

Mueller's eyes searched for contact with Dimitrov's, as if he were seeking confirmation of a similar attitude.

Dimitrov cautioned himself. Beria's sister was married to a Jew, and there were Jews of influence in high places. Stalin's late wife was Jewish. Trotsky was Jewish. Ilya Ehrenburg was a powerful Jewish writer, a favorite of Stalin, and his articles were considered fiery and patriotic rallying cries. Not that he mourned the Jews that had been destroyed by Hitler. Indeed, he had secretly marveled at the efficiency and scope of the destruction. Not a bad idea, he had thought it.

Nevertheless, he decided not to pursue the ethnic aspect of Mueller's admission. It seemed irrelevant to his purposes. Besides, a proper SS man was *supposed* to hate Jews and show them no mercy.

"Were you suspected of these murders?"

"I could never be certain. I didn't stay around long enough to find out."

"Why did you kill them?"

"We had this great spot in Long Island, Camp Siegfried. Trains of brown shirts came every weekend. We had brown uniforms, swastika armbands. We sang Nazi songs. The American flag hung side by side with the Nazi flag. It was great fun. We had rifle practice. I was a crack shot. We started a boycott of all the stores in the area. They had to display this certain label that designated that they were

21

supporters, otherwise we wouldn't go in. The Yids didn't like that and started a counter boycott. There were two ringleaders, the Finkelstein brothers. *Finkelstein.*"

He shook his head and chuckled.

"I followed them home one day and shot them."

He made a gesture as if he were holding a rifle.

"Got them at one hundred yards—bang, bang—right through their Yid heads."

"Surely, there was an investigation?"

"Of course. But the cops, you see, loved us. We knew how to grease the skids. Problem was the Jews called in the FBI. You know the power they have. Control everything in America. Just like in Germany."

Dimitrov made no comment. What lingered in his mind was "crack shot."

"Only my father knew, you see, no one else. This was my own idea. Anyway, when the FBI stuck their nose in, I was shipped to Germany to my father's brother in Munich."

"And the investigation?"

"Came to nothing. I was gone. The rifle was at the bottom of the Atlantic. No witnesses. No prints. "

"And you never went back?"

"I got into this, the SS, the real thing. No more playtime like the Bund in America. Hell, General . . . " He seemed suddenly wistful. " . . . I loved it. We killed so many fuckin' Jews."

He sucked in a deep breath.

"And Russians, *Obersturmbannführer,*" Dimitrov reminded him.

"Hate to say it, but the Führer fucked up. He should have hit England, left Russia alone. Am I right? Look at us. You've got us by the balls. We're over, General, kaput."

He curled his lips in a gesture of disgust.

"So why tell me you're American? What did you hope to gain by such an admission?"

"I'm still alive, aren't I? And here I am sitting in your office."

22

He lifted the nub of his cigarette, held it up like a specimen. "You give me American cigarettes. Okay, General, I've had my jollies. Now, I'm in the survival business. I know what NKVD guys do, you're the cleanup squad, the executioners. Hitler is over. The SS was fun while it lasted. They catch Himmler, they'll tear out his balls. Fact is, General, our boys didn't measure up—all that hailing and goose-stepping, all that ritual. I was one good fucking SS man. I dug the whole thing. I loved it. And I still believe, in the end, we will win. But die for it now? I'm not ready. No, dying is not an option at present. You have a plan to keep me alive. I'll buy that. But die for it? That's another matter entirely."

"You call this loyalty, Mueller?"

This was a man after his own heart, Dimitrov thought, *a brave, arrogant bastard with a survival instinct.*

Mueller sucked in a last puff, then stamped out the nub before it burnt his fingers.

"You got to know when to hold and when to fold. You guys have been making your way across Eastern Europe and now into Deutschland. Here's the way I figure it: It's more than likely your next war will be with the Americans and their European stooges. Wouldn't be such a bad thing if you won. In America, like in Germany, maybe even like in Russia now, the Yids run everything. That's my war. Someday, you guys will get the message and start getting rid of your Kikes, like Hitler. Maybe we didn't finish the job, but someone will. I'm volunteering, General. Besides, it's my only chance to avoid being dead meat."

Dimitrov was astonished by the man's cheek. He admitted that some of the man's slang baffled him, but he had gotten the gist of it.

"Did your father know you were SS?"

"Proud of it. Only he's dead now; I'm a fucking orphan."

"Do you have siblings?"

He shook his head.

"I'm an only child. Poor me." He looked up. "Got another cigarette?"

23

Dimitrov offered him another cigarette from the pack of Lucky Strikes and lit it.

"And your uncle? Was there an aunt?"

"They're still in Munich."

Dimitrov's mind began to race with ideas and possibilities.

"Women? A wife? A sweetheart? Children?"

Mueller smiled.

"I've had my fair share," he chuckled. "Nothing permanent. I've been lucky." He inhaled and looked at his cigarette ash. "I hear your troops have fucked their way across the Continent."

It sounded to Dimitrov like an obvious accusation. He ignored it. He was on another track.

"Let me ask you, Mueller. Would you go back to America?"

Mueller's eyes narrowed.

Dimitrov noted a flicker of optimistic expectation.

"Why ask? You know the answer." He paused. "How would you get me there? You know, without complications."

"Never mind."

"What's the catch?"

"I don't understand."

"Quid pro quo, General. There's no free lunch."

Again Dimitrov was confused by the slang. Mueller apparently understood.

"I mean, what do I have to do?"

"I don't know, perhaps you'd be too much of a risk."

"Risk?" Mueller reflected for a moment. "I get it. I go back to America to do a job for you."

"Something like that."

Dimitrov observed him closely.

"Of course, you could be the wrong choice."

"Your call, General. I'm game if you are."

"Game?"

"American talk," Mueller said. "You see I'm tailor-made to pass. I'm the real thing."

24

At that moment, a sharp knock sounded on the office door.

"Yes?" Dimitrov called.

A voice could be heard beyond the door: "The division awaits orders, comrade."

"Give the order to move them out. I will follow shortly."

Dimitrov got up from behind his desk and signaled to the American.

"Come with me, Mueller."

They moved through the dank, brick-lined corridors, and then to a stairwell, followed by four Russian soldiers with NKVD markings holding automatic weapons. Dimitrov led them to a large holding cell; inside were the forty-odd SS officers. They were seated, packed together with their hands tied behind their backs. The room stunk of feces and urine.

"What a bunch of pigs," Dimitrov said.

Mueller didn't answer, and his face's expression seemed neutral and indifferent.

"Hand this man your weapon," Dimitrov ordered one of the Russian soldiers.

He looked momentarily confused but handed the weapon to Mueller.

"You know how this works?" Dimitrov asked.

"My expertise, General."

"Shoot them, Mueller," Dimitrov ordered, pointing with his chin. "Shoot your SS shit comrades."

Mueller smiled and, without hesitation, sprayed the occupants of the cell with bullets. The men screamed and blood began to puddle on the floor. When the bullets ran out and some men were still alive, Dimitrov ordered the remaining soldier to hand over his weapon. Without missing a beat, Mueller continued the killing spree. Some men were still alive, writhing in pain. Mueller carefully finished them off.

"Now them," Dimitrov said, pointing with his chin at the two NKVD soldiers.

Mueller promptly shot them both then threw the weapons on the floor, now rust-colored, puddling with blood.

"Like a Coney Island shooting gallery," Mueller muttered, as they moved into the corridor, tracking bloodstains on the stone floor. "Hell, they weren't worth shit. We were supposed to win."

This man has possibilities, Dimitrov thought. He would discuss it with Beria.

"Did I pass, General?"

"Not yet, *Obersturmbannführer*, not yet."

Chapter 3

For the first time in thirty years, Winston Churchill couldn't sleep. Even in the bleakest days of the war, he could just will himself into a catnap in limousines, trains, or planes. At night or in his regular nap after lunch each day, he would no sooner hit the pillow, than he would doze off. Now, it was like the days after the Gallipoli disaster in 1915, when he had been blamed for the deaths of over twenty thousand Anzacs. That incident had made him a temporary insomniac.

The poor lads had been mowed down by machine guns from the heights overlooking the Turkish seacoast where they had just landed. Churchill had pondered the disaster for years, reviewing it over and over in his mind. If only Lord Kitchener had sent in the troops at the same time Churchill had directed the Royal Navy to bombard the straits leading to Constantinople . . . Would the results have been different? Despite all that had passed since then, the question came back periodically to haunt and depress him. It had not been his finest hour.

Considering the long history of victories and defeats—including the most recent one, his electoral defeat—his mind still harked back to Gallipoli, always Gallipoli. It eclipsed everything before or since.

Tonight, even the two brandies and sodas Churchill had downed before dinner—and then the bottle of Valpolicella during the meal to wash down the veal—didn't seem to help. Not to mention the two whiskeys and sodas after dinner. He rolled over again in

27

sleeplessness. Having nothing to do, he decided—nothing to plan, nothing to work on, inaction—bred insomnia. He could simply not shake his despondent mood.

The seventy-year-old British politician tossed again in the mammoth bed that had been custom-made for an Italian industry mogul who had built this marble monstrosity of a lakeside villa in the twenties.

Churchill had always heard that after the death of a loved one, there is first denial, then anger before acceptance. He had gone through the process numerous times—with his parents, with his infant daughter, Marigold, who had died at two and a half, and old friends lost in the two bloody wars of his lifetime.

Losing the post of Prime Minister had hit him a lot like a death, for which he was still mourning, locked between denial and anger. Yes, the British gave him credit for winning the war, but didn't they realize they could now lose the peace? Stalin could be a Bolshevik Hitler who would overrun Europe. Who would rally the empire? That Socialist bore, Clement Attlee? Churchill had once referred to him as "a modest man, with a great deal to be modest about." Well, Attlee had gotten his revenge.

Churchill was sweating. He pulled himself out of bed to open the windows to catch the lake breeze. He needed his rest for tomorrow. He was meeting some Brigadier General colleague of Alex, Sir Harold Alexander.

He was sure Alex had taken the Brigadier General aside, imagining what he had told him: "Hold Winnie's hand a bit. He needs tender, loving care. This is not the best time for him."

Churchill felt a brief flash of anger at the imagined conversation.

Well, I'll have a message for him to take back to dear Alex.

He could not abide pity. His countrymen had rejected him and the Conservative Party after the stunning victory over Hitler. As leader of the opposition, he was merely a voice now, powerless, whining, and ineffective. *So much for gratitude!* But hadn't he been rejected many times before?

For some reason, the image of that old bull at that Royal Agricultural Show that he had opened at Kelso years ago when he was an MP for Dundee flashed into his mind; this huge Aberdeen-Angus bull called Canute had been paraded in front of the assemblage. His career as stud was over. He was a spent force now, a relic, just another old bull to be sent out to pasture.

Odd, these memories . . . Not old Winston! he thought, pugnaciously.

But then, Churchill reminded himself, he couldn't take it out on dear Alex who had gone to great lengths to find this vacation villa in Italy. Besides, it was better than being in London, where every street or square seemed to remind him of some critical moment in the recent war.

When he had moved out of 10 Downing Street in July, the head of the Savoy Group of Hotels had graciously let him use his personal suite at Claridge's when he was in London. Unfortunately, the suite had a balcony. One night, when he was unable to sleep, he had walked out on that balcony. For a brief moment, he felt the urge to jump. He could not believe that his depression had reached that point, and it frightened him. He vacated the suite the next day, switching to one that did not have a balcony.

He called these fits of melancholy his "black dog"— oppressive, deep depression that filled him with ennui and self-loathing. Any attempt by Clementine or anyone else to lift him from his morass was resented and met with hostility. His aide, Brendan Bracken, once asked him why he called it his "black dog." He had answered that *dog* spelled backward is *God*—it is the opposite of God, it is hell, a black hell.

He had said, "Brendan, if death is black velvet, depression is a prickly black."

It wasn't simply the Labour victory, which was bad enough, but it was the size of their victory that was so humiliating and appalling. He was entitled to his black dog. Besides, he had had a premonition. It had come to him in a dream and he had awakened with his pajamas soaked with perspiration.

In the dream, he was lying in a hospital bed. He could not move. Suddenly, a white-coated attendant slowly pulled a white sheet over his head. He had little trouble interpreting the dream.

When the early returns were broadcast on BBC, Clemetine had tried her best to console him.

"Winston, perhaps it's a blessing in disguise."

"If so," he had shot back, "it's certainly well disguised."

Attlee of all people! It gnawed at him. Actually, he liked the man. He had been a loyal lieutenant in the wartime coalition. The problem was deeper than just a lost election. The fate of Great Britain was in the balance. Men like Ernest Bevin and Herbert Morrison and their fellow trade union Marxists did not understand the true depth of Stalin's ambition. He had personally taken the measure of the man and his cohorts. Soon the Soviet Union would own Poland, Czechoslovakia, Hungary, Romania, Bulgaria, and the entire Eastern Europe. Perhaps even Germany would fall into its orbit as well, and Greece and Italy, and more—perhaps the world. Shades of Adolph.

Didn't they understand that socialism in Moscow was a different beast from socialism in London? It was predatory, not some utopian dream of social engineering but tyranny imposed by brutality. Russian Marxists believed in revolution by tyranny. They had contempt for free elections or any other freedoms—like freedom of speech, freedom of assembly, freedom of religion. He knew in his gut what Stalin wanted: a Soviet Union that embraced the world.

He had been appalled with the *Herald* and *The Guardian* characterizing Stalin as some warm and cuddly teddy bear. Roosevelt, too, was certain he had charmed Stalin into a true friend. Did the Labour stalwarts and Franklin really believe that?

There, he told himself.

There was the seed of his discontent. There were the thoughts that stole his sleep. There was the origin of his black dog. It was neither disappointment nor rejection nor the futile expectation of his countrymen's gratitude but fear, not merely for his country, for the world. With that epiphany, he fell, at last, into a deep slumber.

It was not the cold dawn light that awakened him but the "old man's alarm"—the clock in his bladder. For him to sleep for eight-and-a-half hours straight was a kind of sexagenarian record. The bathroom bowl reminded him of the lake. Instead of going back to sleep, Churchill decided to take a swim. For the first time in weeks, he felt the first tremulous signs of recovery and, with them, the courage and energy to brave the morning chill.

He remembered the code flashed on every Royal Navy ship in the sea when he became First Lord of the Admiralty for the second time in 1939: Winston is Back!

Perhaps, he thought, *perhaps.*

He donned his old-fashioned, navy, striped bathing suit that covered his chest and made him look like a bloated balloon. Actually, he preferred no suit at all, but chuckling at the thought, decided to avoid alarming the neighbors who might think some odd blimp-like sea monster had polluted the lake.

He cautiously descended the steps of the escarpment that bordered the lake. At the lapping edge of Como's waters, he offered a toe, then a foot. He shivered. Then, shouting lines from Macbeth— "Let me screw my courage to the sticking place!"—in he plunged.

Soon the cold became bearable, and he lay on his back to capture the visual joy of the early-morning sunrise. He knew it was a day of decision, and this brief respite in the lake would, he was certain, clear his mind of the cobwebs of depression.

As he was about to finish his swim, Churchill stopped floating and submerged himself, walking along the pebbly and sandy bottom, then rising to the top. It reminded him of the time he had explained to an acquaintance about the disaster at Gallipoli, his resignation from public life, and the trauma he suffered afterwards.

He had likened it to the experience of a deep-sea diver who has the shakes when he returns to dry land. As he climbed up the cliff steps, he felt no shakes or shivers. Exhilaration was fast replacing ennui and discouragement.

He was reminded, too, of what he had read about those river baptisms they have in the American South. The preacher dunks you and you come to the surface hearing hallelujahs from the congregation. He wanted to cry out his own version of hallelujah and a rousing *Hip, Hip Hooray.*

As he mounted the slope to the villa, he thought of Solomon's words in *Proverbs,* "As cold waters to a thirsty soul, so is good news from a far country."

When he got back to his room, he dried himself and quickly fell into a sound sleep. At ten thirty, Churchill heard a soft persistent knock on the door.

"Signore Churchill."

It was the voice of the maid.

Churchill quickly donned his green dressing gown adorned with gold dragons. The Italian maid carried in an aquamarine tray, the color of the lake, decorated with his favorite flower, the Marigold, the name that he had bestowed on his beloved dead child. Oddly, it reminded him of his dear friend Dwight Eisenhower who had led the Allies to their military victory. Aside from their roles in the war, they had bonded deeply because of this strange coincidence of their children's deaths. Eisenhower had lost his first son, Dwight, within three months of Churchill's daughter's death.

The maid placed the breakfast tray on a table in front of the window. On the tray were two pitchers, one of hot coffee and another of hot milk, two croissants, and a little plate of plum preserves.

He looked at the tray with resignation. He had not been able to get the maid to understand that an English breakfast consisted of eggs, fried tomatoes, bacon, and fried bread; it was futile. But his mood became brighter when he suddenly remembered what Somerset Maugham once told him, "Winston, the only way to dine well in England is to have three breakfasts a day."

Smiling at the recollection, he recalled another breakfast comment when Field Marshall Montgomery came in to find him tucking into bacon and eggs in Number 10. At the sight of what he was eating, Monty fumed.

"That is an unhealthy breakfast. Look at me. I don't eat meat, I don't smoke, I don't drink, and I'm 100 percent fit."

Churchill had growled back, "I eat meat three times a day, I smoke ten cigars a day, I drink, and I'm 200 percent fit."

Sipping his café au lait and missing the morning English newspapers, Churchill was determined to keep his black dog at bay. Later, he decided, he would spend part of the sunny morning hours painting, a passion that he found wonderfully therapeutic.

Painting at the lakeside, Churchill wore the zippered, blue siren suit, which he had designed for himself during the war to allow him to leap from nude to some presentable garb in the case of an air raid or a sudden emergency meeting in the middle of the night. On most occasions, cabinet ministers and generals had found the prime minister in his siren suit when they met with him in the underground war room.

He was proud of his fashion statement, which he called his "rompers," although Clementine had a contrary view. His recollection of her critique always brought a smile to his face.

Once, he had called her from the war room: "Clemmie," he excitedly exclaimed, "how long do you think it took me to get dressed for my meeting with Pug?"

Harold "Pug" Ismay was a General in charge of military strategy.

"At least fifteen minutes," was Clementine's guess, "from taking off your pajamas to getting into your suit."

"Thirty-two seconds—I timed it with my new siren outfit," Churchill boasted.

"But, Winston, you look so ridiculous in it—like a fat penguin who couldn't fit into his usual dinner clothes."

Churchill observed the sun as it began to hide itself in a nest of billowy clouds framed by a blue sky. He daubed some azure tincture from the palette and concentrated on the landscape, taking his mind further and further from the black dog that had plagued him.

Painting, he had learned, offered a different kind of challenge, one that used a different part of his mind. He likened it to a farmer who rotated the fields for the planting of his crops. Painting rested that part of the brain he used in writing by employing another part. While using his hands to paint, his subconscious was working on a speech or chapter he was writing. He knew that while he was creating with his paints, the writing side of his mind was percolating.

He had his daughter Sarah to thank for his taking up painting. Years ago, just after Gallipoli and his being fired as the youngest First Lord of the Admiralty, he had thrashed around for something to keep his mind off his terrible disgrace. The family had gone to the South of France. On the beach, he had spied Sarah's little coloring box. She gave him his first lessons, for which he was eternally grateful.

But painting was only one of his exercises in extending his creative brainpower. At Chartwell, he laid long walls of bricks and would often find other chores to use his hands, especially when his brain needed relief from his intense long hours of concentrating on his creative work. But his most ardent secret personal weapon was his discovery of the benefits of midday napping.

After a short doze in the mid-afternoon, his eyes covered by a black-silk band, he would awake completely refreshed. He likened it to erasing the blackboard in the classroom at Harrow. It was one thing to use the eraser and wipe away what you had written and try to write again, but after sleep, it was as if the blackboard had been washed down clean. Thus, he had discovered, his mind scrubbed clean after a nap. Previous attempts were erased, and he could start afresh. He had kept to this schedule religiously every day of his adult life.

Hours later, he heard Sarah's voice, "Father, your guests have arrived."

His daughter Sarah wore white slacks that clung neatly to her figure. Her chartreuse blouse was a striking contrast to her chestnut hair. Sarah was a part-time actress in her early thirties. She had inherited her father's flair for the dramatic—both in her acting and painting, where she relished the vibrant tones that her father liked also.

His children were all different: Randolph was a journalist like his father had been; Diana and Mary, like their mother, had married politicians, and Sarah had inherited her father's artistic side. He was grateful for her comforting presence.

Clementine had urged her husband to accept Alex's offer of a villa. She thought the sun and painting might break through and wash away his melancholy. When Churchill had agreed, she had declined to accompany him, sending Sarah in her place to act as hostess. Although she had begged off on the grounds that there were still moving chores at Number 10, Churchill suspected that, she, too, needed some time alone.

Dear Clemmie, he thought, missing her terribly.

She had invested her entire life in his career. His pain was her pain, and the loss of the Prime Minister's office had hit her equally as hard, perhaps harder.

Sarah took her father's hand and gently guided him up the slight slope back to the villa. These days, the media characterized him as an old man past his prime, which galled him, but her father didn't look old to Sarah. Sure, his gait may have been a bit shambling and, at times, unsteady. But the pink face was still that of a cherub, with blue eyes that could still twinkle merrily. She adored him.

The villa commanded the top of the hill, yet its stark fascist architecture clashed with the soft curves of the Mediterranean hills and the Nile blue of Como's waters, as if a modern rail station had been erected in marble and then nailed to the top of the hill. Churchill likened it to an alien invader stamping its tyranny on an inhospitable landscape. The villa had once been the headquarters of the British Army in Italy. Before that, it was rumored to be a place where rich playboys took their girlfriends. To know that his large bed had been put to good use amused Churchill.

At the villa, Sarah took command of the military guests and supervised the introductions.

"I'm Derek Luddington, Mr. Churchill," the officer intoned, shaking hands with Churchill.

Luddington was wearing the tan uniform of the British Army. He was coatless in the hot sun, but his shirt was topped with the red epaulets of a Brigadier General. He was slender and of medium height with a neatly trimmed brown moustache.

He introduced his aide, "And this is Major Cope."

"A pleasure to meet you, Mr. Churchill."

Churchill nodded. Cope was a small, dapper man with black hair slicked into two matching halves.

"General," boomed Churchill, "I hope you will convey to Field Marshall Alexander my thanks for arranging this vacation idyll."

"Father," interrupted Sarah, "look what the General has brought you, compliments of Sir Alexander. Some smoked salmon and a bottle of champagne."

Churchill observed that the champagne was not Pol Roger, his favorite, but Veuve Clicquot. He silently admonished Alex, thinking he would have to make do. The gift was hardly mouthwash and would serve well for lunch.

Sarah offered drinks, and the men both ordered gin and tonics. She gave her father his usual brandy and pouring herself a healthy straight scotch.

He knew, of course, the purpose of the visit. Churchill's views had weight in the general's circles. He was an avowed Churchill believer and a good and loyal friend. He had been heartbroken at Churchill's defeat.

For Harold Alexander, only Churchill understood the big picture, and these men were part of the periodic assessment of his friend's insight into the fast-moving events of the postwar era.

They took their seats in the white metal chairs around a circular metal table on the veranda under a yellow umbrella that advertised Martini & Rossi, the Italian vermouth.

The conversation mostly dwelled on the ending of the war in

Japan and the ceremonies of surrender to the Americans and British on the battleship *Missouri*. Churchill remarked how gallant and fitting for Macarthur to let the frail and haggard General Wainwright, who had been imprisoned by the Japanese on the Philippines, receive the sword from the Japanese.

"It wouldn't have happened so quickly without the atomic bomb, would it?" offered Luddington.

"Truman showed some spine on that," Churchill muttered. "I thought he might be dissuaded by those lily-livered intellectuals around him."

Churchill paused and shook his head.

"Beastly weapon! Lucky Hitler didn't get it first. Now the Russians are trying to get it. Can you imagine? Roosevelt was on the verge of giving Stalin those secrets. If the war had lasted, he might have. I hope Truman has the good sense to keep it out of his hands."

"Do you think he has?" Luddington asked.

"Has what?"

"The good sense," Luddington explained.

Churchill chuckled.

"He looks like a Manchester shopkeeper, but his looks are deceiving. He's a lot tougher than he appears—as he has demonstrated."

The men waited through a long pause; then he nodded as if he had given himself permission to expound further.

"I talked to him at length in Potsdam. The only time we were alone was just after we met. He whispered in my ear, 'Mr. Churchill, I must have a chance to speak to you privately.' That night he came to my bedroom, and I turned up the volume of the radio and told him to whisper because I was sure the Soviets had listening devices planted everywhere.

"It was the matter of the superbomb Truman told me. They would drop it only three weeks later in Hiroshima. Then he said, 'Mr. Churchill, I'm going to tell Premier Stalin tomorrow that the bomb is operational. I'm sure he knows what we were up to, but I doubt that he knows it's ready for use.' 'Then don't tell him,' I said. 'Why even corroborate any information about the bomb?' 'Because,' he said, running a chill down my spine, 'those were President Roosevelt's instructions.' He went further. He said that he had uncovered a memorandum suggesting that he offered the Russians the formula for making the bomb. 'And will you obey these instructions?' I asked. 'We shall see,' he said. Imagine that! We shall see. I also told him that if he felt honor bound to tell Stalin that it was operational, then slip it in as nonessential information between other items like MacArthur's Pacific strategy, the Kuril Islands, the Nuremberg trials, the refugee problem."

"Did he do it?" Luddington interjected.

"I can't be certain, although I understand that when the bomb was finally dropped on Hiroshima, Stalin screamed bloody murder at Harriman, the U.S. ambassador in Moscow, because he was not told about the date in advance."

"Do you think Truman would really share those atomic secrets with the Russians?"

"I can't be certain, although I would suspect that Franklin might have done it if the war had dragged on. *Might* have, I stress, although I feel certain I would have talked him out of it. As for Truman, I can't be certain. Not that it would matter. I am no longer at 10 Downing."

Churchill's face reddened with a brief flash of anger. It was the one subject that could threaten the return of his black dog. Sarah sensed this and tried to abort the conversation with cheerful laughter.

"Don't let Father get started on that or lunch will get cold. Come in now."

They rose from their seats and followed her to the dining room. The table was of Venetian origin with ornate carvings on the side panels. Plates of chilled melon and prosciutto were set on mats. Sarah asked the Brigadier General to open the champagne and pour into the fluted glasses.

Churchill held up his glass in a mock toast.

"To the Phoenix," he said, "that great mythical bird, master of resurrection."

The visitors laughed nervously, apparently understanding the reference, which was hardly subtle.

Was it possible, he wondered, *to rise from the ashes?*

"To you, Mr. Churchill," offered Luddington. "If it wasn't . . . "

Churchill quickly interrupted the toast. He knew exactly what was coming. Although the reminder of his leadership during the war could be comforting, he did not wish to dwell on the past, which triggered thoughts of ingratitude and insult.

"To the king," he said, lifting his glass, foreclosing on any future toasts.

"The king," the others chimed in.

As always, Churchill dominated the table talk. Increasingly on his mind was what he saw as Stalin's growing threat. Unfortunately, few were listening. It had been exactly the same in the early days of Hitler. He had been vociferous in his opposition to appeasement, a lone voice. It was happening again. He reiterated his suspicion of Stalin's motives and the danger he posed to the Western democracies.

"Why must I be cast in the role of the canary in the coal mine?" he asked his guests rhetorically.

The two luncheon guests exchanged glances. Churchill was certain that they, too, were inclined to buy the line that he was exaggerating the threat. Such thoughts now permeated the thinking in Great Britain and in America.

"Out of power, finding a pulpit will be more difficult than ever. These are indeed dangerous times. Think of Stalin with the bomb. Imagine him having a weapon that has more destructive power than twenty thousand tons of TNT, two thousand times the power of our own Grand Slam, once the most powerful bomb in the world. Putting that in the hands of the Russians is a frightening prospect."

"But, Father," Sarah said, "Look at it from their point of view. They see themselves as powerless against the Allies. The Americans and us, we own the bomb, remember, that should be enough to hold the Russians in line."

The guests looked at her and nodded.

"Hold Stalin in line? Don't be absurd, Sarah. These people have an agenda to spread their control over the world. Their agents are undoubtedly burrowed in everywhere. They want a Marxist world. Hegemony." He chuckled, "You see? Even my own daughter has doubts. Such is the fate of any sailing ship that tries to buck the prevailing winds. Tack here, tack there, but keep your eye on the objective."

"But, Mr. Churchill," Luddington said. "You are a world-renowned and respected figure. Surely, you can find a pulpit to make your views known. And you are a writer as well."

"Gentlemen, out of power is out of power. I can speak, yes. But my voice as former Prime Minister is considerably diminished."

"My father would rather paint and write these days," Sarah said, with an admonishing glance at her father.

Ignoring her remark, Churchill proceeded to return to his earlier theme, revealing his principal worry: the atomic bomb in Stalin's hands.

"I was told by Edward Stettinius, Roosevelt's last Secretary of State, as well as his aide, Hiss, that a memorandum had been prepared for Roosevelt by Hopkins and Hiss, urging him to give Stalin the secrets. He died before he could act."

"Would Truman do that?" Luddington asked, a deep frown creasing his forehead.

"I think not. Let me amend that. I *hope* not. Can he be such a fool? Who knows? That's what Stalin is demanding, and I understand that the new tenant of Number 10 is sympathetic!"

Churchill paused.

"Quite believable, I'm afraid. Attlee, you know, was always a sheep in sheep's clothing. If either of them consents to such an appalling decision, it would be a disaster."

"Can they be stopped?" Luddington asked.

"Who will stop them?"

"Perhaps you, sir," Luddington said.

"Must I remind you that I am at this point merely an opposition voice in Parliament? Mr. Truman does not call to ask my advice."

"But, Father," Sarah interjected, obviously hoping again to put an optimistic turn on the conversation. "You could accept that invitation in March."

Churchill sighed regretfully.

"Perhaps," he began, and then fell silent.

"Father has been invited to speak at a college in America," Sarah said, directing the news to the guests. "Truman will introduce him."

"Not much of a college," Churchill muttered. "Where in America was it?"

"Westminster College in Fulton, Missouri. Two hundred twenty students."

"Hardly an international forum, Sarah," Churchill replied gruffly.

"But, Father, it is Truman's state, and with him to introduce you, it will become automatically a center of international interest."

"Really, Sarah, hardly Harvard," he persisted. "You'll recall they gave me a degree a couple of years ago."

She produced the invitation, which was typed on White House stationery with a handwritten postscript from President Truman. She read the president's scrawled words, as she had done a number of times since the invitation had been received.

"'This is a very fine old college in my state. I will be there to introduce you.'" She looked pointedly at her father. "Now how can you turn that down, Father?

They had discussed the invitation at length, and Churchill had asked her to find an atlas. He had always been an inveterate reader of maps, ever since his days as a subaltern in India. He had always carried a map book with him.

Sarah had found one in the library, and both father and

daughter studied it carefully. "Father, Fulton is west, actually southwest, of St. Louis, almost a hundred miles or so."

She had pointed a finger towards Fulton and directed her father's eyes to the spot.

"What do the Americans say: A hick town? A hick college in a hick town."

"But with the President introducing you and after your speech, it will never be hick again. Besides, they still love you in America, Father." She paused. "It is called the Green Lecture, and there is a $4,000 honorarium."

"Unthinkable!" he said. "To be introduced by the President and accept money? Absolutely not."

Although he dismissed the suggestion, he had promised to give it some thought, but Sarah had continued to lobby him and now in front of witnesses where he would be more vulnerable.

Churchill chuckled, amused at his daughter's spirit. She had always been the rebellious child. The two guests were silent as they watched this domestic byplay between father and daughter. He turned to his guests.

"You see? Do you think I can withstand this daughterly bombardment?"

The men shrugged, obviously not wanting to get involved in the dispute.

"Then you'll accept?" Sarah persisted.

"Have I a choice, daughter?"

"Only one, Father."

"Well, then . . ." He paused for effect. "Why not? The old Hussar goes west." He laughed. "Guns blazing."

By then the lunch was coming to an end. The men offered their compliments to the cook, and then Churchill asked Sarah to bring him the box of Romeo y Julieta cigars that Herman Upmann had sent him recently. He offered them to his guests who declined. He clipped one, lit the end carefully, and sucked in a deep drag, his face beaming with contentment.

"A cigar, you know, is one of the few vices yet remaining for the advanced in age."

He looked at the men, smiled, and fell into another long, brooding silence. He found himself recalling Potsdam and Yalta, assessing his own behavior. Had Stalin bested them? Should he have been more forceful, less willing to go along with Franklin at Yalta and Truman at Potsdam. He was fast coming to the opinion that Stalin had won the day at both conferences. He took some deep puffs on his cigar.

"I remember once when I was invited to have a drink with Stalin in Potsdam, I felt it was rude not to match him drink for drink of Russian vodka. After we had drained most of the bottle, and Stalin was questioning me in general terms about our intentions in Greece and our position on Poland as he touted the new 'liberation' committee that was running that country, I saw this aide furiously writing down anything and everything that the Russian interpreter reporting my reactions said to Stalin.

"I said to him, 'Premier Stalin, why the need of taking notes?' Next afternoon, Uncle Joe walks over to me with his English translator, pushes his pipe into my chest, and amid chuckles, announces, 'I've destroyed the notes and the notes taker.'"

"He sacked the aide, Mr. Churchill?" asked Luddington.

"Oh, yes, literally, General." Churchill paused for effect. "He had been executed that morning."

"Not *executed?*" said the astonished Luddington.

"Oh, yes, a bullet to his head I'm told. I had the sense that he thought I would laugh." Churchill shook his head and sighed. "This man is a killer. The reports of the Russian offensive last year are appalling: indiscriminate killing, rape, looting. He thought Russians in the lands occupied by the Germans had been brainwashed into the Nazi philosophy. His NKVD troops went on a killing spree targeting Russians and Germans alike. The man is a killer who enjoys killing."

"Chilling," Luddington said.

"Way of life, gentlemen. There is an apocryphal story I have heard about some woman from Zagreb who, when informed about my demise as prime minister, proclaimed, 'Oh, poor Mr. Churchill. I suppose he will now be shot.'"

Churchill chortled and the two men laughed appreciatively.

"This is the way Stalin handles dissent—off with their heads!" Churchill shrugged.

"What did Stalin think of Roosevelt?" Luddington asked.

"He charmed poor Franklin; they really bonded. It was appalling, and yet, he had told others that he thought Roosevelt was merely a rich playboy, soft as butter and easily manipulated."

"And you, Sir?" Luddington let the question hang in the air. "I mean, how did you feel about Roosevelt?"

"You may recall it took me quite a while to get him to act on our behalf." Churchill shook his head. "Nevertheless," he continued, "we became good friends in the process. He was a great man, a master politician."

He grew distant and silent for a long moment.

"God, I miss Franklin; I loved him. England is forever in his debt."

There was another long pause, and Churchill noted that his two guests eyed him expectantly. He was, he knew, holding court and he reveled in the opportunity, not wishing it to end. He signaled by a nod that he was no longer being reflective and would welcome fresh questions.

"And what of Byrnes, the new Secretary of State? Where does he stand in all this?"

He noted that Luddington was being deliberately vague, but he took "all this" to mean the attitude towards the Soviet Union.

Ah, Churchill thought, *British intelligence, for some reason, is probing.*

He wanted to ask Luddington if this visit's pithy fruits would make their way not only to Alex but also to MI6 and perhaps, the Russians. Churchill secretly suspected that Communist moles had invaded MI6.

"Byrnes, yes, Byrnes," Churchill remembered. "Met him

at Potsdam . . . a southerner with a drawl like honey. Truman calls him 'Jimmy.' I'm told he was put out a bit when Roosevelt picked Truman over him for Vice President, an office he had coveted. But then, politics being what it is, Roosevelt chose Truman. Perhaps Roosevelt thought that Truman might be more compliant. Indeed, he kept him at arm's length."

He checked himself. Sarah admonished him with a glance. He was rambling a bit. *Back to Byrnes!* he rebuked himself.

"Byrnes is no political innocent. He was once the majority leader in the Senate until Roosevelt put him on the Supreme Court. Then Roosevelt made him the 'Czar' of war mobilization somewhat like what I had Beaverbrook do for me. Like Max, Byrnes speaks to Truman like a peer with a capital *P*—without a pretense of subservience. I liked that in Beaverbrook—but in our cabinet the Prime Minister is 'first among equals.' Not so in America—the cabinet members are puppets of the President."

"I hear he's not pro-Soviet," said Luddington. "At least, we've been reading that in the articles on Byrnes' trip to Paris where he talked to DeGaulle."

"Perhaps. But they say that 'while Byrnes roams, Truman fiddles.'"

Churchill chuckled at his little joke.

"Remember, he is an instrument of the President, and Truman, for some reason, is wary of standing up to the Soviets. Frankly, his attitude is baffling."

"Surely the Soviets don't want war?" asked Luddington. "After what they've gone through?"

Churchill eyed the man with some curiosity, and then resigned himself to the present reality. Luddington was merely echoing the typical appeasement line that was in vogue on both sides of the Atlantic.

"Oh no," he said with sarcasm. "I'm sure they want 'peace'—a piece of Poland, a piece of Czechoslovakia, a piece of Hungary, tomorrow, the world. Remember that one. What the Soviets want is to 'Bolshevize' the Balkans."

He turned to Sarah, the brief dispute forgotten.

"Do you like that Sarah?"

Sarah shrugged.

"Father, do you think we've kept our visitors too long?"

"Not at all, Sir," Luddington said.

Churchill nodded.

"Sarah is hinting that it's time for me to contemplate the cosmic infinities horizontally."

"Father means his daily nap."

"Yes," said Churchill. "One of the two splendid Spanish contributions to the betterment of the civilized state of man, which I embraced in my early years as a military observer in Spain. One is the siesta and the other the Havana."

Churchill smothered the remains of his cigar in the ashtray and rose to bid farewell to his visitors. They exited with the amenities of thanks to Sarah, as Churchill ascended the marble staircase.

In his bedroom, Churchill changed into pajamas for his afternoon nap. It amused him that Sarah had cleverly persuaded him to accept the invitation to speak at the small college in the Midwest.

But then she did have a point. Truman and he had last met at Potsdam. His sense of history clicked in. Perhaps this could be the pulpit he had wished for.

He picked up the phone. He needed to talk to Clemmie. Luckily, he found her at Chartwell, where she had just arrived from London. Hearing her voice always filled him with joy.

"Oink, oink," Churchill imitated a porcine grunt.

"Meow, meow," answered the voice of his wife.

In his intimate moments with his wife, Churchill would often assume the role of a pig to his wife's cat.

"Hello, pussycat—do you miss my stroking?"

Then he recited a children's rhyme:

"The Owl and the Pussy-cat went to sea
In a beautiful pea-green boat,

They took some honey, and plenty of money,
Wrapped up in a five-pound note."

He continued, "What do you think, Clemmie, of a cat and a pig going across the sea to America? Don't worry. It won't cost any money, it will be all paid for. I've just been invited by President Truman to speak in some college in Missouri. And, of course, the usual honorary degree."

"Missouri?"

"A backwater, I agree. But it does offer an opportunity."

In his mind, he was already composing what he would say.

"We could go early and spend some time with that Canadian friend. You know, that Colonel Clarke of Montreal, who has a winter home in Miami. They've always wanted us to visit them in Florida."

"Splendid! Do us both wonders. But I will have to forgo Missouri. Chartwell does need work, darling. After all, Chequers will be Mr. Attlee's now." She paused. "As for Number 10, we are now officially vacated."

"Did you leave all the silver intact?" Churchill teased.

"Absolutely. But I did take the dozen cases of Pol Roger."

"Ours or theirs?"

"Theirs. I paid hard pounds for it, darling."

"Farewell to the trappings of office."

They giggled like teenagers, after which came a long pause. He could hear his wife's breathing. The silence always meant a worrisome cogitation on her part.

"What is it, darling?"

"This Missouri visit."

"What of it?"

"I'm concerned, Winston. You no longer have the round-the-clock security afforded by the government. I have a favor to ask."

"Of course, darling."

"Take Thompson."

W. H. Thompson was Churchill's personal bodyguard during his days as First Lord of the Admiralty and throughout the war.

47

Churchill had brought him out of retirement from Scotland Yard's Special Branch in 1939. He had served him with extraordinary efficiency, valor, and skill through many a touchy situation during the war and then retired yet again after the war. Despite the normal protection afforded a prime minister, Thompson, with his sixth sense and eagle eye and uncanny prescience, had saved his life more than once during those trying days, a fact that had been assiduously kept from the British public but not from his wife.

"Really, darling. I'm no longer Prime Minister. Who would bother to want to harm this little piggy?"

"Grant me the favor, darling. Allow me the peace of mind."

"Clemmie, really. The West is no longer populated with armed cowboys. Besides, the President has a Secret Service detail. They will be protective of us both."

"I know all that, darling. Still . . ."

"You're worrying unnecessarily," Churchill interrupted. "There is no shooting war going on."

"Please, darling. It's a small favor. Besides, he knows you well, all your little eccentricities."

"Now really, Clemmie. I am a perfectly proper English gentleman—traditional and quite normal to the core."

"Of course, darling," she giggled. "Let's leave it at that. But do take Thompson. Please."

"What of the expense?" he asked shrewdly.

Thompson would have to be paid for by the Churchills. Money was a mania with Clementine. Her grandfather, the Earl of Airlee, had left his wife for a younger woman. The resultant strained economic circumstances had forced Clementine to work as a governess to make ends meet.

"Hang the expense, darling. Call it an investment in our future."

Hearing that, Churchill knew he had lost the argument. Besides, Clementine, like him, was never one to retreat. Faced with her resolve, he knew exactly when surrender was necessary.

48

"Your wish is my command, little pussycat. Just give me a little meow. I miss your purr."

They chatted briefly for a few more moments, and then parted with kisses.

Churchill lay back in the bed. A conversation with Clemmie always lifted his spirits. He pictured her at Chartwell, the chatelaine of the establishment, forever puttering, decorating, and beautifying their lair. He loved the place.

It was his former house in Kent, which had been reluctantly sold when he had become Prime Minister. As PM, he had the use of Chequers, the official suburban retreat in Buckinghamshire.

A group of Churchill's friends had just bought back Chartwell. He had bought the redbrick Victorian house in 1922 without telling his wife. The purchase had been the occasion of one of his few arguments with Clementine. She had counted in her mind the cost of necessary improvements to the nineteenth-century manor house, plus the later costs of entertaining when she'd have to play hostess.

Actually, it was one of the few arguments he had ever won over the former Clementine Hozier. He smiled, thinking about her. She had looked like a more elegant version of Ethel Barrymore, the American actress, who had once caught his interest. The stately feminine member of America's premier acting family had rebuffed his advances saying, "There's is only room for one of us on center stage."

Yes, he remembered, *she had been right about that.*

That little college may be a rare opportunity to take center stage again.

Before he drifted off to sleep, he reminded himself to call Thompson and began thinking again of the speech he would give in Fulton.

It's time to throw my own atomic bomb.

He closed his eyes.

Chapter 4

The small plane landed on a spit of land a few miles south of Konigsberg, which was under siege, bypassed for the moment by the Soviet armies headed toward Berlin. Dimitrov turned up the collar of his big coat and checked his wristwatch. Thankfully, the weather was overcast, cloaking them in even deeper darkness than the moonless night. In the distance, he could hear the faint sounds of the Konigsberg bombardment, although it was impossible to see the flashing lights of the falling shells.

Mueller walked beside him along a worn path leading to the beach. He was wrapped in a heavy civilian overcoat worn over corduroy pants, a heavy woolen turtleneck, and thick-soled boots. On his head, pulled down to his eyebrows, he wore a woolen hat. At every breath, both men exhaled thick vapors. It was twenty degrees below zero.

At the edge of the beach, they peered into the blackness of the swelling sea, the waves undulating toward shore.

"They will be here," Dimitrov said. "I promise you."

In the two weeks since the American's capture, Dimitrov had consulted Beria on the one issue that plagued him. How could he assure total control of the American's actions? Now, that dilemma had been solved, once again through Beria's incandescent brilliance. It was marvelous, he thought, and Mueller had proved quite pliable. Of course, he had no choice.

This was, the man knew, his ultimate test. He wrote in his own hand as Dimitrov dictated his confession to the killing of the

Finkelstein brothers, insisting that it be written down to the last detail, including his membership in the American Bund, and the circumstances surrounding his escape to Germany and his enlistment in the SS.

Beria's extensive intelligence and his people inside the FBI had managed to get their hands on the FBI's report of the double murders. Mueller had expressed astonishment at the depth and breadth of the Russian spy network and gave his consent without question.

"I'm not going to mess with you guys," he told Dimitrov. "Rest assured, Comrade."

He diligently wrote down every word Dimitrov dictated, including some embellishments of his own expanding his anti-Jewish sentiments.

The damned Yids deserved what they got, he wrote.

Dimitrov, of course, approved. The man's Nazi credentials needed to be impeccable, and the letter was signed Franz Mueller, *SS Obersturmbannführer.*

"Good," Dimitrov said, reading over Mueller's confession and remarking on the clarity of his handwriting.

Although he had no need to explain the tactic, he did so anyway.

"You play games with us, Mueller, we will see that this confession falls into the right hands. You will be a wanted man."

"Nothing like insurance," Mueller snickered.

"Either that or a bullet," Dimitrov said.

Mueller had no need to prove his instinct for survival. Besides, his mission was clearly defined. He was to be a human weapon, hidden, cocked, and ready. An American, an unreconstructed Nazi, and a killer—Dimitrov saw him as a perfect combination to deflect accusations away from the Soviets. And what if Mueller were to tell his story? Who would believe such a fairy tale?

"So, who do you want me to knock off?" Mueller had asked.

His role was no mystery, only the designated target.

51

"Roosevelt? Marshall? Eisenhower? All three? Give me the list. Eisenhower is still busy here in Europe, but Roosevelt would be the grand prize. My view is that they are all Jews creating havoc and masquerading as decent people. It would be my pleasure to destroy them."

"Not so eager, Mueller. You do what we tell you and when. Nothing more. If we discover any deviation or the slightest hint of freelancing or disloyalty, you will be dealt with. Do you understand?"

"Of course, General."

Dimitrov had outlined other embellishments. They were as elaborate as they were detailed and repetitive, they had to be committed to memory and reiterated to Dimitrov ad nauseam.

The submarine would pick him up at the designated spot west of Konigsberg. With luck, he would make the Canadian coast in two weeks. A carefully drawn map of the drop-off area was provided, this, too, had to be committed to memory. An American Chevrolet would be waiting at a designated spot near the drop point, marked *X* on the map. Its trunk would be stocked with German weapons, carefully chosen: a German PPC 7.92 Mauser engraved with the SS insignia and armed with a telescopic sight with enough rounds of ammunition and, for self-protection, a Luger.

Also in the trunk would be ten thousand U.S. dollars in small denominations and enough Canadian currency to see him to the border. He was, of course, provided with a U.S. passport in the name of Frank Miller, a social security card, a car registration, a D.C. license, and a map of the Washington metropolitan area. He was to drive to a storage site in Langley Park, Maryland, and sequester the guns and ammunition in a rented facility, the key to which would be with the car keys. Then he was to proceed to the District of Columbia, and check into the YMCA on G Street, a block from the White House.

"So it is to be the President?" Mueller said, interrupting the elaborate explanation the first time it had been offered.

Dimitrov ignored the interruption and went on with his

instructions. He noted that Mueller was listening carefully, his eyes narrowing with concentration. Dimitrov knew the man was rolling over questions in his mind.

Beria, using all of his creative skills as a spymaster, had worked out all other details. Even Dimitrov had been surprised at the priority Beria had given the idea, although he, too, was not privy as yet to the designated target.

"How then will I be summoned?" Mueller asked. "You know, for the deed?"

He seemed to be enjoying the cloak-and-dagger aspect of the assignment.

"You will be given two telephone numbers. You will call daily. If one does not answer, call the other. Vary the phones. Use booths. You will ask for 'Fritz.'"

"And then?"

"You will say, 'This is Karl.'"

"Nice German names."

"Exactly. The voice will say, 'Fritz is not here.'"

"No further conversation?"

"None. The call will be aborted immediately from the other end."

"I see," Mueller said. "You will want to be in touch, be sure I haven't skipped."

Dimitrov smiled and ignored the comment.

"And when will I get my assignment?" Mueller asked.

"You will be told all in due course," Dimitrov said.

"So I just wait?" Mueller said.

"Until summoned."

Again Dimitrov watched Mueller's expression.

"Just wait?" Mueller reiterated. "How long?"

"You have an appointment somewhere, Comrade?" Dimitrov chortled, enjoying this bit of humor. Then he added, "I told you. Until we say."

Dimitrov paused, again trying to anticipate Mueller's questions.

He continued, "You must relate to no one. No relationships, none at all. No fucking."

He paused and smiled.

"Become a priest in your body."

"Beat the monkey. Is that what you mean?"

"I think I understand. But then, I am certain you have had more than your share of the real thing."

"Not more than you Russians."

Dimitrov didn't react. Rape for the soldiers were their principal form of revenge. It was considered their right. They had screwed their way across the battlefield. The SS, he knew, was not immune to such gifts for their troops.

"So my name is Frank Miller. Where do I come from? What is my new history?"

"You are an American. Make up your history. Change it to fit the circumstances. Frankly, I hope you will not need to explain it."

"How can I get in touch with you?"

"You can't."

"So I am to be an inanimate object, a live weapon. I must keep it cocked and ready until you choose its target."

He made the sign of a pistol with his fingers.

"It sounds so . . . so childishly simple . . . and a little ridiculous."

"Exactly—deliberately childish and simple. As for ridiculous, we shall see."

Beria, after all, was an expert on such matters, running a vast worldwide spy network—actually, a spy network within a spy network. The man was clever and cunning, a genius. One day, Dimitrov speculated, he will be Stalin's successor, and he, Dimitrov, would be his trusted lieutenant, powerful and feared. It was his dream.

"And if I'm caught, General?" Mueller asked.

"Depends, Mueller. If caught *before* the act, you will probably be a corpse. If caught *after*, you could be lionized in some quarters, perhaps notorious, famous forever."

"And if I run?"

"You will not run far."

Dimitrov liked the man's cool arrogance and humor. The preparations had been elaborate, indicating that Beria considered this assignment a matter of great importance. Yet he could not contain his speculation as to whom Beria had in mind for Mueller's mission. One of ours? Or one of theirs? Beria did not discriminate. Enemies were everywhere, within and without.

Dimitrov knew that there were a number of other potential Soviet assassins loose in America and elsewhere, but this one would be special, an unreconstructed Nazi. It occurred to him that he was the only living soul who was exposed to Mueller, who knew his face. He felt great pride in this illustration of Beria's faith and trust in him.

"And in the meantime?" Mueller asked.

"Fill your time. Read. Go to movies. Beat your monkey." Dimitrov chuckled. "You SS are supposed to be masters of discipline. Obey Mr. Himmler's rules: Live clean. No whiskey. No drugs. Concentrate all your thoughts on killing your enemies. Think Jews. Think Bolsheviks. Enjoy your hate, Comrade. It will keep you warm."

"It will indeed, Comrade," Mueller snickered.

"Exactly. Hate will keep you alive."

Dimitrov had observed the man's ruminations in his expression.

"And after? If there is an after?" Mueller asked.

"You will have earned our gratitude," Dimitrov said.

Mueller started to speak, then aborted what he was going to say.

"Yes," Dimitrov said, certain of what Mueller had in mind. "What is the American expression about a hook?"

"Off the hook," Mueller said.

Dimitrov put a hand over his heart.

"When the job is successfully achieved, you are, yes, as you say 'off the hook.' You have my word."

Mueller frowned, telescoping his disbelief.

"I will owe my life to your word? What does that mean?"

"We will destroy your written confession."

The man is not a naïve fool, Dimitrov thought, considering all the possibilities of an aftermath. For Mueller, he knew, there could be no future.

"So that is the carrot?"

"I'm sorry, I don't understand . . ."

"To keep me motivated."

Dimitrov said, "You will have to trust me, Mueller."

"Do I have another option?"

Dimitrov shrugged, smiled, and shook his head from side to side.

Suddenly, they heard the low hum of an outboard motor. A small rubber boat came into view. Beyond the boat, they could see nothing in the blackness. They moved toward the edge of the beach and Dimitrov took a flashlight from his overcoat pocket and blinked it. The boat headed toward the beach.

Dimitrov turned toward Mueller.

"I wish you luck, *Obersturmbannführer.*"

"Give my regards to the Führer, General."

He stood for a moment facing Dimitrov. Then raised his arm.

"Heil Hitler!"

Chapter 5

"So why did he accept?" Todd Baker, managing editor of the *Washington Star* asked, sitting on the edge of Spencer Benson's desk.

"Harry is introducing him," Spencer Benson said.

"They've announced that?"

"Not yet." Spencer winked. "I have my sources."

Benson smiled his cat-who-ate-the-canary smile. He was sandy-haired, brown-eyed, freckled, and still boyish in his late thirties. His smile was lopsided, and when he grinned, his eyes squinted. People said he had an endearing air about him, useful to disarm interview subjects, which was his specialty. He was the *Washington Star*'s top feature writer.

"Makes sense," Baker said. "Missouri is Harry's home state. The Midwest is in."

"And Churchill is out," Spencer reminded him.

"You think you can wheedle some idea of what he will talk about? He's in Miami with his wife."

"So I've heard. But I'm told he's not doing interviews."

"He loves interviews."

"I suppose he's being coy."

"Come on, Spence, you've got the inside track. You don't have to say what we're really after. Feature is your turf, not hard news. Be a coup for us."

"We're not dating anymore, Todd. Besides, Sarah is on the West Coast making a movie."

"So you are in touch?"

"We're still friends," Benson muttered, blushing.

A month of passionate intensity didn't make a lasting relationship. It was a fling. She was a delight, but her own person, not given to anything permanent—too rich for his blood. Drank too much. Wore him out in bed. And she had too many active lovers. Not his style. He was a one-woman-at-a-time man. Besides, he had obligations to his two children who lived in Bethesda with his ex-wife.

"As the Brits say: give it a go," Baker said with authority. "I'm looking for a news peg. Maybe you can fish it out of him. Why this little college in the middle of nowhere? Why now? What's the big deal? Fish around in Washington. You've got connections; use them."

His first call was to Donald Maclean, first secretary of the British embassy. Lord Halifax was the ambassador but dependent on Maclean to run the embassy. Sarah had introduced them at the height of their affair, and he invited them to a plushy dinner at the embassy. Maclean had called him after the dinner, and they had had lunch at the Cosmos Club, a male bastion for both the intellectual aristocracy and the powered meritocracy.

He was a charming, urbane, upper-class Englishman who cultivated journalists. Physically impressive, with his slim build, swept-back blond hair, six-foot-four height, always dressed elegantly in exquisitely tailored Saville Row pinstripes, he was straight out of central casting for the authentic version of the quintessential British diplomat. He knew everyone, was socially ubiquitous, and was rumored, despite a wife and children, to be a womanizer. There were also dark whispers about his being something of a switch-hitter sexually. But then, the Brits private school system was notorious for such propensities.

"It baffles me, Donald," Benson said, offering his boyish smile. "Why this little college in the boonies?"

"A favor to your President," Maclean said. "Favors, Benson, the system runs on them. Harry probably owed one of the trustees

58

something from his Prendergast days. His buddy Vaughn was probably involved. Mustn't forget old Harry is a ward healer at heart. He obviously promised them a big fish. Winnie will flash his V and puff his stogie, and the great unwashed will go wild."

Maclean hesitated, then speared the olive from his martini, popped it in his mouth, and shrugged.

"What could he possibly say that he hasn't said? He's no longer the PM, out of favor, yesterday's dishwater."

"Power exists in his words, Donald. You can't just write him off."

"You're right, of course. You can never write off the old boy. He's done us a great favor, rallying the troops, a real cheerleader for the empire, the vaunted empire."

Maclean shook his head and snickered.

"I'm afraid the bloody old empire is going to shrink a bit in the next few years, Spence. Those Tory lions are not in vogue these days. The future is elsewhere."

He stopped abruptly as if he were choking off a desire to say more.

"Never ceases to amaze me how you Brits could turn that party out of office after they were instrumental in winning the war. Not exactly a grateful nation."

"You forget, Spence, acrimonious British politics was suspended during the war. The Brits were one, and Winnie was the conductor of our patriotic orchestra. 'Blood, sweat, and tears,' remember that?" he gave a good imitation of the former Prime Minister. "What can he possibly say that we haven't heard before? Hit on the Russians? He's done that before. We are in an era of good faith, Spence. We love our Russian friends now and have great residual feeling for their enormous sacrifice. Uncle Joe is still a cuddly old bear. Our former PM is running against the tide, old boy."

"Maybe so, but . . . "

Maclean was not to be stopped.

"The Russians can barely pull themselves together. The

destruction of their country has been massive. They deserve our pity and our friendship. Whatever he says won't make a dent, except in the most rightist circles. Spencer, we are moving in the opposite direction. The Socialists are in charge in Britain now."

Benson dismissed his talk as butt kissing for the new government, bureaucratic ass kissing.

"The king is dead, long live the king."

"Still, why Fulton? I can understand Harry's motives, but why Churchill? Is he merely obliging a friend?"

"Oh, I doubt they're friends," Maclean said. He lowered his voice, "Truman has nothing in common with the old Tory. I'd say he and Churchill are oil and water. Imagine the grandson of the Duke of Marlborough and the son of Lord Randolph with this . . . "

Maclean left the sentence unfinished, then sipped his drink, and began again.

"FDR must be spinning in his grave for perpetrating this unintended consequence. For whatever political reasons that flogged him on, the poor man deliberately tapped a border-state nonentity. Beware of what you wish for, Spence."

Not wanting to turn off a source, Spencer held back any hint of resentment. He didn't like this charming but snobby Brit to badmouth his presidents—not that he didn't partially agree. But Truman's decision to drop the bomb showed extraordinary courage and did end the war.

Maclean had emptied his martini glass, and Benson sensed that he would order another.

"Not for me," he said quickly.

"Let's order then," Maclean said, adding, "I wouldn't give the speech that much credence, Spencer. He lowered his voice. "Let's face it, Benson. The man's an icon. Trust me, his fame will fade in time. But in terms of power politics, I'd say he's out of the loop."

Maclean's dismissal of Churchill struck him as ingenuous.

The lunch left him troubled. When he got back to the office, he put in a call to Sarah Churchill. Forgetting the time difference, he apparently roused her from sleep. He knew she would be testy and hung over.

"Why can't the world operate on one time zone?" she said, hoarsely.

"I'm so sorry, Sarah. Could you call me later at the paper?"

"No, no, Spence. Just give me a few minutes to pull myself together." She giggled. "I am alone, darling."

He waited through a long pause, but the tinkle of ice in her glass gave a clue to what was happening.

"So, how are things in the capital of our colonies, darling?"

"Hopping," he said, with some indifference. He wanted to avoid the small talk and get right to the point.

"I'd like to interview your father, Sarah. Soft stuff. A feature on what the great man is doing in his retirement."

"How endearing."

"It's business, baby. You're my source."

"You mean sauce or source?" she teased. "I did enjoy you as the former."

"Your deflecting, Sarah," he said, with mock sternness.

She sighed and paused. He could picture her taking another sip of Johnny Black, her father's choice as well.

"Both he and Mother are in Miami. I'll be visiting them in a few days. Got a week's reprieve from this dreary flick we're doing. I need family solace to compensate for a wretched script."

Spencer knew that despite outbursts of rebellion, Sarah sought her parent's comfort in times of stress.

"Really, Sarah. Can you set it up for me?"

"Using me, are you, Spencer?" she giggled. Obviously, the alcohol was improving her mood. "But then you can use me anytime you feel the urge."

"Too rich for my blood, Sarah," he muttered, but with a deliberate lilt.

He was indeed using her and had no intention of getting back on her treadmill of perpetual need. But then he did understand that she had a heavy burden to bear, considering her father's celebrity. She was without illusions about being a stick figure in her father's spotlight. The role had considerably stunted her sense of self-worth.

"My understanding is that Father does not want to give any interviews. Not before his speech in . . . " she groped for the name.

"Fulton, Missouri."

"Sounds right. Oh yes, Westminster College. I thought it would be nice for him to go, poor dear. He's rather flummoxed with his move from Number 10, although he's getting over it. For what it's worth, I encouraged him to go. The President himself is making the introduction."

He was surprised at her knowledge. Perhaps the relationship with her father was closer than he realized.

"What will he talk about?"

He hoped his inquiry sounded casual, only mildly interested.

"As always, darling. The big picture."

"State of the world?"

"What else? Obviously, he does not wish to leave the world stage. He has a great sense of the dramatic . . . as if you hadn't heard."

"Runs in the family, Sarah."

"His stage is a lot bigger than mine, darling."

There it was, he thought, a tiny chink in the family armor, a brief glimpse of resentment, perhaps jealousy.

"Please try, Sarah. Put a feather in my cap."

"Only if you tickle me with it, darling," she said, ending the conversation with polite amenities and no promises of assistance.

He had almost given up hope, when Sarah called him a few days later from Miami.

"Come on down and toast your buns, darling."

"You've done it?" he asked expectantly.

"I was a bit oblique. Father is having his portrait painted. He's sort of trapped. Loves the idea of the result but not the process. I told him I had this very intelligent newspaper friend from Washington. I think the Washington bit got him interested."

The paper booked him a stateroom on the Miami overnight train, and he spent the time pouring over material he had managed to cull through the *Star*'s extensive files on Churchill and some books he had cadged from his contacts at the Library of Congress. He figured that knowledge of Churchill's early days might be ingratiating as an opening gambit. The man's career was amazing. More than once, he had risen from the ashes like the proverbial phoenix.

Churchill had been attacked unmercifully in his early days in politics. As First Lord of the Admiralty he was excoriated for the Gallipoli disaster, then flayed again as Chancellor of the Exchequer during the Depression. Economists blamed his gold policy for the debacle. Then came attacks by Socialists who railed against his colonialist objections to ending British Raj in India.

Adding insult to injury he had been bludgeoned for his furious objections to Chamberlain's pro-peace policies, which he had characterized as appeasement. The man had been a punching bag for most of his political career. The Russians particularly amused him by battering him for his damning of the Molotov-Ribbentrop Pact that had divided Poland. And, of course, Mr. Goebbels was predictably harsh, portraying him as a satanic monster.

Some of the information he learned about Churchill was extraordinary: He had missed death numerous times. During World War I, he had left a bunker five minutes before it was blown up. He was nearly killed during the Boer War, captured, imprisoned, and then escaped. Again, he was nearly killed in an automobile in Manhattan on a lecture tour in the States.

Little-known, odd facts tickled Benson: In 1900, Mark Twain introduced Churchill at the Waldorf Astoria in New York while on a lecture tour describing his exploits in Africa. Churchill was a correspondent in Cuba during the time Theodore Roosevelt led his Rough Riders up San Juan Hill. He was a close friend and admirer of Lawrence of Arabia. His research on Churchill was so extensive; Benson barely slept on the journey.

Sarah picked him up at the station in a pre-war Lincoln

Continental convertible. Wearing white shorts and a green jersey to set off her green eyes, she looked radiant. He kissed her on both cheeks in the Continental manner.

"You look like a million, Sarah," Benson said, meaning it.

The sun was bright, the air clear. Sarah's hair caught the breeze of the speeding car as it moved through the Miami streets. She asked about the trip, his children, the usual amenities, and he probed in kind.

"Father is sitting this morning for Douglas Chandor, the portrait painter," she said. "He was a bit crotchety earlier, but a touch of brandy settled him down. Douglas has him all decked out in a winter suit, not exactly the proper attire for this climate."

"Have you explained why I'm here?" he asked, hopefully.

"I told him you're my journalist friend from Washington, and you're researching a future article. I wouldn't be too specific about your intentions."

"Will he be amenable? I mean, he's sitting for a portrait, and Mr. Chandor might object."

"Not at all, darling, Douglas doesn't mind. And Father will welcome the interruption. As I told you, he hates the process, especially his costume. Father is into legacy these days."

Sarah introduced Benson to Mrs. Churchill, whom they met just as they entered the house. Her silver hair and aristocratic poise was a well-known photographic image, mostly taken while welcoming her husband home from his many journeys. She was shorter than he imagined. Mrs. Churchill smiled, nodded politely, and reached out her hand.

"So good to meet you, Mr. Benson. Sarah has told me a great deal about you." She looked beyond them to a waiting limousine. "So sorry, but I must be off. The ladies of Miami have kept me busy. Today we are touring an art museum. They have been so generous."

"A great deal about me?" Benson whispered to Sarah, when Mrs. Churchill had moved out of earshot.

"Mother is an old political pro. She understands the protocol of ingratiation. I merely told her you are a friend, only that. We Brits are expert apple polishers, polite to a fault. It masks our disdain." She laughed, tucked an arm under his, and moved him through the house.

They found Churchill sitting in an enclosed glassed-in terrace. Just outside was a large swimming pool in an area surrounded by a high wall fronted by tall, exotic plants.

The artist had placed him in a large chair, where he sat somewhat stiffly, using a magnifying glass to read the *London Times*. The magnification apparently was necessary so that Churchill would not break the pose. He was dressed to the nines in a navy blue, pinstriped, woolen suit, a gold watch chain slid through a middle button of his vest. He wore a maroon polka-dot bow tie on a white shirt.

A fan hummed behind him. His baby pink complexion belied his seventy-one years. In his right hand, he held a lit cigar.

"Father, this is Mr. Benson."

Churchill looked up from his reading. The artist, a short squat man with a tiny moustache, concentrated on his work behind a large easel.

"It's all right, Mr. Churchill," the artist said. "You can stand down."

Churchill shrugged and pulled a smile of relief, showing a wet lower lip, in which he quickly slipped his cigar for a brief puff.

"This man is a tyrant. Look at this costume. I am a chained prisoner in a tropical cell."

"It will look wonderful in the portrait, Father. Or would you rather be painted in the altogether?"

"With an arrow and quiver, I could pass as Cupid."

He took a deep puff on his cigar then used it as a pointer to a chair. Benson settled in and took out his dictation-style notebook.

"I'll leave you two together."

Sarah kissed her father's cheek and patted Benson on the knee.

"I was one, you know," Churchill said, when she had sauntered off.

"One what, sir?"

"Foreign correspondent. Pretty good one, I must say."

"I'm well aware of that, sir. I spent the night reading very extensive material on your career."

"How boring."

Churchill winked and smiled. He took another deep puff and exhaled a cloud of smoke. Benson felt his cerulean blue eyes assessing him.

"I can tell you this: It is far better *making* the news than merely taking it down," he said.

"Unfortunately," Benson responded. "I have never had the opportunity to do the former."

"The *Washington Star* is it? Sarah said something about you wanting to do a story about how this old, has-been hulk is faring in his so-called tranquil retirement."

"That would hardly be my theme, sir."

"Tranquility!" Churchill boomed suddenly, as if it were an expression of contempt. "There is nothing more tranquil than the grave. It is not my intention to repair there in the near future." He paused and then muttered, "Although there are some who would like to hasten such a journey."

Benson was taken aback by the sudden outburst and wasn't sure how to respond. Churchill suddenly relaxed and took another puff on his cigar, blowing the smoke upward.

"I hadn't planned any meetings with the fourth estate for the time being. But my daughter is quite persuasive. I thought perhaps, in a fair exchange, you might give me some insight into what's happening in Washington."

"Be my pleasure, Mr. Churchill."

"How is our new president faring these days?" Churchill asked. "We did get a chance to know each other in Potsdam. Perhaps if I hadn't attended and stuck to my political last, I might still be living at Number 10."

A brief shadow of regret seemed to pass over his eyes,

dulling them for a moment. He paused, recovering, and then asked cheerfully, "Do you think Mr. Truman has a chance to be elected on his own?"

Benson felt flattered by the question and determined to give the answer his best shot.

"Too early to tell, sir," Benson said. "He's got two years to solidify himself. At the moment, I'd put him in the political danger zone. There are stirrings on his left and right flank. He may find himself in a real fight. I think it will be a Republican win, although I'm only speculating. The bomb thing gave him heft, but most pundits think his days are numbered in the White House."

"Hazardous business, politics."

He shrugged and looked upward as if consulting a muse.

"Politics is almost as exciting as war and quite as dangerous. In war, you can only be killed once but in politics many times." He shook his head and smiled. "I do admire the man. Took a lot of gumption to make that decision to drop the bomb. Franklin might have done it, although one can't be certain, but it was Truman after all who gave the order. The destruction it wrought was beyond belief. Truman was told about its frightening power, and it certainly did get the attention of the Japanese warlords. To his everlasting credit, that decision finished the war in the East. Indeed, many a parent or wife or sweetheart or child of an Allied soldier owe the man a debt of gratitude."

"To you as well, sir."

"You think so, Benson? In their wisdom, the British public thought otherwise."

"History will be a better judge, sir."

"Can one depend on the judgment of history? I have found that a contemporary outlook far different than our own always determines history. History might judge Mr. Truman as a brutal murderer of thousands of innocents in a horrific *Götterdämmerung*. And I? Already there are rumblings that I am responsible for the destruction of Dresden. As if what their bombers did to Coventry

67

and London was playacting. Without the passion of our desperate struggle, how would it be possible for future historians to summon up the raw emotion of our time? They will look at our struggle through the wrong end of the telescope. Perhaps even Hitler will be cleansed of his legacy of evil. Indeed, people might say he didn't finish the job of the so-called final solution."

"You're being very pessimistic, sir."

"Not really. Even revisions get revised."

Benson knew he had to steer the conversation beyond the historical. His editor had given him a specific assignment. With time fleeting, he plunged ahead.

"Tell me about what you'll be doing and saying at Westminster College in March," Benson said, hoping he was being casual and only mildly interested.

His mind had focused on a quote he had read on the train, attributed to Edward R. Murrow, saying that Churchill had "marshaled the power of words and sent them into battle."

Churchill nodded and shrugged.

"Oh yes, they're giving me a doctorate."

Churchill flicked an ash from his cigar into a nearby ashtray. His lower lip jutted downward into a scowl.

"Defeat, you see, allows one to reap the benefits of death prematurely—portraits, dedications, honors—it's like watching one's own funeral."

He grinned suddenly, his eyes sparkling.

"Getting yet another honorary doctorate here in Miami. Clemmie says I'm addicted to the irony, since I was such an awful student. No one who has ever passed so few examinations has received so many honorary degrees. Douglas tells me it's because I like the costumes."

He bent closer to Benson in an attitude of confidentiality.

"I'm only enduring this torture because Chandor has promised to give me some painting tips. Isn't that right, Douglas?"

"I must say, Mr. Churchill. Your paintings are wonderful."

"Who can argue with such praise? The truth is my figures are awful. That's why I always paint landscapes."

"And trees don't talk back or chatter away," Chandor said.

"What will be your theme?" Benson asked, trying to make the idea seem a casual thought.

"My theme?"

"In Fulton. Your speech."

Churchill smiled. His cigar had gone out and he relit it, savoring the smoke.

"Depends," he said, cryptically.

"Depends on what?" Benson pressed.

"On the moment," Churchill said, with an air of dismissal.

Benson was reminded of his deflective remark to Sarah. Churchill was quite obviously deflecting. But Benson persisted.

"I'm sure everyone will be most interested in what you have to say, Mr. Churchill."

"Nonsense, Benson. I speak to the wind these days."

"When Churchill speaks," Benson said, determined to restore himself in better graces, "the world listens." Ironically, his remarks offered another opening: "Your speech in Fulton, sir, could provide an opportunity."

"I see my daughter has gotten to you, Benson. She sees it as a seminal event, what with Mr. Truman present to introduce me."

"I would say that you could make it a historic event if you so chose."

Churchill puffed deeply on his still-lit cigar and blew out a stream of smoke. He seemed suddenly distant, lost in thought.

"What is your assessment of the attitude toward the Russians in Washington, Mr. Benson?" he asked, after what might be called a pregnant pause.

The inquiry seemed of very distant interest to the matter at hand, but Benson went along.

"So far, so good," Benson said, cautiously. "There are, of course, those on the right who are rabidly anti-Communist and won't trust the Russians on anything. And, of course, there are many on the Left who approve of our relationship with them. All in all, I'd say there is a wide centrist reservoir of goodwill that still exists toward the Russians."

Churchill grew pensive.

"Your General Patton wanted to go right in and fight them."

"Surely that wasn't your view, Mr. Churchill?"

A deliberate journalist's ploy, he offered it with trepidation. Churchill observed him, his eyes narrowing.

"Remember, Benson, I was in your profession once."

Churchill seemed to turn inward, and Benson did not press the point. He sensed that the old man had put up his guard.

"Put it this way, Benson. These are troubled times. We have won the war. The larger question is: Can we win the peace?"

"Who do you mean by *we*, sir?"

Churchill's eyes narrowed. His cigar had gone out, and he used the pause to relight it and puff deeply.

"Why belabor the obvious, Benson? *We* are Western civilization. *We* are those who stand for the great democratic values of freedom and the rule of law. Come, Benson, surely that doesn't need any further explanation."

His sudden testiness quickly subsided, and Benson tried again.

"Do you think the preservation of those values is in doubt, sir? Is this what you will speak about in Fulton?"

"That depends."

"On what?" Benson pressed.

"On Cassandra's mood on that day," Churchill chuckled, his brief burst of temper gone.

"And what will she be prophesying, sir?"

"Endless questions, Mr. Benson! The journalist's lot is questions, questions, questions."

"That's our job, Mr. Churchill. If we don't ask questions, we don't get at the truth."

"Ah, the truth. There is a conundrum. Make it up, lad. I did when I was in your profession."

"Mr. Churchill is being playful this morning," Douglass Chandor said, peeking from behind his big canvas.

"I was just trying to get your perspective, sir," Benson said, defensively.

It was obvious to him now that he was not going to get the story he came for. Churchill, as if reading his mind, offered more meat for deflection.

"So what does one do in one's dotage?" Churchill said, deliberately answering an unasked question about how he spent his time. "I paint. I write. I dictate, by the way. I continue to be a member of Parliament and the leader of His Majesty's opposition—although, at the moment, we Tories are in shambles. I enjoy good spirits and good food, and the love and devotion of a fine family."

He lifted the *London Times*.

"I keep up with events. I receive honorary degrees. My friend Chandor here is immortalizing me. And I will be crossing America with Mr. Truman, although I will not be joining him on his daily constitutional. Does he continue that practice?"

"Without fail, rain or shine."

"Do me the world of good, I suppose, but I get my exercise being a pallbearer for my friends who swear by calisthenics and exercise," Churchill said, patting his ample girth. "Unfortunately, the man rises at dawn. I work on a rather different clock."

He smiled and directed his remarks to Chandor.

"What say you, Douglas?"

He turned again to Benson. "I know what he's doing. He's making me look like a bulldog."

"I'm trying my best, Mr. Churchill," Chandor said, dabbing his brush against the canvas, stepping back to assess his work.

"I am more a lion than a bulldog, Chandor. Frankly, I prefer the lion."

"Then roar away, sir," Chandor chuckled, obviously enjoying

the banter. "Your recess is over."

"Well, then back to the grindstone," Churchill said, resuming his pose and picking up the *Times* and the magnifying glass.

"Nice meeting you, Mr. Benson. I hope you have a pleasant stay in this tropical paradise."   Benson rose. He knew when he was defeated.

"I hope I have given you enough meat to put on the bones of your story."

"I was hoping . . . " Benson began.

"Springs eternal, Mr. Benson. Springs eternal. I look forward to meeting you again."

Benson nodded. He was dismissed.

Churchill took another deep puff on his cigar and looked toward the painter.

"Am I in the correct pose, Chandor?" Churchill asked.

"It will do," Chandor said.

Benson backed away. The interview was over.

Words, words, words, Benson said to himself.

***

"I hope you got what you needed," Sarah said.

"Very informative."

He hadn't told her the true objective of his mission. Nor did he wish to show any disappointment. She had gone out of the way to arrange the interview, and he wanted to show a pose of gratitude and to hide his disappointment at the results.

They were sitting in the corner of a dark cocktail lounge at a small beach hotel that Sarah had booked for him. They were on the second bottle of vintage champagne, an expense-account perk, most of which was imbibed by Sarah. Noting her condition, Benson suggested dinner.

"In a bit, darling," Sarah said, her tongue slightly heavy.

He knew the signs. In her cups, she would eschew food, and

he could look forward to a late hamburger in his room. Although they were once lovers, he had no intention of spending the night with her.

He hoped she wouldn't get sloppy drunk, although she was quickly heading in that direction. Soon, he knew, she would get maudlin. He hated her in that mood.

"I could never marry a man like you, Spence. Never."

"That again?" he sighed.

"Too focused. Too absorbed in your work. You never smell the roses."

"Like your father?"

"Not at all. For Father, his work is the roses. He lives in a rose garden."

"Tell you the truth, Sarah, I wish I had his range of interests."

"My father is a genius," Sarah said. "He has one problem."

Benson's journalistic instinct suddenly went on full alert.

"And what is that?"

"Too bloody formidable. We all love him dearly, but being his offspring is a trial. It has bent us all."

She grew distant for a moment, then reached for her drink, and upended it.

"No more, Sarah," Benson urged.

"You're right," she giggled. "Time for scotch."

She signaled to the bartender to bring her a scotch highball. Benson resigned himself to a long night.

"Did he activate his Cassandra mode?" Sarah asked.

"As a matter of fact," Benson shrugged.

"He'll be right again in Missouri," Sarah said.

Again Benson's journalistic instincts rose.

"Right about what?"

"Blasted Stalin. Blasted Russians. I think it's the root of his depression, what he calls his 'black dog.' Thinks they outsmarted us. Calls them liars, ruthless buggers. Not to be trusted. He was all for going in and taking Berlin before them and moving into Yugoslavia and Czechoslovakia when we had the chance. Thinks Eisenhower and Roosevelt were patsies, although he adored them both. Mostly, he thinks he was bamboozled."

She swilled down the scotch. He was baffled by her knowledge of these recent historical events.

"Thinks Attlee is a fool, soft on the Russians. Worse, he thinks Truman might, for some harebrained political tradeoff, give Stalin the secrets of the bomb. Imagine that! Says Roosevelt promised it and could have done it. He's hoping to foreclose on that possibility. You can't imagine how Father thinks about these people—Stalin and his gang. I have the sense that he really wants to deliver a smashing psychological blow, warn the world about the Russian menace."

"But they did suffer terribly, and the Red Army did bear the brunt of the burden."

"He acknowledges that, of course, but insists that we might have lost the peace. For their failure at the conference table, the Western democracies could pay the piper . . . unless they wake up and face this new menace."

"Pay the piper?"

"Lose the world to them, the Red menace."

Sarah lifted her hand to signal for another scotch. But Benson did not want to break her thought pattern and motioned to the bartender to slow down the order. Although she had imbibed a great deal of alcohol, her speech was remarkably lucid.

"I think he now sees Fulton as a launching pad for his views. I'm only speculating, of course. At this stage, no one knows what he is going to say. Perhaps not even he does. But I feel certain—call it gut instinct—that he wants it to be a real bell ringer. My father believes that words are more lethal than bombs. He wants to use words to blast open the truth about the Russians."

"Which is?"

"I just told you, Spence. He believes they want to take over the world."

"Tomorrow the world . . . just like Hitler."

She nodded.

"To my father, the war is not really over."

Benson looked at his watch. It was past midnight. The train was to leave the Miami station at eight in the morning.

"Let me get you home, Sarah," he said, gently.

She nodded and sighed. He felt deep compassion for her, sensing her general unhappiness. He helped her to her feet, paid the check, and with her leaning heavily on him, led her to her car.

As he drove, she put her head on his shoulder.

"It's really hard for anything to grow in the shade of a big tree," she whispered.

He helped her up the stairs of the villa and used her key to open the door.

"Did I reveal too much?" she asked.

"Not too much," he replied.

"I hope you'll respect our friendship, Spence."

As a journalist, he knew what that meant.

"Of course."

She smiled, kissed him on both cheeks, and passed into the house.

Chapter 6

Instead of two weeks, the journey to reach Canada took more than a month. Mueller, now Miller, spent the trip mostly in isolation. The captain and crew of the sub had obviously been instructed to keep their distance and communicate only in the most rudimentary way. He took his meals alone in the officer's mess, and most other communication was avoided. It didn't matter. No one aboard spoke English, and he had been instructed not to speak German.

His biggest challenge was to ward off the boredom and cope with the discomfort in the terribly cramped quarters he had been given. His only respite from the suffocating atmosphere was when the sub surfaced and he was allowed to climb on deck to breathe fresh air.

There was only one English book aboard: *Of Human Bondage* by Somerset Maugham, which he read repeatedly and practically memorized. He supposed he should be grateful, although he attributed his miraculous survival record to his old standby, his absolute conviction that he was born under a lucky star.

He looked back, with some nostalgia, free of remorse. He had been a good Bund member and an exemplary and heroic SS man, a true believer. He had no illusions as to why this battle would be lost. The Jews would win. Despite all the superhuman efforts to eliminate their influence, despite the elaborate killing mechanisms, despite the effort by Hitler to rally the world against this scourge, despite the mass executions by bullets and gas, the Jews were sure to win what, in his mind, was merely the first round.

Perhaps the Nazis, in the end, were not clever enough, not ruthless enough, not single-minded enough, and too soft and weak to accomplish their purpose. Those like himself, who were spared—he was certain—fate had picked to survive, to continue to carry out the mission, or face the prospect of being forever enslaved by the Jew and his twisted agenda.

He felt nothing for the SS men he had murdered in the prison. They deserved their fate. They had not been worthy of the battle. They had buckled, lost their courage. They deserved to bite the dust.

He approved of the mission the Russians had devised for him. It defined why he had made such an effort to survive. His role was to continue the battle. He had a clear view of his real enemy, the enemy of all white people everywhere. The Jews had deliberately set about to corrupt the blood of other peoples, while they kept themselves pure and watched with glee how the blood of the other races created a world of degenerates. They had engineered the bastardization of the human race.

He welcomed the idea of killing anyone who did the Jews' bidding, especially their leaders, the Jew Roosevelt and his henchmen, Marshall and Eisenhower, and that fat tub of lard, Churchill. The Russians, too, were on his list, manipulated by Jews. Marx was a Jew. Trotsky was a Jew. The Jews invented Communism. The protocols of Zion proved what they wanted: world domination.

He dismissed the apparent loss of the war as merely a phase in the struggle. The mixed races had won temporarily. The Slavic and Mongoloid hordes and the American half-breeds and their allies had been the Jews' soldiers. He would carry on the battle until it was joined again. His father had understood; a Jew had cheated him out of a job. A hit-and-run driver—certainly a Jew—had killed his mother. He had their number. He had no illusions.

He lived with a pure blue flame of purpose. His hope was that the Soviets would be coldly efficient enough to set him up to kill one of the top kike leaders or surrogates. Not that he had much faith in their skills. Dimitrov was a lackey for his boss, Beria, who ran their secret police and was probably a Jew himself.

After the sub was two weeks without radio contact, it surfaced at an apparently prearranged rendezvous site near a Russian warship that signaled Roosevelt had died. The captain seemed genuinely sad at the news and managed to convey the information to Miller, who turned away quickly. He did not want the captain to see his smile.

Good riddance, he thought, *another Jew gone.*

Finally, the journey ended. The sub surfaced in the dead of night, and he was put ashore on a barren beach on the coast of Canada, exactly as planned. The sub commander shook his hand and wished him good luck in English, which surprised him.

The sun was just rising when he found the car in the exact place that was designated a two-mile walk from where he had landed. Checking the car carefully, he opened the trunk and found a duffel bag filled with the promised weapons. Beside the duffel was a smaller one in which he found the Canadian and U.S. dollars.

The efficiency of the Russians surprised him. Their superiors had told them that the Reds were a gaggle of ignorant peasants; they were partially right. Dimitrov, though, was one clever bastard. He knew the Americans would be coming for them one day. They were planning ahead and he, Miller, was their advance unit.

Indeed, the Russian spy network was a masterpiece of planning—probably run by Jews for their own sinister purposes. One day they would have their comeuppance. At least in this area, Miller convinced himself he and Dimitrov were both on the right side.

Dimitrov had told him that America was riddled with Russian spies and that he would be under constant surveillance. He doubted that, although it remained to be seen. He would reserve judgment.

The car was a Chevrolet, a late-thirties sedan with District of Columbia license plates. It had a full tank of gas and worked perfectly. He headed south in the direction of Montreal, keeping well within the speed limits. Checking his map, he figured that he would be in Washington in four days.

As he drove, he turned on the radio and flipped the dial until he got a decent signal. Music played he hadn't heard for years: Bing Crosby, the Andrews Sisters, Kate Smith. He was particularly amused by "Praise the Lord and Pass the Ammunition." Despite his cynicism, the songs triggered his memory. Although his mother had died when he was five, he imagined that he could remember the tactile sensation of her embrace, its enveloping warmth, and the scent of her body.

In the depth of his dreams, he often saw her watching him, her lips moving, and her smile broad and loving. Her pictures were in his father's house, and in his dreams, she seemed accurately portrayed and very much alive. At times in these dreams, she lifted her arms and beckoned him, and he came forward into her embrace. Often, he awoke and found his face wet with tears. He did not have these dreams about his father, whom he respected, revered, and obeyed, but he could not summon the same emotional connection for him as he had with his dead mother.

He was surprised that these songs could stir such sentimental thoughts. When he was just about to turn off the radio, an announcer broke into the music and said Berlin had fallen and the führer had reportedly committed suicide.

His SS training conditioned him to show no emotion when confronted with defeat or failure and to use it to restoke resolve. He had been taught to idolize the führer and he did in his gut, but he took the news of his death as a signal to redouble his determination. That, he decided, was the message of his reported but as yet unconfirmed suicide. It was an act of victorious self-discipline. He had preserved his honor and avoided humiliation. Miller lifted his arm in salute.

Heil Hitler!

After the news was announced, the voice of the new American president, flat and twangy, came over the air. His name was only vaguely familiar. Miller flicked off the radio. Who needed to hear what he had to say? He knew it would soon be over when he left Russia.

Phase one kaput, he sighed, imagining the führer's disappointment at the weakness and resolve of his armies. *Probably died in despair. He had the right idea, but he should have waited until he had conquered England before taking on the Russians.*

In a small town about thirty miles from his starting point, he found a grocery store and loaded up on food for the journey. He was especially in need of fruit and meat, which had been in short supply on the sub. He bought milk, bread, cold cuts, and cheese to carry him through for the rest of the journey.

He had been instructed to make his first contact call during the first day of his landing in Canada, which he did at a telephone booth at a filling station. He had been provided with numerous packs of coins both Canadian and American. They had thought of every detail. The operator instructed him on the amount, and he obliged. The phone was answered after five rings.

"This is Karl. I am looking for Fritz."

"Fritz is not here," a voice said. The phone rang off.

The process amused him, and he laughed out loud. It seemed so childish, more like a game. But then he had never been an undercover agent before. He decided he was going to enjoy the role.

For the next three nights, he slept in roadside cabins. Getting across the border was no problem at all. The border guards asked some benign questions, which he answered easily, then waved him through.

After going through the border crossing, he passed a sign that read Welcome to the United States of America and was decorated with crossed American flags. He felt no sense of homecoming, no joy of return. At that moment, he told himself, he was a man without a country.

The drive was uneventful, and he reached the storage facility in Maryland late in the afternoon of the fourth day of driving. Signing in on a clipboard handed to him by an indifferent clerk, he found the bin that had been arranged and carefully sequestered the duffel bag filled with his arsenal. He divided the money, pocketed some, and put the remaining money in with the weapons.

That done, he drove through Washington and following the

map provided, proceeding to the YMCA on G Street. Driving past the White House on Pennsylvania Avenue, he noted that the YMCA building was a short walk away.

The proximity prompted speculation that his intended victim was the president of the United States, an idea that shot a thrill up his spine. With Roosevelt dead, he had no idea who that might be, but it was enough to know that it was the leader of the nation the führer had called "corrupted by Jewish and Negro blood."

Parking the car on the street, he checked in to the YMCA and was given a small room overlooking the front of the building. The room contained only a single bed and a small chair and desk. It had no phone or connecting bathroom.

He slept soundly and awoke early, doing all of his morning ablutions in the communal bathroom. There was one other man shaving beside him who wanted to strike up a conversation. Miller made it quite clear by his perfunctory response that he had no interest in friendship or dialogue. He was following orders and had no intention of reaching out to anyone.

Outside, the late-April weather was clear, and he wore a sweater against the morning chill. He bought a guidebook at the Peoples Drug Store across the street, and thumbed through it as he ate his breakfast at the counter.

He assumed that the reason he had been required to check in at the YMCA was because it was so close to the White House and other important government buildings.

Dimitrov's orders had been simple: "Await further instructions."

No timetable had been offered. But his assumption that his victim was to be the president of the United States was an exciting prospect, and he decided he would familiarize himself with the area.

He spent the day walking in the neighborhood, observing the Ellipse, which was the area around the White House. Although he was able to spot antiaircraft gun emplacements in various places in the area, he was surprised at what he, as a military man, judged very bad security. It was laughable. Considering the destruction that took place in Germany, he marveled at the peaceful nature of Washington. It seemed like a sleepy city, despite the appearance of many uniformed people. He could not believe the Americans—considering what was going on in Europe and the huge army they had fielded on that continent and the Pacific—could be so phlegmatic and indifferent to what was happening.

He was further astonished the next morning when he awoke early and resumed his surveillance of the area. The streets were deserted, but ahead he saw a knot of people moving like a centipede along the streets. As he got closer, he noted that some of the people carried cameras and were snapping pictures as they moved.

Ahead of the group, walking swiftly, was a man in a suit wearing a large, brimmed, tan hat square on his head. Miller had no idea who the man was but suspected he might be someone important, because he was being followed by a gaggle of people, some with Speed Graphic cameras, who moved at all angles to the walking man, taking pictures.

Occasionally, the man tipped his hat and acknowledged those who waved or smiled back at him. Moving quickly to get a closer view, he asked one of the passersby who the man was in the large, brimmed hat.

"Him? That's Harry Truman, our president," the man grinned and shook his head in obvious criticism of Miller's ignorance.

"The president?"

Miller was aghast. Walking in broad daylight? In the middle of wartime? The man was obviously mad.

"He's taking his morning constitutional," the man said. "Military style—one hundred twenty steps to the minute."

"Surely not the same route every day?" he asked.

"Sometimes. Sometimes not."

Miller felt a trill of jubilance speed through him. If this man were indeed his target, it would be simple to find a sniper's nest in one of the many high buildings that lined his route. He wished he could discuss this with Dimitrov. They could get the matter over with in a few days. Of course, he had no way of reaching Dimitrov. Nevertheless, convinced that his mission was to assassinate the president, he was determined to continue his "research."

He made it his number one priority, and since he had no fixed schedule, he arose each morning and tracked the president from the moment he came out of the side gate of the White House until his return about forty-five minutes later. In order to know in advance when the president was not in residence at the White House, he became an avid reader of all four Washington papers.

Following the war news diligently, he was perpetually baffled by the reports of the situation in Europe and in the Pacific, as contrasted to what he determined was the bucolic atmosphere of the nation's capital. He suspected, of course, that there was a lot going on behind the façade of the government buildings and the long rows of temporary buildings that lined the area near the Potomac.

When the president was not in residence, Miller explored the Pentagon, a huge building that employed thirty thousand people. A bus stopped at a tunnel under the Pentagon, and there, too, the security was lax, and he was able to lose himself in the crowds that worked there and explore the entire building. Indeed, he quickly discovered where the offices of the men who ran the U.S. military were located.

Another remarkable discovery was that the addresses of all of America's high officials was hardly a mystery, and he spent many a day passing their homes and fantasizing how simple it would be to send a squad of assassins to kill them all. Why hadn't the führer done this? It was baffling.

Since his instructions were to merely wait and to check in daily, he followed them to the letter.

During this early time of his assignment, a great deal was happening in Europe and Japan. In May, as expected, Germany surrendered, and the Allies turned their attention to Japan. The president, Stalin, and Churchill met in Potsdam to divide the spoils and carve out zones of authority. He felt certain that the defeated Germans would secretly begin to prepare for the next war against the real enemy, the Jews.

During the Potsdam Conference, Winston Churchill's party was defeated, and a new man, Clement Attlee, became prime minister. *Good riddance to that fat tub of lard,* he thought.

When the president was not in town for his early-morning constitutional, Miller explored the area for places where he might get the best shot. When the president came back to town after Potsdam and resumed his walks again, Miller was able follow him at a short distance, changing his own pattern so that it would not appear obvious that he was stalking him.

At times, he approached Mr. Truman head on, and once greeted him with "Good Morning, Mr. President."

Truman nodded and returned the greeting. As the summer months began, the weather grew unbearably hot. Washington was built on a swamp, and the humidity was deadly. His little room became an oven, and he spent more and more time in movie houses, which provided the only public air-conditioning in town. When the weather hit over 90 degrees Fahrenheit, most of the government workers were sent home.

Dutifully, he called his anonymous contact each day, sometimes varying the given telephone numbers. His routine was essentially boring, and he was growing increasingly impatient and uncomfortable. He became interested in the Washington Senators baseball team and bought himself a little radio to hear play-by-play descriptions of the games. Needless to say, he "beat the monkey" with increasing frequency.

Because of the various regulations concerning parking on city streets, he began putting the car in public parking garages, varying his routine, and turning over the motor periodically.

At the beginning of August, the Americans dropped an atomic bomb on Hiroshima, Japan, and a few days later one on Nagasaki. Why hadn't the führer developed such a weapon? It now made the United States the most powerful nation on earth.

The Jews had made the bomb. Oppenheimer, a Jew, had organized it from scientific work originally done by Einstein and other Jews. This meant that the Jews had the secrets of the bomb and could blow up anyone who stood in their way. And that little lackey whom he had followed on the Washington streets during the morning was the most powerful man on earth.

What were these stupid Russians waiting for? He was ready and primed to assassinate this man. He had the opportunity, the weapon, and the best possible spot to do the job. Normally, the president walked out of the southeast gate of the White House at six o'clock every morning, accompanied by four Secret Service men. At the gate, a group of reporters and photographers awaited his arrival.

Sometimes, he turned northward and began his walk crossing Pennsylvania Avenue, moving briskly through Lafayette Park, and continuing along the city streets. At times, he turned southward and walked along the Ellipse from which one could clearly see the back of the White House beyond a long expanse of lawn. He smiled and waved at people he passed. He amazed Miller; the führer had never been so accessible.

He wished he could discuss his plan with someone in authority. Nevertheless, he remained obediently at his post making his daily calls, receiving no instructions. He wondered if he had been forgotten. It was possible that he was written off as valueless. Perhaps they had changed their mind.

"Just wait."

Dimitrov's words rang in his ears. He wondered if this was his fate and his future: to wait, to wait forever.

Once, he varied his telephone call, and when it clicked on instead of asking for Fritz, he said, "I must speak to Dimitrov."

The phone call aborted instantly, and he returned to his regular routine.

Then, in early December, his life took a strange turn. The president had varied the route of his constitutional because of some construction. As always, Miller kept himself at a distance, moving at a varied pace, sometimes fast, sometimes slowing to avoid attracting any undue attention of Mr. Truman's small Secret Service detail. At one point, while looking in another direction, he fell hard over the wooden barrier in front of a construction ditch.

He knew he had broken bones. He heard the crack. His right arm was lifeless at his side, and his foot was twisted completely around. His sock and shoe were bathed in blood, and the pain was intense. Luckily, someone driving along the still-deserted street had seen him fall. He was a black man who had stopped the car and called to him.

"You okay, buddy?" the man asked.

He was middle-aged, wearing the blue-gray uniform of a post office worker.

Miller was tempted to say "fine" but it was obvious that he could not walk, and his right arm was useless.

"I think I broke something," he retorted, barely able to speak, convulsed with pain.

His body was bathed in sweat, and he felt on the verge of fainting.

The man reached out a hand and grasped Miller's uninjured hand and pulled him into a vertical position. His rescuer was a big, obviously strong man. He managed to heft him over his shoulder and put him in the rear of his mail truck.

"GW hospital is a minute away," the man said. "I'll get you there."

The man raced the truck to the emergency exit of the George Washington University Hospital on Logan Circle and went inside, and soon two burly men in white coats helped Miller onto a gurney. He was sweating, almost semiconscious. The pain was unbearable, but he felt the movement of the gurney speeding him to an unknown destination.

Then he passed out.

Chapter 7

Benson had come back from Miami on the train, arriving the day before. That morning, he had checked in with his editor to discuss his interview with Churchill.

"He was having his portrait painted, Todd," Benson told him, "and was quite evasive about the speech."

He had debated with himself all night on the train if he should violate Sarah's conversational confidences made under the influence. Even now, with his editor sitting in front of him, he had not reached a decision.

"Not the slightest hint?" Todd asked. "Why so close to the vest?"

"You know he dictates his own speeches and doesn't like to preempt his own drama."

"Did you get an impression, something instinctive?" Baker asked.

He remembered Sarah's words almost verbatim and had written them down after getting back to his hotel. He had called her upon arriving in Washington, but she had already gone back to Los Angeles. He hoped he would not lose a good friend—*and a source,* he added cynically to his thoughts.

"My impression, Todd," he said, after a lengthy pause, "in the light of his deliberate evasion, is that he is planning a significant speech."

"What exactly does that mean?"

"Maybe something critical about the way the peace is going,

the division of Berlin by the Potsdam Agreement. Maybe something very unpleasant about the Russians."

He waited for a reaction from his editor.

"He's always been critical of the Russians."

"Still it's only speculation. I don't think you could build a hot news story on a mere reporter's impression without quoting sources. And I've never felt comfortable not using real live sources. I hate quoting anonymous sources."

He knew he was being ingenuous, since the paper often quoted anonymous sources, albeit sparingly. But he knew that if Sarah got wind of a story about her father wanting to create a stem-winder that would rock the world and practically indict Stalin for stealing half of Europe, their friendship would be over. He didn't want that to happen. It would always be a journalist's dilemma.

"Tell you what, Todd," he said. "Suppose I sleep on it. The speech is more than a month away. I know what you're looking for. Also, Todd, I've got some good stuff for a Churchill feature. Maybe I can get Sarah to arrange some photo stuff to go with it."

"How is your friend?"

"Great," Benson said, as he walked away to see Maclean.

They met in Maclean's opulent, paneled first secretary's office in the British embassy on Massachusetts Avenue. The redbrick dwelling with stone dressing featured a pillared, classical Greek front. The combined residence and diplomatic office, which he had once described in a feature story, suggested an English manor house in the time of Queen Anne.

A large desk dominated the thick-carpeted room. To one side was a spit-shined, long, oval conference table, and the other side contained a sitting area with dark leather chairs and couches and a large, square cocktail table.

Benson noted a number of pictures with Maclean, his wife, and children, as well as photos of him with various members of the royals, including the king and queen, and Churchill and Anthony Eden. It was an impressive stage setting for the tall, handsome Maclean.

Maclean ran the embassy for the ambassador, Lord Halifax, a tall, austere man whom Benson had met and who spent much of his time riding to the hounds or other familiar pursuits of the British aristocracy. He had been Chamberlain's foreign secretary and had hoped to be Churchill's. But after Dunkirk, when he had advocated making peace with the Nazis, Churchill had sent him off to Washington.

Donald Maclean, in his capacity as first secretary, was always the first to arrive at the embassy and the last to leave. No diplomatic activity between the Americans and the British took place without his knowledge.

Benson's appointment had been timed for teatime; and almost as soon as Benson arrived, a tall, attractive, dark-haired, young woman brought in a tray filled with tea things and small cakes and sandwiches in the age-old tradition.

"This is Victoria Stewart," Maclean said, making a sweeping motion toward the woman. "Spencer Benson, a good and trusted friend."

He patted the reporter on the upper arm.

"So pleased to meet you, sir," she said, offering a broad smile.

"So how was your little tête-à-tête with the great Winston and the magnificent Sarah?" Maclean asked.

The young woman carefully poured the tea and politely asked for the usual preferences of milk and lumps of sugar.

"Impressive," Benson replied.

"And what will the old man talk about when he greets the great unwashed in Nowheresville, Missouri?"

Benson was impressed with Maclean's command of American slang.

"My sense of it is that it will be a real Soviet basher."

"Really?" Maclean said, with a heavy touch of sarcasm.

With well-manicured fingers, he lifted a tiny cucumber sandwich, pausing for a moment to ask a question.

"Did he tell you that?"

"Not in so many words," Benson said.

The woman poured the tea and offered the milk and sugar in the polite English style.

"Will that be all, sir?" she asked.

Maclean nodded and observed her as she left with what seemed like more than routine interest, arousing Benson's suspicion that there was more here than meets the eye.

Maclean daintily slipped a sandwich into his mouth and washed it down with a sip of tea.

"Just your conclusion then?" Maclean pressed, returning the cup and saucer soundlessly to the table.

Benson again mulled over Sarah's words. He weighed the harm of revealing them in this venue. It wasn't as if he were quoting it in his story.

"I had a drink with Sarah while I was down there. She alluded to it."

"Alluded?"

"She seemed convinced her father was going to be rather harsh."

"On the Russians?"

Benson nodded.

Maclean turned away and looked into his teacup as if some response was hidden there.

"Nothing more specific?"

"Just an allusion."

Maclean grew oddly pensive.

"At our lunch at Cosmos, you predicted it," Benson said.

As in all relationships with sources, it was business under the guise of socializing. Each wanted something from the other. Benson was looking for a quotable source.

"That wasn't for attribution, Spencer," Maclean rebuked, his expression suddenly wary.

"Of course not, Donald," Benson said. "As always, we are on background here. And confidential."

He was, of course, disappointed. A quote from Maclean would take him off the hook with Sarah.

"It is inevitable, Spencer. Darling Winnie has been pissed about Uncle Joe for endless reasons. Stalin blamed him for delaying a second front. Indeed, he actually called him a coward to his face, which infuriated the old man. Later, Churchill wanted the Allies to take Berlin before the Soviets. Patton was hot to go, and Churchill— it is rumored—agreed. He apparently pressed Roosevelt to take such action, but Roosevelt, who thought good old Uncle Joe a kindred soul, turned down the idea. Of course, the PM yielded, with—I may add—a Latin quotation: *Amantium irea amoris integratio est.*

"Meaning?"

"'Lovers' quarrels always go with true love'," Maclean snorted, as if it were a private joke. "Nothing like an English education."

"Makes me feel somewhat diminished," Benson shrugged.

"And diminished you should be."

His hand reached again for the cup and saucer. Benson followed suit, although his tea was already getting cold.

"Churchill, it is common knowledge, hates Stalin. Thinks him a cruel, heartless bastard." Maclean continued, "When Stalin suggested that one hundred thousand German officials and military officers be lined up and shot at the end of the war, the PM was so appalled he left a banquet in disgust and went into one of his black dog depressions."

"How do you know this, Maclean?"

"Foreign office gossip. Even when Stalin told the old man he was only joshing, Churchill was unappeased. Secretly, he was rumored to be soft on Germany, which, by the way, gave Stalin the heebie-jeebies, fearing that Churchill would push for a separate peace with Hitler."

"You are a fount of Churchill lore, Maclean."

The men picked up their cups and saucers simultaneously and eyed each other over the rims. Maclean was the first to break the brief silence.

91

"Then there were the Jews," Maclean said, lowering his voice and swiveling his neck for a furtive look around, although there was no one in the room.

"The Jews?"

"Churchill lobbied Roosevelt to do something about the Jews. They all knew that Hitler was exterminating the whole race, burning them in the ovens. Roosevelt didn't want the distraction of doing something about it to deflect attention from the main point: winning the war. Stalin agreed.

"Churchill wanted the world to know what was happening, thinking that it would give a boost to our will to win. Churchill, once again, reluctantly surrendered. It was also suspected that our PM was not fully in accord with unconditional surrender, on the grounds that it would prolong the war. He was getting flack from the British people in the streets who were growing weary of the conflict. But then, it did conflict with his 'never give in' cheerleading, and he acquiesced. Not that it mattered. They turned him out anyway. So you see, there were differences between them."

Benson had the impression that Maclean was egging him on, pouring out information, offering areas of response in the hope that Benson would reveal more than he was willing to impart. He knew the Washington ping-pong game; only the little white ball was potentially inside information, a tit-for-tat pas de deux.

"If I read you correctly, Maclean, you think that Churchill, no longer constrained by the diplomatic niceties of being prime minister, will use the occasion to blast away."

"Hardly at the Americans. I'd guess that he would hold his fire there, but the Russians would be fair game. He's always hated Communists and, you must remember, he fought with the Whites attempting in his words "to strangle them in the cradle.""

Maclean chortled, as if he were ridiculing the idea, adding with what might pass as glee, "Without success."

"How far do you think he will go with Truman standing by?" Benson asked. "Considering the present climate is distinctly pro-Russian."

"As you say, he is no longer constrained. Even the great ones have a soft spot for vengeance. My sense is that he might be so blinded by old prejudices, he may well not recognize that the Soviets could have earned their new spheres of influence."

Benson found this latest wrinkle of Maclean's somewhat off-key and perhaps a reflection of the Brits' current political agenda vis-à-vis the Soviet Union—or his own.

"But he is out of power. In our last conversation, you dismissed his having any real impact for that very reason. Have you changed your mind?"

Maclean smiled and took another quick sip of his tea and put the cup and saucer on the table. Benson detected a sudden change in the man's expression. His face seemed ruddier than usual as if some internal mechanism was heating his blood.

"Does it sound so? I'm not sure. With old Winnie, there's no telling. There seems to be a groundswell of interest in the old man's prognostications. Perhaps it comes from some pity over his political defeat. But with Truman introducing him, he will be in the spotlight of the world stage. When he addressed the American Congress in '41, he brought the house down. His weapons are quite formidable."

"Weapons?"

"Words, my dear Benson. Although being turned out of office may have diminished his power, Winston is a master of words. And words—as we have heard ad infinitum—are mightier than the sword. 'We will fight them on the beaches,' et cetera, et cetera. Who knows what would have happened to our tight little island if we Brits had not heard those words?"

Maclean reached for another cucumber sandwich and popped it into his mouth.

"His words could be a fatal stab into the heart of our plans for the postwar world. We need harmony, Spencer, not divisiveness."

"You think his words can be that influential?"

"Without the shadow of a doubt, my journalist friend. Without the shadow of a doubt."

93

Chapter 8

By the time Benson had left, the February light had faded into early high-winter darkness. Maclean had confirmed his own gloomy premonition, which he had shared at lunch that day with Alger Hiss. He opened the calendar on his desk and noted the date that Churchill was to arrive in Washington, some three weeks hence. Then he picked up the phone and dialed a number, hanging up after two rings. The phones he knew were allegedly secure, but he had long ago learned the value of overdoing caution. Two rings were quite useful and safe as a signal, and he used the method often.

Then he called his home. He and his wife, Melinda, had moved into a rented house on Thirty-Fifth Street a month before. Up until then, she had lived with her mother at her farm in Western Massachusetts.

But Donald had needed an excuse to leave Washington for New York, where Soviet control was maintained, usually staying at Melinda's stepfather's apartment on Park Avenue. His cover had been his need to visit his wife during her pregnancy. Although he rarely saw her on his frequent visits, he was never questioned by anyone about his visits.

With the impending switch of Soviet control to its embassy in Washington, his trips to New York would end. This had meant moving Melinda and their children to Washington and slowly varying his routine, establishing his relationship with new handlers at the Russian embassy in Washington. At that point in time, the transfer had not been completed, and he was still reporting to his handler in New York.

"Darling, I'll be going up to New York tomorrow early," he told Melinda. "Could you pack an overnighter like a dear?"

"Now that I'm here, Donald, why the need to go up to New York?" she had asked. "Besides, we're expected at the Stimsons tomorrow."

It was an important dinner, he reflected. Stimson was secretary of war, and the chitchat would be valuable. He weighed the alternatives. New York, he decided, was more pressing.

"Dear Stimmie. Surely, you can find a suitable replacement in twenty-four hours?"

"Can't be helped, darling. Important state business."

He looked into the mouthpiece and smiled. He had to meet Volkov, his handler. Maclean's information was, in his judgment, important enough to send along. There were too many crucial matters at stake.

In his role as first secretary, he was privy to all decoded messages. Arriving early each morning, he was able to read all the overnights, which gave him the clearest possible picture of what was transpiring on this side of the Atlantic from both a British and an American perspective. On his frequent trips to New York, his efficient Soviet handlers were able to get the news back to Moscow quickly.

He was quite proud of his achievements. Earlier in the year, he had managed to get his hands on sensitive Churchill communiqués to Truman that were useful to the Soviets in their strategy vis-à-vis Poland. The Americans truly believed that Poland would regain her freedom as an independent state. When the Americans would one day learn the truth, it would be too late. Poland would be well within the Soviet sphere.

He loved the excitement of it, the sheer exhilaration of deceit. Others were involved as well, some of them quite high up and in the know, like Alger Hiss, now involved with the creation of the United Nations and a man with whom he met frequently. Both men were convinced that the Soviet strategy and its socialist underpinnings would carry the day in the postwar world and that their mutual countries were doomed to eventual collapse. Risks had to be taken to further the Soviet advance, and he was not averse to risk, including those of a sexual nature.

He had been committed to these ideas since a student at Cambridge and had been both lucky and clever enough to make his special contribution. So far, he had totally escaped detection. He supposed that someday the string might run out, but he kept that possibility at bay. Besides, there was a heroic component to these peregrinations, and he reveled in his role as a queen bee in the honeycomb of the Allied hive.

Victoria came into his office. He watched her parade across the room, deliberately exaggerating the movement of her hips, very aware of his observation. She had locked the door after her and drew the blinds. Most of his colleagues had gone. The ambassador always left early. Indeed, he spent more time riding horses than in the embassy and was often the honored guest at embassy dinners and private homes. She opened the liquor cabinet and poured them each a couple of fingers of scotch.

"Cheers, darling," she whispered, kissing him on the lips.

He opened his mouth, and they tipped tongues. The seduction of his gorgeous secretary had been both useful and pleasurable. Her affable socializing with the staff, particularly the secretaries of Lord Halifax and those who served the intelligence officers, had been remarkably helpful.

Of course, she knew nothing of his real intent or his role as a Soviet spy. He had explained that she was, in effect, the first secretary's eyes and ears, not that she knew the implications of what she transmitted. Aside from secretarial school, her liberal education was minimal, and her interest in world politics indifferent. Her working-class accent was jarring but added to her sex appeal.

His intrigues, he assured her, were for his own advancement and, of course, for His Majesty's benefit. To do his job expeditiously as first secretary, he needed to know as much as he could learn about the motives and agendas of his colleagues.

In these sensitive times, he told her, he needed the extra dimension of human intelligence to enhance his job, and she had eagerly provided it. Most of it, he understood, was merely raw gossip. Some of it was useful. Some not. She hadn't a clue which was which. Indeed, she loved doing anything if it pleased him and inured to his benefit.

"Anything, darling. I'll do anything," she had assured him.

And that included especially sex. Besides, her discretion was impeccable and her sexual appetite extraordinary.

"I'm off to New York tomorrow," he told her, after they had taken their first sips of the scotch and begun to stoke up the sexual fires.

"Why don't you take me along, darling? We could make love all night."

"And bugger things up?"

She kissed him deeply and began to caress his penis, which had erected swiftly. She had that effect. To both of them, this time was known as the "quickie hour." She kneeled, unbuttoned his pants, pulled them down, and began to administer fellatio.

He caressed her hair as she warmed to her work.

"Absolute wizard," he whispered, feeling the full effect of her ministrations.

"In me, darling," she said, after a few moments.

Then she moved to the couch, lifted her skirt, pulled down her panties, and inserted him from the rear. He seconded her quick climax, during which his hand covered her mouth. She tended to be a bit of a screamer, and they had worked out this method to insure silence.

"I love it like this, darling," she told him after they had rearranged their clothes. "So wonderfully impulsive."

"Agreed," he said.

Venue was always difficult in this crowded city, where living space was still hard to come by. She lived with two female roommates in an apartment house near Dupont Circle, and a hotel room would

97

be too dangerously indiscreet. Their copulations of necessity took place in his car, his office, or on rare occasions, in apartments of his colleagues who were out on leave.

She had conspicuously avoided the *L* word, although her feelings were obvious. His were more physical than involving, and he loved burning both ends of the candle, regardless of gender. His discipline and focus on his mission were intense enough to quash any entangling and dangerous emotional involvements although he also knew he was prone to sexual risks. He supposed there were those in the embassy who suspected an affair, but her believable denials to her secretarial colleagues kept the confirmation unreliable.

"The first secretary is a family man; however, I would if asked."

She told him this was her usual response when one or another of her colleagues broadly hinted at their suspected affair.

He knew, of course, that there were dark rumors that he was attracted to men as well. She had probed him on that point and would have gladly participated in a ménage à trois, but he denied the allegations. He had become very good at compartmentalizing, and Victoria was not the only extracurricular body he was involved with.

"You must have stashed another lover up there," she would joke occasionally, about his frequent New York trips.

The joke did not hide a whiff of jealousy. He had the sense that her aggressive sexual repetitions on his return might be more of a test of his possible depletion than simple sexual enthusiasm. At those times, it was his turn to make jokes.

"Note that I always return with a full tank."

"Contents noted. That's why I always plan for a long drive when you return."

"To prove speed," he chortled.

"And endurance."

His New York trips were not completely devoid of sexual experience. In his compartmentalized life, he saved New York for his taste for men. He had found that one gender actually enhanced the desire for the other.

One feasts on many flavors, he assured himself, proud of his capacity to perform.

His wife, Melinda, had been placed in yet another compartment. Their marriage had always been a bit rocky, but he did not want to upset that compartment, which might have caused unintended consequences. He was very careful about unintended consequences.

At this moment, he was priming Victoria for a special assignment. Churchill, who dictated his writings, including his speeches, had not, because of the personal expense, brought along his usual stenographers. He had, therefore, requested the services of the best typist and stenographer at the embassy. As first secretary, the request had come to him, and he seized the opportunity.

Victoria, whose stenographic and typing skills were superb, was a perfect choice for the role. She was also skilled and thick-skinned enough to take the old man's legendary impatience.

Besides, he had been charged by his handlers to obtain a copy of the speech in advance. It occurred to him that at times unintended consequences were miraculous.

The early morning Congressional Limited to New York landed him at Penn Station at approximately eleven in the morning. In this period of transition, their method of communication was to meet at a series of out-of-the-way coffee shops in different parts of Manhattan. He was careful to arrange some appointments at the British consul's office in the afternoon to add an official cover to his movements. If further discussion were needed with Volkov, they would meet again at a designated restaurant, but always in a public place. At night, he would sleep at his wife's stepfather's apartment on Park Avenue.

He had long ago developed a sixth sense regarding human surveillance and was well aware of all the accepted methods of physical avoidance. His mental antenna was always extended, and he never got careless or inattentive. Volkov, he knew, was a long-time Soviet operative whose cover was as a proprietor of a small stationery store in Greenwich

Village, which Maclean had never visited. Nor was he curious as to how his information was transmitted to Moscow for analysis.

Volkov was thoroughly Americanized and, like Maclean, was a family man with two young children, a role that, if investigated, would be a perfect cover. While Maclean had never probed, Volkov told him he lived in a two-family house in a nondescript neighborhood in East New York. He admitted to having been born in Moscow and apparently had managed to get back a number of times both before and during the war. Beyond that, Maclean knew nothing of the man's background, except that he was extraordinarily intelligent and well informed and undoubtedly, because of Maclean's importance, held a very high rank in the NKVD.

Nothing was ever conveyed in writing between them, and they were extremely careful in their choice of conversational venues. Maclean was never addressed by his name, only his code name, "Homer." Although obscure coffee shops and restaurants were useful, much information was always exchanged outdoors. Like Maclean, Volkov was equally skilled in countersurveillance. Both knew that American and British intelligence, while fairly sophisticated, could not match the Soviets in efficiency and scope. The Soviets had taken full advantage of their relationship with their allies. They were embedded everywhere.

They met at a coffee shop on Seventh Avenue a few blocks from Penn Station and slid into a back booth. New York was one of the few places in the world to have a plethora of coffee shops. Many had only counter service and were called "one-armed beaneries." Some, like the one they were currently using, had a few booths available for table service. The agenda of their meeting was no secret to either of them.

"They are very concerned, Homer," Volkov said, opening the conversation.

"Apparently so."

"Above all, as I gather, they do not want public opinion to harden against us at this juncture."

100

"Or at any juncture for that matter."

"It is especially sensitive now," Volkov said. "The Americans are still overwhelmingly pro-Russian. A change will come, I am sure, but at this moment, anything very negative is not propitious."

When the waitress arrived, they stopped talking and ordered coffee and sandwiches, more as a cover than for eating.

"Have you his schedule?" Volkov asked.

"He will be staying at the embassy," Maclean said. "The ambassador will not be happy; the man can be disruptive and imperious. Then he is set to go to St. Louis with the President by rail, then change trains to Jefferson City, then drive by car to Fulton to speak at the college on March 5."

Volkov nodded.

"They want specifics on the content," Volkov said.

"They are right to be concerned," Maclean said. The waitress came and went with coffee. "His speech, I feel certain, will not be helpful."

Volkov nodded. He was a heavyset man with jet-black hair and wide-set eyes, a flattened profile and big chin that reminded Maclean of a boxer's face. When he talked, a gold tooth flashed disconcertedly and glistened when he smiled, which was rarely.

"Do you have any clue as to the content?" Volkov asked.

"My journalist friend who spent time with him a few days ago said he was quite mum, although apparently the daughter revealed that it would be devoted to his distrust of Soviet intentions. Remember, he is no longer constrained."

Volkov grew thoughtful.

"They are apparently concerned as well with his impact on Truman. There are lots of issues in the balance." He lowered his voice. "The bomb has changed everything."

"My understanding is that we are getting closer."

"I am sure," Volkov acknowledged, although Maclean was certain that Volkov was not in the loop on that piece of intelligence.

Nor was he. So far he had provided a great deal of nontechnical

101

information on the American program and had actually visited some of the facilities in the production chain. Proud of their being the sole possessor of the bomb, the Americans were eager to exploit the PR advantages and a bit more open than they should be on security. Of course, the Brits were their partners and had provided technical help to the bomb's development.

"Without an operational bomb, we are still very vulnerable," said Maclean. "Although the program of agitation to bring U.S. troops home is progressing well, they could still be formidable. The Brits, too, are accelerating their removal of troops from the Continent, but the threat is still there. The bomb will always be a factor until there is parity."

"One day . . . " Volkov said, swallowing his words.

"As night follows day," Maclean muttered.

"In technology and science, nothing remains hidden for long." Volkov lowered his voice. "Beria is on the case; he makes things happen. Our colleagues are everywhere."

"And well worth the risk. We are the future, Volkov," Maclean said. "I wish Mr. Churchill would go home and lay his bricks. His speech cannot be helpful; his words can be a formidable weapon."

"Exactly, Homer," said Volkov. "Which is why they want content. That is their reason for urgency. They have pressed me and I, in turn, ..."

". . . are pressing me."

"Can you deliver?"

"Haven't I always?" Maclean said.

Volkov smiled, showing the flash of gold tooth.

"No offense meant, Homer. We are always pleased by your devotion. But we also know the man's habits. He dictates and revises and is secretive about what he is going to say."

"I am well aware of that, Volkov," Maclean said. "I can assure you, I will have his content well before he gives his speech. It is all arranged."

He thought of Victoria and speculated suddenly on—as

Shakespeare would have characterized it—"country matters." Victoria had the sexual power to arouse a blind man. Churchill? The image faded. There had never been a breath of scandal about the old man. Volkov, perhaps seeing a sign in his face, intruded.

"What are you thinking, Homer?"

Recalled to the reality of place, Maclean smiled.

"I am merely speculating. What do you think they have in mind?"

"That is not our business," Volkov said, his forehead creasing in a deep frown.

"Something extreme?" Maclean asked.

He remembered his comments the other day to Benson—*words, words, words.* Again, lines from Shakespeare intruded on his thoughts as if he were a schoolboy again:

POLONIUS: What do you read, my lord?

HAMLET: Words, words, words.

(*Hamlet, Act 2, Scene 2*)

Maclean chuckled as he recited the lines and the attribution.

"Ah, the glories of an English education!"

"You mention Hamlet, Homer . . ." Maclean watched as Volkov drew in a deep breath. " . . . Do you recall what happened to him?"

Volkov's comment surprised him and forced his mind to light on an image of the former prime minister supine and bleeding.

"Good God!" Maclean said. "Surely, you're not speculating . . . " He cut himself short. "It is not easy to contemplate, Volkov. I'm still an Englishman."

"No offense, Maclean." He sucked in a deep breath. "Let us leave such ideas and action for others."

"I agree. We should not dwell on consequences. It is not on our résumé."

A cold chill suddenly assailed him. Thinking the interview over, Maclean stood up.

"One more thing, comrade," Volkov said, his voice lowered.

"The venue change has been made. You will no longer have to visit here."

"So this is the last time?" Maclean said. "I rather enjoyed our little visits."

He did feel an element of regret. He would miss his little jaunts to the bars along Third Avenue under the El and Greenwich Village, a man hunter's paradise. In Washington, he would not have such freedom.

"You are a great soldier, Homer. To you, a great debt is owed. Someday you will look back with great pride."

"Some day," Maclean agreed, dead certain that he would celebrate at the final victory.

Chapter 9

Miller had the sensation of forcing himself upward out of a sea of molasses. He felt trapped, unable to pull himself out of the viscous muck. Then consciousness began, slowly at first, then rising painfully, like the lifting of a heavy curtain. The blackness began to disintegrate and awareness began to filter through his mind.

With the suddenness of an explosive charge, he found reality again and tried to sit up. But there was a weight on his chest that prevented upward movement.

"Easy, Mr. Miller," a murmuring voice said.

He felt a cool, caressing hand on his forehead. His eyes fluttered open, and he saw the face of a tall, young, blonde woman in a crisp white nurse's uniform. Her large blue eyes observed him, and she was smiling broadly, showing white, even teeth. He noted a dimple in her cheek.

A white angel, he thought, as the image popped into his mind.

Bits of memory collided in his brain. Reaching out, he felt what he assumed was a plaster cast running from his neck to his waist. More attempted movement indicated another cast that ran from his foot to his lower calf.

After a few moments, his mind cleared, and he remembered what had happened and became fully cognizant of his predicament. He was suddenly assaulted by irony. He had come through bloody battles without a scratch. How could this happen?

The blonde nurse pushed aside the curtain that separated him from another bed. An older man lay on his back snoring, his mouth open, as he slept.

"*Vas ist das*," he muttered, without thinking.

The nurse seemed confused by his comment and stuck a thermometer between his lips. Watching her, he noted that she was wearing a nametag pinned to her ample bosom; "Stephanie Brown" it read.

"Nothing fatal, Mr. Miller," the nurse said cheerfully. "Broken humerus and ankle—the ankle is the bad one, compounded. Bones set and casted while you journeyed in oblivion."

He was beginning to remember drifting in and out as a doctor swathed him in some moist substance that smelled odd. *Wet plaster*, a voice had said.

With the nurse's help, he was assisted into a sitting position. He felt nauseated for a moment and waited until the feeling passed. Then he assessed his condition.

He looked down at his left foot, right arm, left ankle. Ambulation would be difficult. And he was right-handed.

"Consider yourself lucky."

"Lucky? Ridiculous!" he muttered, thinking about his mission.

There was no way he could get around, and certainly, he was unable to pull a trigger.

"You'll be one-armed for about six weeks," the nurse said. "The ankle might take longer, but when you heal, you'll be as good as new."

"Did you say six weeks?"

"For the arm. But people heal differently. You look like a healthy specimen. Yes, six weeks for the arm."

She looked at him with inordinate interest, broadly smiling.

"And the ankle?"

She shrugged, lifted him slightly, and fluffed the pillow, then eased his head down again.

"They tell me it was a very bad break. Where were you going? How did this happen?"

"How long before it heals?" he asked, ignoring her question.

"I'm only a nurse, Mr. Miller. Depends. Probably, if you're lucky—and you are—say a couple of weeks longer for the ankle. X-rays will decide. You'll be fit as a fiddle when you heal. Knock plaster."

She knocked a knuckle on his chest cast; it made a hollow sound. He did not respond to her attempt at humor.

"Hey, cheer up, fella! Could have been worse."

He was beginning to assess the full consequences of his dilemma. If they decided to act while he was out of commission, he was—the word slipped out of his mouth—"Kaput!"

"Not at all," she said, understanding. "Put it this way. You're on hiatus."

Then he remembered that he had not made his call.

"How long is it since I came to the hospital?" he asked.

"Early this morning. It is now evening. But you're in no condition to leave. Maybe tomorrow."

He looked outside to confirm her information. It was dark.

"With the shortage of doctors, one orthopedic physician was available. And this bed was empty."

She touched his cheek. Her hand felt cool.

His sense of awareness was expanding rapidly. He was wearing one of those hospital robes that tied in the back. In his mind, he quickly catalogued the content of his wallet and his pockets. He had a roll of cash fashioned by a rubber band, and his wallet contained his forged papers. Nothing more. He was relieved. It was doubtful that his personal effects could arouse suspicions. He wondered how much she knew.

He was recalling events quickly now. He had been following the president and had fallen into a construction ditch. He needed to know how much they knew.

"I was careless," he said. "I fell into a hole."

"It happens. Some man brought you in. Apparently, he left as soon as you were delivered."

107

"Did he say anything? Leave his name?"

He was conscious of a brief flash of paranoia. Had they been watching? Was he being followed?

"I don't think so."

Miller retreated quickly. It was of no consequence. The man was a stranger.

"I wasn't in the ER. Happens frequently. Someone has an accident and is brought in by a Good Samaritan. You're a very lucky fellow."

"My clothes?"

"In the closet, Mr. Miller."

She pointed to a closet beside the bathroom. He could make out the white porcelain of the toilet, the sight of which sparked an urge to urinate. He nodded and attempted to rise, and she helped him to a sitting position. He swung his left leg cast to the floor and with difficulty managed to get into a standing position. The blonde nurse handed him a single crutch and assisted him as he hobbled to the toilet.

He noted the faint aroma of her scent, subtle but pleasant. She was strong, as tall as him. She guided him carefully into the bathroom, closing the door discreetly. As the first drops fell into the water, he suddenly felt dizzy and had to brace himself against the wall to keep from fainting. As he steadied, the awareness of his predicament panicked him.

"I need a telephone," he said, when he managed to leave the bathroom, his urgency palpable.

"I'll try to get one. There is a connection beside the bed."

"Thank you," he muttered, as she helped him make it back to the bed.

He sat down heavily and contemplated his situation. Above all, he needed to connect. That was his principal priority. If he hadn't been followed, they must not know his physical situation.

She brought him the phone, and he got through to the number. Thankfully, the voice responded and after the usual routine, the connection was broken.

After his call, he lay down on the bed, exhausted. The downside to this dilemma was the possibility that he would be summoned to perform his assignment during the time of his recuperation. He toyed with the idea once again of breaking the protocol of his communications and trying to connect with Dimitrov. Whatever was in the planning stage would have to wait. Besides, he needed to be limber to make his getaway. Perhaps if he displayed more panic and anxiety, Dimitrov might find a way to get to him.

He took some comfort in the research he had already done concerning the president. He had mapped out the possibilities, although he hadn't completely worked out his exit strategy. Truman was a sitting duck, but if Miller couldn't run, he would be dead meat.

"Can you call someone to take you home tomorrow?" the nurse asked interrupting his thoughts. It struck him that her face with its high cheekbones, her large blue eyes, and her blonde hair were the Aryan ideal.

At first, he wanted to answer her question in the negative. No, he decided, he would have to manage.

"Yes," he lied.

"Good," she said. "You'll be needing help for a while. You'd be better off if someone wheeled you around for a while."

"A wheelchair? No way."

She put her hands on her hips in mock dismay and shook her head. It struck him suddenly that she was attractive, and he noted the fetching sweep of her figure that gave a curvaceous shape to her nurse's uniform. Briefly, they exchanged glances. He felt himself blush.

"You guys! So wary of showing your vulnerability."

He sensed that she caught his observation and was attempting to engage his interest beyond her nursing role. Remembering Dimitrov's caveat, he forced himself to dismiss the idea. Perhaps he was exaggerating, he decided. Nevertheless, he cautioned himself and deliberately did not continue the dialogue, conscious that she was waiting for a riposte.

"Your choice," she shrugged, turning away.

He spent a restless night. Once, he got up and attempted to maneuver himself to the bathroom. With his upper right side immobilized and his lower left shaky because of the cast, the crutch was of minimal help. It took him nearly a half hour to make it to the bathroom, a distance of no more than ten feet.

Because he was right-handed, eating by himself was also a problem; and he messed himself up by attempting to eat his breakfast with his left hand. Seeing this, the blonde nurse came close to the bed and began to feed him. He was conscious of her proximity.

"You broke the wrong arm," she said, chuckling. "Take the opportunity to learn to be ambidextrous."

Moving closer, she caressed his left arm. Her scent reminded him oddly of apples.

"Good advice," he muttered awkwardly.

She lifted a forkful of scrambled eggs and put it in his mouth.

"You're such a good boy," she joked.

He was able to pick up the toast without difficulty.

"Thank you, Mama," he said, feeling oddly giddy.

"Where are you from?" she asked.

"Been everywhere," he said, deliberately curt, hoping to discourage any further questions. But her proximity was definitely making an impression. "I'm passing through."

She nodded, apparently getting the message. He did not respond with any counterquestions. Above all, he resisted starting a dialogue, although he was now fully aware of her interest—and his own. It was, for him, a new feeling.

When she had finished feeding him, he stirred and attempted to leave the bed.

"I'm going," he muttered. "Got to get dressed."

She brought out his clothes on a hanger. There was a cellophane bag attached, which contained his wallet and cash.

"We're honest here," she said, reading his mind.

He fumbled with his clothes.

"Let me help," she said. "I won't look, I promise."

She reached for his underpants, bent down, and helped put his legs through the openings. She turned away, but he flushed with embarrassment. Using her shoulder for support, he managed to pull up his underpants with one hand. She maneuvered him through the process.

"Have you alerted someone to pick you up?"

He nodded in the affirmative, but she apparently detected something tentative in his mimed answer.

"Are you sure?"

"I have made arrangements," he said, conscious of her probing look.

Again, they exchanged glances.

"To meet you in the lobby, I hope."

"Yes," he nodded. "I arranged for that."

She helped him get into his slacks, which barely managed to slide over his leg cast. The shirt and light windbreaker were another challenge since he did not have an arm handy to put through the sleeve.

For a brief moment, their eyes met again, and his stomach tightened and an uncommon wave of panic crashed over him. It was disconcerting. What he was experiencing had never happened to him before. Again, Dimitrov's cautionary remarks assailed him. When he was fully dressed, she brought him a pair of crutches and showed him how to use them. He found it awkward and painful.

"I'll get a wheelchair," she said. "Hospital orders. We roll you to the door. Once you're checked out, you're on your own."

He could not take his eyes off her as she moved out of the room, noting the sweep of her hips and the grace of her movements. She disappeared for a few moments, then came back with the wheelchair and helped him into it.

"I'll wheel you down, and you can be discharged and meet whoever is going to take you home."

He nodded his thanks and felt himself being pushed along

the corridors, the crutches on his lap. She moved the chair to the discharge office and helped him through the process. He paid the bill with the cash. Happily cash was cash. Not like a check. It left no trace.

"I appreciate everything you've done," he said, as she moved him into the lobby near the main entrance of the hospital.

He was determined to act naturally, observing the expected amenities, aborting any undue curiosity on her part. He knew he had to disengage.

"You said you were being met," she said, suspicious now.

"Perhaps they haven't come yet."

He knew he was caught in a dilemma and was running out of options.

"Maybe they're not coming," he muttered.

It soon became apparent that he had to confront his situation.

"I'm staying at the YMCA. It's not too far. If you can get me a cab, I'll be fine."

Without questioning him further, she moved him outside, in front of the hospital entrance, and hailed a cab. She helped him inside, handed him the crutches. To his astonishment, she got in beside him. He had briefly protested but she was adamant and gave the cabdriver instructions.

"This is beyond the call of duty," he told her, baffled by his unwillingness to resist.

"I know," she said, as the cab drove off.

"I'll help you upstairs," she said, when the cab, after a short ride, pulled up in front of the Y.

He maneuvered himself into the lobby with the crutches and her guidance.

"No women allowed upstairs," said the officious clerk at the desk.

"I'm not just a woman," she said. "I'm a nurse."

But the man at the front desk was insistent.

"I have eyes," he said. His face was pale and thin, pimply,

and he had a snotty attitude. "No women, nurse or not."

"I'll be right down, I promise."

"I can lose my job," the man said. "There is a housing shortage. You'll get me in trouble."

"Just this once," Nurse Brown said.

"It's all right," Miller said. "I can manage."

She was adamant.

"I am a nurse. I am caring for an injured man."

"No women upstairs. That's the rule."

Miller kept his temper. It wasn't easy. He wanted to grab the man and crush his windpipe as he had done with others many times before. He wished she would desist, but he didn't want to cause a scene. Again, he remembered Dimitrov's warning.

"Okay, once," the man agreed, retreating.

After she had gotten him into his room, he thanked her again.

"You've done enough, Nurse Brown," he said. The effort of getting from the hospital to his room had tired him.

She stared at him silently for a long moment and shook her head. Then he watched her observe the small room with disapproval.

"You have no one in town? No one to help?"

"They probably didn't get the message," he lied.

"What is it with you?" she rebuked.

"I'll be fine."

"How will you eat?" She looked around the room. "Is there a phone?"

He shrugged, shook his head in the negative, and forced a smile.

"I'm not your responsibility, for crying out loud. I'll get by. You're probably being missed at the hospital."

"Probably," she said.

"Do you treat all of your patients like this?"

"Only the needy ones."

"I'm not needy," he protested lamely. "I'm okay now. You've done enough. Hell, it's only broken bones. I'll manage."

She reached out with one hand and touched his forehead. Her hand felt cool, gentle, refreshing. Beware, he warned himself.

"You're sweating. It takes an effort to move around. And the casts don't help."

"Stop mothering me, nurse."

"Stephanie."

"Stephanie."

"I'm not mothering you . . . " she paused . . . "Frank."

He sensed the pull between them.

"I think I better leave, before they throw you out for breaking the rules. That man downstairs seems like a stickler."

"I appreciate this," he said, hesitantly. "Let's leave it at that. You don't owe me this. I can take care of myself."

He hoped he was being firm enough. He toyed with the idea of insulting her. She was paying him too much attention. Perhaps she worked for them, a plant like him. Which *them*? The Americans? The Brits? The Soviets? In this business, it helped to be slightly paranoid.

"Okay then," she said.

Inexplicably she held back, observing him. They exchanged furtive glances. But when their eyes met, he was the first to turn away.

"You . . . you're an enigma, Miller."

She sighed, turned away, and let herself out. Relieved at first, he was soon baffled by his reaction. He hadn't wanted her to leave. He dismissed such a sensation as weakness.

So far in his life, he had avoided any emotional attachment to a female, except as an object of sexual pleasure. When he felt the need, he had simply taken, by force if necessary. Physically, he knew he was the Hitlerian ideal: tall, blond, and well built. He knew he was attractive to women. So far, it had been a one-way street.

As an SS officer, he had enjoyed being displayed and lionized in his well-tailored, immaculate uniform. Mostly, he had reveled in the mystical rituals, the pomp, the parades, the camaraderie, the sense of mission. He had especially enjoyed the combat, the thrill of conscious heroism, exhibiting bravery, and the personal glory he felt in killing the enemies of the Third Reich. He had been happy doing his duty, showing no mercy, pity, or compassion for the enemy, owing allegiance to his führer and the higher purpose of creating the dominance of the master race, of which he was a prime example. Such a sense of duty had been his pride. These things were now in the dust heap of old memories, and he avoided recalling them.

He was used to being admired by women and had taken full advantage of such admiration. As for what was referred to as "romantic love," he had neither experienced nor wished for it. He was often disgusted by its display. His sexual fantasies dealt with images of half-dressed women being fucked in different positions. Rear entry particularly excited him. He recalled incidents where he had ripped off women's clothes and fucked them in the ass. He forced women to fellate him and swallow his ejaculation. Images like these helped him to masturbate. None of this had anything at all to do with romantic love.

He had believed that such personal sentiment was unmanly, irrelevant, and unnecessary. Besides, such sentiment was dangerous and debilitating. Romantic love, he was convinced, like religion, was an opiate. It enfeebled people, made them fearful and decadent. The Jews used such emotions to fill people's heads with enslaving ideas, like inventing the movies, which glorified individual sentiment and promoted the idea of romantic love. It was nothing more than a mind drug.

Yet, try as he could to rationalize his odd, new feelings, he could not banish thoughts of Stephanie Brown.

In the morning, he struggled to get out of bed. Because of the difficulty, he had not undressed. With his crutches, he managed to reach the bathroom but it was too awkward to wash or shave. With effort and the use of his crutches, he made it to the elevator. The man at the desk ushered him over and gave him a paper bag.

"From Florence Nightingale," the man said, smiling lasciviously. "She brought it herself. I let you get away with it

115

yesterday, seeing your situation. No more—nurse or not."

Miller grunted, ignored the man, and looked inside the bag. There were sandwiches, candy bars, and two pints of milk. He had intended to go to the Peoples Drug Store across the street for a sandwich and to make his call. Instead, he used the open pay phone in the lobby and went upstairs to his room to eat.

The delivery repeated itself for the next few days. He was baffled by her conduct, but he accepted her largesse out of necessity. Suspicious of her motives, his gratitude was complex. After a week of these food gifts, she appeared in the lobby herself, holding the bag.

"Why are you doing this?" he asked.

Nevertheless, he was glad to see her. She looked wonderful: fresh and smiling. She wore black slacks and a turtleneck sweater that emphasized her full bosoms. He hadn't realized how really tall she was.

"You look terrible," she said, ignoring his question.

"I hadn't noticed," he lied, feeling awkward and scruffy.

He had paid no attention at all to his appearance.

"At least, you've been eating," she said.

"Okay, so you have my thanks."

He continued to hold the bag of food.

"How about you go upstairs and clean yourself up, and let's get out of here for a while."

She had her hands on her hips and spoke in a mock commanding tone.

Good idea, he thought and then shook his head, refusing the offer.

He shrugged and they exchanged glances, but he did not move.

"Go ahead. I'll wait."

He wanted to tell her she was wasting her time. Instead, he said, "In this condition? Go where?"

"It's a nice day. I'm on the nightshift. The weather is perfect. I have a wheelchair."

She pointed to a folded wheelchair leaning against the wall.

"Do you good to smell the roses," she giggled girlishly.

116

"It's December," he said. "There are no roses."

"We'll make believe. Besides, it's unseasonably mild."

"I didn't ask you to come," he muttered.

"So I'm a pain in the butt. Now, go get cleaned up."

He turned and pressed the elevator button. Each day he was having less of a struggle. The chest cast was more burdensome than the ankle cast, but he was, with the help of one crutch, soon able to take halting steps. The elevator door opened, and he pressed the button of his floor. As the elevator ascended, he decided to join her. Uncomfortable about his easy compliance, he was unable to resist.

He cleaned himself up in the communal bathroom, shaved, and managed to get into clean pants, a shirt, sweater, and windbreaker. He groomed himself carefully, taking his time, a reminder of his SS glory days. He half hoped she would grow tired of waiting.

He was wrong.

"You clean up nice," she said. She led him to the wheelchair, which she opened, then patted the seat. "Enthrone yourself."

The man behind the desk shook his head. She threw him a haughty and contemptuous glance, then moved the wheelchair into the street.

She had been right about the weather, which was uncommonly warm for December. She wheeled him slowly past the Ellipse in the direction of the Potomac. They passed rows of temporary office buildings.

"Remember your stroller days?" she said, moving at a swift pace, stopping finally at a bench overlooking the tidal basin and the Jefferson Memorial, its white marble gleaming in the sun.

"Lovely, isn't it?" she said.

He hadn't said a word since leaving the Y. The situation was both mysterious and frightening. He tried to put it in the context of an intrigue, giving it a business twist, eschewing any emotional content. He forced his thoughts to deal with what her motives could be. Surely, he tried convincing himself, she had glommed on to him for a reason. Either the Americans were on to him, or the NKVD was concocting another plan. He had acquiesced, he assured himself, to get to the bottom of such suspicions.

Trust no one, Dimitrov had cautioned.

If she were an enemy, he would have to find a way to either evade her or dispatch her. Sitting here in the open, with little chance of being overheard, he speculated that she might be the conduit for more instructions from Dimitrov. It was inconceivable that her attraction was casual.

"So why are we here?" he asked, observing her in profile.

She turned to him and smiled.

"You're a strange one," she said. "Why not just enjoy it?"

Was she being cagey? He wondered. Or playing with him?

"I'd like to know why," he said.

Despite the pleasure of her proximity, he could not shake his suspicions.

"So would I, if you must know," she chuckled. "I'm not sure myself. It's a bit of a mystery, even to me."

"What is?"

"Never mind."

He saw her flush, as if little patches of rouge had been applied to her cheeks.

"Maybe you're a challenge," she mumbled. "Maybe that's it."

"A challenge?" He was baffled.

"Am I making a fool of myself?" she asked.

He shook his head and sucked in a deep breath.

"You're making a mistake," he told her.

"You're probably right."

They sat quietly, he in the wheelchair, she on the bench. From their vantage, they could see the low line of the Pentagon. He was conscious of her disturbing presence beside him.

This is stupid and wrong! He rebuked himself, still unable to fully trust her motives.

Then suddenly, he felt her hand touch his and caress it. He dared not look into her face, but he felt the inspection of her eyes.

Inexplicably, he allowed her fingers to entwine with his. He felt her hand's pressure in his and, to his surprise, returned it. She said nothing, turning her head away, watching the lazy flow of the muddy Potomac. As the sun declined, the air turned cooler.

"Are you cold, Frank?" she whispered.

It felt strange to hear her speak his name.

Franz, he wanted to tell her. *My name is Franz.*

"I'm fine."

He felt more confusion than chill. What was he doing here with this woman, holding her hand? He knew it was dangerous, but the fact was that he felt no danger, only a strange feeling of exultation.

"Are you cold, Frank?" she whispered again, her lips close to his ear.

Something was changing too rapidly for him to assess. By using his first name, she was accelerating the level of intimacy.

He shook his head but said nothing. He was too busy sorting out his feelings. He wanted to address her by her first name, Stephanie. He wanted to say, *Stephanie.* But he held back.

"Hungry?" she asked. "We could go to a restaurant if you'd like." She looked at her watch. "I'm free until six."

Actually, he wasn't hungry. Food was the last thing on his mind.

"That would be nice," he heard himself say, knowing now he was being carried by a momentum he could not resist.

Again he cautioned himself. *She might be here for a purpose. Be wary.*

They sat for a while longer, holding hands but saying little. He was determined to keep silent, hoping that she would soon tire of his lack of communication. Neither did he wish to ask her any questions about herself, fearful of starting a dialogue.

Finally, after a long period of silence between them, she stood up.

"Let's get something to eat," she said.

He nodded his consent.

She wheeled him to a modest restaurant on Pennsylvania Avenue, where he insisted she leave the wheelchair outside and clumped his way inside.

"Machismo," she giggled.

It was true, he agreed. Actually, he hated the idea of seeming dependent, especially on a woman, although secretly he was beginning to enjoy the attention.

The restaurant had plastic tabletops and middle-aged female waitresses. They both made quick choices of the blue plate special: fried chicken, spinach, and cottage-style potatoes. While waiting, their eyes met across the table and held.

"It's nice being with you, Frank," she said, as if it were a confession.

She paused, obviously priming herself.

"What I don't understand . . . " Hesitating, she explored his face. " . . . Don't you have anybody in Washington . . . "

"I'm fine," he interrupted. "I told you, I'm just passing through."

"From where to where?" she asked.

He continued to look at her, not knowing exactly how to respond. Apparently, she was ahead of him.

"It's all right, Frank. I was being nosy. Your prerogative—I won't pry."

For the moment, her statement satisfied him. But he was certain that she would continue to be curious. Better to put the onus on her, he decided.

"Why did you become a nurse?" he asked, deflecting the conversation.

He admitted to his own curiosity now, still unsure about her role.

"There was a shortage," she replied. "And please, I don't want to sound noble. Some day, I think I'd like to go to medical school, become a doctor. When things settle down."

She seemed to be talking in shorthand, which raised his suspicions again.

When he asked no follow-up questions, she continued, "I mean I like nursing. I guess I'm a natural caregiver."

He waited with trepidation, wondering when she would begin to pry again, wary of the ultimate response: *And you?*

The blue plate special came. The chicken was stringy and the cottage fries greasy, but they did not comment on it and picked at their food. But when they looked at each other, their eyes held.

Miller had never been in this position before. He felt the odd pull of it, the strange sense of inchoate longing.

"Been in Washington a year now. Actually, in two weeks it will be my anniversary," she said, suddenly as if in midsentence.

He suspected she was talking about herself to induce him to speak about himself.

"Do you like it here?" he said, deliberately focusing the spotlight on her.

"Lots of stuff happening. They say that now that the war is over, they might be reducing staff here. There'll be plenty of work at the VA hospitals, lots of wounded men to be cared for. I used to work in Massachusetts. We treated everybody, POWs, too."

"Germans?"

Without thinking, he had blurted the question.

Her eyes widened, and she nodded and smiled.

"Some Italians, too. The human body is the human body; we're all flesh and blood." She knocked on his cast through his shirt. "Even you—big, silent Frank Miller."

Oddly, he felt a sudden unburdening, a release. He heard himself chuckling.

"Well, well," she said. "The man doth smile."

She looked at her wristwatch, the face of which was on the underside of her wrist. He noted that her fingers were long and graceful, tapered with short nails. Leaving most of their food untouched, he paid the check, clumped his way outside, and got into the chair.

Keeping silent, she rolled him into the lobby of the Y.

121

"Have a good ride, Miller?" the clerk at the desk said.

They both ignored the comment.

"Remember the rules."

There was a little room off the lobby and away from the prying eyes of the man at the desk. She wheeled him there, and he got out of the wheelchair, which she folded and leaned against the wall.

Then she turned to face him. He felt his stomach tighten and beads of sweat roll down his back under his cast. They faced each other for a long moment.

"I'm glad I came, Frank. I wasn't sure."

He stood silently looking at her, rooted to the spot. His strange yearning seemed to overwhelm him, but he could not bring himself to react.

"I'm glad you did," he stammered.

His knees started to tremble. Reaching out, she moved toward him, and they kissed, a long deep kiss, yet another totally new experience for him. He felt her hand caress the back of his head.

"Tomorrow," she whispered. "I wouldn't want to cause you trouble with the management."

She disengaged reluctantly and started to move away, then she came back, and they kissed again. Her pelvis pressed against him, and he was certain she felt his erection, which, inexplicably, embarrassed him. She moved away, looked back, and waved, then was gone.

Back in his room, he lay down on the bed without undressing and tried to make sense out of this uncommon encounter. What did it mean? He could not relate it to anything he had ever experienced. Try as he might to put it out of his mind, he could not succeed. His reality seemed skewered. This situation was interfering with his concentration. He tried going through the machinations of an impending assassination attempt on the president but could not get a potential plan straight in his mind.

He was still erect. But it was a different kind of desire, something more than merely the anticipation of impending pleasure. There was more to this, a lot more. He reached for his penis with his left hand. It was too awkward for him to masturbate. Besides, the expression "beat the monkey" seemed too crude to associate with her. He felt oddly ashamed.

She came the next day and the next. He made his regular call before she arrived, and they spent the day together. Strange things were happening. The mission, which had totally absorbed him since arriving in the States, seemed to fade into the background of his life. He was well aware that one day, he would be summoned, but the anticipation seemed to be getting less real.

Before his accident, he had been totally focused on the impending assignment. Now, he no longer bothered to read the papers or listen to the radio. What was happening in Europe was of little interest; even Dimitrov's face faded in his memory.

It had been months since he had arrived in Washington. If it weren't for his daily call, he might have thought that he had been forgotten.

Stephanie was what absorbed his full attention. He felt charged, invaded. It was getting increasingly hard to be evasive and was becoming less and less difficult to clump around. She wheeled him around Washington, and they kissed and fondled each other wherever they could snatch some privacy. At times, they indulged themselves in mutual masturbation, but it seemed demeaning and unsatisfactory.

It was awkward and frustrating for both of them. She lived with three other nurses in a one-bedroom apartment in Northwest Washington. The housing shortage was acute. He had been lucky to get his room at the Y, but he suspected that his so-called sponsors had pulled strings to get him in. Apparently, they wanted him based at that specific spot. He suspected that he might be under surveillance, but he soon dismissed the idea.

"We could go to a hotel," he suggested.

She told him it would be uncomfortable for her. House detectives might make trouble. She could lose her job. It would have been an unacceptable risk for him as well.

Dimitrov had warned him that once he got the car to Washington, he should use it only as necessary for the mission, the less exposure the better, with no risk of being stopped and ticketed for a violation. What would be the harm, he decided, provided he could handle it in his present condition? After all, he had been careful on his trip from Canada. Besides, the car was America's love chamber. In Germany, the cars were too small and cramped.

His revelation about the car surprised her.

"Can you drive?" he asked.

She shook her head in the negative. "Too busy to learn."

He was able to manage it, and they began to drive and park along deserted roads in Virginia. They began to make love in the car.

"I'm not very experienced, Frank," she told him. "I'm also a virgin."

"Is that important to you?" he had asked.

"It was," she said. "Until now."

He did not press the point. Yet their lovemaking was passionate, and they satisfied themselves in ways that did not interfere with her virginity.

"Are you sure, Frank?" she would ask at times, when they had reached a point where a little more effort would have settled the question.

Of course, his being in a cast was inhibiting, even when they moved to the backseat. They never undressed completely. Besides, they each felt the tension of accidental discovery.

He remembered an expression from his teen days in America: "Everything but." Even the girls at Yaphank were guarded about their virginity, although it was at Yaphank that he had lost his with an older girl. He had been fifteen; the girl was seventeen.

Back in Germany, Himmler had created camps where SS men and carefully screened girls were available strictly for propagation purposes. There was no love involved; it was sex by the numbers. He had been paired with a girl from Munich who was hell-bent on having a baby for the führer. It hadn't been a very satisfactory episode, barely pleasurable, and he learned later, she hadn't conceived. Remembering that, he did not press the issue. Besides, an accidental pregnancy would be a complication he did not want.

Despite their physical intimacy, he kept himself carefully guarded, always leaving open the possibility that she might be an agent, a mole like himself, planted to find out what he was up to. And yet, when he held her in his arms, he could not imagine someone so beautiful, open, and loving could stir such suspicions.

Of course, there was dialogue between them, but he kept any answers deflective and evasive. He was wary of revealing anything of his past, his point of view, his beliefs and prejudices, his hatred of the Jews and all mongrel races, his absolute belief that the destiny of the pure Germanic race was to one day rule the world, that Adolph Hitler's defeat was merely a temporary pause in this great crusade.

Surely, he was convinced that she was of Aryan stock. She was blue-eyed, and he noted that her pubic hair was golden. Her breasts were full, large, delicious, and he treated her nipples like a suckling child. Together, with their classic Germanic looks, they could make beautiful Aryan children. Such projected thoughts surprised him. Despite all his discipline and self-control, something had occurred deep inside him, beyond his control.

She made some small effort to probe beyond the scrim of his silence; and in order to protect himself, he invented a line of half-truths. He had grown up in New Jersey, which was true, although he was not specific. When she asked about his parents, he said they were both dead, which was true. He gave his correct age of twenty-seven, which she could find out if she went through his forged identification papers.

"Have you plans for the future?" she asked, numerous times.

That answer departed from any semblance of truth. In his mind, he remained an SS man, a soldier, a knight in a holy cause. Instead, he invented another persona. He told her he had planned to study architecture, build things. He was on his way to California— it could have been anywhere. He had spent the war years in the merchant marine on Victory ships. But when she probed beyond the thin slice of information, he balked and changed the subject.

Rather than questioning her, he waited until she volunteered. She was twenty-two, had grown up in Newton, Massachusetts. Her father was a physician, her mother a housewife. She had two brothers; both had been in the army. Yet, he detected hesitation, which instigated brief episodes of heightened suspicion, and he could not contain his curiosity.

"Why me?" he asked. "Why single me out?"

"That again." she sighed.

"You must have had reasons. You see many patients in the hospital."

"I can only say, my darling, the human heart cannot be explained. It takes you on strange journeys when you least expect it."

He admitted some difficulty with the explanation.

"But why *me*?" he pressed.

"I can't explain attraction, Frank. I was just drawn to you, I guess. Maybe you were sending out signals. Who knows? Maybe you looked needy. But there is no denying you struck a chord. I'm sorry, but I guess I yielded to an impulse."

She started a playful chain of kisses from his forehead to his lips. Then she stopped and observed his face.

"And to you," she said.

He laughed and kissed her forehead.

"I guess I was a vulnerable target."

"Are you sorry?" she asked coyly.

"No," he admitted, but it was another half-truth.

"Could be, we bit off more than we can chew," she told him.

He was baffled by her comment and, in an odd way, relieved. To explore it further seemed as if they would be poking into dangerous ground.

Accept the present, he urged himself. *Savor it. Enjoy it.*

He loved these halcyon days, the joyful pleasures. At times, she begged him to penetrate her. For some complicated reason, he held back. Perhaps, it was some sense of distorted honor, or, he reasoned, she was entitled to some sacred, personal place, something untouched and pristine. Such thoughts baffled him.

Considering his situation, he dared not speculate beyond the moment. He was a caged predator, programmed to kill, trapped by his past, and condemned to an uncertain future. He berated his foolishness for this involvement. Dimitrov had been absolutely right. Such relationships were dangerous to him and a hindrance to his mission. He had stepped across a red line.

When left alone at night, he contemplated what had become a dilemma. He could not find the will to break off this debilitating complication. When she left him, his longing was like some disease he could not shake. Was there a cure?

Worse, he had discovered certain tenderness, a vulnerability that he did not know he had. He tried demonizing her, imagining her as some ruthless Delilah who had blinded him, a Mata Hari, a Jezebel, an evil castrator of the flower of German youth. Unfortunately, all his accusations melted under the power of his longing.

Six weeks passed like lightening. He clomped around with less and less difficulty and was able to do away with crutches. A wheelchair had long been abandoned.

When the six weeks were up, at her insistence, he went back to the hospital. He was x-rayed and the cast on his arm was removed. As she had predicted, the x-ray of his ankle had revealed that the healing process was not complete.

"How long?" he had asked, remembering his mission.

The doctor had shrugged. "No way of knowing."

Each day he called his unknown contact was a telling reminder of his involvement. He wished it were over. His relationship with Stephanie threatened to change everything. He felt he had been turned inside out, as if his meeting Stephanie were the start of a new life.

She was transferred to the dayshift, and they changed their routine, although the car remained their love chamber. For some reason, the night increased the intensity of their feelings. He spent his days anxious with expectation. Although he continued to make his daily call, the idea of his mission seemed to fade, then disappear. His past seemed like a dream. He paid little attention to current events. He couldn't care less. His one focus, his one obsession was Stephanie Brown.

One night in January, they had parked on a deserted country road in Virginia. The air was crystal clear, and fresh snow began to fall on the windows of the car. The heater was on, and they felt encapsulated and alone. In the backseat, they made love.

"Frank, please. Now! I want the memory of this. I want to mark its significance. I want to seal our love."

Love? The word frightened him. He had never before been confronted by the power of this emotion.

"Please—for us, darling. For me, this is the most important thing in my life."

He was confused by her assertion. She maneuvered herself under him and inserted him. He felt the barrier, and she surged up to meet him. She groaned briefly, and the barrier gave way.

"Thank you, darling," she whispered.

He felt her tremble.

Later, driving through the light snow toward Washington, she leaned against him.

"I love you, sweetheart," she said.

He did not respond. To utter such a word would be a mark of hope for a future that he knew he yearned for desperately and for which he dared not hope—not yet.

She sighed, and caressing her face, he noted that she was crying.

"Tears?"

He felt her nod. He supposed they were tears of happiness; he was wrong.

"There are obstacles ahead, Frank."

He didn't understand.

"We come from different ends of the spectrum."

"What does that mean?"

He was confused.

"I played with fire, but I couldn't help myself."

"What are you talking about?"

"I've been less than forthright, darling. I'm not what I appear."

He was tempted to say: *Neither am I.*

She was silent through a long pause.

"I'm Jewish, Frank. My family would never approve."

Chapter 10

Dimitrov stamped his feet on the hardened snow outside Beria's dacha thirty miles from Moscow. Despite his thick, fur-lined boots, fur hat with earlaps, and his heavy, fur-collared overcoat, his breath seemed to freeze in his lungs. From where he stood near the side entrance of the large dacha, he could see the high-voltage electrified fence through the tall evergreens that lined the property.

When summoned in this way and directed to the edge of the side porch, Dimitrov knew that Beria had something of extreme importance to impart. That they were to discuss this outdoors in subzero weather, free from any possibility of bugging devices, invested the subject matter with top-secret urgency.

Dimitrov had to pass through two gates guarded by more than a dozen NKVD uniformed soldiers at each gate. He presented his pass for careful scrutiny at both checkpoints. There were no exceptions to this procedure, despite Dimitrov's confidential relationship and high rank. He ran what was often jokingly referred to as the "NKVD within the NKVD," but everyone knew he was Beria's man, even though Beria had theoretically given up the post as Stalin's boss of the NKVD apparatus. Beria's tentacles were everywhere, and with the exception of Stalin, his power was absolute.

He was now the man in charge of getting Russia the bomb. Stalin was obsessed with that mission, deeply angered by the Americans' arrogance about their possession of it. According to Beria, who revealed this information to Dimitrov, Roosevelt had told Stalin in Yalta that they were working on this superbomb, and the American

130

president had indicated that he would share it with the Soviets. Of course, that was at a time when the battle was still ongoing, and Stalin was pressing Churchill and Roosevelt for a second front while Russia was in agony. Things had changed considerably since the president's untimely death. As for this new American president, it was still too early to tell if he would honor his predecessor's intentions.

Dimitrov heard a door close and, turning, saw Beria step outside. Steamy vapor poured out of his mouth, and as he approached Dimitrov, he took off his pince-nez and wiped off the condensation, putting them on again in his one-handed way.

Moving his head in the direction of a partially snow-cleared trail that snaked through a thickly wooded forest of evergreens, Dimitrov took his place next to Beria, and the two men followed the path. Surrounding the house and eyeing the two men were a number of NKVD soldiers holding submachine guns at the ready. Beria took no chances. This was not the first time that the two men used the outdoors for their discussion. Beria was paranoid about bugging, which was ironic, since he was the champion bugger of them all. This was often a joke between them.

"Even paranoids have enemies," Beria chuckled, as they moved deeper into the forest. At times, he often made jokes about himself. Dimitrov exhibited the required appreciation.

Dimitrov's role was to eliminate obstacles in what they referred to privately as the offspring countries, those who were destined for growth within the Soviet family: Hungary, Romania, Bulgaria, Poland, their part of divided Germany, their zone in Berlin, as well as Lithuania, Estonia, and Latvia.

According to Beria, who often shared this information with Dimitrov, everything was going well. The ranks of "antis"—thanks to Dimitrov's dedicated actions—were thinning daily. Beria's gratitude, expressed often, filled Dimitrov with pride and, of course, tangible honors.

Because of Dimitrov's efforts, Beria stressed, the Soviets were pulling the strings in all the recently liberated countries, some

131

of whose citizens were avid Nazi sympathizers who had mounted armed divisions in the service of Hitler's cause. Under the guise of rooting out such elements, Dimitrov's men showed no mercy and gave no quarter. The campaign, for reasons thoroughly and secretly explained by Beria, was to be deliberately kept clandestine. Stalin did not wish to be considered heavy-handed while enjoying the residual support of his wartime allies.

In terms of his career, Dimitrov had, indeed, picked the right horse. Not only was Beria in Stalin's confidence, there was talk that at some point in the future he might be Stalin's successor. Of course, such speculation was unspoken, although Beria often hinted at the possibility. Such hints raised Dimitrov's expectations that he would one day take over the command of the entire NKVD apparatus.

Dimitrov enjoyed Beria's confidential commentaries on the latest geopolitical strategies employed by the ruling comrades. Such information corroborated Dimitrov's status as a loyal associate.

Today was no exception, and as they walked, Beria revealed that the Soviet's worldwide propaganda effort was winning more and more adherents to the Communist cause.

"The corrupt capitalist states were falling under their own weight," he explained, shaking his head and patting Dimitrov on the shoulder. Beria nodded in emphasis and chortled—a signal that his superior was going into a gossipy "behind the scenes" mode—especially at his observations at Yalta where he had been in attendance. These were the revelations Dimitrov treasured most.

Stalin's manipulation of Roosevelt had been masterful, Beria told him, gleeful in his rendition. Roosevelt had seemed to Stalin a buffoon who told long anecdotes and could not hold his liquor. Stalin had remarked privately on the president's preference for the martini, which he had dubbed an effeminate drink.

Churchill on the other hand, with his scotch, brandy, and champagne, was characterized as a shrewd, cunning, and dangerous poser. His capacity for alcohol, at first, seemed astonishing. The more he seemed to imbibe, the more eloquent he became. Beria had deduced, after careful analysis of the minute observations by his operatives, that the prime minister had faked his capacity. In other words, to Beria, Churchill was a hostile menace, a powerful dissimulator with a satanic talent for persuasion and a potentially destructive influence on Soviet plans for the future.

He had been a thorn in their side since the beginning, and Stalin blamed him not only for deliberately stalling the second front but secretly trying to sow dissent between him and Roosevelt. Worse, Beria explained, he wanted to make nice to the Germans.

"You know why?" Beria told him, again and again.

Dimitrov had been party to many a diatribe against Churchill by Beria.

"Churchill wants a Germany that will serve as a bulwark against the Soviet Union. He distrusts us to the point of fanaticism. We were partners only because Hitler was a military moron, taking on the Soviet Union when he could easily have conquered Britain despite that breast-beating 'blood, sweat, and tears' speech. It was all horn blowing and crap. Hitler would have gone through England like a hot knife through butter."

Once, Beria told him that the assassination of Hitler was put on the table for discussion. Churchill turned it down on the grounds that the führer was making so many military blunders it was best to keep him alive rather than risk the chance that the German military would fall under the command of a really competent general.

Dimitrov basked in Beria's trust.

Beria had been told that Hitler's body was unquestionably identified by his jaw and dental work, which were now kept under guarded wraps in a Kremlin vault. This was deliberately hidden from public view because Stalin wanted the German people to believe he was still alive. He needed to convince Churchill and Roosevelt that the Germans were fighting harder because they believed that the führer would return; and therefore, he provided them with a reason why it was necessary for the Red Army to sweep deeper and with more urgency into the Nazi state to quell all expectations of a Nazi comeback. Beria took credit for the ploy, which Stalin had called brilliant.

Although Churchill was out of power, Beria considered him even more dangerous as an anti-Soviet propagandist.

"He has always been anti-Soviet and one of the prime organizers of the White Russian pigs who tried to thwart the revolution."

This was one of Beria's favorite accusations.

The NKVD files, he revealed to Dimitrov, were filled with secret Churchill material that confirmed his anti-Soviet feelings. "Kill the Bolshie" had been his mantra. It was he who, along with Patton, wanted to thwart the Red Army's advance to Berlin. Secretly, they both wanted to push deeper into Germany and entertained the idea of taking on the Red Army. Such pressure did not move Eisenhower and Roosevelt.

"Did you know, Ivan Vasilyevich, that Churchill, to press his case against us, suggested privately that with the new superbomb they were building, they could have easily defeated us. With that atomic bomb, they could have succeeded, destroying our major cities in minutes. One day we will have it; I promised this to Comrade Stalin. We will have it, and that will no longer be an issue. Believe me, we have people inside their labs who are providing us with information. In due time, we will have it, despite Churchill's Red-baiting eloquence."

To Beria, Churchill was the ultimate enemy, in or out of power. Once he got started on the subject he was unstoppable.

"Under his guise of bonhomie and outward show of affection for Stalin and despite his kind words, Churchill was playing a double game. To me, it was absolutely clear. I don't trust him. He is an obstacle, a weapon as potent and destructive, perhaps, as the big bomb itself."

As they walked through the forest path, Beria informed Dimitrov, "I told Stalin himself just the other day that Churchill should be eliminated, pushed off the world stage as quickly as possible. We had a great debate on this issue. Actually, he is amused by this silly chubby man with the pink cheeks, his big cigar, and his stupid finger sign."

Beria made the V-for-victory sign and chuckled.

"Only he is not a joke, and Stalin knows that. In or out of office, Churchill is a menace. Stalin agrees. In private conversation with me, he cited the power of his words. He referred to Lenin, whose speeches were electrifying, and of course, Marx and his books. No one could dispute the power of the words coming from the pen of this obscure apostate Jew, who was able to articulate the true path for all of us who demand justice and an end to slavery by the powers of entrenched privilege."

Dimitrov had heard differing versions of Stalin's opinion on Churchill, but they all added up to the same thing: He was a continuing hazard and obstacle.

"Comrade Stalin does not believe Churchill is finished. He thinks Attlee and Truman are both no better than shopkeepers. He doubts the Americans would be stupid enough to keep Truman in office. The same will be true of Attlee. England is in even worse economic shape than us, and their system will throw him out in the next election and turn again to Churchill. We mustn't let that happen, he told me. Of course, I agreed."

Beria continued, "So far, Churchill's ant-Soviet remarks have been publicly muted, although in his Parliament he is sometimes vehement in his criticism. Even Attlee heeds the bluster and has publicly declared our party as undesirable, preferring his own socialist system. But this speech in America could be a public attack on us with the whole world watching. I have urged Comrade Stalin that we must take steps."

Beria lowered his voice and sucked in a deep breath.

"He is worried that Churchill will spread his lies and make us out to be devils. The man is an imperialist provocateur who has nothing but enmity for our cause. If he regurgitated his views in our domain, he would be dead meat." Beria smiled. "He doesn't understand the extent of our reach; one day, he will."

"Surely, Lavrentiy Pavlovich, you explained to Stalin the beauty of our plan using our captive SS officer?"

"A great leader must not be burdened with details. He knows his trusted lieutenants will carry out his wishes to the letter."

Beria paused.

"We agree in principle. We have always agreed in principle."

Dimitrov was confused and waited for a further expansion of his remarks.

"Ivan Vasilyevich," Beria explained. "There is no substitute for . . ."

He made a motion with the edge of his hand across his throat.

" . . . It is far cheaper and more effective to physically destroy your enemies. Dead is dead, comrade. The dead don't make trouble. It is a messy business, and only the most dedicated and courageous can do the job properly. Some brand me a tyrant and executioner, but history will prove that I have served our cause with honor and courage. Our enemies are everywhere. They want to see our movement expire. Generations of capitalist propaganda have created a gigantic army of destructive fools. Their system is decadent and serves only those who exploit and rule."

He paused.

"I don't have to tell you this, Ivan Vasilyevich. We are making new history here. The disease affects the herd, and the sick ones must be culled and destroyed."

Beria grew suddenly silent as they walked. Only the crunch of the snow under their boots broke the silence.

"We must rid them of their mouthpiece," Beria ejaculated, raising his voice.

Dimitrov knew, of course, who was meant.

"Is it being contemplated?"

"Let us say the idea is in the oven," Beria said.

Dimitrov laughed politely.

"Churchill?"

"Not yet."

Beria paused and looked up at the pale sun beneath the low clouds. Dimitrov saw the reflection of the sun on Beria's glasses. He shielded his eyes and turned in another direction.

"He will be making a big noise next month in America. What he plans to say will be a deciding factor."

"Do we know?"

"We have indications, but we do not know exactly. Our understanding is that it will be a diatribe against us."

"Will you know in advance?"

Beria smiled.

"Well in advance. We will be very well informed."

Dimitrov nodded. In these matters, he did not pry, waiting instead for Beria to volunteer information. For a few minutes, as they walked through the forest, Beria was silent. Then he stopped and faced Dimitrov.

"No one else can be trusted with instructions, Ivan Vasilyevich. Pack your toothbrush and be ready."

Chapter 11

Maclean had fully briefed Victoria on what to expect. She had been surprised when he announced her assignment to take Churchill's dictation.

"Why me?" she had asked, although she could not deny a feeling of pride.

"Because you are the most intelligent, most efficient, and most skillful," he said, smiling while adding, "and most attractive." He paused and chuckled. "I volunteered you."

"Kind of you," she said, with mock severity.

"It wasn't easy. Thompson checked you out quite thoroughly."

"Thompson?"

"Churchill's man, officially his private bodyguard, but much more than that. He is a former member of Scotland Yard's Special Branch and quite legendary. On and off, he was been Churchill's bodyguard for years. He is all eyes and ears and has a canny sense of detail. Churchill called him out of retirement when he became prime minister and was with him during the war. He retired again and has been called back by Mr. Churchill to be with him during foreign trips." Maclean paused. "Churchill trusts him totally. The man is passionately protective, the best in the business. And I am sure he is armed."

"I'm hardly a threat, darling."

"To him, everyone is a threat. He put me through a relentless interrogation about your background and qualifications. He has gone over your personnel file with a fine-tooth comb and has questioned me at length about your skills and general attitude."

Maclean winked. "I told him everything."

"Everything?" She winked back.

"Everyone is entitled to some secrets," he said slyly.

"I suppose I should be honored, darling. Did this canny gentleman tell you what I'm to expect?"

"As a matter of fact, he did. Here again, he was quite thorough. He explained that Mr. Churchill would be irascible and sometimes difficult. He is used to his regular English secretaries, all of whom know his habits. Undoubtedly, he will expect you to react like them, which will be impossible. You must be patient and unflappable. At times, he will be difficult to follow. He has a bit of a stammer."

"Churchill a stammer? Really, darling? Churchill?"

"According to Thompson, it becomes particularly prominent when dictating."

Victoria raised her eyebrows.

"He will dictate a line, say it again and again, then change it and go through the routine yet another time. Thompson acknowledged that this could be terribly difficult for a typist or a stenographer, even one as efficient as you on both scores, Victoria. The point here is that we need . . . "

He frowned, paused, turned away, and then came back with a smile.

" . . . *I* need," he said. "I need you, Victoria, to stay on the job. If he is dissatisfied, you will be sacked. He is very serious about his speeches. They are his stock-in-trade as a politician, and he knows it."

He seemed more tense than usual, and his warnings were making her nervous.

"I won't let you down, darling. I promise."

Ignoring her comment, he continued.

"His final draft . . . Thompson was rather explicit about this . . . must be typed out as if it were verse, and you will have to make these line judgments based upon his cadences. The chances are he

139

will go over them again and again and make changes. Expect to do numerous drafts."

"Why a verse format?"

"I suppose he thinks of his speeches as poetry, poetry as words meant to be read aloud as if they were rhymed and metered. Thompson says that every line must be a phrase and no line must end in a preposition or an adjective. Apparently, Churchill will make this point ad infinitum. Oh yes, I've forgotten, the verse lines must not begin with a capital letter. Do you understand, Victoria?"

"Of course, I understand. But I must say the details are so precise, it's alarming. Do you think I'm up to it, darling?"

"You must be, Victoria."

He looked at her in a sharp businesslike way. His blue eyes blazed with intensity.

"Must? My God, darling, my fingers will shake and my knees will wobble. Perhaps Thompson deliberately made it sound too formidable."

"He wants you to be prepared is all."

"I've taken dictation from the best, darling," she snapped. "You, too, can be a difficult composer. I told you. I won't let you down. Frankly, darling, you make it sound like a matter of life and death."

He swallowed hard, and she saw a nerve palpitate in his cheek, a common tic when he was tense.

"Victoria, this assignment is important. I don't want you to be intimidated or humiliated. All I ask is that you stay the course."

"Stop worrying, darling. I will not let him intimidate me, and I have no intention of being sacked."

She winked at him and blew him a kiss across the desk.

"Does he like girls?" she asked, seeking to lighten his mood and calm him as well.

"He adores pretty girls and once courted Ethel Barrymore, and rumor has it that he has a crush on Vivien Leigh. He might be free with the compliments and seem flirty, but he will never make a pass. He is devoted solely to Clementine. There has never been a breath of scandal about him."

"Didn't you tell me I was irresistible?" she said, pursing her lips and winking again. "And competent in other areas as well."

She opened her mouth and licked her lips in an unmistakably erotic gesture. He did not react.

"This is serious, Victoria," he said, resuming his instructions. "Mostly, Thompson tells me, he will be dictating in his bed. He might decide to dictate to you while you type his words rather than take shorthand. At times, he told me, he has actually dictated to female secretaries in his bath."

"You're not serious?"

"I am, indeed."

"I hope he doesn't try it with me."

"If he does, I seriously doubt you will become distracted by temptation."

"One never knows," she giggled.

He ignored the remark and continued, "But he will probably dictate mostly while he is sitting up in bed. He often takes his breakfast there as well."

"And where will I be?" she said, facetiously.

"Here again, Thompson was quite detailed. If he chooses direct-to-typewriter dictation, you will work at a little table near his bed, where he will have fitted you with his preferred typewriter whose brand escapes me. He will smoke his cigar, and the room will fill with smoke. If he is interrupted by a phone call, he will bark into the phone and feign annoyance. But he will interrupt himself frequently with anecdotal experiences, reminiscences, and frequent quotes from Shakespeare and his favorite poets." He chuckled. "We have some interests in common. The man is a vast storehouse of knowledge, an entertaining talker, a raconteur of fearsome talent and innate timing. He will do this often, tell wry little jokes, offer descriptions, make inquiries."

"Inquiries?"

"He will want to know where you are from, what your parents do, where you went to school. He is endlessly curious about everybody and everything. But Thompson warns, beware of the timing and propriety of making inquiries yourself. He is cunning, clever, and guarded. Above all, remember that the man's ego matches his charm; both are massive and extraordinary. This is a unique human being, bigger than life. But if you are inattentive or make careless errors, he can be lethal."

"I am always attentive," she said, with real indignation. Then she smiled. "Especially on certain special occasions."

Pad in hand, she stood up and stuck out her tongue.

"Really, be serious, Victoria."

"Darling, I promise not to embarrass myself."

She was well aware of the nature of security precautions, but the thoroughness of her vetting made her uncomfortable and slightly nervous.

"Or, for that matter," she added, "I promise not to embarrass the first secretary for his choice."

Maclean's forehead creased suddenly, and he nodded as if to himself. It was a gesture that struck her as something she had not seen before.

"Let's face it, Victoria. He is the great Winston Churchill, admired by millions. Thompson was only doing his job. The fact is that Churchill does have enemies, many enemies."

"I suppose we all do," she sighed, thinking of Maclean's wife, Melinda. Had they been discreet? Did she know? And if so, would she be an enemy? Quickly, she dismissed the thought.

"You will have to revise and revise, type and retype."

"I will do as ordered, sir," she teased, her initial fears dissipating.

He hesitated, nodded, leaned over, and caressed her cheek.

"You are wonderful, Victoria," he said, bending toward her and kissing her deeply on the lips. "You are my one true friend."

"Friend?" she whispered. "Surely you can do better than that."

He kissed her again, then stood up, and paced the length of the room, his usual gesture when he was deep in thought. Finally, he turned.

"There is one other area of discussion," he said. "They insist upon confidentiality."

"Of course," she commented, hardly surprised.

"Victoria, darling. I will need a copy of the speech."

Suddenly, she was totally confused. They exchanged glances. There was no mistaking his determination.

"But if they insist on confidentiality . . . " Victoria said.

"I know, darling. It does sound . . . well, I suppose, unethical. But I'm afraid it is necessary. As you know, my job as first secretary requires me to properly monitor such material. After all, Mr. Churchill is no longer prime minister, and I now serve Mr. Attlee's government. Do you see?"

"I do, of course. But how can I violate their trust?"

"It has nothing to do with trust. The matter is a question of national security. You will be doing a patriotic duty for His Majesty's government. Please, darling, don't be alarmed at my suggestion. It's a question of being forewarned about themes and subject matter that might deviate from current government policy. The ambassador and I will be meeting with Mr. Churchill tomorrow and will discuss matters that bear on the speech. Policies change with governments. There is no longer any wartime coalition with Britain, but to the world, Churchill is still perceived as speaking for our country."

He paused, and then added, "Seeing the speech will give me a leg up in such a conversation. You will be providing yeoman service."

"Surely," she snapped. "You're not going to tell him that you've read the speech."

"Absolutely not," he replied. "It would be unthinkable to compromise you in any way."

His explanation seemed reassuring. He had raised security questions and she trusted him implicitly. In her mind, her loyalty was to her boss. Indeed, as his lover, she would put any request he made above all else, whatever the circumstances.

"How would you suggest it be done? You say Thompson is all eyes and ears."

"I doubt very much if he would do a body search."

"Well then," she giggled coyly. "I know exactly where I shall hide it."

"And I will eagerly search amongst the various treasures."

She swiveled her hips and offered a smart salute.

"You're the captain of this ship, sir," she said. "Your wish is my command."

She stood up, her dictation book in one hand and a sheaf of pencils in the other.

"The copy," he reminded. "An affair of state."

"An affair," she said winking. "I like that."

***

With some trepidation, she knocked on the door of the ambassador's suite.

A tall man came to the door. He wore a double-breasted, pinstriped suit and looked more like a businessman than a bodyguard. His eyes revealed an acute sharpness of observation as he inspected her. Forewarned by her lover, she knew he would carefully scrutinize her. His glance washed over her like an x-ray exploring every detail of her person, her inner life, and thoughts. She had never felt more naked.

"I'm Victoria Stewart," she said, feeling a slight tremble in her voice. "First Secretary Maclean sent me."

"Yes, the secretary. I'm so very pleased to meet you. Mr. Churchill will be with you shortly."

He offered a surprisingly warm and ingratiating smile that began to put her at her ease.

He directed her to an impressive sitting room dominated

by a painting of Wellington and set up with a series of comfortable conversational settings. She sat on a straight chair, which seemed appropriate to her station, noting that Thompson had taken a wingchair at the other end of the sitting room. He crossed his legs and picked up a copy of the *London Times,* which he had obviously been reading before she arrived.

She heard sounds coming from an adjoining room, one of which she recognized immediately as the unmistakable voice of Churchill.

"You've come highly recommended," Thompson said, his face poking from behind the paper.

"I'm honored, sir."

"I suppose you've been fully briefed and know what to expect."

"Yes. The first secretary has been thorough," she said crisply, knowing that Thompson had vetted him carefully about her background and skills.

"Above all, he expects confidentiality."

"I understand, sir."

The words seemed to catch in her throat.

"He is a hard taskmaster."

"So I understand."

The door to the adjoining room opened, and a distinguished-looking man with a military-trim moustache walked across the suite and nodded in her direction and passed out of the suite.

"Dean Acheson," Thompson said, after he had gone. "American State Department."

"Ready," a voice boomed from the bedroom

"Off you go," Thompson said, "into the lion's lair."

She stood up and entered the bedroom. Churchill sat in bed, his back supported by a leather headrest. He wore a colorful silk dressing gown with a dragon pattern. He was smoking a long cigar. In front of him were a tray and the remains of his breakfast. Newspapers and some official-looking documents lay helter-skelter

145

over the comforter. Beside the bed was a small desk on which sat a typewriter and a sheaf of paper.

"You are?" he barked, making no attempt to charm.

But the twinkle in his eyes belied his stern look.

"Victoria Stewart, the first secretary . . . "

"Victoria, is it? I was born under her reign. Fine woman. A progenitress of royal crowns across Europe."

Victoria had seen him in person before but certainly never in bed. He had the fierce look of a chained bulldog.

"Sit," he ordered, pointing to the desk.

She sat down, put a paper in the roller, and waited. She noticed that Thompson had moved into a corner of the bedroom and ensconced himself in an upholstered easy chair.

"They all have issues," Churchill said, shaking his head and looking toward Thompson. "A fine man, Acheson. Man of principle. Not fond of Franklin. Wants me to insert something about the United Nations in my speech." He shook his head. "Has a point. I will do it, of course. Such an organization might very well be worth the candle. Will it work or become a debating society? One never knows. Indeed, it might get us into heaven at long last, or at the very least, keep us out of hell." He chuckled.

Victoria eyed the blank paper, primed to begin, but Churchill went on.

"This Acheson. His Christian name is Dean—never ceases to amaze me how my mother's countrymen name their offspring after titles. I've met 'Kings,' 'Dukes,' 'Earls.' But then, there is a certain logic to 'Dean.' He is the son of an Episcopal bishop and dean is the next rank under bishop, as earl is to marquis. Maybe he was christened Dean because he was the son of a bishop."

Listening, Victoria remembered her boss's cautionary tale about Mr. Churchill's habit of anecdotal asides. Suddenly, he observed her with intensity and smiled with obvious ingratiation.

"My dear, if you can take dictation as well as you look, we shall get along famously. Where are you from, Miss Victoria Stewart?"

146

"Chelsea, sir."

"Were you there during the blitz?"

"Yes, I was. Our home was destroyed, but we all survived."

"Hitler was quite ruthless," Churchill nodded, shaking his head.

"And I do remember," Victoria added, "'Never was so much owed by so many to so few.' Stuck with me, sir."

"As it should, my dear, as it should. Those were indeed dark days, very dark. People must never forget that."

"No, sir."

Churchill's cigar had gone out. Thompson moved quickly forward, clicked a lighter, and brought the flame forward to light the cigar. Churchill looked at the burning end then puffed contently.

"Thompson here is my companion in vice. He encourages my habit."

"Against your doctor's orders, Mr. Churchill," Thompson said, revealing the easy closeness of their relationship.

Maclean had characterized him as Churchill's shadow and bodyguard. She understood the reference but questioned why he needed a bodyguard. He was no longer prime minister.

"Clementine has great faith in his guardianship," Churchill said. "Having been through a number of wars, imprisoned, shot at, an easy, bulky target, one would think Providence alone would continue its fine work of protection."

"Even Providence needs an occasional helper, Mr. Churchill," Thompson said, straight-faced.

It was obvious to Victoria that this was a much-repeated routine between them.

"Shall we begin, Miss Stewart?"

Victoria braced herself in her chair, her fingers poised on the keyboard. Churchill began to dictate. She could tell even at this early stage that he had probably worked out the pattern and construction of the speech in his mind. She had the impression that he had already gone over the lines in his head, and when he spoke finally, he was merely unreeling the words solely for the benefit of the typewriter.

She worked diligently, thankful for the many pauses. Although, his interruptions, asides, and anecdotes, as Donald had warned her, made her anxious. Apparently, he needed the diversions to restoke his mind.

At first, she took down the words by rote, concentrating on the sentences, some of which came out in a stammer, then raging forward with such sudden passion that she could barely keep up. When a page was finished, she paused to put in another.

"Faster, please!" Churchill snapped. "You must insert the paper faster."

"Yes, sir."

She typed at breakneck speed. At times, spent after a sudden burst, he paused and would relate an anecdote that seemed totally irrelevant to the text he was creating.

In one such pause, he said, "Did you know, Miss Stewart, that Winnie the Pooh was named after me?"

"Why no, sir," Victoria said, stunned not by the assertion but by its total irrelevancy to the speech.

"Oh, yes. The playwright, A. A. Milne, is my good friend." Churchill chuckled. "He told me that his two-year-old son, Christopher Robin, called a toy bear he had given him 'Pooh' in baby talk. It was the closest he could get to 'bear.' But Alan thought the bear should have a name so he called him 'Winnie' after me."

He shook his head, obviously enjoying the sudden flight into nostalgia.

"Once in the war, I instructed that lines in *The House on Pooh Corner* be code words for our British operatives in France for their radioing back of information. They had all grown up, you see, with Christopher Robin and Winnie-the-Pooh. Some priggish bureaucrats in Whitehall objected, but I overruled them. I told them that the Nazis would never figure it out—they have no sense of whimsy."

He was silent for a while then began again. She braced herself for the onslaught. The words came roaring out.

"The Soviets have divided Europe into two halves and put up

a fence . . . " he paused " . . . an iron fence." He shook his head. "No, strike that . . . a barricade." He shook his head in frustration, "Strike that." He mulled it over further. "Shield?" He shook his head. "Leave it blank, Miss . . . we'll look it over in draft." Then he continued, " . . . has descended across the Continent. Behind the line, lie all the countries of Central and Eastern Europe, their populations now in the Soviet sphere, and all are subject, in one form or another, not only to Soviet influence but to a very high measure of control from Moscow."

His stammering and many hesitations made it difficult to follow, but she was certain that she could figure it out when she typed a clean copy. He shook his head, obviously dissatisfied with the phrasing.

"Needs work," he grumped.

At times, he would ask her to strike out whole sentences and complain about the slowness, although she was going as fast as she could. After a while, she only typed two or three dashes to indicate the deletion.

Throughout the dictation, Thompson calmly read the paper, looking from behind it only when something was said that particularly perked his interest. During one long burst, he listened with rapt attention, his brows creased in concentration.

"In a great number of countries, far from the Russian frontiers throughout the world, Communist fifth columns are established and work in complete unity and absolute obedience to the directions they receive from the Communist center."

"If I might comment, Mr. Churchill," Thompson interrupted. "Isn't that inflammatory?"

"I hope so," Churchill replied, remarkably tolerant of Thompson's remark, indicating the closeness of their relationship. "This must be said: it is the essential point of the exercise."

"With due respect, Sir. There are inherent dangers . . ."

Churchill shook his head and pointed at Thompson with his cigar.

"The man's an old worrywart, a male Cassandra. I am the

very model of inflammatory," Churchill said, offering a mischievous grin. "It is the nature of the business at hand. I am not an ostrich, Thompson."

He grew thoughtful for a moment then intoned:

"Hang out our banners on the outward walls;
The cry is still 'They come:' our castle's strength
Will laugh a siege to scorn . . . "

He grinned.

"God help us if the Macbeth outcome repeats itself in our case."

"Forewarned is forearmed, Mr. Churchill," Thompson said, retreating from his earlier comment, surrendering totally.

"You see, I've rebuked him into submission."

Thompson shrugged and turned toward Victoria.

"Discretion, Miss. What you hear in this room is for your ears only. And the words you are recording are for your eyes only."

"My keeper," Churchill mused. "He sees conspiracies everywhere."

"I've learned that concept at your knee, Mr. Churchill."

Churchill sucked on his cigar and puffed deeply.

"I'm sure Miss Stewart has been thoroughly instructed by the first secretary on the nature of her role here."

"Absolutely, sir," she said, agitated by the necessity to dissimulate.

But then, her relationship with her lover was grounded in secrecy and deception. It was indeed conspiratorial. *In for a penny, in for a pound,* she thought, dismissing this sudden pang of conscience.

Although she was privy to the various intrigues swirling about the embassy and was reasonably informed about what was going on, she was well indoctrinated and aware of her discreet role as an embassy secretary. She had been carefully vetted and investigated by the hiring authorities at the foreign office.

At this stage, her interest was solely and exclusively on her lover and his concerns, which she deemed in the best interest of His Majesty's government. She felt certain that the reason for his request was exactly as stated, to protect the former prime minister from the blunders of overdramatizing and exaggeration. Besides, she felt slavishly and emotionally bound to honor Maclean's every request in all matters.

Of course, she was, while hardly interested in the details, fully cognizant that her boss was an advocate for good relations with the Russians. He seemed to go out of his way with his colleagues to press that point home. In his letters and in the minutes of meetings she had taken, his mantra was to maintain the wartime bond with Moscow. She felt certain that, as he had stated, he would raise the matter with Halifax or with Churchill himself if the speech raised issues contrary to the policies of the government. It had no relevance for her. What Maclean wanted, she would give him.

Although Churchill tolerated Thompson's interruption, it did set his mind going in yet another seemingly disjointed direction.

"I wish I could have been more forthright at Yalta. Unfortunately, Roosevelt and Stalin were dominant, and I found my role to be that of a gadfly. Some of the byplay was appalling. Stalin, I realized, was bloodthirsty. Although he treated it as a joke after I called him on it, he was all for the assassination of all Nazis above a certain rank. He wanted to dispatch a hundred thousand on a killing spree. I wanted to regurgitate! When he asserted this, I had to leave the room."

He shook his head and his expression struck her as one of profound regret.

"Franklin disagreed, of course, but not in such a public and emotional way. He truly believed that his infinite charm and good humor would seduce the marshal into coming his way. Stalin played along, as I see it now. Worse, I was not as forceful on key points. The man didn't trust me anyway, so where was the loss? We should have taken Berlin."

His cigar had gone out. He looked at it, and Thompson quickly obliged when he put it back in his mouth.

"Twenty-twenty hindsight is a curse to be reckoned with.

Perhaps, we can undue some of the damage," he muttered, then shrugged and turned to face his typist, who remained poised and ready.

But he continued to digress: "But you see, we wanted Stalin's help with the Japanese."

He took a deep puff on his cigar and expelled the smoke at the side of his mouth. Then his eyes seemed to glaze over, a clear indication that his mind was elsewhere.

"That bomb," he said. "Can you imagine? It wiped out ninety-five percent of human life in four square miles. And that is not the end of it. We are learning about radiation sickness and its terrible effect. Nevertheless, Truman's decision to use it was necessary. The war might have been prolonged for months, perhaps years."

He turned suddenly, shook his head. Victoria, by then, knew the difference between his digressions, offhand comments, and asides and the speech text. Suddenly, he plunged again into the speech.

"It would nevertheless be wrong and imprudent to entrust the secret knowledge or experience of the atomic bomb, which the United States, Great Britain, and Canada now share, to the world organization that is now in its infancy."

He shook his head as if to emphasize the point, then continued, "It would be criminal madness to cast it adrift in this still agitated and disunited world. No one in any country has slept less well in their beds because this knowledge, and the method and the raw materials to apply it, are at present largely retained in American hands."

He paused again, obviously forming the words in his mind before expelling them. The reference to the horror of the bomb seemed to animate him and his phrases now had a pugnacious quality. He was less stammering, more relentless. Perhaps it was his delivery, but the meaning of the words did penetrate her understanding. She noted peripherally that Thompson was raptly attentive, but made no comment. He apparently knew when his interruptions would be welcome and when not.

Churchill, totally concentrated now, continued: "I do not believe we should have all slept so soundly had the positions been reversed and some Communist or neofascist state monopolized for the time being these dread agencies."

Victoria felt chilled by his words.

"Last time, I saw it all coming and cried aloud to my own fellow countrymen and to the world, but no one paid attention. Up until the year 1933 or even 1935, Germany might have been saved from the awful fate that has overtaken her, and we might have been spared the miseries Hitler let loose on mankind."

He seemed suddenly deeply troubled, hesitated, shook his head, and said, "And our tight little island might have been spared so much agony and destruction."

Suddenly, he turned to Victoria with a sweeping gesture.

"'This blessed plot, this earth, this realm, this England.'" He cleared his throat. "John of Gaunt's soliloquy in *Richard II.* I love those magical lines."

His eyes moistened, and taking out a large, white handkerchief from the pocket of his dressing gown, he blew his nose.

Toward afternoon, Churchill seemed to flag.

"I must have my bath," he muttered.

Victoria stiffened. *Not that,* she thought.

Thankfully, Thompson summoned her to another room in the suite with a desk and typewriter. Sandwiches and tea were laid out beside it.

"He will expect the draft of what was dictated this morning to be cleanly typed and ready when he finishes his nap."

Victoria eyed the pages and nodded.

"Must I type it in verse?" she asked.

"Only the last draft," he replied. "We'll begin again after lunch. Prepare to work late, Miss Stewart. The PM likes to finish a first draft so that he can work on it in bed before retiring."

"I understand, sir," Victoria said.

He started to leave, then stopped for a moment and addressed her.

"I am sure you understand now why confidentiality is so essential."

They exchanged glances.

A chill of anxiety gripped her. It had not occurred to her that Maclean's request was such a profound betrayal of trust. She became agitated and felt a hot flush rise to her face. Thankfully, Thompson had quickly departed.

***

After lunch, the routine began again. This time, Churchill was fully dressed in vested pinstripes and a polka-dot bow tie. He had piled a number of books on a table before a mirror and recited the lines from the cleaned-up copy as if he were talking to an audience, sometimes approving and sometimes disapproving.

She had typed a carbon and inserted it into the typewriter, making changes as ordered.

"Did you get that?" he would snap occasionally.

"Yes, sir," she would respond—a bit of a white lie, which she hoped to correct during his many asides.

At times, he would interrupt his so-called rehearsal with a rebuke.

"You are an atrocious speller, Miss Stewart. *Habeas corpus* is not *corpse*. You do know the difference?"

"Sorry, sir."

At another point, he snapped.

"Versailles, my dear! May I suggest you consult an atlas? There is no *y* in *Versailles*."

"I will find an atlas, sir."

Her stomach had knotted at the rebuke, but she remained calm.

She noted that every nuance of language, every phrase, every cadence was carefully gone over, then repeated, and then gone over again. She made changes as he barked them out. This went on until it

154

began to grow dark outside. Churchill turned to her and nodded, then turned to Thompson who had remained in the room.

"I must have my bath," Churchill said, moving to the bedroom.

"I thought he had one earlier," Victoria said, when he had gone.

"Two a day, my dear." He paused and looked at her. "Says they are marvelously relaxing and clear the mind."

She made no comment and suppressed a giggle.

"You weathered the storm. Good show!" He smiled.

"Thank you, sir."

She assembled the carbons and brought the pages to the typewriter in the other room and proceeded to make yet another clean copy.

It was nearly midnight, and she had just finished typing the full first draft. Thompson's glance washed over them as she handed him the pages. She had typed two carbons, and one was neatly tucked into the band of her panties.

"He'll expect you by eleven," he said, looking at this watch.

She was tired and nervous; not only by the work itself, but also by the heightened anxiety of knowing she was willfully disobeying an explicit order of confidentiality.

She felt caught in the vise of a dilemma. While she loved Maclean, desperately and intensely, she felt uncomfortable about providing him with the draft of the speech.

She had, of course, no reason to doubt her lover's motives; he had explained the reasons.

After being dismissed by Thompson, she went back to her office to retrieve her coat and hat and get back to her apartment near Dupont Circle. She intended to walk the distance to clear her head of the cigar smoke and the sense of anxiety that was beginning to disturb her. Her intention was to give her lover the copy in the morning.

Taking dictation from Winston Churchill was something to be remembered and cherished. He had been portrayed as difficult but was less so than she had expected. She had found him both charming and accessible, and she was certain that she had done her job—the small spelling errors notwithstanding—with great efficiency. She felt, too, a sense of patriotic pride, knowing that she had participated in some enormously historic and important event. By then, contrary to her usual indifference to the subject matter, she had absorbed the material and knew that he would be saying something momentous, something extraordinarily important to the fate of the world.

As she prepared to leave, the door to Maclean's office opened suddenly, and her lover stood in the opening, his hair tousled.

"I must have dozed off, darling," he told her, beckoning her inside the office. "You look like you need a drink."

Seeing him, as always, filled her with strong emotions. She was totally committed to him in every way. Although startled, she was glad that he waited for her. She followed him into the office and he poured two scotches. She had already slumped into the leather couch, and he joined her and handed her the drink.

"It was hard work, but quite exhilarating. What a fine mind and gift for words the man has."

"He is a true Renaissance man," Maclean agreed, sipping his drink. "Was he difficult?"

"As they say, his bark was bigger than his bite." She laughed suddenly. "He takes two baths a day. Imagine!"

"And the speech?" he asked, taking a few swallows and putting his glass on the table beside the couch.

"It should be a real bell ringer," she said. "Of course, he is only in his first drafts, and I'm sure there will be refinements. He is working in bed on the last draft I typed as we speak. Thompson says that tomorrow, he will probably finalize the speech, and then I'll be typing it in verse form, as we discussed. I'll say this for him, he's amazingly thorough." Although she was tired, the drink revived her. He took her in his arms and kissed her deeply. She fully expected and looked forward to a sexual experience for which she was fully prepared, despite her exhaustion. She caressed his crotch, felt the reaction, and started to unbutton his pants. He resisted, gently removing her hand.

"You have a carbon copy of the speech, of course?" he said, the request casual.

156

She felt a sudden stab of shame. She was betraying a trust and it made her uncomfortable, notwithstanding her betrayal of her lover's wife. But that was different, not deliberate, like this.

"Are you sure, Donald?" she asked.

"About what?"

"The speech. They were quite adamant about its confidentiality."

"I explained all that," he said, his expression serious.

In his eyes, she caught a glint of annoyance.

"I'm sorry, darling, but I do feel somewhat uncomfortable."

"This is diplomatic business, Victoria. I gave you explicit instructions. Why do you think you were placed in this position? Really, darling, I mean it. Did you get a copy of his speech?"

He articulated the last sentence with demanding slowness.

"I understand all that, darling," she whispered. "It just makes me . . . well . . . queasy."

He stood up suddenly and walked to the end of the room. She had seen the gesture before but not in her case. This was the way he assuaged his anger and got it under control. After a moment, he came back and faced her, looking down at her while she sat stiffly on the couch.

"Victoria, I must demand to see the speech. Frankly, your reluctance baffles me. You owe your allegiance to me, to the embassy, to His Majesty's government. Mr. Churchill is no longer prime minister. It is I . . . we . . . who must protect Great Britain from danger. Indeed, because he is a British subject and a member of Parliament, our job extends to protecting him from . . . well . . . from himself. If I see anything in the speech that hints of a problem for us or for him, I give you my solemn word the ambassador and I will discuss it with Churchill tomorrow. No, I will not refer to the speech itself, only to the thematic material. Do you understand this, Victoria, or must I reiterate?"

His tone was deeply disturbing. Being his clandestine lover was the most important part of her present life. She had been a poor

157

girl from Chelsea, the daughter of a bus attendant and a seamstress. She had gone to secretarial school in England and had graduated at the top of her class and, after a series of jobs at the foreign office, had jumped at the chance for the U.S. assignment.

To have attracted such a fine, intelligent man as Donald Maclean was a coup for a woman of her class and background. She reveled in the attention but dared not think too far ahead, although she longed for a more permanent place in his life.

She knew she was attractive, blessed by good looks and a sexy body. Maclean was not her first lover, and she prided herself on her ability to provide sexual expertise and maximum satisfaction. She wished that she was better schooled in current events and deeply admired her lover's supposed grasp of these affairs, although her emotional and sexual involvement was her principal interest.

She reprimanded herself for her daring to question his good judgment. Nothing must come between us, she decided.

"I understand, my darling. I don't know why, but I just needed your reassurance."

She looked up at him and smiled. Then she raised her skirt.

"Come and get it, darling," she said, snapping the elastic of her panties.

He looked down at her, shook his head, and laughed.

"You silly goose," he said, as he reached out for the speech and slipped it out of her panties.

"Is that it?" she said, spreading her legs.

He reached out and caressed her hair.

"For the moment, my darling," he said, "for the moment. I'll say this, you couldn't have put it in a more worthy place."

"Is that a rejection?" she muttered, with mock severity.

"More like a postponement," he said, his eyes already concentrated on the text.

"I was expecting some celebratory gesture," she pouted, pulling down her skirt.

She could see that the speech had absorbed all his interest.

She watched him as he read.

"Beautifully composed. Don't you think so, darling?"

Despite her surrender, she continued to feel conspiratorial, much like a spy. She lifted her drink from an end table and continued to sip it as she observed him.

At times, as he read the speech, his comments were vocal, although she had the sense that they were for his ears only.

"Fifth column," he said aloud. "I don't believe this! My God, he has indicted Stalin and the Soviet Union."

She paid no attention to his outburst; it did not concern her. She assumed that he would keep his promise and discuss this in general terms with the ambassador and Churchill, in the hope of dissuading him from taking a position that was contrary to current national policy. It was not her place to reason why. She was a mere tiny cog in the vast and complicated diplomatic gears of the embassy.

Finally, he was finished. There was no mistaking his rage. His face was flushed, and his expression contorted with anger. He seemed to ignore her presence, concentrating instead on some inner dialogue.

"The man has signed his death warrant."

They were whispered words, but she heard them clearly. She wished she had not heard them, and she had the impression that they had slipped out inadvertently. At times, he did this as if his mind could not contain the thought unsaid. Sometimes, she reacted.

"What did you say, darling?"

"Oh," he sounded surprised. "Did I say anything?"

They exchanged glances, but she thought better of making any comments. She had done her job.

"May I go now, darling?" she asked.

He raised his head. He was still concentrated on the speech.

"Of course, darling."

He seemed distracted, but he offered a distant smile then slipped the speech pages into a large manila envelope.

She freshened up in the adjacent ladies' room, and then came back to her office to retrieve her coat. Opening the door to his office to say good night, she noted that he had gone.

"Has the first secretary left?" she asked the uniformed guard at the entrance.

"You just missed him, Miss," he said pleasantly. "Call you a taxi, Miss?"

"No, thank you," she said.

Despite her fatigue, she needed the fresh air to clear her lungs. Gulping deep drafts, she felt revived somewhat and increased her pace.

She headed down Massachusetts Avenue toward Dupont Circle. It was a moonless night, and the light from the streetlamps threw eerie shadows along her route. Although the streets were deserted, she felt no anxiety or fear. Wartime Washington was a safe city, and she had never been accosted or threatened. Indeed, she had taken this late-night walk to her apartment often.

At times, after a late-night tryst, Donald would often drive her to her apartment, and they would linger in the car before she departed, often for a farewell—and quick—episode of lovemaking. She smiled at the memory. But she felt a flash of annoyance that since he had left at nearly the same time, he could have offered her a lift tonight.

She had barely gone a few hundred yards when she saw Donald across the street. He was standing in the shadows at the edge of a circle of light thrown by the street lamp. It seemed odd to see him standing there at this hour. In his hand, he held the familiar envelope. She was about to cross the street when another man approached, and they shook hands. Puzzled, she moved behind a line of shrubs that rendered her less visible, although she could see the men clearly.

She had never questioned any action of her lover in connection with his job; nevertheless, she could not contain her curiosity. It struck her as odd. The encounter between the two men seemed so . . . she searched for the word . . . so clandestine. Normally, she might not have given it a second thought, but it seemed so out of the ordinary and strange that she could not contain her curiosity. She watched as the men exchanged a few words and the large envelope passed from her lover to the other man.

Then each man parted in opposite directions, the first secretary back in the direction of the embassy to pick up his car and the other man on foot toward Dupont Circle. At this point, she still could have made herself known to Maclean, but the inexplicable circumstances caused her to hesitate. For reasons that she explained to herself as pure curiosity, she headed in the same direction as the stranger.

Exhilarated by the fresh air and a bizarre sense of adventure, she followed the man as he turned on Twenty-Third Street and headed south, then turning left on M Street and right again. His walk was purposeful and concentrated, and she followed at a distance, hugging the shadows, just managing to keep him in sight. Considering the exhaustion of her day, her rising energy level surprised her.

On Sixteenth Street, she paused, noting that he was walking on the east side of the street. To keep free of observation, she walked on the west side of Sixteenth, but she kept him clearly in view.

In the distance, she could see the bulky outline of the Hilton on the corner of K Street and assumed that the man was heading for the hotel. Once entering, she knew he would be lost to any further observation.

Why was she doing this? What was she thinking? Perhaps, it was Thompson's caveat about keeping the speech confidential and the guilt of her violation. But giving the text to Donald hadn't felt like a violation, more like a little white lie. It was quite another story to see it pass into the hands of this stranger.

Short of the Hilton, the man turned left and entered one of the more ornate buildings that lined the street and was gone. Moving quickly, she reached the building. Her agitation was palpable. Her heartbeat banged like a drum in her chest, her stomach knotted, and her breath came in gasps.

The man had entered the Russian embassy.

Chapter 12

Dimitrov had been urgently summoned to Beria's office. A plane had been sent, and he had arrived in the early morning hours, surprised that Beria was already there, behind his desk, looking pale and unshaven, slightly nervous.

"Stand ready, Ivan Vasilyevich," Beria said, his first words. "We might be activating your mole. I am seeing Stalin in an hour. Is he ready for immediate deployment?"

The reference to his American mole caught Dimitrov by surprise. He had received periodic reports that Mueller was in contact, but nothing beyond that. He could only assume that Mueller had done as ordered: Wait. Be ready. Dimitrov had no reason to think otherwise.

Beria took off his pince-nez and polished them with a cloth, then put them on again in a one-handed motion. Dimitrov waited politely for Beria to speak. He watched his face as he organized his thoughts. Then Beria slapped his hand on a sheaf of papers he had on his desk.

"We must put an end to this garbage," Beria cried, his voice rising.

Dimitrov was confused.

"Winston Churchill will be speaking in America in six days," Beria began, shaking his head and again slapping the sheaf of papers.

He thumbed through them, then picked out a sheet and read aloud, his words ringing with contempt: "'However, in a great number of countries, far from the Russian frontiers and throughout the world, Communist fifth columns are established and work in complete unity and absolute obedience to the directions they receive from the Communist center.'"

Dimitrov remained silent, knowing Beria's reactions, especially his anger, which was just entering its pre-eruption phase.

"We on one side, they on the other," Beria offered a tight smile, another forerunner to an eruption. His seething rage was simmering. "So far. The man is not a fool, he knows that this is just the beginning. Soon they will not be able to hide behind their bomb. Very soon."

"Here," Beria jabbed his finger into the text. "Here is what he has to say about it."

He read aloud, his temper still brewing in the pressure cooker of his emotions: "No one in any country has slept less well in their beds because this knowledge, and the method and the raw materials to apply it, are at present largely retained in American hands."

Beria shook his head and hissed through his teeth. "And this: 'I do not believe we should have all slept so soundly had the positions been reversed and some Communist or neo-fascist state monopolized for the time being these dread agencies.'"

Suddenly he stood up from his seat behind the large, carved desk, and holding the text of the speech, he stormed about the office. He had reached the boiling point.

"This arrogant bastard of a pig's mother!" He speared his finger into the air as if he were pointing at the specter of Churchill in the room. "Wait until we have the bomb, you stinking, fat, drunken sot! You filthy swine, you know one day we will have it and will have snatched it from under your fat ass."

He looked at Dimitrov. "You heard his words, Ivan Vasilyevich. Now, I ask you, does this filth deserve to live? Such words are like daggers into the heart of our great Russian people. Let him spit on us with his lisping, mincing lies. If he were here now, I would cut out his golden tongue."

He continued to look over the text.

"And here," he cried, his voice rising. "Listen to this: 'From what I have seen of our Russian friends and allies during the war, I am convinced that there is nothing they admire so much as strength, and there is nothing for which they have less respect than weakness, military weakness.'"

He spat on the paper. "It is a call to war. Make no mistake about it. The man wants war with us."

He flung the text of Churchill's speech into the air, and the pages scattered around the office. Then he stamped on any within the reach of his feet.

"Shit! Shit! Shit!" he cried.

Dimitrov had never seen Beria in such a rage. It struck him, too, that Beria's anger was triggered simply by the power of words; and such utterances by a master wordsmith like Churchill on a world stage seemed as dangerous as the most powerful of weapons.

"We will let the world know what comes to those who mouth such swill." He looked at Dimitrov. "Now you see why I must convince Stalin that this mission is necessary? A bullet is too good for this filth. And it must happen before the entire world—center stage."

Behind his glasses, Beria's eyes were beaming directly into Dimitrov's. "Do you see, comrade?"

"Yes, I do."

His anger spent, Beria returned to his desk and sat down. He appeared to be calming rapidly.

"Are you satisfied that you have chosen the right man for this job?" Beria asked, in an abrupt businesslike tone. "We must be beyond suspicion."

"I am," Dimitrov said, with conviction.

There were doubts, but he pushed them aside. His bet had been made, and he needed to defend it.

"Stalin will not ask me about the specifics of my plan. I feel certain he will agree with my assessment, but he will need reassurance that this will not come back to bite him."

164

"I understand, comrade."

"Any hint of our involvement will be fatal . . . " Beria paused . . . "to both of us."

"Of course."

"So you are certain you have the right man?" Beria asked again.

"I am certain. The man is a committed Nazi," Dimitrov explained, "a fanatic, a Hitler loyalist, a Jew hater. He is the perfect choice. He will probably believe that he is settling a score for the führer by killing one of the leaders who brought him down. In my opinion, he will greatly enjoy the killing part."

Beria pondered the explanation.

"Well, then . . . " Beria began, "Churchill is slated to speak in a few days before a college in the Midwest of America."

Dimitrov listened intensely to the details of the event, obviously based on material gleaned from Beria's extensive worldwide intelligence sources. His strategy was fairly straightforward, dealing mostly with logistical facts. The actual planning of the assassination itself would have to be left to the discretion of Mueller.

"I want this pig bastard shot in the midst of his speech, with the eyes of the world upon him. Do you think your man can do this?"

"I am sure he will do his best, comrade. Naturally, nothing can be guaranteed."

"And if he is caught alive?" Beria asked, mostly for reassurance, since the matter had been discussed months ago.

"Who will believe his story? It will seem fanciful. He is a committed SS officer, and we have his signed confession to two murders that can be planted. Clearly, it would be an act of vengeance. Now, there is the matter of money, comrade; it was part of the package," Dimitrov said, to refresh Beria's memory.

"Yes, of course. How much?"

Dimitrov calculated a sum.

"Fifty thousand U.S. dollars. Not traceable."

Beria nodded.

"No problem."

"They will think it was being paid by an organization of former Nazis. I understand that there is an efficient, well-financed pipeline to South America."

Beria sighed and closed his eyes, illustrating his concentration. Dimitrov wondered if they had missed any details, although the actual act would have to be planned on-site by Mueller himself. Then Beria spoke again.

"Stalin will, providing he is persuaded to move forward, vigorously deny any connection to what he will most certainly characterize as a sordid crime of pure vengeance. Other factors will deflect suspicion. He and Churchill actually liked each other, and there is much evidence to validate that. During Churchill's visit to Stalin, ample eyewitness reports and notes attest to their friendship despite ideological differences. And in the aftermath, surely Stalin will march behind his bier and speak at his grave. Believe me, I know the man. He will create a great show of mourning. No one will ever connect us to this deed."

He nodded as if to reiterate the point to himself.

"And if he is successful and gets away?" Beria asked.

"If Mueller is lucky enough to find an escape route, he would spend his life as a hunted man."

As a gesture of friendly cooperation, Dimitrov had calculated that his own agents would inform opposite numbers among the U.S. and British intelligence services as to the man's identity, past murders, and background as an SS man. A revenge scenario by a committed Nazi would be a logical explanation for the assassination.

"Hopefully, he will be found by us first and killed."

Dimitrov added, "Like Trotsky."

He noted that Beria was pleased by the reference.

Beria rose and came around from his desk to embrace Dimitrov in a bear hug.

"We will know soon enough," Beria whispered.

Chapter 13

In the morning, she arrived at the embassy a little before eleven. She had barely slept, and even the four cups of coffee she had consumed that morning had left her slightly listless. All night long, as she tossed restlessly in her bed, her mind concocted various scenarios to explain what she had observed. Unfortunately, each scenario ended in illogic and self-incrimination.

Perhaps, she should confront Donald with what she had seen and ask—no, *insist*—on an explanation. Clearly, he had given Churchill's text to someone who worked at the Russian embassy. Was it her place to ask why?

This business of diplomacy, as Donald had explained it to her, was a choreographed dance between states, each vying to know the others' motives and agendas. Since time immemorial, it's been that way, he had explained. Remembering his remarks did not ease her anxiety. She wondered if she should inform Thompson about what she had seen. She was both confounded and demoralized. Could what she had seen have a negative effect on Mr. Churchill—or worse? She dismissed the thought as too painful to contemplate.

Maclean had not yet arrived in the office. She arrived at Churchill's suite promptly at eleven and Thompson ushered her into the bedroom.

Mr. Churchill was in his green, dragon-decorated dressing gown and busy devouring a huge English breakfast of eggs, sausage, kippers, toast, and tea. Beside the teacup was a small pony of brown liquid that she assumed was brandy.

His glasses had slipped to the tip of his nose, and she noted that her draft was beside him on the table, and he was making notes in the margins and occasionally mumbling words. He looked up when she came in. After admitting her to the bedroom, Thompson once again sat in a chair in the corner observing his charge.

"Marvelous, marvelous, marvelous," Churchill said, greeting her with a grin. "You have done well, dear girl."

He shook his head, looked at the pages again. "I cannot for the life of me come up with the right phrase to describe a separation. I just cannot arrive at another appropriate word for *fence*. Besides, that entire paragraph seems stilted . . . It will come. Surely, it will come."

He cleared his throat and read a portion of the speech aloud.

"A shadow has fallen upon the scenes so lately lighted by the Allied victory. Nobody knows what Soviet Russia and its Communist international organization intend to do in the immediate future or what are the limits, if any, to their expansive and proselytizing tendencies." He paused and nodded. "Yes, I like that." He turned to her.

"What do you think of it, Miss Stewart?"

"I . . . I . . . "

"Speak up, woman!"

"I thought it was wonderful, sir."

"Ought to give the Russians something to chew on."

"Yes, sir."

The image of Maclean giving his speech to someone from the Russian embassy gnawed at her. Had she betrayed this great man?

He put the papers down on the tray, then put it aside, rose from his bed, and left the room for the bathroom. From the sound coming from it, she supposed he was running his bath.

Left alone with Thompson, she followed him into the sitting room where they sat opposite each other.

"He likes you, Miss Stewart," Thompson said, lowering his voice. "I've made arrangements for you to accompany us to Missouri on the president's train."

She felt a sharp trill of excitement.

"Really?"

"He is sure to make last-minute changes. Then he will need you to type the stencils for the mimeograph process. We normally provide an advance to the press to be distributed an hour or so before delivery."

She was so excited; it made her forget her anxiety.

"I can't tell you how grateful I am. I've really enjoyed taking his dictation."

"You're lucky. He is usually a terror. He is remarkably restrained, a tribute to your efficiency."

"I appreciate that, Mr. Thompson."

"Above all, he trusts you. That is always the biggest hurdle. He makes these gut-reaction decisions."

"Is he usually right?" she asked.

He looked at her and smiled. "Frankly, Miss, I agree with him."

She felt a strange sinking feeling and a lightness in her head. *Trust* her? Despite all her rationalizations, she was ashamed of her conduct and what she had seen. It must have shown in her complexion.

"Are you okay, Miss?"

She nodded, recovering quickly.

"Oh, yes. I guess it was the excitement of being asked to accompany Mr. Churchill to Missouri."

After a while, she felt the lightness disappear, although the accelerating pangs of conscience did not. On its heels, a shred of memory intruded. Maclean's phrase, "signed his death warrant," rose in her mind, agitating her further.

"Is Mr. Churchill well protected?" she asked, then remembered suddenly Thompson's role.

"I should hope so," Thompson said. He offered an inexplicable wink and smile. "That is my mission."

"Just you? One man?"

169

"I admit, young lady, that it does seem rather light-armored. But I assure you, I know my business." He paused and studied her. "You seem anxious."

"I hadn't meant . . . " she said haltingly, sorry she had brought up the matter. "But yesterday, you talked about . . . well . . . certain passages you thought were inflammatory. It implied . . . well . . . danger. What I mean is . . . is Mr. Churchill at risk of harm?"

Thompson chuckled.

"My dear young lady, your concerns echo those of his wife, his children, his friends and associates, everyone, even his enemies, of which he has many. Mr. Churchill is a fatalist. He has been castigated, imprisoned, nearly killed in motor crashes, by illness and bombs. He has been insulted, reviled, and threatened. He has been through every imaginable crisis: wars, depressions—what have you—victories and defeats. He has been exposed to assassination all his life."

At his use of the word, she froze. Her own speculations had not gone that far.

"Even in the recent war," Thompson continued, "he would leave his bunker, tour our ravaged cities to give comfort to our citizens, spend time at Chartwell, and visit the battlefield. There was ample opportunity for assassination. Even Hitler's sinister gang never got to him."

"But, surely, people have tried?" She could not resist keeping the subject alive.

He grew pensive, his eyes narrowing.

"Generally speaking, there has been only one assassination of a prime minister, Spencer Percival in 1814. A disgruntled businessman shot him at the entrance to the House of Commons. The United States has had three presidents killed while in office. Of course, we've had royal bloodletting galore in our early days, although not in recent years."

He stopped his history lesson abruptly and studied her face.

"Why such concern?"

"No concern, really," she said, trying to maintain a casual air. "Curiosity is all. Won't the Russians hate his speech?" she asked, her implication clear.

"You heard him. He hopes so. Perhaps, such tough talk will make them mend their ways."

"Won't they want to silence him?"

"There you go, Miss. He is not easily silenced."

He crossed his legs and went back to reading his paper, and she was left to contemplate the dilemma caused by the previous night's experience. Perhaps she was overreacting to something that was easily explained.

Soon Mr. Churchill came into the sitting room, dressed in what was his regular attire: the pinstriped, vested suit and a polka-dot bow tie. His complexion reminded her of a satisfied, overstuffed, and contented baby. Seeing him so decked out, calm, almost jaunty, the worries that had briefly plagued her disappeared.

He held the sheaf of papers that constituted his speech.

"I've made numerous chicken marks, Miss Stewart, and I've fiddled a bit over the ending."

There was no typewriter available in the sitting room, although there was one in the private room where she typed clean copies. She hurriedly opened her dictation book and assumed the position. But he did not begin.

"You see, a speech must be like a Beethoven symphony—you can have three movements, but there has to be one dominant melody."

And then he intoned, "Da da da dum," the chord from Beethoven's Fifth Symphony, often called the Victory Symphony; in Morse code, the sound stands for the letter *V*.

She nodded as if she understood fully what he meant, which she didn't.

"There is a kind of scaffolding of rhetoric," he went on. "The steps are: strong beginning, one dominant theme, simple language, lots of word pictures, and a strong emotional ending."

He spoke now directly to her. "We must have a stronger ending."

Then he began to dictate, his voice booming as he paced.

He lifted his right hand and gave his famous *V* salute and chuckled. Then he looked at the papers in his hand and read a portion to himself.

He smiled, nodded, pulled out a leather case where he kept his cigars, and clipped off an end. Thompson was quick to bring his portable flame. Churchill puffed contentedly, looked at the ash, and spoke.

"Let's draft this and see how it plays," he said, pulling out his watch and looking at it. "We'll be off to the White House shortly, Thompson. Halifax will be joining us. But first, I must call Clemmie."   He turned and walked back to the bedroom.

The mention of the ambassador reminded her of Maclean.

"Has the first secretary called yet today?" she asked innocently, remembering Maclean's words of the night before.

"Not that I know of. Why would he do that?"

"I thought . . . "

She aborted her remark and went to the little anteroom and began working on the latest draft. The concentration left her little time to deal with her dilemma.

When she returned to her own office later in the day, she knocked at Maclean's office door, and he ushered her inside.

"Did he make many changes to the draft?" Maclean asked.

"Some," she said.

"Nothing major?"

"Nothing major." She paused. "I could insert the changes in your draft."

"Not necessary, darling."

"I know, but you might as well have the complete draft."

"It's fine, darling, really."

He seemed preoccupied, and she was on the verge of leaving, when she suddenly felt compelled to question him.

172

"I spoke to Thompson this morning," she said, hesitantly, uncertain about how to appear casual in approaching the subject.

"Yes, darling," he said, expectantly.

"I wonder . . . well, I was thinking . . . you said last night that you were going to discuss the draft with . . . "

He was silent for a long moment, then nodded and smiled.

"Why are you fussing about that, darling?" he replied. "Such matters are delicate policy conversation—purely sensitive diplomatic activities, hardly worth your concern."

She felt that he was being dismissive and found herself coping with a rising anger.

"Donald, I violated their wishes. Surely . . . "

"Please, Victoria," he said, engaged now. "There is no need for this discussion now."

He reached for some papers on his desk and began to read.

She stood stiffly before the desk unable to move.

"We'll talk later, darling. This is important. Now, please."

He waved her away.

She sucked in a deep breath and watched him. She did love him. Indeed, she would do anything he asked of her, and he knew it. He was the love of her life. But she could not reconcile what she had seen last night with her own eyes. She was tempted to tell him what she had observed but was unable to find the words.

He looked up from his reading and looked at her intensely.

Was her consternation well hidden?

"What is it, Victoria?"

"I just feel uncomfortable, darling. They keep harping on confidentiality."

"I do understand, darling."

She felt a lump grow in her throat and screwed up her courage.

"Have you discussed it with the ambassador?"

He studied her, his brows knit as he shook his head in an attitude of impatience.

173

"What is going on with you, Victoria? I told you my reasons." Suddenly, he sucked in a deep breath. "You didn't mention this to Churchill or Thompson?"

She felt a sinking feeling in her stomach. How could he imagine such a thing?

"Of course not," she said, holding down her anger.

He seemed relieved. Then he smiled.

"You're troubling yourself over nothing, darling. Why are you so concerned? There's nothing for you to fret over. I would suggest you stop worrying yourself about this. You are doing your proper duty. So am I. Always remember, we are doing His Majesty's business."

He stood up, approached her, and embraced her in his arms.

"Trust me, darling, please."

He kissed her deeply, and she responded.

"I'm sorry, darling."

"Are you reassured?"

She hesitated for a moment and drew in a deep breath.

"Yes, darling. I am."

Am I really? she asked herself, unable to reach absolute certainty, although in his arms, her comfort level had risen dramatically.

They kissed again and disengaged. She started to move away, then turned to face him.

"They're taking me with them to Fulton," she said.

He smiled.

"Ripping!" he said. "Absolutely ripping! It should be a wonderful experience." He winked at her and smiled. "Of course, I shall miss you."

"And I you."

"I'll get to see him deliver the speech we made together."

"Wonderful, darling. You'll be part of history."

She nodded and left the office, reassured but still discomfited.

Chapter 14

Miller had barely left his room in the last two weeks, except to make his call and eat sandwiches at the Peoples Drug Store across the street from the Y. He had been pinned on the razor's edge of confusion. Abruptly, like a surgeon who cuts out a cancer, he had sliced Stephanie out of his life—or had tried. The pain of the incision was relentless.

At first, he thought it was a ploy. They, the mysterious Soviet intelligence forces that hovered over his life, had deliberately aborted the affair. A Jew—what could be more clever? She had done her job well. But a Jew?

Yet the logic of it evaded him. Perhaps she had been what he had deduced all along, a counteragent, an American plant. It was another suspicion he could not reconcile rationally.

His hatred of the Jews expanded in his mind. They were cunning, always one step ahead. No matter how many were killed, there were always more. Who knows how many they needed to sacrifice to achieve their dream of world domination? He remembered *The Protocols of the Elders of Zion,* which he had read again and again.

No, he decided, she could not be a Jew. She was posing as a Jew to force him to deliberately break it off, which he had done, ruthlessly, refusing all contact.

This theory seemed to gain headway in his mind as he turned it over and over. Besides, she didn't look at all Jewish. Physically, she was the perfect Aryan woman. Had they deliberately cast her to lure him on? She did not carry the obvious stain of their likeness:

the jet-black kinky hair, the long hawk-like nose, the mark of their predatory nature, the smell—this latter characteristic based upon his own instinctive scent, which confirmed he could distinguish a Jew by some special olfactory emission like that given off by a nigger.

She was a genuine blonde. He had seen her light patch of pubic hair, and his uncut penis was evidence of his racial truth. Considering how she had lavished attention on that part, she certainly could have no illusions about his origins. Why had she chosen that moment? Nor had she raised any questions about her own antecedents or political views, telling him that she avoided such information as too upsetting to dwell on.

"I do not wish to dwell on the dark side of the human condition," she had told him once. "I am in the healing business."

He hadn't challenged such statements, which—thinking about it in retrospect—could have been yet another ploy to avoid any subject that might make him suspicious of her motives. On his part, he did not reveal anything of his own views, anything at all that might give himself away.

On the other hand . . . he was full of "other hands" . . . she might have reported to her superiors that he was not worth the surveillance, that it was time to drop him as a suspect. A suspect who did or will do what? No matter where his thoughts and suspicions took him, he could not abort his longing. She had cast a spell over him, made him crazy with an overwhelming sense of possession and, now, loss. Or was it lust? Even that accusation was flawed. He knew what real lust was; he had had lots of experience with lust, the sexual compulsion that drove one to pursue immediate gratification. Whether forced or consensual, the objective was never considered beyond the act of pleasure itself, like masturbation, except with a piece of living female flesh.

There was more here than merely that. Perhaps they had perfected a love potion that had enslaved him in this terrible emotional prison.

His first instinct, when she told him, was to put his hands

176

on her throat and crush it between them. It took all of his willpower to resist the temptation. Instead, he turned the idea around, cursing himself for his naïveté. He should have obeyed his first instincts before he had become enmeshed in this emotional booby trap. Dimitrov had warned him. He should have heeded his advice.

That first night after the confession was torture. He had dropped her off at the hospital without a word.

"I understand," was all she said in parting, obviously misreading his reaction.

He had held back from taking any action. He needed to think it through, but after a sleepless night of contemplating a plethora of scenarios, he was no closer to a definitive conclusion than he was at the moment of her revelation. Actually, it was less of a revelation than a rejection. Something was wrong here, something sinister and dangerous. A ruthless Jewess was fucking up his head.

When he came down the following morning to make his daily call, the clerk at the desk signaled with his eyes toward the reception room where they had first kissed. She was sitting in the corner of the badly lit room. Her face was pale, and she was unmistakably upset and forlorn. Her eyes were puffy and red. Quite obviously, she had been crying. Seeing her in this condition, all the angst of the night before swept away. He wanted to take her in his arms and comfort her. At the same time, he was ashamed of such weakness and sentimentality.

"I'm sorry, Frank," she said, her voice tremulous. "I should have told you. But . . . " She paused. "I . . . never expected. I mean . . . I was the aggressor here. I didn't think. Then the reality hit me."

"What reality?"

"You could never understand, Frank. Maybe it will be different some day. But Jewish parents, my parents, would never accept the idea. Never. I had never gone out with a gentile boy. They would have disowned me."

Again he held himself back. Disowned you? Run you out of their disgusting tribe. Once a Jew, always a Jew. Such talk was

177

beyond logic. There was only one conclusion. America was infected with these people. They controlled everything, directed everything. When would the Americans wise up? There was an evil disease in their midst. He told himself this, but observing her now, he could not reconcile such thoughts with the present reality.

They were a dangerous people. Hitler had been right to characterize even the slightest hint of their tainted blood as a plague, worthy of elimination. The method of disposal, gassing and burning, had been exactly correct. Reduce them to ashes. That was the only way.

"It hit me suddenly. There's no future for us, Frank. I faced the reality of it, and it's very painful."

She looked up at him with tearful eyes.

"The truth is that I can't . . . " She started to cry, her face a portrait of suffering. "I love you, Frank. I love you with all my heart and soul. I love you, and I don't care what my parents or anyone else thinks. I want to be with you."

He watched her for a long moment. He was at odds with himself. He wanted to move forward, embrace her, smother her with kisses, and ask for forgiveness, although he could not find a reason. Was it possible for her to exist outside the circle of his hatred for her people? No, he decided. He could not excise his convictions. He had been invaded, attacked.

"Leave me alone," he said after a long pause. "I don't want to see you again."

"But Frank . . . " she began, her eyes clouded with confusion.

She seemed stunned by his assertion, but he had made his choice and was determined to stick to it. Besides, she was in love with a fiction. She had no idea of his background and his mission. Or did she? She had been only mildly curious, which could have meant that she knew who he was and why he was here and the truth of his intentions.

Yet, despite his assertion, he continued to stand there as if attached to the floor. He watched her nod, a gesture that bespoke an abject total surrender. A sob began to trickle up from somewhere deep inside him. Finally, he found the strength to turn away.

"I understand, Frank," she whispered. "Believe me, I will not bother you. I'll respect your wishes."

***

After two weeks of agony, and despite his meandering analysis of her intentions, he still did not reach any conclusions, nor could he get her out of his mind. She dominated his thoughts and emotions more than ever, as if she had injected him with bacteria, which was devouring him.

As for his so-called mission, after so many months, he began to believe that it had been put on the shelf. Was he free of them, he wondered? What were their intentions? He had been fully prepared to do whatever deed he was assigned. After all, they had him by the balls. All he wished for now was to get it over with.

Other thoughts began to plague him. Suppose he was freed from their clutches? Was it possible to start a new life here? Had she planted such thoughts in his mind? Months before, as he was herded into that prison in the dead of winter, he was certain that his life was over. Along with his fellow officers, he was resigned to such a fate. The war was over for him. Life was over. *Obersturmbannführer, you are dead meat,* he assured himself, although for some reason, he was unwilling to accept the idea. Instead, he had opted for a chance at life and did his dance before Dimitrov.

But what kind of a life? Then he had seen himself as preserving his life for the extension of the real war, the war against the Jews. Was he relenting suddenly, mesmerized by this manipulative, sinister Jewess?

Eight weeks had passed since his arm and ankle had been put in a cast, two weeks since the cast on his arm was removed. It was still not perfect, but certainly workable. He could aim a rifle and pull a trigger.

He had been warned that the ankle would take longer, and

his mobility was still constrained, although he was able to clump around easily and without pain. He decided he would remove his ankle cast himself. He was strong. He was lucky. Surely, the bones had knit enough for him to take a chance. Besides, he did not wish to go back to the hospital. The sight of her might be a match to dry tinder. Why tempt fate?

Instead, he went to a nearby hardware store and bought a wooden mallet and a rug cutter that might be adequate for the job. In his room, he managed to slice through the plaster and remove the cast. Although it was a relief to remove it, as he expected, the muscles and tendons had atrophied. He was able to walk, somewhat unsteadily, but that, he was certain, would get better with time.

Although the accident was the cause of his present dilemma, he had the urge to show Stephanie his unfettered self. She had only seen him as an invalid.

He began a process of self-rehabilitation, taking walks, first for short distances, then longer. The arm was growing stronger, and he was quickly regaining full mobility. The ankle was healing more slowly. Each morning, he seemed to need more and more time to unstiffen the ankle and get moving. He was conscious of a progressing limp. Yet he felt certain that he would work his way through it. He began to rely more and more on aspirin to relieve the pain.

The weather had turned icy cold. Although he tried in his mind to resume his so-called research into the president's schedule, he noted that, at least on very cold days, Truman did not take his walks. Miller also found it difficult to renew his interest in world events.

Still, although he fought against it, railed against it, hated it like an addict hates and loves his habit, he could not resist the temptation to pass the hospital where she worked. For days, he stood outside in the cold morning air to catch a glimpse of her as she came off duty, cursing himself for his weakness. He likened his situation to being caught in a magnetic field, unable to resist the unseen power of its pressure.

Hiding behind a car or a tree, he occasionally caught a glimpse of her, watching her move into the distance. His heart jumped in his throat, his knees trembled, but he could not bring himself to reveal himself.

His mood shifted between longing and boredom. He felt as if he were in a state of suspended animation. At times, he felt a loss of identity and would often wake up from a nightmarish dream panicked and in a cold sweat, wondering who he was.

His leg pain was increasing and his dosage of aspirin had to be increased. He acknowledged that he might have been premature in removing the cast, but he felt convinced that his luck would not desert him and that the ankle would heal with time.

One morning in the lobby of the Y, just as he began his call, he felt a tap on his shoulder. Turning, he saw a man who was vaguely familiar. He was clean-shaven and wore a fedora pulled low over his head and a light topcoat. For a brief moment, Miller was puzzled, and then it struck him.

"We meet again, *Obersturmbannführer.*

Chapter 15

"Mr. Miller, is it?" Dimitrov said, offering a thin smile. His eyes narrowed, and he looked from side to side. He motioned for Miller to follow, which he did.

Dimitrov walked briskly to the edge of Georgetown, not looking back. With his stiff leg and increasing pain, which even larger doses of aspirin could not mask, Miller had trouble keeping up. Dimitrov turned left on M Street and then right to enter the footpath beside the old canal. Only then did Dimitrov stop, waiting for Miller to catch up.

"So we meet again, Mueller." He paused. "Miller, I mean." Dimitrov inspected his face. "You don't look so good."

"I'm fine," Miller muttered.

They began to walk together along the footpath as if they were two old friends reuniting. Miller was conscious of using all of his willpower to disguise the limp in his leg.

"It's been a long time, General," he said.

Miller was astonished and puzzled by Dimitrov's presence. He hadn't expected his instructions to come directly from him. Dimitrov looked different in his ill-fitting civilian clothes, more like a government flunky than the powerful NKVD general Miller had confronted in Germany.

Dimitrov checked behind him from time to time, obviously to be certain they were not followed.

"We're ready now," he said.

"I hadn't expected it to be you," Miller admitted.

"Your mission is too important to trust to others."

Dimitrov lowered his voice, although there seemed no necessity for doing so. They were beyond the capacity of audio surveillance.

"Should I be flattered, General? I thought I had been forgotten. I was getting ready to walk away."

"We would have found you, Miller. We have a long arm."

They exchanged glances. Dimitrov's eyes narrowed as he inspected him.

"Are you ready?" Dimitrov asked.

Miller nodded. He needed to put this mission behind him, although he did not know what he would do next. He thought suddenly of Stephanie and his stomach tightened. Why now, at this moment?

"You must listen carefully and absorb these instructions," Dimitrov said. "If you have questions, ask them now. We won't be in contact again."

"No more calls?"

"Finished," Dimitrov said.

"Good," Miller said, confronting Dimitrov's icy stare. "I was running out of dimes."

The little joke fell flat. For some reason, he felt deeply alien to the situation, as if he were hovering above, watching, not participating. He felt Dimitrov's intense stare, like harsh pinpoints of light beaming directly into his eyes.

"You will kill Winston Churchill," Dimitrov said.

Miller was thunderstruck. It was a name totally out of the blue.

"Winston Churchill?" Miller cried.

Dimitrov put a finger on his lips to quiet him.

"But I assumed . . . " He interrupted himself. " . . . I thought Truman. He presents an easy target on his walks."

Dimitrov grunted then looked behind him again. They were moving north on the footpath, which was deserted.

"What you assumed is irrelevant. I'm here to give you instructions, not to explain motives." He paused and looked directly into Miller's face. "Your assignment is to kill Winston Churchill. Do you understand?"

"Why Churchill?" Miller blurted. It seemed a strange choice. The man was no longer prime minister.

"Your only business is to kill him. Beyond that, don't trouble yourself."

"All right then. Where is the target? Am I now to go to England?"

Dimitrov laughed slyly, looking around him.

"Not more than a mile from here at the British embassy."

Dimitrov paused and Miller felt the intensity of his stare washing over him like a prison beam. "But the deed will be done elsewhere."

"Where?"

"Fulton, Missouri."

"Where is that?"

"In the middle of this country."

They continued to move farther along the footpath. For a few moments, they maintained silence between them. Miller tried to absorb the information. For years, Churchill and Roosevelt had been the face of the enemy. Now Roosevelt was dead. In Germany during the war, Churchill was cast in the newspapers and radio as a blustering fool, a fat, incompetent, drunken pig. He was ridiculed, laughed at, derided.

The mention of his name stirred old memories. When the troops of the SS saw newsreels of him, they laughed at his stupid cigar, his two-fingered V sign, his silly derby hat. Himmler had called him a Jew lover and promised to hang him by the balls after the war.

Yes, he decided, his sense of mission rekindled and inspired, he would gladly put a bullet in that bastard's skull.

"It won't be simple, Miller. Not just bang bang, you're dead."

"I don't understand."

"We're asking for a public execution."

"I'm not following," Miller said, confused.

"You must listen carefully. This requires your utmost concentration."

"Of course."

They walked on for a few moments more. It was hard going for Miller. The pain in his ankle grew more intense. Dimitrov looked behind him a number of times then began his explanation and instruction.

"You will proceed immediately by car to Westminster College in the town of Fulton, Missouri, where Churchill will speak on March 5."

"Is that all?"

"Not quite all," Dimitrov said. "Churchill will be traveling with the president in his private railroad car. They will stop in St. Louis, go on to Jefferson City, then drive to Fulton, where they will have lunch at the home of the college president and then go on to the college hall where Churchill is to speak. There will be elaborate preparations. You must arrive in Fulton in time to investigate the town, the surrounding area and the general conditions, and plan your attack."

Miller listened with deepening interest, making tentative plans as Dimitrov spoke.

"Six days," Miller calculated. *Short notice,* he thought. "Why there? If he's here in town, . . . "

"Please, Mueller." He checked himself. "Your assignment is to kill him while he is speaking."

"In public? With an audience?"

Dimitrov nodded.

"In the hall where he'll speak," he continued, "*while* he speaks."

Miller was confused.

"Why such a public exhibition?"

"The eyes of the world will be on this man."

"But dead is dead. Isn't your objective to silence him?"

"We're looking for the maximum impact. We've chosen not merely the target, but also the moment."

Miller was baffled.

"Is this a game, General? Kill Churchill while he's speaking? I think you exaggerate my potential. Am I supposed to be flattered? It sounds as if I'm to be sacrificed."

"Sacrificed?" Dimitrov shot back angrily. "*Obersturmbannführer*, I gave your life back to you. I have kept my word. It's up to you to keep yours."

Miller felt a rising anger.

"And if I refuse?"

"You've seen too many American movies, Miller. You have no choice. You must be aware of that."

"Kill me now, what happens to your plan?"

"We'll find another plan," Dimitrov said, calmly. "But we're betting on your survival instincts."

"Is that a compliment, General? You make it sound so simple."

Miller's mind was a jumble of alternatives. But he was quick to recognize Dimitrov's strategy. *Okay, it's risky* . . . but Miller sensed something missing, a detail withheld . . .

"It's a hard gamble, General." He paused. "You've given me nothing but a date—no details, no maps. You're setting me loose like . . . Alice in Wonderland."

"Exactly."

"It's stupid. I'll be caught or killed."

"Maybe. We're all taking risks."

"You? You'll be back in Europe, fucking some fräulein."

Dimitrov ignored the comment.

"Think in these terms, Miller: You'll find your way into the hall, where there will be great excitement. The great Churchill will rise and speak. His speech, whatever it is, will be interrupted by great applause. When he spoke to the Congress of the United States, his speech was practically drowned out by applause. There's no reason to think it won't be the same. The noise of applause will mask the fatal shot and, if you're clever and have planned well, you'll escape. Newspaper people will be in attendance, newsreels will be running, and the film will bear witness. After the shot is fired, there will be confusion, perhaps hysteria. You'll find a way out. Your only instructions are to shoot, hit your target, leave your weapon to be found, and lose yourself in the melee. You're a bright young man, one of Himmler's young stars. Surely, you can figure out a workable exit plan."

"Leave the weapon?"

"As you know, it's a Waffen-SS-issue rifle, and marked as such."

He pulled out another packet from his pocket and handed it to Miller. It was flat, an envelope wrapped in a cellophane pouch. Miller studied it.

"You will leave this note beside the weapon."

"What does it say?"

"Death to tyrants! Heil Hitler!"

Miller shook his head and smiled.

"It's a child's game," he muttered. He felt himself getting testy. The painkilling effects of the aspirin were wearing off.

Dimitrov ignored the comment.

"It's theater," he said. "A revenge shooting by a disgruntled Nazi. That's what we want the world to think."

"So blatantly obvious," Miller said, adding "And if I'm caught?"

"Don't be," Dimitrov said, between clenched teeth. "This is our risk."

"At that point, I become a target." He paused and exchanged glances with Dimitrov. "Of yours."

"You're too gloomy, Miller. It's doubtful that your story, even if it were the absolute truth, would be credible. And, of course, we would deny everything."

Dimitrov suddenly grasped Miller by the arm in a gesture of camaraderie.

"Game or not, it's most direct, simple. You can do this, Miller. Don't look so discouraged. Of course, there will be the president's security which will also guard Churchill." Dimitrov snickered, "Churchill travels with a single bodyguard. He must think he is immortal. We'll show him how wrong that is. Am I correct, Miller?"

Miller shrugged. The question was not worthy of a direct answer. He decided to eschew any counterarguments, which were futile at this point. For him, it was a game of survival. The stick was well defined, but for some reason, Dimitrov was withholding the carrot.

They had continued to walk. Miller was in agony. The footpath was still deserted except for a lone walker in the distance. Then, as he had expected, it came—the carrot.

Dimitrov took a thick, folded manila envelope out of an inner pocket.

"There are fifty thousand U.S. dollars in this envelope. As for your confession, it will be destroyed, you're freedom assured. You will never hear from us again."

He paused, and Miller felt the man's eyes inspecting his profile, since he had refused to turn to him full face. "You have my word."

"Your word! From an NKVD general? That is laughable. What is that worth?"

"I understand your skepticism. But consider this: You will have the money and the identity to live another life. The reward seems ample and just."

"And I will *never* hear from you again?" Miller persisted.

He remembered having asked for such assurances before.

"Never. Live your life, Miller. You will be a rich man. Marry, grow fat, and have many children."

The word "marriage" conveyed a bizarre idea.

"Are you married, General?"

Dimitrov smiled and nodded.

"I'm married to my work," he said.

At that moment, perhaps reacting to the word *marriage*, he thought suddenly of Stephanie Brown, her image bursting into his mind. For a moment, it obliterated all other issues, and a sense of profound longing gripped him once more. Dimitrov had continued to speak, but Miller was not absorbing the information. Suddenly, he gave voice to a thought that seemed to have jumped into his mouth.

"And if I fail?"

"We'll try again," Dimitrov chortled, "with or without you." He shrugged. "But let's not look on the dark side. Succeed and I'll keep my part of the bargain. You must trust me, Miller."

To trust this ruthless NKVD general was, he knew, ridiculous. These people were not to be trusted. But, he calculated, there was always the chance that, if he did survive this assignment, he might find his way out. Hadn't he done so before? As always, he would trust to luck. Perhaps in another life, he had been a cat with nine lives. He chuckled at the thought.

Still he had the sensation of living in a parallel universe. In that other universe, the mysterious and profound yearning was like an incurable affliction. This strange longing nagged at him. He felt shackled, trapped, caught in a vice. *She was not a Jewess, no way, couldn't be.* His denial expanded in his mind. He needed to divorce her from the profound hatred he held for the people whose attachment she claimed.

"All right then, General," Miller said, stifling, as best he could, this other self.

At this stage, he needed to focus his concentration, absorb the details. This mission might be his ticket to freedom after all, his gateway to another life. Forcing his concentration, he pressed Dimitrov for more and more specifics. Dimitrov obliged.

They had been walking for more than an hour when Dimitrov reversed direction, and they both headed back toward where they had entered. The pain was unbearable. He fingered the aspirin bottle in his pocket, knew he needed more, but did not want to reveal his affliction to Dimitrov.

"Have you the picture now?" Dimitrov asked. "As you can see, a lot will depend on your own planning and ingenuity."

Miller nodded. At this point, it was still very tentative. He needed to focus on method and strategy. As for the target itself, he harbored enough hatred and contempt for the man to reject any sentimentality. To detest one's target, especially this fat fool and poseur, was especially motivating.

Then another idea entered his mind. He had been waylaid into believing that his life might change direction, and he would reject his prime motivation. Whatever happened, whatever rewards he had and would garner, the essence of the mission was the glory of the deed itself.

As these thoughts tumbled in Miller's mind, Dimitrov spoke again, "Here is something more for you to chew on, comrade. Your target is a Jew-loving Zionist. He believes in a Jewish homeland. He wanted to save the Jews from the wrath of your darling führer. Now there is something to prod you forward."

The barb had, indeed, found its mark. Despite the cynical transparency of the comment, it helped seal the bargain.

How far he had traveled from the idea that gave his life meaning! Churchill, this fat, Jew-loving mountain of flesh, was, with his sniveling, fancy words of hate for Germany and the führer, the ultimate enemy, Satan with a cigar. To kill this monster would be the most sublime moment of his life.

They reached the spot in Georgetown where they had entered on the footpath.

"Well, comrade," Dimitrov said, holding out his hand. "I assume nothing less than success." He grasped Miller's right shoulder. "Please, no brazen gestures."

Miller leaned over and put his mouth to Dimitrov's ear.

"Heil Hitler!"

Dimitrov smiled and shot him a look of mockery.

"That war is over, Comrade."

"We shall see."

He stood for a long time watching Dimitrov's fading figure as it headed east on M Street. When he was out of sight, he upended the aspirin bottle in his mouth.

***

Miller saw the vapor trail from his mouth as he waited near the entrance to the hospital, hoping for Stephanie to emerge. He was well aware that he was caught between a rock and a hard place. Yet he needed to resolve this situation. Never before in his life had he been confronted with such a debilitating compulsion.

The unseasonal cold snap seemed a metaphor for his situation. It had come upon them suddenly, a condition for which he was totally unprepared. He ascribed the increasing pain in his leg to the cold.

He recalled Dimitrov's sudden reappearance in his life. It was both unwanted and unexpected, and it ricocheted through his mind like a wild bullet determined to find its target.

He saw her emerge from the hospital, wearing her nurse's uniform under her coat, and move to the corner of Twenty-Third Street in anticipation of crossing. He felt rooted to the spot. The night had been agony. No matter how he tried, how he forced his concentration on both the realities and the glory of his mission, he could not eliminate Stephanie from his thoughts.

Dubbing this effort a reasonable compromise, and since he was leaving at first light for Missouri, he could not see the harm in a brief farewell. The car was loaded and ready. He had retrieved the weapons from the storage locker, and they were locked in the trunk of his car along with the envelope of cash.

He followed her to where she stood waiting for the light to change and tapped her on the shoulder. She turned, alarmed at first, then bewildered. His own reaction to being this close to her again was confusing, and he was astonished at its effect on him. His lips trembled as he spoke.

"I came to say good-bye," he whispered.

"Good-bye?"

Her eyes probed his and became moist.

"I . . . I'm going away," he stammered.

"Where?"

He shrugged but could not bring himself to answer. Then, moved by some inchoate, overwhelming wave of emotion, he said, "Can we talk?"

She nodded.

"I have my car," he said, pointing with his chin.

Without another word, they moved to the car and got in. He started the motor and drove around the circle to Twenty-Third Street. Surprising himself, he noted that it was their usual route to Virginia, around the Lincoln Memorial, to the bridge over the Potomac. Her presence so close to him seemed to paralyze his tongue.

"So where are you going, Frank?" she asked, her hand touching his arm.

He sucked in a deep breath.

"I told you I was just passing through."

He saw her nod and swallow and then felt her fingers tighten on his arm.

"These last few weeks have been a nightmare, Frank. It was as if some piece of me was missing." There was a long silence. "And you, Frank? Have you written me off?"

"I missed you," he confessed reluctantly, surprising himself. "Of course, I missed you."

"I love you, Frank. When you sent me away . . . well, my world collapsed. I never expected this to happen. Never. Believe me, Frank, I . . . "

She could not continue. Suddenly, he reached for her hand and brought it up to his lips.

192

"Oh God, Frank, this is so unfair. I've been so stupid, locked into these old-fashioned ways of my parents. I need to be with you, Frank. I don't care anymore for those old ways. My heart is telling me the truth. Please, Frank, let me obey my heart."

He was confused, his mind ablaze with contrary images and wild thoughts. Was there such a thing as a heart to be obeyed? He felt his inner discipline crumble. Why hadn't he found the will to overpower this feeling?

They drove across the bridge, and he found himself on Lee Highway heading south. He felt torn, confused, utterly baffled, lost in his own skin. He turned the car into a country lane and stopped the car. They reached for each other and the power of their embrace astonished him.

"I love you, Frank, with all of my heart and soul. I love you."

He listened to her voice but could not find any responding voice within himself, although his feelings for her were profound.

"Take me with you, Frank. Please, darling, take me with you."

The possibility had lain dormant in his mind; now it exploded, the incentive both mysterious and powerful. Again he could not bring himself to speak.

She moved toward him and lifted her white nurse's skirt and began to unbutton him. It was not lust, not merely desire he told himself, it was validation—for her as well as him. It was as if he were being reborn. The past, the old ideas, the bitter Jew hate seemed to be quickly disappearing.

"Not here, Stephanie, not here."

He restarted the car and headed back to the highway, his thoughts buzzing with possibilities. She sat beside him as he drove, caressing his penis as if it were somehow a symbol of their unity, the connection between them. He had never before thought of this in such mystical terms. What had he become? Who was he?

"There." She pointed to a lighted sign ahead. "Cabins."

He left her in the car and went to the small office where he paid cash for a cabin. An old man took his five dollars and handed him a key.

When he returned to the car, she looked troubled.

"You were limping, Frank."

"Gets stiff sometimes."

"Was it x-rayed?"

"I'm fine."

"You didn't come back to the hospital, Frank. I assumed you found a private doctor."

"I did," he lied. "It's just stiff. The doctor said it would take time."

"Yes, it does," she agreed, frowning, obviously troubled.

"I'm fine," he said again. The reminder made the pain worse.

He parked the car in front of the cabin, and they entered.

Although the cabin was cold and damp, they reacted as if they had suddenly arrived in Valhalla. He felt suddenly replaced—the old Franz Mueller and the new Frank Miller fading into nothingness— and a new person emerging to fill his outer skin. They clung together, naked, merged now into a single being. Connected! I am home now, he told himself.

"I love you, Frank," she whispered, lost in passion.

"And I, you," he cried, repeating it again and again. "And I, you.

He wanted time to stop, to freeze the moment.

Even after they were sated by orgasmic fury, they stayed connected and entwined.

They had not bothered to pull down the shade in the cabin. They dozed, contented, dreamy, isolated. Opening his eyes, he saw the morning winter light wash over them. Her eyes were open, her head turned upward, as if she had been watching him all night. She lay in the crook of his arm, her fingers caressing his body.

"Take me with you, Frank," she persisted. "Please, Frank, take me with you."

As far as he could remember, he had never doubted that his course was the right one. Was disbelief entering his consciousness?

194

Or could it be that there were exceptions to his conviction that all Jews were vermin to be exterminated from the face of the earth. Were there no exceptions? Had some errant gene found its way into the evil mix that could neutralize the beast within and create an alien species? Stephanie had to be an exception, misplaced, an aberration. In her, the errant gene was absent. She was misplaced, he was certain. She was a full-blooded Aryan. She had to be. How could he feel this if it were not so?

He could not, of course, take her with him. But there was the possibility that when his assignment was over, he might return here, a free man, able to make a free choice, to live a complete life without fear. Perhaps, if he broached it, she would stand beside him in all his future battles with the enemy. In her mind, hadn't she already rejected a kinship with her misbegotten people? Could he hold out such a possibility? Questions . . . questions. He needed to find answers.

They made love again, then, their bodies' rage depleted, they simmered, still entwined, unwilling to disengage. Suddenly, as if an explosion rocked the room, she cried out.

"No," she screamed. "It can't be."

His left arm had embraced her, and his right arm lay relaxed above his head. She screamed again, her eyes focused on the space under his arm. He had forgotten the blood type number the SS had tattooed under his arm.

She was on her hands and knees inspecting the tattoo under his arm.

"It can't be! I'm dreaming!" she shouted. "I've seen that before. I know what it is—SS. I saw this mark on those Germans in the New England hospital. I know what this is. How could this be?"

He had been caught completely off guard. It was indeed an SS regulation, the pure-Aryan, pure-blood-type tattoo, proudly recorded, a ritual marking that accompanied induction.

She looked at the tattoo in horror, mesmerized, unable to take her eyes off it. He brought his arm down, but she continued to stare, her hysteria unabated.

"I can explain," he whispered lamely. Explain what?

"You're SS. I can't believe it! SS are Jew-hating killers. You sent my people to the ovens. I don't believe this. When they were prisoners, I wouldn't nurse them. I wouldn't touch them."

She jumped from the bed and began to gather her clothes.

"You're SS, a monster!" She shrieked, repeating the words over and over again. "You're SS! Forgive me, God. I'm so ashamed."

She moved away from him, to a corner of the room.

"I can't stay here. You're SS. I don't believe this! I've been sleeping with the devil."

He came toward her, and she began to shriek again, shaking, "Get away from me. Please don't touch me."

"Stop," he commanded. "Stop this."

She began to scream again. He felt disoriented, a fire of rage in his gut.

"Jewish bitch," he cried, reaching for her.

As he came forward, she waited, terrified. Then with all the strength she could muster, she kicked him in the genitals. The blow stopped him. He doubled over but quickly recovered and came at her again.

She fought hard, punching him. Then she tried to gouge out his eyes. Despite her strength, she was no match for him. He hit her in the face, and her head thudded against the wall. Then he reached for her neck.

The fight was still in her. She renewed her struggle, twisting and turning, trying to maneuver herself out of the power of his grip.

Unwilling to stop her vain attempts to get out of his grasp, she fought him with all her strength.

"Enough," he hissed the words into her ear, but she continued to struggle. His hands closed on her throat.

As he increased the pressure, she began to weaken. He heard a cracking noise and she slumped against him.

"Filthy Jew," he whispered, letting her limp body drop to the floor.

196

Chapter 16

Harry Truman, president of the United States, in a neat, double-breasted suit and a splashy-colored tie, stood just inside the rear car of the Ferdinand Magellan, the seven-car, bullet-proofed, armor-plated train commissioned by his predecessor. He was impatiently waiting for Churchill to arrive. Because the train was so closely associated with Roosevelt, Truman felt uncomfortable. It was only the second time he was on board, having used it once to make a quick whistle-stop tour at the urging of Roosevelt during his campaign for vice president.

Shedding the Roosevelt mantle was Truman's most difficult chore. Although he did admire the former president and owed him for appointing him vice president, he continued to be resentful of the man's death at such a critical time. It was a foolish resentment, he knew, but he had been completely unprepared, and the year of catch-up had presented him with enormous challenges. It might have been less of a chore if he had been fully briefed beforehand.

Nevertheless, despite his initial bewilderment, his confidence in himself never flagged. He wished he had been in the loop during the eighty-eight days of Roosevelt's presidency, twenty-five of which he had been away.

He had met with Roosevelt as vice president only twice before he died. He remembered how shocked he was seeing him face-to-face on his last visit. The hollow cheeks and pallid face suggested he was dying, although at the time, Truman had never acknowledged it to himself. Nor, he supposed, had Roosevelt.

Obviously, the man knew he was sick and kept it a secret from the public, who never saw him in a wheelchair. Did he believe he was immortal? Why he never prepared his vice president for the postwar world was a mystery to Truman. He had been chosen for political reasons and was considered, even by himself, as strictly a political prop.

Above all, Truman knew that good health was essential to the enormous pressures of the presidency. He was well aware of his own strong constitution, and his vigorous daily walk and occasional swim in the White House pool was part of a regular regimen. Roosevelt had been too ingenuous about his declining health. There was evidence as well, that Churchill, despite his pink cherubic complexion had sporadic heart problems. On a previous visit to the White House during Roosevelt's time, he had been rumored to have had a mild heart attack.

For this reason, his own trusted physician, Doctor Wallace Graham, was aboard the train, and he had made arrangements for emergency medical services to be on hand and available at the college.

Despite his freak advancement to the presidency, Truman thought, in hindsight, that Roosevelt's running for a fourth term had been a fatal mistake. Unfortunately, the dead president was a one-man band and, as a consequence, never gave himself permission to contemplate dying in office and leaving his handpicked vice president in charge.

Truman knew what was being said behind his back at the time: *failed haberdasher, good old boy flunky for the Prendergast machine, badly educated, not a college graduate, an inconsequential Senator from an insignificant border state.*

Roosevelt, they said during the campaign, *will stick him in the closet and close the door on him for the next four years.*

Worse, he had not been privy to any cables informing Roosevelt of the war's progress and the complicated issues that the Allies and their fair-weather friend, the Soviet Union, would face when the fighting was over. The gaps in his knowledge of the war years and the machinations of the White House were profoundly complicated, and he knew it. It was this shortfall of knowledge that bothered him most.

There was also the lack of personal chemistry between him and Churchill. A unique chemistry had bonded Roosevelt with Churchill and, giving credit where credit was due, helped make the great Atlantic Alliance workable, which was essential to winning the war in Europe in the end.

There were so many things to learn.

Sure, he revered and respected Roosevelt, but the ball was in his court now and heeding the sign he placed on his desk, The Buck Stops Here, he had no illusions about what he was up against.

At the time of Roosevelt's death, he had no knowledge of the building of the atomic bomb. He was flabbergasted to hear about it two days after he was sworn in and more stunned to learn about its destructive power.

What appalled him further was that, according to intelligence reports, the Russians had known about its development since 1942. One of his aides had discovered an unsigned Roosevelt memo, prepared by Harry Hopkins and Alger Hiss, indicating that he was open to sharing the method for making the bomb with Stalin. Apparently—Truman had learned at Potsdam—Stalin fully expected the Americans to share information on new weapons with the Russians. Had Roosevelt privately suggested such an arrangement? Had Truman been expected to make good on such an alleged promise?

Five months into his presidency, he had been called upon to make the most momentous decision in the history of the world. While sailing home from Potsdam, he gave the order to drop the bomb on Hiroshima. Despite the tragic carnage, he had lost no sleep over it. The best estimate was that the invasion of Japan would cost five hundred thousand American casualties, a situation to be avoided at all costs.

Unfortunately, to his chagrin, he had to make the decision twice since it was obvious that the stupidly stubborn and fanatic

Japanese warlords needed more convincing. He'd let history make its own judgment of his actions. His decision had ended the war; wasn't that the primary mission of the Commander-in-Chief? Would Roosevelt have made the same decision? Of course! Why then develop the bomb in the first place? He felt certain that if the war in Europe had continued, Roosevelt would not have hesitated to drop the bomb on Germany. Nor would he.

In the end, it was his decision to make, his decision alone, and he would stick by it to his grave.

Churchill was late and the president was getting impatient. He turned to his friend and military aide, General Harry Vaughn. The heavyset man was his lifelong friend from their Missouri National Guard days. In the lonely mental sepulcher of the presidency, Truman welcomed the warmth and comfort of an old buddy.

Unfortunately, much to Truman and Vaughn's distress, *The Washington Post* referred to him as "the president's poker-playing crony" as if it were one word. It was true, of course. Playing poker was one of the President's greatest pleasures, and Harry Vaughn was a regular. Poker gave Truman a chance to unwind from the rigors and intensity of the presidency, and playing with pals had been a weekly ritual on the presidential yacht.

He was looking forward to a game later during the eighteen-hour railroad trip. Perhaps, he could persuade Mr. Churchill to join the table. He was purported to be somewhat of a gambler.

"Where the hell is he?" the President smirked. "You'd think he was still Prime Minister."

"He'll be here. I'm told he's always late," Vaughan said.

"You got me into this, Harry," Truman said, referring to Vaughn's ties to Westminster College. Vaughn had suggested Churchill as speaker and Truman as introducer, to show his personal clout to his buddies on the college board of trustees and to the President of the college, "Bullet" McCluer.

After all, what good was it to be in the White House and close to the president if you couldn't flex your muscle now and then

200

and show the home folks you were, as they used to say: A Big Man on Campus?

Truman was growing testy at Churchill's tardiness. He watched the various members of the press milling around the gated entrance to the track. A few Baltimore & Ohio cars had been attached to the train for members of the press. A large group of onlookers had gathered to watch the proceedings, hoping to get a look at Churchill.

"Did you read his speech?" Vaughn asked.

"He won't show it, and I would prefer not to read it, knowing how he feels about the Russians. I'll bet he'll give Stalin holy hell for the way the Commies are behaving these days. He never did believe the bastards would live up to their agreements. He has a point, but this is not the time for us to slam them; there is a lot of sympathy for them still. They made a hell of a lot of sacrifices. Dammit, they lost seven million men on the battlefield, not to mention all the civilians the Germans killed. You can't take that away from them."

"And they raped their way through Germany," Vaughn grunted.

"If conditions were reversed, and *our* soil was plundered and *our* citizens butchered, who knows what our boys might have done."

"We're not that kind of people, Mr. President."

"Read history, Harry. As a committed Baptist, I guess you might say that I like to see the good in people not the bad. But as a student of history, such a view is suspect. It is not a pretty story."

Truman removed his glasses from his myopic eyes and wiped the lenses, squinting into the distance, then carefully put them on again.

"Be nice to know what he's going to say, especially since you're going to introduce him," Vaughn said.

"*Introduce,* Harry, but not *endorse.* There is a difference. You got me into this, my friend—you and your buddies at the college. I'll tell you this. He's a rouser, a great showman, and a master wordsmith, but a bit of a snob, talked down to me at Potsdam. Those old Tories still think America is one of their colonies. All right, he was a pain in the ass. Hell, he kept pushing Eisenhower to go straight for Berlin."

"Not a bad idea if you ask me," Vaughn said.

"Hell, we'd be fighting the Russians," Truman said. "It was a quagmire for Hitler and Napoleon, why not for us?"

"We had the bomb. We could have wiped the floor with the bastards."

Truman looked at his old friend with mock severity.

"Better not bandy that stuff around, Harry."

Despite this mild admonishment, Truman had no illusions about what direction Churchill would take in the Fulton speech, and he was fully prepared for a highly charged lobbying effort on Churchill's part urging him to get tougher with the Russians. He fully expected Churchill to mount this onslaught on many fronts, sometimes subtle, sometimes blunt and blatant, but relentless and directed towards a single goal. Truman knew he had a nose for such salesmanship and felt clever enough to parry whatever thrusts Churchill made in his direction.

While he was inclined to agree, his political instincts told him America was not ready to acknowledge any strong antagonisms to a valiant former ally. Already there had been ominous warnings from the U.S. diplomat George F. Kennan who was running the embassy in Moscow in the absence of the ambassador Averill Harriman. Kennan had warned, in what had become known as the "Long Telegram," that the Russians were becoming a destabilizing influence in the postwar world.

At this juncture, he was happy to let Churchill do the heavy lifting, although he didn't want it to be too heavy. This was not the time to bash good old Uncle Joe.

There were other problems on his mind as well, purely political. The Democratic Party was split down the middle, with the Left making noises to run their own candidate and the Right threatening a similar assault. He was particularly upset with the former vice president, Henry Wallace, whom he had appointed secretary of commerce. He was a damned fool and a tool of the hard

Left and could be a potential opponent. He'd have to ask him to resign. As for that band of die-hard segregationists on the Right, they were a tough bunch, on the wrong side of history and fighting a lost cause. He had no choice but to fight them on both fronts if he wanted to stay in the White House.

He was, after all, in the persuasion business and knew he had to woo some of the Lefties and Righties into the Democratic center if he had any chance of another term. While he agreed somewhat with Churchill's known opinions of the Russians, he knew that any really hard criticisms now would push the Wallace supporters even further Left. As a political realist, he would, if the speech were too blatantly hostile to the Russians, have to distance himself from its full import.

Suddenly, they heard a rousing cheer and cries of "Winnie! Winnie!" Through the train's window, he saw Churchill being led through the crowd by a police escort. The former prime minister acknowledged the cheers and made his familiar *V* sign, which stimulated even more applause.

"Son of a bitch has a flair for the dramatic. Makes me look like a bit player at a minstrel show."

Churchill moved along the platform accompanied by Thompson, his bodyguard, and a young woman, presumably his secretary. He was followed by a crowd of press people, photographers snapping pictures and shouting questions at him, the dominant theme of which was the content of his upcoming speech in Missouri. From his vantage, Truman was able to hear the shouted byplay.

"Will it be another 'blood, sweat, and tears' speech?" a reporter shouted.

"No blood, but lots of sweat and tears."

The reporter who shouted the question looked confused.

"It's what goes into composing a speech," Churchill said. "Mostly sweat and tears."

"What are you going to talk about Mr. Churchill?"

Churchill apparently recognized the reporter who asked that question.

"Was it . . . Benson?" Churchill asked.

"I'm going with you," Benson said. "Can you give us a hint as to what your speech will contain?"

"A lesson in history, Benson."

"But what lesson, sir?"

Churchill's blue eyes twinkled.

"'For now sits Expectation in the air,'" he called out, impishly.

The reporters laughed. Exercising his sense of the dramatic, he paused in front of the observation car so that the photographers might get a glimpse of the presidential seal affixed to the gate.

As he posed, the reporter who had been identified as Benson sidled over to the young woman near Churchill.

"We've met, haven't we?" Benson said.

She glanced at him, blankly at first, then obviously remembering.

"Oh, yes, I do remember."

"The first secretary introduced us. I see you've been promoted."

"Not really. Temporary duty. I'm taking Mr. Churchill's dictation."

"Are you? Any crumbs for this hungry reporter?"

"Sorry. My duties are confidential."

Benson nodded. She moved closer to Thompson, who had observed them.

"See you in Fulton," he waved.

"You know him?" Thompson asked.

"Met him at the embassy."

Thompson turned away.

Posing for the photographers, Churchill gave his *V* sign again, and then following the policemen, he entered the observation car where the president and other U.S. officials had assembled to greet him. Churchill was introduced to Admiral Leahy, who had worked with Truman during the war, Charlie Ross, his press secretary, Harry

Vaughn, his military aide, his physician, Wallace Graham, and his young naval aide, Clark Clifford.

The press were herded away into their special car attached to the Magellan, and Thompson and Victoria were shown to Churchill's quarters and their own.

"Mr. President," Churchill said, shaking hands.

"Mr. Prime Minister," Truman acknowledged.

"Kind of you, sir," Churchill said, smiling. "Would that I were."

He surveyed the interior of the observation lounge, which was fitted with comfortable blue chairs and couches.

"Nice digs, Mr. President. Better than the ones I had as PM. I am also partial to trains and not a great fan of the 'infernal combustion engine.' Besides, my wife has forbidden me to fly. And I never disobey Clementine."

Nothing went past Churchill without some anecdote or bon mot, Truman knew. The man was an inveterate, habitual, and dominating talker, and Truman was prepared for being talked at ad infinitum throughout the trip. Not that he objected to the onslaught of words. The man was enormously interesting and surely thought he was the most captivating person in the room, which he was. Truman, always honest with himself, acknowledged that he was no match in the talk department, although he did believe he might give the man a run for his money, especially after two or three bourbons.

Sitting down on one of the blue chairs, Churchill put the stump of his cigar in an ashtray on a small side table. The president sat facing him, while the others moved to other seats in the lounge.

The train began to move out of the station and pick up speed.

"I noticed that you posed before the presidential seal," Truman observed. "You may not know this, but I just had it changed."

"Changed?" Churchill seemed curious.

"Before the change, the eagle was turned to face the arrows. I had it changed so that it now looks at the olive branch."

Truman felt proud of his change. It reflected America's thrust toward peace.

"With all due respect, Mr. President," Churchill said. "I'd rather you had the eagle's head on a swivel so that it could turned between olive branches and arrows depending on the situation."

Truman chuckled appropriately and fully understood the observation as Churchill's opening lobbying sally. After all, as a captain in the earlier war, he was an expert in artillery combat.

"Let's have a drink," offered Truman, assuming that such a suggestion would be an icebreaker for them both during the long journey. He turned to his guest. "Mr. Churchill, we are going to be together on this train for some time. I don't want to rest on formality so, I would ask you to call me Harry."

"I would be delighted to call you Harry." Churchill paused. "And you must call me Winston."

"I just don't know if I can do that. I have such admiration for you and what you mean, not only to your people, but to the country and the world."

Churchill smiled. "Yes, you can. You must or else I will not be able to call you Harry."

"Well, if you put it that way, Winston," Truman said, secretly pleased. "I will call you Winston."

A white-coated black man approached and each ordered their drinks. Churchill called for scotch by brand, Johnny Walker Black, illustrating the desired measure by fingers, with "water, no ice." Churchill chuckled. "When I was in South Africa as a young man, the water was not fit to drink. I have felt that way about water ever since, but I have learned that it can be made palatable by the addition of some whiskey."

The group, anticipating the legendary wit, laughed appropriately.

Truman ordered bourbon and branch water.

"Branch water?"

"Any clear water that contains liquor," Truman said. "A Southern expression." He bent closer to Churchill. "Most of us here are bourbon drinkers. I hope some smart fellow did his research and discovered your preferences," Truman said.

By observing him at Potsdam, he knew that Churchill had a predilection for Johnny Walker Black scotch whiskey and Pol Roger champagne, both of which Churchill imbibed in what appeared to be large quantities. He hoped the train was stocked accordingly.

At that moment, the train slowed and stopped. General Vaughn bent and whispered something in Truman's ear. They had stopped at the Silver Spring station, a few minutes ride from Union Station.

"A crisis, Winston," Truman said, smiling. "We've had to send someone to the liquor store to get your favorite brew. Sorry about this."

"A crisis indeed, Harry," replied Churchill.

He leaned toward Truman, as if to stress the confidential nature of the impending remark.

"My wife's family is from Scotland, and she made the beverage mandatory before we were married. 'Winston, she said, scotch is the mother's milk of Scotland.' Long ago, I surrendered to her wisdom. While I have no Scottish blood, I was born on St. Andrew's Eve, and he's the patron saint of Scotland. Besides, I once represented Dundee, a Scottish constituency, for years, and of course, I married Clemmie, a Scottish lassie. And, I note with some pride, that many with Scottish names have been president. Monroe, Jackson, Polk, Buchanan, Hayes, and McKinley."

As a student of American history, Truman was impressed and said so.

"I am particularly fond of Polk," Churchill said.

To Truman, this was yet another subtle barrage. Truman's admiration for Polk was well known. Churchill was demonstrating his gift for ingratiation. So he was right on target, and Truman succumbed gladly.

"So am I, Winston. He is the most underrated of our presidents. After Washington and Jackson, I'd put him at number three."

"Ahead of Franklin?"

"History might judge otherwise," Truman said quickly, knowing of Churchill's special affection for Roosevelt.

He was instantly sorry he had graded his preferences, but felt it necessary to embellish his point about Polk.

"He was no orator like you, Winston, or Roosevelt, but he was a man of action not words. He served only one term. He said in his inaugural speech exactly what he intended to do. Actually, it was one of the shortest on record. He proposed four things and, by God, he did them: annex Texas, abolish the national bank, lower the tariff, and then settle the Oregon boundary dispute with you people. He beat the Mexicans for California and got you to give up Oregon under threat of war. He was one tough SOB."

Relating it to present circumstances, Truman sensed that the reference to Polk was Churchill's way of plumping for more aggressive action when it came to the Russians. Truman preferred to steer the conversation in another direction.

The train began to move again, and Churchill was presented with his drink, from which he took a deep sip.

"Once again the Americans have come to the rescue," Churchill said.

Everyone laughed.

"We are on a very historic route, Winston," Truman said. "It's the very same track that carried another president to his final resting place, Springfield, Illinois."

"Lincoln," Churchill said. "He wrote the finest speech ever written."

"Wrote it himself," Truman said. "Takes two talents, writing and speaking—like you, Winston. I'm afraid I'm somewhat lacking in both departments."

He instantly regretted the comment, remembering that Bess had always said he was too self-effacing, accusing him of keeping the light of his candle hidden under a bushel. He chuckled at the memory of his mother-in-law who thought her daughter married beneath her.

Churchill closed his eyes for a moment and then nodded.

"A house divided against itself cannot stand," he intoned. "Could be a metaphor for today." Truman was confused by the comment but let it pass. Churchill was an encyclopedia of quotations.

The waiter came with refills for their now-empty glasses. Churchill raised his.

"To victory," Churchill intoned.

"Victory?" Truman said, perplexed. "I thought we already won."

"Not that victory, Harry," Churchill said. "I'm talking about the current engagement. I don't believe it can be described as the end. It is not even the beginning of the end, but it is, perhaps, the end of the beginning."

Truman clearly understood the reference.

"I guess we Americans are by nature more optimistic, Winston," Truman said.

They drank. Truman offered no response, nor did he have any doubts about what Churchill had meant.

Navy bean soup, Truman's favorite, followed by ham and cheese sandwiches, was served at lunch.

During the course of the lunch, Truman described the small Westminster College in glowing terms, describing it as "a jewel of place, small but prestigious." His research on the former prime minister had revealed that one of Churchill's favorite American movies was *Kings Row.*

"Did you know, Winston, that the author of the book *Kings Row,* Henry Bellamann, was a graduate of Westminster?"

"Was he? I must confess I have seen that movie a number of times. I thoroughly enjoyed it at each viewing."

"He had called Westminster 'Aberdeen College,' and used Fulton as his model."

"Interesting," Churchill mused. "I remember that scene in which the character woke up to discover he had lost his legs. What was the name of that actor?"

"Reagan, I think," Vaughn said. "I forget his first name."

During dinner, Churchill continued to push his case against the Russians and steered the conversation to the atomic bomb.

"How are we ever going to prevent others from getting it?" Churchill had asked.

"We can't," Truman admitted. "We might keep the lid on it for a few years, but sooner or later, some country will obtain it, by hook or by crook."

"And what of the Soviets?" Churchill asked.

"Five years, at best . . . or worst. It's out of the box, Winston. There's no stopping it. But we've certainly got to postpone the inevitable as long as we can. If the war had dragged on and Roosevelt was alive, it might have happened sooner. Hell, he might have given it to them."

Truman was certain that Churchill caught the implication of his remark, the allegation that Roosevelt was alleged to have wanted to share atomic secrets with good old Uncle Joe.

"You said by hook or by crook, Harry," Churchill said, picking up on the nuance. "It is not the hook to be feared, Harry, rather the crook."

"I agree. Our people have told me that we are inundated with Soviet spies and sympathizers. Our country leaks like a sieve, Winston. My number-one priority is to beef up our intelligence services. During the war, they were directed against the Germans; the Soviets were given a pass. No more."

"I'm afraid we are in the same boat," Churchill sighed. "When it comes to spying and enlisting cohorts, the Russians are masters. They have burrowed in for the long haul. And speaking of weapons of destruction, the Germans created the most horrendous weapon of all. They transported Lenin in a sealed railroad car to Russia like a plague bacteria. This one act has created a worldwide epidemic."

"That's a pretty grim assessment, Winston."

"I know. My spiritual mother must have been Cassandra."

210

Truman listened patiently to what amounted to Churchill's continuing brief against the Russians. It was a steady drumbeat and went on until mid-afternoon while the train sped along the tracks.

"You make it sound as if any productive relations with the Russians are hopeless, Winston," Truman said.

Despite his resistance, Churchill's argument had made an impact on him.

"One would think it would be to Stalin's advantage to maintain good relations with us at this moment. His country is devastated. Hell, we can help him get his country back on its feet. I mean he can't just close the curtains and lock out the light."

"Harry, trying to maintain good relations with a Communist is like wooing a crocodile. You do not know whether to tickle it under the chin or beat it over the head. When it opens its mouth, you cannot tell whether it is trying to smile or preparing to eat you up."

"You're not going with that one in Fulton are you, Winston?" Truman asked, suddenly uncomfortable with his aggressive attitude. "Pretty strong stuff. I'm not saying there might not be truth in it, but it seems a bit over the top at this moment in time."

"Rest assured, Harry," Churchill said. "I hope to be more artful."

"I'm sure you will be, Winston," Truman said, not entirely relieved. "I prefer to be more optimistic. I know, I know, you Brits think your old colonials are naïve and given to rosy scenarios. Frankly, Winston, I think you should be more positive. Hell, we have the United Nations organization now. It may be a crude setup, but hell, we all can talk to each other."

"Talk?" Churchill chuckled. "The cacophony will be fearsome."

"Better to talk than shoot, Winston. What do you see down the road for that organization?"

"I always avoid prophesying before the event, because it is much better policy to prophecy after the event has already taken place."

Truman laughed.

211

"You are a card, Winston."

"Let's hope it's not the joker."

"Speaking of cards, Winston. Can we interest you in a bit of poker after dinner tonight?"

Churchill rubbed his chin and smiled.

"Be happy to join you. Gin and bezique are my principal gambling vices, although I have been known to be quite keen around the poker table."

"Is that a challenge?" Truman asked.

"We accept then," Vaughn said, with a chuckle.

"I must warn you, Winston, we take no quarter."

"Nor do I, Harry. Nor do I."

"A well-known fact, sir," Admiral Leahy added.

"I'm sure we won't break the Bank of England, Winston," Truman said.

"Not that we won't try," Vaughn chortled.

The convivial conversation continued for a while longer, then Truman noted that Churchill's energy seemed to flag.

"I guess we should allow Mr. Churchill a bit of rest before dinner."

"Capital idea, Harry." Churchill stood up. ""I'm a siesta man, Harry. Clears the cobwebs. Makes me a more interesting companion at dinner."

He paused for a moment, his eyes glazing over as if his thoughts had drifted suddenly. Then he spoke, "You said curtains, didn't you, Harry?"

Truman shrugged, baffled by the comment. Churchill turned and left the car to be ushered to his designated compartment.

Chapter 17

Miller carried the lifeless, nude body of Stephanie Brown and put it into the trunk of his car. She had given him little choice, and his survival instinct had kicked in. Unfortunately, he had to wait until dark. His testicles still ached from her blow, but in the interim, he was able to put the entire episode into perspective.

He had been a fool, trapped in an emotional prison by a conniving and manipulative Jewess. With her dead body only a few feet from where he sat in the only chair in the cabin, he felt and truly believed that his action had caused the poison to seep out of his body and mind.

His SS tattoo, he reasoned now, had saved him from certain disaster, as if the führer were protecting him from becoming entangled with the devil. Like the feelings induced by the mystical rituals of the SS, he sensed some otherworldly meaning in the murder of this Jewish temptress, as if it were necessary for him to experience this killing as a test of his dedication to rid the world of this filth. These people were evil, cunning, sly, and duplicitous, and he had almost been seduced into their net. At this moment, he could not imagine ever having had such a strong feeling of attachment to a woman. But the fact of her gender was less compelling than the reality of her race.

Finally, he had cleansed himself of her and broken the spell of her erotic attraction. Now, he must dispose of her body and put the whole episode behind him.

Emptied of this obsession, he could now turn himself to the matter at hand, his assassination of Winston Churchill. A plan was forming in his mind. He had studied the road maps and figured out the best route to Fulton. The *Washington Post* that morning had written that the president and Churchill would leave by train in a couple of days, which would give him a good head start. With luck, he could make it to Fulton in twenty-four hours, stopping occasionally for brief naps.

He needed to get there to explore all the aspects of the so-called landscape. He would have to visit the hall where Churchill was slated to speak and explore the surrounding area. His principal preoccupation would be the matter of his escape. He would treat the attack as a military operation, scouting the terrain for the weakest link, finding the most vulnerable moment to attack and retreating intact to fight again.

After putting the body in the car trunk, along with her nurse's uniform, underwear, and white shoes and stockings beside her, he took off. He decided to drive at least five hundred miles, the halfway point to Fulton, before he would begin to consider where to dump the body.

Driving carefully, keeping well within the speed limits, he headed west on a route he had mapped beforehand. To eliminate the possibility of running out of gas, he topped off his tank a number of times along the road and stopped in a small town for bread, cheese, fruit, milk, and a large supply of aspirin to sustain him for the entire journey. At a hardware store, he bought a large spade.

He reached the five-hundred-mile point in late afternoon. Taking advantage of the waning light, he drove along country roads looking for an area that appeared deserted and infrequently used. He found what he was looking for just as darkness descended. In the pitch-black of the moonless night, he dragged the body into a copse surrounded by trees and dug a hole deep enough to contain her remains.

The effort exacerbated his leg pain, which he partly assuaged with aspirin. The drug seemed to be having less and less effect. He was well aware that once his mission was over, he would have to seek medical care. Obviously, he had removed the cast before his leg had fully healed.

Working diligently, he dug until he was satisfied with the length and depth of the hole. Then he rolled the nude body into it, covered it with the removed soil, and patted it down so that it would be level with the ground, returned the spade to the trunk, and headed back to the main road.

This done, he wiped the event from his mind. He likened it to burying garbage. Like the people he had killed in battle—those whom he had personally executed and the men he had killed in the German prison cell—he felt nothing for them. He was now free to concentrate fully on his mission.

He reached Fulton on March 3, two days before the speech was scheduled. The small town of eight thousand was clearly buzzing with anticipation. Crossed flags, the Union Jack, and the Stars and Stripes were posted along most of the streets. Posters with Harry Truman and Winston Churchill's pictures were plastered on every available storefront. His first action was to buy a Fulton newspaper.

The paper contained articles on every aspect of the event, which was expected to draw twenty-five thousand people, including a large press contingent and dignitaries that would tax every facility in the town.

The event was to be held in the college gymnasium, the largest building on the campus, which could accommodate approximately twenty-eight hundred people. It seemed to Miller a paltry number, considering the people involved.

An overflow would be able to listen via loudspeaker at the Swope Chapel on the campus, which could hold an additional nine hundred people. According to the newspaper, nine voluntary committees had been established to plan and monitor the event.

Miller could now understand part of the reasoning behind the Russians' insistence that the deed be done during the speech, when the ears and eyes of the world would be focused on it, an event in which he, of all people, would have the most significant role. It was

215

also obvious that the Russians needed to pin the deed on a disgruntled Nazi and deflect any suspicion from themselves, hence their obvious indifference to whether or not he was caught. The placement of the rifle and the note would offer clues to enhance the motive. He was well aware of the strategy, but he was determined, come what may, to survive.

That the town would be jammed was a point of optimism for Miller; the more crowded the better. He imagined doing the deed and getting lost in the swelter of people. Still, what was planned was a far cry from the huge Hitler rallies he had attended, giant spectacles that brought huge crowds together to honor the führer and hear his immortal words. Even now, his pulse quickened with the memory of the führer's voice and the great rolling cry of "Sieg Heil!" as if one voice had risen to reach the heavens.

According to the articles in the newspaper, this little Presbyterian college of not more than two hundred twenty male students had seized the attention of the world. He noted the weather report: sunny and warm.

The articles contained every detail of the event and saved Miller the trouble of inquiring further. Timing of the event, rules of admission, and other specific details and explanations were well covered. Also published was a detailed map of the gymnasium building, complete with the numbered layout of all entrances and exits, the seating plan, and other details, including the locations of bathrooms and the first aid station. Studying the map in depth, he carefully tore it from the paper, folded it, and placed it in his pocket.

He inspected the town, pondering his exit strategy if he were lucky enough to make it after the initial impact of the deed. Then he drove to the Westminster College campus. The area was filled with activity, which centered on a flat-roofed building, obviously the gymnasium in which the event would be held. He found a parking space not far from the building.

In front of the gymnasium, people were unloading metal folding chairs and bringing them into the building.

"Can I help?" he asked one of the adult men who carried the chairs to the gymnasium.

"Of course," the man said. "We're all volunteers."

He couldn't believe his good fortune. Lining up behind those who were receiving metals chairs from the truck, he took two in each hand and moved to the gymnasium. His leg ached, but he managed the process. It was essential that he inspect the interior of the building.

Carpenters were constructing a two-tiered wooden platform. Electricians were stringing up a public address system. Rows of metal seats stretched from the front of the platform and were building toward the rear. Along the sides of the gymnasium were rows of wooden bleachers. It would be a tight fit for what was going to seriously tax the facility's space.

Following directions, he placed the chairs where he was told and roamed through the premises. Few paid him any attention. Workmen were also building a platform behind the rostrum, presumably for important officials. A smaller platform was being built in the rear. A man supervised the construction and occasionally glanced at a blueprint.

"What are you building?" Miller asked innocently.

"Platform for news photographers and others from the press," the man said, without looking up from his blueprint.

He noted two high, double-door entrances at the front of the gymnasium and two single-door entries at the sides of the gym and two entrances at the rear behind what was obviously to be the speaker's platform. Consulting his map, he noted that the narrow doors were locker rooms, one for girls, one for boys. The boys' locker room had been designated a first aid station. He supposed that the gymnasium was sometimes used for events for a nearby girls' college.

Above the floor and not designated on the map was a scoreboard that he noted was not electrified but apparently relied on large cardboard signs that were inserted into frames to reflect the scores of basketball games. Above one of the frames was a sign indicating that the home team was called the Blue Jays. He noted the backboards and hoops at either end of the gym, partially hidden by bunting. The scoreboard piqued his curiosity. How did one get there to change the numbers? There had to be a space up there for someone to insert the scorecards.

Amid all the carpenters banging away and the various workpeople and volunteers, no one paid any attention to him, and he was able to walk through every door without anyone stopping him. If they did, he could always feign ignorance. Everyone seemed absorbed in his or her own work.

He explored both locker rooms and discovered that there was an inner door in each that opened to the back of the gymnasium, leading to a parking lot. Intrigued by the scoreboards on either side of the gymnasium, which seemed a perfect sniper's perch, he decided that there must be some entranceway that permitted someone to get up there. There were no visible doorways from the floor. It took him a while to figure out that there must be an access stairway somewhere in the locker rooms on either side of the gymnasium.

Entering the boys' locker room first, he noted a narrow doorway concealed behind a bank of lockers. On either side of the door were two metal rings that had obviously at one time been used as loops for a chain to be held together by a lock. There was no lock in place at the moment. He opened the door, which led to a winding metal staircase.

With effort, he painfully climbed the staircase that ascended to a small area behind the scoreboard, just enough for someone to crouch behind. There were two stacks of scorecards neatly placed in bins alongside the opening. Obviously, a single operator could watch the game and slip the scorecards into their metal frames so that the spectators could keep track of the score. He poked his head into the opening. From there, he could see the entire length of the gym with a bird's-eye view of the speaker's platform now being constructed. He was elated; he had found the perfect sniper's perch.

He descended the steps again, timing the descent. It took him less than five seconds to reach the door. Cautiously, he opened the door a crack, and since a bank of lockers hid the entrance to the stairway, he could slip in and out unobserved. Still, he had not yet worked out a way to get in and out undetected. Also, he was certain that the president's security detail would sweep the area thoroughly prior to the event and check every entrance and exit, including the one he had just come from. He needed to come up with a plan that would neutralize their inspection and keep their focus off the possibility of any foul play from that location.

Another fortunate stroke of luck was that the door to the outdoors was close enough to the edge of the bank of lockers to provide quick access to the parking lot. As he moved toward this exit, a couple of men were measuring the width of the door opening.

"Just makes it," the man who had measured the doorway said to the other as he read the tape. "We can get a wide stretcher in if we have to."

"Let's hope we don't have to," the other man said.

"Never know," the first man said. "Best be prepared."

"We'll park a couple of ambulances from Fulton State outside."

"Just a precaution," the man with the tape measure said. "Hell, it's the president of the United States and Churchill."

"What if someone else needs help, a spectator with a coronary?"

"We'll have extra people on duty, doctors, nurses. Strict orders from Washington."

The men left the locker room and went out the back door, leaving Miller to contemplate how his mission was to be accomplished and his escape secured.

He returned to the floor of the gymnasium and reconnoitered the area, wracking his brains on methods and strategy. He felt confident that he could do the job. Wasn't he born under a lucky star? Then he inspected the girls' locker room. There, the entrance to the scoreboard stairs was impenetrable. A bank of lockers was pushed tight against the doorway. Apparently, this area was to be reserved as a VIP holding area, from which Truman and Churchill would make their dramatic entrance.

Helping with the chairs again, he fell into line with the others and placed the chairs in rows. People were now putting bunting on the platform. He stood in the back of the gymnasium and observed the scene.

"Biggest thing that ever happened to Fulton," a woman said behind him. "I'm so excited, I can't stand it."

He wasn't sure if the remark was meant for him, but he turned to face her anyway. She was middle-aged and gray-haired.

"It will certainly be a blast," he said, enjoying the irony.

After his inspection of the scene, he returned to his car and drove about twenty miles out of town until he came to a spot that he had seen on his way to Fulton. It was a dirt road that led through a forested area. He had to drive a few miles into the forest where the road dead-ended. No structures were visible, and the road, although hard-packed, looked somewhat overgrown with scrub from lack of use.

He stretched out in the rear seat and slept for a few hours until dawn provided enough light for his needs. His leg was stiff when he awoke, and he downed a number of aspirins in an increasingly difficult task to mask the pain.

Opening the trunk, he removed the weapons he had not touched since he had arrived in Canada. A film of oil remained on the rifle and the pistol, and looking around for a rag, he noted that he had forgotten to dispose of Stephanie's clothes, her nurse's uniform, underwear, and shoes.

He took her panties and used them to wipe the rifle and pistol clear of oil. Then he stripped both weapons and checked every part. Both were SS issue and he had expert knowledge of how they operated. He peered through the barrel and double-checked the firing mechanism, loading the six bullets into the magazine.

Although he knew he was taking a chance, he needed to check the sighting of the rifle and carefully picked a target that was approximately the same distance between the scoreboard and the speaker's podium. Ahead, in the quickening light, he saw a bird's nest built into the crook of a tree. He crouched, aimed, and fired. He had always been a crack shot, but he missed the first shot, adjusted the sights, fired again, and hit the nest on the second try. He shot again and hit the target a second time, dislodging the nest from the tree.

What he had to do was hit Churchill in the head with the first shot, a shot that would blow away his brains. His escape depended on his hitting the man on this initial try. A second one would put him at risk.

There were, of course, other details to be considered. So far his plan was too sketchy and unclear. He needed time to think, and he felt certain that, with careful planning, he could accomplish the mission. There were numerous other considerations as well. Would Dimitrov keep his word? He did not discount the possibility of the Russians sending their own assassin to track him down. He had money and mobility. The United States was a big country. He'd find a way to get lost in it, assume yet another identity, and continue the inevitable battle against the enemy. But that was not his immediate concern.

He opened the trunk, stuffed the panties in his pocket, and carefully laid the weapons inside. Again he noticed Stephanie's nurse's uniform. Only then did the idea occur to him. He had solved yet another problem.

Chapter 18

Victoria sat opposite Thompson in the sitting room of Churchill's railcar suite, waiting for his return.

After dinner, Churchill had changed into his blue siren suit and gone off to play poker with Truman and his companions. He had asked that they be available in case he needed to go over the last drafts of the speech before it was mimeographed for the press.

Victoria's mind was elsewhere. No matter how hard she tried to rationalize her lover's action, she could not ignore that he had voluntarily handed over the speech to the Russians. She had seen the handover with her own eyes, and while she would have been willing to believe that he was carrying out an official act, the remark he had inadvertently made while reading the speech—"He has signed his death warrant"—echoed and re-echoed in her mind.

Donald had often told her that diplomats were masters of obfuscation and intrigue and often acted in ways that could strike an unschooled observer as strange and mysterious. Who was she to question the actions of the first secretary of the British embassy? He was an acknowledged star of the British diplomatic corps, someone on his way to the top of his calling. Lord Halifax, the ambassador, trusted his judgment without question, and charged Donald with keeping all facets of the embassy running smoothly. Indeed, to all intents and purposes, Donald Maclean ran the British embassy and could be considered one of the most important people in Washington.

The phrase *death warrant* could not be excised from her thoughts. What did he mean? Considering that both Churchill and

Thompson had reiterated the necessity for confidentiality, she could not reconcile Donald's act or those chilling words with any benign purpose.

He had told her he was going to discuss the thematic aspects of the speech with Churchill or, at the very least, persuade the ambassador to discuss it with him. None of these things had apparently occurred. Or perhaps they agreed with the former prime minister's thesis, although the remark about a death warrant seemed to negate that theory. Something was awry. She couldn't shake an uncommon sense of terrible discomfort, a kind of anxious desperation.

Yet she continued to resist sharing this information with Thompson. He might think she was imagining things or it might set off unnecessary and possibly false alarm bells. After all, the Russians had been friends and allies. By imparting the information, she would, in effect, be involved in a double betrayal, both of her lover and Mr. Churchill.

She could not deflect her uneasiness.

"You look a bit distracted, young lady," Thompson said.

Sitting opposite her, he had apparently been observing her closely for some time.

"Do I?" she asked innocently, knowing his assessment was exactly correct.

Guilt was having its corrosive effect. However she tried to put it aside and rationalize it in the name of love and loyalty to her boss, it continued to gnaw at her. She needed Donald by her side to reassure her by his presence and to reiterate his explanation.

"Just an idle observation, Miss Stewart. It's the curse of the detective. Always needing to look beyond the human façade. Forgive me."

After a long silence, she found her mind too fatigued with speculation about her lover's motives. But in the process of blocking one path, she found another equally disturbing.

"You've been with Mr. Churchill a long time, Mr. Thompson?" she began.

"Very long, my dear—earlier in his career when he was First Lord of the Admiralty in the first war and later when he called me back in thirty-nine. I was with him during the entire time of his service as prime minister." He sighed and smiled. "We've been through a great deal together."

She noted his great pride in his service, and she had no doubts about his affection for and absolute loyalty to Mr. Churchill.

"I suppose you've seen him through all kinds of danger."

She was surprised at her own comment, since it revealed a level of anxiety that she had deliberately repressed.

"My goodness, yes," Thompson said. "You cannot imagine the close calls we've had. He is a stubborn man, courageous and quite fearless. During the blitz, I could not get him to be cautious, and often he would refuse to go down to a shelter. Considering his extensive travels during the war by land, sea, and air, it's a miracle that he's still alive."

"I guess you must have an eagle eye for danger, sir," she said, watching his face.

"Maybe so. At times, I've had to be rather heavy-handed to get him to change a schedule, switch modes of transportation, restrain him from moving into crowds—even though they were mostly adoring crowds. Many times I've had to deliberately inhibit his movements to get between him and potential harm."

"Which would put you in the line of fire," she said, suddenly feeling chilled.

"I would take a bullet for that man anytime or anyplace," he said emphatically. "He is a great man."

"Give up your life for another man, Mr. Thompson? That is quite a sacrifice."

"To give it up for him would be an honor."

She felt a sudden sense of panic and sucked in deep breaths to calm her. But she had apparently triggered in him a new train of thought.

"Odd, isn't it? None of the great wartime leaders—Stalin,

Roosevelt, Mr. Churchill, de Gaulle—were ever harmed during the war. Only Admiral Darlan, the Vichy collaborator who later betrayed the Nazis and collaborated with us, was assassinated."

"I suppose they were well protected," Victoria said.

"The marshal and the president had elaborate protection."

"And the Prime Minister?"

Thompson chuckled.

"He had me."

She offered a smile and a humorless laugh.

"Of course, when he was prime minister he was officially protected, but I was always on hand to watch over him."

"Has there ever been an attempt . . . you know what I mean . . . on Mr. Churchill?" she asked hesitantly.

He studied her face for a moment then turned away to contemplate the passing scenery. After a while, he looked at her again. His expression seemed severe.

"This is a matter we never discuss. Not ever."

"I'm sorry, Sir. I hadn't realized."

"There are subjects beyond revelation," he said. "In the public arena, they power suggestion and, unfortunately, emulation."

"I think I understand, sir."

She wasn't exactly certain, but she presumed he meant that any public discussion of such an act or the possibility of it occurring would give evil people ideas. From his sudden change of attitude, she felt certain that attempts had been made on Mr. Churchill's life that, quite obviously, had been thwarted and, presumably, never publicized.

"I'm sorry, sir. I'm afraid I have set off some gloomy thoughts." She shrugged. "I have no idea why I brought up the subject."

Again, she repressed a desire to tell him about her lover's action and his odd statement. The idea was obsessing her. At the very least, she thought suddenly, she should have pressed Donald for an explanation of why he would give the speech to the Russians. Surely, he owed her that. After all, they did share the secret of their affair. Surely, that meant something.

She felt suddenly stifled and vulnerable. The temptation to reveal what she knew was overwhelming. She needed to be alone and think this over.

"Will Mr. Churchill be needing me tonight?" she asked, anxious to be off.

"I expect he'll be quite late—poker game, you know. If he needs you, he'll call."

She bid him good-night and left the compartment.

Inexplicably, the young woman had triggered in Thompson's mind recollections publicly repressed but never far from his thoughts. Yes, there were narrow escapes from the obvious: U-boats tracking ships and trains on which the prime minister had traveled, planes on which he flew.

He remembered the case of poor Lesley Howard, one of the great English actors, whose plane had gone down over the Atlantic. Thompson was dead certain that the actor's plane was thought to be carrying the prime minister. Then there were the many instances when he toured the battlefield with General Eisenhower or went round London during the blitz.

Most of these episodes would, one day, when all the intelligence of both sides was sorted out, become the stuff of history. The other episodes, he hoped, would never see the light of day. His job was not only to guard the prime minister and foil any attempt to assassinate him, but prevent the attempt from becoming known. Some were not even revealed to the prime minister or his family.

An implicit policy of Special Branch was that all such incidents be shrouded in secrecy and not recorded anywhere, leaving no trace. The most serious of these attempted murders occurred at Chequers, the PM's official country house. Before Churchill would embark to go anywhere, Thompson would carefully check the route, surveying possible clandestine targeting places. Secretly, he would pay a visit to the most dangerous spots, often working by pure instinct.

If he were suspicious, he often sat in a car where he could deflect a bullet before it hit Mr. Churchill. Yes, he would gladly put himself in harm's way to protect his charge.

It was, of course, almost impossible to guard his man during the numerous stump speeches he made running for Parliament. But if the Prime Minister were to speak in an enclosed space—the House of Commons excepted, since that was thoroughly vetted by MI5, he was always careful to scout the premises in advance, checking even after his colleagues had scoured the area. He rarely trusted anyone to "cleanse" an area completely.

He trusted no one to be as thorough as himself. At one speech in a hall in Hampshire, his attention had been drawn to a man who seemed innocent and harmless, but for some reason he seemed to radiate suspicion. Thompson got to him just in time. He had a live grenade in his pocket and admitted later, in a private, merciless interrogation carried out by Thompson himself, that he was an assassin hired by the Gestapo; his reward, whether he lived or died, was a lifetime stipend for his family. He had been committed to an insane asylum for life.

Once at Chequers, a gardener who had miraculously gotten through the clearance process, had been observed on the grounds near a hedge through which could be seen Churchill's study. Thompson, who knew the spot intimately and checked it out whenever the prime minister was in residence, found the man poised with a rifle ready for a shot at Mr. Churchill. Thompson quickly dispatched him to oblivion. In that case, he had done the cleanup job himself.

There were other incidents as well, all kept secret. At times, Special Branch would alert him to a dire possibility, and he would quickly follow through, sometimes on the sketchiest of clues but which offered just enough intelligence to stop the potential assassin in his tracks.

He felt no compunction or remorse at preemptive strikes aimed at preventing an assassination of the prime minister. *Better left unsaid and unthought of,* he told himself. He recalled two other incidents of potential assassins being dispatched without any official reporting. Only he knew those; he tried never to think about them. Sometimes he succeeded, sometimes not, like now. What he feared most was that someone might read his thoughts. Of course, it was ridiculous, but then many fears were. Again, he tucked them away in his memory vault.

Hearing this lovely young woman expressing such anxiety over the fate of Mr. Churchill felt chilling. Perhaps, something was in the air. He believed implicitly in such psychic moments, a kind of telepathy that could never be explained. Such precognition baffled him, but he never distrusted the feeling when it came over him. He would never share such ideas with anyone, not even his wife—and certainly not Mr. Churchill, who would have called them poppycock and nonsense. Nevertheless, his own proofs were unassailable.

More than once, he knew, such sensations—such mysterious insight and awareness—had saved Churchill's life. In his heart of hearts, he knew his job was a calling, ordained perhaps by supernatural forces commanding that he protect this great man and assure him a long and productive life for the benefit of all mankind. Thinking such thoughts often brought tears to his eyes.

Twice he sat by Mr. Churchill's bedside when he was at death's door, once when a car in New York had struck him in the thirties and during the war when an attack of pneumonia had brought him close to the brink. He had prayed all night, not simply to the Anglican God of his church, but to all gods of all religions everywhere. He had come to believe in the very fabric of his being that as long as he was on the job, Churchill would never have to worry about his mortality.

His thoughts were interrupted by the arrival of Mr. Churchill. His face was flushed, and he seemed to carry with him an air of amused reflection, as if he were chuckling at some joke known only to him.

"I'm afraid, Thompson, I did not carry the day for Albion."

"You lost, sir?"

Churchill nodded and smiled sheepishly.

"Like swimming with sharks, Thompson! The Yanks bested me. They are masters of deception and bluff." He chortled. "And there were the usual language difficulties. They call the knave a 'jack' and a sequence a 'straight.' Imagine?"

"It is not only the ocean that separates us, Prime Minister."

"The price was well worth the lesson. Truman is canny and bold, shrewd and cautious, and at times, is excellent at the bluff. The Americans are quite sentimental and lacking in cold-blooded ruthlessness. They felt sorry for this old English gentlemen's poker incompetence and began to let me win when my chip pile had shrunk to disastrous proportions."

"How, sir?"

"One of the fellows, Ross, the president's press secretary, let me bid up my knave against his ace, then when the pot was large enough, the man, clearly holding the winning hand, folded. It happened often enough until they felt that I had partially recouped. I won one large pot with a pair of deuces. I did not let on." Churchill began to laugh uproariously. "Of course, they did not let me carry the day. As I left the table and had barely closed the compartment door, I heard Vaughn say: 'We didn't want him to brag to his limey friends that he had beaten the Americans at poker.' I must say I loved the experience. This Truman, Thompson, is genuine, a true man of the people. Poker, Thompson, is a great teacher of character."

He looked animated, not at all tired. He sat in a chair for a long time lost in thought. Then he looked around the compartment.

"Where is Miss Stewart?"

"I'll get her, sir," Thompson said. "She knows she is on call. We must get the speech stenciled and mimeographed for the press."

He found her compartment, which she shared with one of Mr. Truman's secretaries.

"Be right there!"

She arrived flustered and distraught. Churchill paid little attention to her. A typewriter sat on a desk in a corner of the compartment. Thompson could see that she hadn't prepared herself mentally for such swift action.

"Step lively, please," Mr. Churchill snapped. "You have the text?"

"Yes, sir."

"Let me have it."

He put on his reading glasses and glanced over the text. Then he nodded and whispered the line, "'A house divided against itself cannot stand.'"

"Shall I put that down, sir?"

"No. I was quoting Lincoln, one of their few presidents who wrote his own speeches. It brought something to mind."

He looked over the text again.

"I am troubled," he muttered, "over the paragraph where I talk about the division of Europe. Iron fence seems so . . . so unmemorable. I actually used the line in an earlier letter to Truman, but I just don't like it."

"I'm afraid, sir, we have to sign off on the speech tonight. Tomorrow, we will be in Fulton."

"It will come to me, Thompson."

"It always does, sir."

"Well then, I guess I have no choice. Of course, it won't prevent an insertion when I deliver the speech."

"Not at all, sir."

"Well then, proceed," said Churchill. "Nevertheless, in my mind it is still a work in progress."

She began immediately to type the final draft onto a stencil. It had already been arranged that Thompson would have the stencils run off on the press office mimeograph machine on the train. He would gather up all the copies and guard them until the time for their release.

"And after you finish that, Miss Stewart, type the working text I will use. Do you remember the instructions?"

"Verse form, sir. I do remember."

230

Churchill nodded, reached into an inner pocket, and pulled out his leather cigar case. He clipped off the end of a cigar, and Thompson was quick with his lighter. Churchill puffed deeply and observed the ash, then fell into a deep silence for a few moments.

"Damn," he said suddenly.

"What is it, sir?" Thompson asked.

"I was thinking of my toast to Stalin in Tehran. Words . . . " He paused and shook his head.

"I was present, sir."

"Yes, of course, Thompson. I do remember."

He nodded his head, a gesture, Thompson knew, of recollection. The man had an uncanny memory. He watched as Churchill lifted his hand as if he were holding a glass and making a toast.

"'I sometimes call you Joe,'" he began, recollecting, "and you can call me Winston if you like, and I like to think of you as my very good friend' . . . What hypocrisy! Then, I said: 'The British people were turning politically pink' . . . ending with . . . 'Marshal Stalin, Stalin the Great' . . . The memory of the toast often stirs up my black dog." He looked up suddenly. "He could be infuriating! Once, in front of Roosevelt, he actually called me a coward. Later, he told me—after I walked out of the meeting—that his translator had misinterpreted his words."

"You did your best, sir," Thompson said, trying to refocus Churchill's dark thoughts.   Considering the importance of the upcoming speech, Thompson was determined to do anything in his power to stop the black dog from attacking Churchill. He sensed that his recollections of Tehran were bringing him farther down.

"The sad fact of it, Thompson, was that I liked the man, despite my distaste for everything he stood for and represented. When I visited him in Moscow, I thought we had really bonded. He had a certain attractive air." Churchill grew pensive. "Franklin liked him as well, perhaps too well. Dear Franklin!"

He sighed and sucked in a deep breath.

"Now there was charm personified. With Stalin he was clearly seductive, using all of his skills of allure and bewitchment as if that was all that was needed to win him over. There were moments, Thompson, when I felt like a rejected suitor." He chuckled. "'Oh, beware, my lord, of jealousy. It is the green-eyed monster which doth mock the meat it feeds on.' Can you imagine? Jealous of Stalin for attracting my friend."

Thompson was not shocked at the metaphor. Churchill was an incorrigible romantic.

"Stalin trumped us, Thompson. Power was his true mistress."

"This speech should balance the scales."

Churchill puffed deeply on his cigar. Thompson sensed that he was fighting hard to repress his black dog.

"Do you think the United Nations will be a true family of nations, able to resolve domestic spats and assure a peaceful future?" Churchill asked. "Truman is quite hopeful."

"And you, sir?"

He shrugged. He put on his glasses and read through the text of his speech that he still held on his lap. Then he spoke the words dealing with the United Nations: "We must make sure that its work is fruitful, that it is a reality and not a sham, that it is a force for action, not merely a frothing of words, that it is a true temple of peace, in which the shields of many nations can someday be hung up, and not merely a cockpit in a Tower of Babel."

He put the text down again.

"I truly hope that the future will match my words. Sure, Thompson, it is always wise to look ahead, but difficult to look farther than one can see. I wish I were more sanguine about the future."

"Surely, you don't think that someday there will be another war, sir?"

"Will it matter what I think now?"

"Of course, it does, sir," Thompson said, "Your remarks could set the world on a course that could have an enormous impact on the future."

"'There is a tide in the affairs of men,'" Churchill said.

Thompson had heard this quote from *Julius Caesar* many times before.

"Well, then, sir, we are in high tide."

"Perhaps, Thompson," Churchill said, standing up and walking to the adjoining bedroom.

Thompson watched the young lady typing away with great diligence.

"He will be fine, Miss Stewart. Not to worry."

"Yes, sir," Victoria said, but her response seemed tentative.

Chapter 19

Miller awoke from a dreamless sleep in the backseat of his car. The pain in his leg had accelerated, and his ankle had begun to swell. Swallowing a few aspirin tablets, he untangled himself, managed to get out of the car, and limped around until he was able to walk.

One more day, he thought, trying to will his mind to withstand the pain.

Resisting pain had been one of the hallmarks of his SS training. Yielding to pain was a violation of the code. One endured pain. Maintaining silence under extreme torture was a fundamental caveat. "Death before dishonor" was the mantra.

"Heil Hitler!" he shouted into the still morning, as he moved in a widening circle around the car.

Before falling asleep, his mind had buzzed with various scenarios designed to accomplish the deed. Only when the final details had emerged—etching a matrix of action in his brain—was he able to sleep.

The killing of Winston Churchill had taken on the trappings of ritual, and his mind hearkened back to the earliest days of his SS indoctrination. Himmler had imbued them all with a sense that their existence had been ordained by destiny. Their godhead was Adolph Hitler, master of their lives and future. They were the chosen, the pure-blooded-Aryan ideal, the perfection of the master race.

He realized now that he had been tested and preserved for a reason. Their defeat, too, had been a test of their endurance. Now these mongrels, these Jew-loving pigs, the puppets that unwittingly danced to the strings of the sinister Yids would learn the power of vengeance. The death of Churchill, Churchill the poseur, Churchill the golden-tongued serpent, would validate their resurrection. Because Franz Mueller was one of the chosen, he was confident of his survival. His planning was, he was certain, being dictated by the godhead assuring his survival. *Adolph Hitler lives in me,* he told himself. The Russians were merely tools of Hitler's will.

"Sieg Heil!" he shouted into the rising sun. "Sieg Heil! Sieg Heil! Sieg Heil!"

The sound rolled over the deserted landscape. He felt charged with the electricity of ecstasy.

He drove the car into town and had coffee and scrambled eggs at a counter in a crowded luncheonette. The cacophony of voices around him seemed to merge into a single word: *Churchill.* Obviously, this was the most important event that had happened in Fulton since its first settlers had arrived.

"Here for the big brouhaha, buddy?" the waitress behind the counter asked.

He nodded and smiled.

"Town's gone crazy," said the waitress.

"It's a great honor," said a uniformed mailman, sitting next to him. "Somethin' to tell my grandchildren."

He made no comment. They would not only remember the day, they would remember the moment.

He paid the check and, following the plan that had etched itself in his mind, walked down the main shopping street, going over those items that were essential to his plan. In every store window was a sign proclaiming Churchill Day.

By all means, Churchill Day, he snickered.

He passed a clothing store with two mannequins in the window—one male and one female. He was particularly interested in the female mannequin and the wig that adorned her head under an Easter bonnet. He noted that a chain hung down on one side of the door to the shop with a lock hanging on one of the loops. This struck him as prescient, since the locking system was the same as he had considered for the door to the scorecard perch.

Then he went into a hardware store and bought a length of chain, a lock, and a metal cutter. In the Woolworth store, which dominated the main shopping street, he bought white stockings, white shoe polish, a lipstick, and a hand mirror. The clerk had looked at him curiously but executed the purchase without comment.

He was enormously satisfied at the imagination and verve of his plan, which seemed to be dictated by some mysterious outside source. Dimitrov had left him to his own devices. Years back, when he had killed the Finkelstein brothers, he had been somewhat imaginative, but that paled beside what was planned here. It was as if a play had been created in which he was the principal actor.

He found a parking space on the campus, already buzzing with activity, but something odd was happening. Some people were bringing metal chairs out of the gymnasium, and others were bringing metal chairs in.

"What's going on?" he asked one of the volunteers.

"They're putting in smaller chairs and taking out the larger ones. They're going to seat nearly three thousand people, shoehorn them in."

Good, he thought.

The shift gave him a greater opportunity to get lost in the increased activity. Yesterday, he had spotted the truck with rolls of bunting. It was gone now, but at the side of the building, he noted a pile of unused bunting. He lifted one of the rolls and put it on his shoulder and walked to his car. His luck was holding. No one paid him any attention.

He put the chain and the lock in his pocket, and then opening the trunk of his car, he removed the loaded rifle. He inserted the rifle in the roll of bunting, then closed the trunk and put the bunting roll back on his shoulder. He carried it to the rear of the building where the entrance to the locker room was located.

Two policemen manned the entrance. On the door was a sign with a red cross, indicating that it was designated as the first aid station, which the map in the newspaper had indicated. The policemen were chatting and disinterested and let him by with a smile and a friendly salute. The locker room was empty, although the door to the main gym was open, and he could see the people working frantically to rearrange the metal chairs.

He found the narrow door to the scorecard site and, slowly and carefully, ignoring the pain in his leg, climbed the metal stairs to the little platform where the scorekeeper would normally sit. Having scoped the site earlier, he lodged the rifle in its bunting in one of the containers that held the scorecards, arranging it for easy access.

He widened the opening in the bunting roll, and slid out the rifle to determine the timing and smoothness of the action. He did this a number of times. Then he pulled it out, aimed carefully at the approximate place where Churchill's head would be on the podium, and tested the telescopic sight. From this vantage, he could not miss.

If only the bastard were in the crosshairs now, he thought.

By standing two steps down from the platform, he was able to render himself invisible to those on the floor of the gymnasium, although there was a small risk that the tip of the barrel might be seen from the raised speaker's platform. A quick test determined that the risk would be minimal, depending on how fast he could sight the scope and get off the crucial shot. Besides, all eyes would be on Churchill. He discounted any potential observation. After all, there was no game in progress. Why would anyone be looking up?

He knew that he had to be quick, steady-handed, and precise. He had enough confidence in his marksmanship to do the deed on the first shot. If he were forced into a second shot, it would considerably lessen his odds of escape. There could be no third shot. The issue of timing was crucial. He would have to pull the trigger at the exact moment when the applause level was highest and could mask the rifle report. He expected a great deal of loud applause. After all, the speaker was Churchill, the great Churchill.

Fat bastard, he croaked.

Getting down the winding staircase would take seconds, although the condition of his ankle was worrisome. He would prime himself well with aspirin. His hope was that the ensuing shock of seeing Churchill collapse would create enough commotion—perhaps, a panic—to give him more cover.

The aftermath would be the most difficult part. The medical team that would be stationed in the locker room would be springing into action. His plan called for him to take advantage of these events.

He left the rifle encased in its bunting disguise. Moving carefully down the winding staircase, he reached the door and looked around. A number of volunteers were milling about, apparently using the area as a smoking lounge and getting respite from the work of moving the chairs. No one paid any attention to him.

Closing the door behind him, he leaned against it and unscrewed one of the metal loops embedded on either side of the door, leaving it within two threaded turns, then pulled the chain through the loops and clamped the links together with the lock. He tested the looseness of the loop, which came out easily, then screwed it back in just to the point where it held. Then he stood around, a casual observer taking a brief respite from his chores.

"Gonna be one great day tomorrow," a man said, directing his attention to Miller.

"Greatest," he commented, enjoying the irony. He chuckled.

It will be the shot heard round the world, he thought, remembering the reference to the assassination of the Habsburg archduke in Sarajevo, which set off World War I. This, he decided, would be the first shot of World War III.

He knew issues still needed to be resolved. As for the crucial shot, he felt certain he could do it, but the aftermath concerned him. Anticipation and alternative solutions had been the hallmark of his military training. In matters of combat, the original battle plan, however carefully worked out in advance, was sure to change in the first few minutes of combat. He related this lesson to the mission at hand.

He expected the crowd to surge, and he was certain that the president's security detail had considered the possibility and had planned for some form of crowd control in case of emergency. Of course, he was probably overestimating their efficiency, but over anticipating was another hallmark of his military training.

The detail would quickly spring into action to protect the president and concentrate on getting him out of the hall, probably using a route through the girls' locker room at the other end of the gym.

He had already determined that the girls' locker room would be the logical place through which Churchill and the president would enter and the area that would receive the president's Secret Service detail's most careful inspection.

The body of Churchill on the other hand would be speedily moved through the locker room in which he was currently standing. Medical personnel would obviously have priority here. But while he was certain that a number of alternative protective strategies had been considered by the security detail, the immediate aftermath would be confusion and bewilderment. In that moment of chaos was his window of opportunity.

But getting out of the gymnasium—although important— would not be his most crucial challenge. Once they had determined the reality of the situation, they would begin the manhunt for the assassin. A cordon would be established, roadblocks set up. All transportation for miles around would be monitored. With luck, he would find a parking space close enough for a fast getaway, but he doubted he would try to leave town. He would need to find a safe place to hide nearby until the initial surveillance ended.

He left the locker room, saluted the policeman guarding the door, and limped his way to the car and drove off. He stopped by a grocery store, bought a loaf of bread, cheese slices, a bottle of milk, and a large bottle of aspirin. The pain in his leg had intensified, and the ankle swelling was increasing. Again, he forced himself to ignore the pain.

He reviewed the scenario in his mind repeatedly. Had he missed something?

At a gas station, a boy came out to fill up the car.

"How are things in D.C.?" the boy asked.

He was startled by the assertion. Then he remembered that the car had D.C. plates, a missed detail that had to be corrected. Parking the car at the edge of town, he made cheese sandwiches, ate them, and washed them down with milk. Then he dozed until dark.

After midnight, he drove back into town, first stopping in a deserted side street to remove the license plates of two parked cars. He put one set on immediately and put the other set under the front seat, although he was still uncertain if he would chance trying to drive away after the mission.

Fulton's main shopping street, despite the event that was to take place in the afternoon tomorrow, was deserted. He parked in front of the clothing store whose windows were displaying the mannequins. Using his metal cutter he cut the chain that locked the front door of the store, pried it open, and headed for the display in the window. With care, he removed the mannequin's hat, then slid off the wig underneath and carefully replaced the hat.

Closing the front door, he managed to refit the lock into the chain links. Returning to the car, he drove to the campus. Both police and National Guardsmen, who had apparently blocked the entrance to any nonessential traffic, were now manning the lot where he had parked earlier.

Various cars and trucks were parked around the gymnasium entrance, which was lit by searchlights. Foot traffic was not being monitored, and workmen came and went without being stopped. He had planned for this contingency. Parking the car on a deserted part of town, he polished his shoes white, and while they dried, dry-shaved with his safety razor. Then he put on the mannequin's wig and made up his lips while looking into the hand mirror.

He rolled up his pants legs and, after cutting the toes off the white stockings, rolled them on. His leg had swollen considerably, and putting on the stockings was excruciatingly painful. Then he put on Stephanie's nurse's uniform over his own clothes. It was an incredibly tight fit. Thankfully, Stephanie's big bosoms gave him enough space to fasten the top buttons.

Reasonably satisfied with his costumed transformation, he was able to pass through the checkpoint at the rear of the campus with merely a wave. He parked his car in the lot close to the back entrance of the locker room. Opening the trunk, he removed the food and carried it through the back entrance with another wave and a smile. His disguise, despite his discomfort, had worked.

There was now major activity going on in the first aid station. Two metal tables had been installed. A doctor was talking to a nurse at one end of the locker room. Again, no one paid any attention to him. He was merely a nurse going about her business. He ducked behind the locker bank to the door of the scorecard perch, easily removed the metal loop, then leaving a space for his arm, moved into the stairwell and managed to rescrew the metal loop in place again. Unless someone pulled hard on the chain, to all outward appearance, the door would appear chained from the outside.

If they were efficient, they would surely visibly check the door to the scorekeeper's perch. He was hopeful that the lock and chain would create the impression that the door was secured.

With effort, he climbed the winding metal staircase, reaching the little platform at the top. The rifle was secure in its place within the roll of bunting. He took out the pistol he had pocketed and placed it beside him, along with his cheese sandwiches, his milk bottle, and his container of aspirin.

Below on the gymnasium floor, the activity continued. The hall was festooned with the flags of both countries. Electricians were setting up microphones on the two-tiered platform from which Churchill was to speak.

His leg had swollen, and the aspirin was having less and less effect on the pain, despite increasing the dosage. He set his mind to transcending it and waited.

241

Chapter 20

Churchill, apparently unable to sleep, returned to the sitting room, dressed in his siren suit. He had with him a world atlas, which he carried with him on all trips. With Thompson helping, they proofread Victoria's typed stencils. Occasionally, one of them would find a spelling error, and Victoria Stewart would correct it.

With a brandy beside him, his cigar lit, and his glasses perched on the tip of his nose, he read the last page of his speech and grew reflective, then read the closing few lines aloud: "If we adhere faithfully to the Charter of the United Nations and walk forward in sedate and sober strength, seeking no one's land or treasure, seeking to lay no arbitrary control upon the thoughts of men; if all British moral and material forces and convictions are joined with your own in fraternal association, the high roads of the future will be clear, not only for us, not only for our time, but for a century to come."

He nodded his approval and looked at Thompson for comment.

"Quite eloquent, Sir," he replied.

"Eloquent, Thompson?" He removed his glasses and peered into his own reflection in the darkened window.

Victoria, the corrections made, sat silently, awaiting further instructions. Her mind, at this stage, was seething with uncertainties. For some reason, her sense of menace had accelerated.

"It is a mistake to look too far ahead. Only one link in the chain of destiny can be handled at a time."

Although the statement was addressed to no one in particular,

242

Thompson apparently felt the need to comment.

"Well, sir, in a hundred years, no one of us will be around to test the accuracy of your prediction."

Victoria sensed that the remark was designed to lighten Churchill's mood. It did not seem to make a difference. He seemed gloomy, his demeanor a far cry from his earlier buoyancy.

"You have a point, Thompson, but the speech is dark enough without ending on a note of pessimism."

"You sound tentative, sir."

Churchill fell into a long profound silence. Then he spoke.

"'The weight of this sad time we must obey. Speak what we feel, not what we ought to say.' I'm afraid the habits of a lifetime of politics hold sway in those words. And yet, it could be true that, in historical terms, a hundred years is a mere snapshot." He seemed to perk up. "And, of course, I have referred to caveats. But there is no doubt that the Russians will throw obstacles along the way. And who knows what will transpire in the wake of changes in the world order? The British Empire is crumbling, Thompson. I am afraid that world, where we held sway, is over. But what will happen to those pieces of empire when we vacate the premises? God knows."

He upended his brandy pony.

"Another, sir?" Thompson asked.

Churchill shook his head and stood up, then turned to Victoria.

"I have forgotten to provide a title for the speech. I wish to call it "Sinews of Peace." He smiled. "Shades of Cicero—he used that phrase. Perhaps some Latin teacher at the college might understand the irony." He chuckled. "Poor Cicero! He was assassinated."

He opened the atlas and turned to the page containing Europe and studied it, then ran his finger over the map, tracing it.

"Indeed," he mumbled. "We are a divided continent."

"Your iron-fence reference, sir?"

Churchill nodded, shook his head, then grew silent.

"I'll have the speech reproduced for the press, sir," Thompson said.

"Keep it under wraps, Thompson."

"I shall guard it with my life, sir," Thompson said, with a touch of amused sarcasm.

Churchill smiled and nodded, opened the door to the bedroom and, still carrying the atlas, closed it behind him.

The remark about the assassination of Cicero opened a wellspring of anguish inside Victoria. She typed the title of the speech on the first stencil, then slumped over the typewriter, and began to sob hysterically. Tears rolled down her cheeks. She couldn't stop herself.

Thompson seemed alarmed. He pulled a clean white handkerchief from the upper pocket of his jacket, gave it to her, and wrapped her in a fatherly embrace.

"I can't," she began. "I'm so sorry."

"Easy, young lady. It's the strain. You've been working very hard."

"What he said . . . " she sobbed barely able to catch her breath, " . . . about Cicero."

She wiped her tears and took deep breaths. He released her and poured her a brandy.

"Drink this, Victoria. It will put you to rights."

Inexplicably, it was the first time he broke his formality and used her first name. She sipped the brandy, noting that her hand shook. She felt the warmth suffuse her and took a deep breath, the compulsive emotional outburst waning. Her head was clearing. She knew the source of her sudden eruption.

"I have betrayed you," she said, her voice reedy, her stomach tightening.

Thompson looked at her, his forehead showing lines of confusion.

"Betrayed?"

She started to speak, stopped before she could get out any words, then pulled herself together, and spoke finally.

"I have not kept your confidence, Mr. Thompson. The guilt is upsetting me terribly."

244

A sob began deep inside her. To tamp it down, she took a deep swallow of the brandy.   "Perhaps I have fallen into deep waters. I feel as if . . . as if I've been drowning."

"Easy now, Victoria. Speak calmly. You say you have betrayed us. How?"

"I've given a copy of Mr. Churchill's speech to the first secretary, against your orders of confidentiality."

Thompson shook his head. He was obviously confused.

"Knowing the confidential nature of your assignment, did he request it?"

"He did."

"Did he tell you why?"

"He said that he wanted to be sure that the speech conformed to the current policies of Mr. Attlee. If it had not, he told me he and the ambassador would discuss it with Mr. Churchill—in general terms, sir. The first secretary promised he would not reveal what I had done."

Thompson shook his head and looked at her sympathetically.

"Well, then," he said in a soothing tone. "You reacted to an order from your immediate superior. I understand your dilemma, Victoria. Confronted with such a choice, I might have done the same myself."

"No, you wouldn't, Mr. Thompson," she whispered. "Not you. I should have informed you of his request from the beginning. I didn't. I deliberately betrayed you."

Thompson grew thoughtful.

"I suppose Mr. Attlee and the opposition are by now completely aware of the text. I can assure you that neither the ambassador nor Mr. Maclean have discussed any matter of policy with Mr. Churchill."

"There's more," Victoria said.

"Oh?"

Thompson looked at her sharply. She hesitated and swallowed.

"The Russians have it as well."

Although he maintained a calm façade, she saw a pulsing tic suddenly begin in his jaw.

"How do you know?"

"I . . ."

She hesitated. This was the hardest revelation of all. She was having second thoughts, silently begging her lover for forgiveness. Perhaps it was all appropriate conduct for a high-level diplomat. Hadn't he explained that diplomacy often took bizarre turns? She felt certain he was innocent of any wrongdoing and—she hoped—when all this was over, he would understand why she had to unburden herself.

She told Thompson she had inadvertently seen the first secretary hand the speech to a man whom she followed to the Russian embassy.

"It might have been perfectly appropriate," she said. "I'm not sure."

Then she remembered the words that had bitten deep into her psyche.

Must I? She asked herself then blurted the words.

"When he read the draft, I had given him, he said . . . " She emptied her brandy glass. " . . . he said that Mr. Churchill . . . " She could not continue.

"Yes?" he prodded.

"He said that Mr. Churchill had signed his death warrant."

Thompson seemed stunned.

"Good God!"

"He blurted it out," she explained. "He often does that when angry."

When pleasured, too, she thought. He could be ardent and uninhibited at the supreme moment—she, as well. Unfortunately, the memory only added to her guilt, like a double-betrayal.

"Are you sure you heard correctly?"

She nodded.

246

"It frightened me, Mr. Thompson. I'm still frightened." She shook her head. "I'm so sorry, so terribly sorry I didn't speak sooner. It was driving me mad."

She watched as Thompson grew thoughtful, then he turned to her.

"It seems so . . . out of context. Perhaps he was reacting to something specific to the speech itself. Stalin, for example."

"I hadn't thought of that," she admitted, although it did not assuage her fear.

He rubbed his chin and frowned.

"Marshal Stalin is not my concern," he said.

He seemed suddenly distant, obviously wrestling with the ramifications of what she had revealed.

"Will you tell Mr. Churchill?" she asked.

He grew more pensive, then turned and looked out the window into the darkness, seeing little but both their reflections in the glass. Then he turned to her, his eyes met hers, and she could feel the power of their penetration.

"I need your trust, your absolute unequivocal trust. Can I ask that of you?"

"Considering what I've told you, can you or Mr. Churchill have any faith in my reliability?"

He smiled and patted her arm.

"We are both believers in redemption, Victoria."

"I appreciate that, sir," she said, drawing in a deep breath. "And I'll do anything to prove myself. As for trust, depend on it."

"This, Victoria, is between you and me."

She nodded vigorously, exhilarated by a strong sense of solidarity.

"For now, Mr. Churchill cannot be privy to this, not on the eve of this important event."

"Of course, sir. I completely understand."

"On the matter of this Russian connection, may I say, it might be perfectly innocent, some diplomatic folderol; nevertheless, it does deserve some attention. Are you with me on this as well, Victoria?"

He surveyed her face with intensity as if trying to read beyond her expression.

"It might clear your mind of any uncertainty about the first secretary. Or . . . " he paused, as if pondering her reaction, " . . . it might not."

Inexplicably, the consequences of her affair with Donald Maclean and the betrayal it entailed crossed her mind. She was thinking of his wife, Melinda, an unwitting victim of their clandestine passion. What Thompson was asking now was for her to keep yet another secret. But this time, she felt no guilt, rather an enormous sense of her own personal value, something that she had never calculated before.

"I would welcome that, sir."

"It may, at first, seem bizarre, perhaps unseemly to ask of you. But you must trust my judgment on this, Victoria, and follow my instructions to the letter. Am I clear?"

"I'm ready to cooperate, sir."

She felt certain that her belief in her lover's loyalty would be fully vindicated.

Chapter 21

"You say this reporter is a friend of the first secretary?" Thompson had asked.

She had been surprised that he had dredged up this tiny detail from an overheard remark by Benson at the station. The man doesn't miss a trick, she thought. His assumption had been prescient.

He had apparently worked out a scenario in his mind as if it had been a contingency plan all along. She listened carefully, answering every question he had posed.

"One of his many press contacts, but I think much closer than most. The first secretary introduced me to him. They seemed to share camaraderie, he called often, and they lunched frequently. As I understand it, he is a special friend of Sarah Churchill."

"How special?"

"Beyond simple friendship, but one can never be certain."

"Are you implying an affair?"

Considering her own relationship with the first secretary, it was a subject she did not wish to broach.

"I really don't know. But we do know that Mr. Benson has interviewed Mr. Churchill in Florida and has been quite aggressive in trying to obtain a copy of his speech. He asked Mr. Churchill about it at the station before we left Washington, and he pressed me for information as well." She paused. "Of course, I told him nothing."

"That chap," Thompson had replied.

He explained to her what he had in mind. At first, she was baffled by the idea, but as he continued to flesh out the details, she grasped the full import of the plan and was fully primed to pursue it. In her mind, the plan would surely vindicate her lover and buttress his explanation.

"Do you think he'll react?" Victoria asked.

From her perspective, it was designed to manipulate the reporter to investigate the political motive behind the handover to the Russians. If the act were merely informational, a courtesy from the Attlee government, the issue would be fully explained.

"For the press, the only lure is the story and, above all, getting it first. To have a private source is like reaching nirvana."

He had gathered up the stencils and started to leave the compartment.

"And the other?" Victoria asked.

"What other?"

"The 'death warrant' comment."

Saying it aloud, as Maclean had done, was particularly chilling. Thompson looked at her, said nothing, and left the compartment.

***

It took her sometime to locate Benson. Some of the press were still imbibing at the bar. One of them, with an unmistakable leer, directed her to Benson's compartment but not before he got off a drunken comment and a wink.

"He's sharing, but perhaps you know that."

She offered no reply and quickly found the compartment. Stunned by the sudden intrusion, Benson came out in his robe over his pajamas, his hair tousled, looking slightly groggy. He stood in the corridor with her.

"I have something of interest," she began.

"You certainly have that," he said.

"Don't misinterpret. I'm talking story here—an exclusive," she snapped.

He lifted both hands in a gesture of surrender.

"Sorry," he said. "I'm still in my dream."

"This is no dream."

"I'm awake now."

He ran his fingers through his tousled hair.

"I'm taking a big risk."

Her gestures became deliberately furtive. She looked up and down the corridor and spoke in a low whisper. His interest piqued. The press, as Thompson had explained, loved intrigue and conspiracy, and she was determined to play her part well. Thompson had been specific, highly detailed in the manner she was to approach Benson.

"Can I can count on your confidence?" she pressed.

"And what can I count on?"

She had expected it.

"Mr. Churchill's speech in advance. You're an afternoon paper. The speech is being mimeographed as we speak. You will have it enough in advance to make your first edition—ahead of the pack."

He nodded and seemed satisfied.

"Now what is this about?"

"I'm out of it. Do you understand? I need your solemn promise."

"You'll take my word?"

She nodded and waited until some press people passed. Unfortunately, the corridor was not the best of venues. Some members of the press sauntered through, returning from the club car or using the facilities at either end of the train. Watching both ends of the corridor, she spoke in low tones.

"There is a possible security leak in the British embassy in Washington."

He scratched his head and looked puzzled.

"How do you know this?"

"The Russians have the full text of the speech."

He raised his eyebrows.

"Ahead of us? Doesn't seem cricket."

251

He grew thoughtful, again rolling his fingers through his hair.

"Perhaps it's deliberate on the part of the embassy, a courtesy of sorts—something like that. Hell, we're still allies."

She had expected more curiosity and emotion in his reaction. Before she could comment, he spoke again, as if prodded by second thoughts.

"The speech. Is it very anti-Russian? What I mean is . . . is it a real blast?"

"Yes, it is, very much so."

"It was expected, of course."

"Maybe so, but it is believed that the impact will be enormous, Mr. Benson."

"Remains to be seen," he said, with an air of dismissal.

She watched his face. His expression seemed no longer guarded.

"A security leak, you called it? Doesn't seem like that big a deal."

"The text was known only to three people—Mr. Churchill, Mr. Thompson, and myself. It's a genuine mystery; no one at the embassy could possibly have known about it."

She had worried about that part, a blatant lie. But Thompson had convinced her of its necessity. She watched his face and waited for further reaction.

"Why do you deem it so important? They'll have its content soon enough."

"It was supposed to be confidential."

"In Washington? A difficult chore at best."

"You don't think it's serious?"

"It's not exactly, for example, like passing the secret of the bomb. It's only a speech. I'm not putting it down completely, but it's no longer wartime and the Nazis are defeated."

"You don't sound very interested."

"I am. Don't misunderstand. I'm a natural skeptic. Who do you think was the culprit?"

"Beyond what I've told you, I can't reveal any more. Trust that my information is authentic."

"Why can't you tell this to the first secretary? He's your boss."

"Above all, I must not be involved in the information chain. You must keep that confidence, Benson. I've pledged confidence to Mr. Churchill. It would be unseemly if I'm seen as a press informer." She paused. "You on the other hand, do not need to be constrained. You can always say you picked up a rumor and were making inquiries."

"Are you dead certain of this?" he asked again.

"If I didn't think it was important, I wouldn't have awakened you in the middle of the night."

He looked at his wrist, noting that his wristwatch was still in the compartment. She wore hers. It was three in the morning.

"We hit St. Louis in a couple of hours. There's a brief layover. You can call from there," Victoria suggested.

He looked at her and nodded.

"I appreciate this, Miss Stewart." He hesitated. "Although I'm somewhat baffled. Does Mr. Churchill know anything about this?"

"Absolutely not."

"And the speech?"

"In your hands by St. Louis."

He looked at her, smiled, and shrugged, and then ran his fingers through his hair, opened the door to his compartment, and went in.

Chapter 22

Blurry with sleep, Maclean reached in the dark for the phone on the bedside table. Considering the London time difference, he was used to being awakened in the middle of night. It was one of the reasons—among many—that he and Melinda slept in separate bedrooms.

"Spencer?"

He was genuinely surprised. An ominous chill shot through him. A newspaperman's call in the middle of the night always spelled trouble.

"Sorry, Donald," Benson said. "I suppose it could have waited, but having read Churchill's speech, I thought it worth the candle . . . waking you."

"They've released the speech?" Maclean said, curious.

It would not have been released until an hour before it was to be delivered. Something was amiss. His heart began to pound with anxiety.

"Quite nasty to our Russian friends, talks about an iron fence coming down in Europe—we on one side, the Communists on the other. Very inflammatory in today's political climate."

"An iron fence?"

He was not confounded by the reference. He had, after all, read it in draft.

"Shall I read it to you?"

"Not now, Spencer. I'm a bit cloudy at the moment."

"In a few more hours, everyone will have it anyway," said Benson. "Stalin will be furious."

254

Maclean felt himself growing impatient.

"It's the middle of the night, Spencer. Surely, we can discuss the speech in the morning."

"There could be a security leak in the embassy, Donald."

Maclean tried to keep his voice casual, his dismissal natural, but he was stunned by the assertion. How could Benson possibly know that the Russians had the speech?

His stomach tightened. Were they coming close at last?

"A security leak? I don't understand."

"The Russians have been given an advance copy of the speech."

It was hardly a revelation, and he groped for a response.

"Of course, they would. You have a TASS reporter on board."

"No, Donald. I'm the only journalist with an advance copy. The Russians have had it apparently a couple of days. My sources tell me that the speech was confidential. No one, including President Truman, had a copy."

His pores opened. He felt icy perspiration running down his back.

"Where did you get this, Spencer?"

"We don't reveal our sources, Donald. You know that."

"Have the Russians confirmed it?"

"I haven't asked, but they usually stonewall."

"And how may I ask have you got a copy? It won't be officially released until much later."

"Sorry, Donald. Lucky, I guess."

"Did you get it from the Russians?"

There was a long pause in the conversation as Maclean tried to sort out the information. Who could possibly know? Had he been seen the night he handed over the speech? And if he was, could they know what was in the envelope he had handed over? Was he under surveillance? Were they onto him? He was panicking.

His mind groped for an explanation, and he could not ignore the possibility of Victoria's involvement. But the idea could not cross

255

the threshold of suspicion. Considering her access and the delivery of the speech to him, he could not connect her to such subterfuge. He felt certain that her interest in him was purely a matter of love and lust, her involvement far removed from the political realm.

No, he decided, absolving her in his mind. *Couldn't be.*

Then it occurred to him that the Russians might have betrayed him deliberately. Perhaps he was being scuttled, no longer relevant. For the first time in many years, he was genuinely frightened.

"Of course, I have to look into it immediately."

But the real question in his mind was what Spencer would be writing in tomorrow's paper.

"Do you intend to print this?" Maclean asked, cautiously.

"I'm on the story, Donald."

"But you do need some confirmation."

He noticed a sudden reediness in the quality of his voice.

"I was hoping for some further enlightenment."

"Frankly, Spencer, the news comes as a shock . . . if true. Our security procedures are superb. Perhaps someone in Mr. Churchill's circle might have leaked the speech inadvertently."

"Why inadvertently?"

Maclean was seeking some logical explanation to satisfy Benson.

"Could you give me some time to work on this, Spencer? I have to check with the ambassador."

"And MI6."

"Of course. If true, this is a serious charge. A security breach in the British embassy is not unheard of, but not while I've been in charge of operations here. All I ask, Spencer, is to give me time to investigate. I'm sure there is a very simple explanation. Perhaps even Churchill himself . . ."

He was grasping at straws, deflecting suspicion. At least, he was not confronting this newspaperman face-to-face. His expression would be a dead giveaway.

"Why would he give them a preview of a decidedly anti-

Russian speech? No, Donald. I doubt that. I think you have a problem right inside your shop."

"Yes, yes, of course. I'm afraid there are so many things going through my mind at once. Who benefits? That is the question I always ask myself."

"That's a mystery novel cliché, Donald. Frankly, in this case, I can't see the benefit to anyone."

"Nor can I," Maclean answered swiftly.

He was bewildered, yet he mustered the courage of deceit and explained to Benson that as far as he knew, only two people were involved in the creation of the speech, Churchill and Victoria. Thompson, he pointed out, would be perpetually hovering nearby, but it was impossible to believe that such a loyal watchdog could betray any confidence of Churchill's.

Who then would have been Benson's source? Maclean felt a terrible chill of fear. How could Benson know the Russians knew?

He had taken Victoria's copy and given it to his handler. She had told him it was the only one of two carbons, and she had given the other carbon copy to Churchill, as well as the original. He was both baffled and frightened. Was he now supposed to walk the plank on something as absurd as this?

"I need time, Spencer. I'll get to the bottom of this, I promise you. And if there is a leak here, I will deal with it posthaste," Donald said, hoping he sounded determined.

After hanging up, he dressed and called the number that signaled his handler to meet him at a spot they had predesignated for emergency assignations, an all-night restaurant near Union Station that served the adjacent main post office and nightshift railroad workers. So far, they had never used the venue.

His handler had arrived first and taken a table in the back of the restaurant. Because of the shifts of the workers, some of the patrons were eating breakfast, some lunch, and some dinner. Unlike Volkov, the new handler was known only as Boris. He was the man to whom Maclean had given the speech. Taking a seat at the table, he

257

recounted his conversation with Benson in hushed tones.

Boris was fortyish, with a heavy face in which small eyes darted ferret-like from side to side. Obviously, the man was nervous and apprehensive, this being a first in their brief relationship.

"Who told him this?" Boris whispered.

He had a voice like sandpaper, even in a whisper.

"That's exactly the point. I don't know," Maclean said. "I could assure you, it wasn't me; and no one at the embassy had a clue, except, of course, Mr. Churchill, my secretary, and Mr. Churchill's bodyguard, Thompson."

"Your secretary, perhaps?"

He was aware that would be Boris's first conclusion.

"Doubtful," he said, mulling over the possibility briefly.

He wondered if they knew of the affair—and if they did? Wouldn't that reinforce their belief in her absolute fealty to him? He decided to let the matter lie.

"She has access to you. She knows your movements."

He tamped down a desire to laugh. Yes, indeed, she knew his movements but in an entirely different context.

"Wrong turn, Boris. I have been at this a long time and have had numerous secretaries and assistants. I consider myself an expert in evasion. Hell, I live in the heart of the beast."

Perhaps he was protesting too much. He could not rule out their knowledge of his affair nor of his other sexual activities. He had not been overly discreet, but it had never been raised as an issue between him and his handlers. He assumed that they trusted his intuitive sense of danger.

"I am here to counsel, comrade, not to accuse. What about this man Thompson?"

"No way. He would be the last on the list of suspects. The man is loyal to a fault."

"So how could it happen? Perhaps your newspaper friend is pulling your leg?"

"Benson?"

258

It surprised him that he had taken Benson's word at face value. But it could have been a possibility. The man had gone to great lengths to find out what Churchill intended to say. Newspapermen, after all, were forever trying to manufacture conspiracies, which always made good copy.

"You have a point, comrade. I won't reject that possibility. Perhaps I have been duped."

Maclean searched Boris's face. His eyes narrowed. No one could misinterpret the expression. It was one of suspicion. Boris shook his head adamantly.

"Granted, it could be someone on our watch. I don't think so. Why would they want to hurt our cozy relationship? You are too valuable. Unless, of course, someone has gotten wind of your . . ."

"Connection?"

Boris chuckled.

"I give you my word, it went directly upstairs by safe Teletype. Believe me, we are just as paranoid about security as you are."

"Where upstairs?"

"To Beria's office directly, high priority. I typed it myself— no middle people—too sensitive. We have confirmation of receipt."

"Perhaps there is someone close to Beria," Maclean suggested. "A true believer, like you, Boris."

"Are you suggesting that there is an American spy in Beria's office?"

"Who then?"

"Perhaps your countrymen are fishing."

"For what?"

Boris shrugged and smiled, showing a glistening gold tooth.

"For you, comrade."

A chill shot through him. For years, he had lived with a sense of false serenity. He had never been really panicked or fearful of discovery. In his mind, he had even worked out an exit strategy. Indeed, Volkov had promised him that if they were ever onto him, he would be welcomed in Russia and lionized as a hero of the Soviet Union.

But he was also aware that, sometimes, in the interest of security, intelligence agencies were frequently duplicitous. He studied Boris for a long moment. His expression revealed nothing. He was quite obviously a trusted NKVD officer with a long record of achievement, someone who would give nothing away in any circumstances. Of course, one never knew who would be a defector someday, who would be a loyal agent, who would play hardball to the end in the face of death and torture.

"I have a suggestion, comrade," Boris whispered.

"I welcome it, comrade."

"Search for the leak at your end."

He had just filled his mouth with coffee, which he spat back into his cup.

"Are you serious? I'm the leak?"

"Go after it with a passion, make it a cause célèbre. Inform the ambassador that you will leave no stone unturned. You might have to transfer some people to other posts. Make a bit of noise, Homer."

"I couldn't accuse without evidence," Maclean protested, smiling suddenly. "We are a virtuous people," he added sarcastically.

"You have a long tradition of theatre, Homer. Make use of it."

His colleagues were indeed cunning. Of course, that could be exactly the solution he was groping for. He would put Spencer Benson in the loop of his making, confide in him, lead him into the dark.

"A fine option, Comrade."

"Rattle the cage. Show zeal and determination."

Maclean nodded.

"Sound and fury signifying nothing," Boris winked and giggled. "It is after all, only a speech. Just words."

"Not just words, comrade. Churchill's words."

Chapter 23

Churchill was in a funk. He had declined breakfast with Truman on grounds that Thompson knew too well. He hated having breakfast with anyone—"far too early for speech," he had averred many times over. In bed alone, Thompson knew, was his favorite place for breakfast.

Unfortunately, his breakfast had been served cold, and he was generally upset to have his usual routine shattered. He could not have his bath on the Magellan and hated the shower, which was too tight for his bulk. This was, Thompson understood, a very bad time to confront him on what he had learned the night before. But it could not wait.

Of course, he would not broach the element of danger. He did not wish anything to interrupt Churchill's concentration on the day's events and his speech, which would be heard by millions throughout the world.

He had wrestled with the information throughout a sleepless night and had concluded that Donald Maclean, as far-fetched as it appeared, was, in some manner or form, formal or informal, a Soviet sympathizer or, at worst, a Soviet agent.

Of course, he had no definitive proof, and he had taken it upon himself to send Victoria on a mission that—he was dead certain—was a red herring. What he needed most was Churchill's validation that he had done the right thing.

During his war years with Churchill, he had observed the prime minister's obsession with intelligence and the necessity to cover the enemy's ground with agents. On his orders, hundreds of agents were parachuted into occupied Europe and MI6 had planted numerous spies within the Nazi bureaucracy, although he had soon discovered that the Nazis were quite good at ferreting them out and turning those who chose to survive into double agents.

Churchill had pressed for and directed the breaking of the Enigma code, a masterful achievement of organizing the best young minds in England to work around the clock and successfully make this important intelligence breakthrough. Thompson felt on fairly safe ground bringing his discovery and the action he had taken to the attention of Churchill.

The information equation, Thompson knew, would be unbalanced. He could not inform Churchill of the "death warrant" remark conveyed by Victoria. That was the most worrisome aspect of her information. Having spent his life unraveling crimes and dealing with potential assassinations and conspiracies, real and imagined, he had developed what he termed a healthy sixth sense to detect real danger.

It would be a profound neglect of duty to ignore the reported remark and the real possibility that Maclean had not only read the speech but also passed it on to the Russians. Why? In an exercise of detective deduction, he had to assume that the "death warrant" remark was connected to the inflammatory nature of the speech itself. The text was, indeed, a gauntlet thrown down, a damning accusation, a revelation of sinister motives, an indictment, and the opening bell of the first round in a long contest. What it suggested to him was that the Russians had marked Churchill and his golden tongue as too dangerous to leave alive.

My God, he cried aloud, castigating himself for what might be an overheated exaggeration.

But it was here that his deduction hit a dead end. He could not see the gain for the Russians. The speech and the act would point directly to them. They might lose more than they could possibly gain by exposing themselves as ruthless killers. He decided to leave that matter for others to mull over. His job was to protect the life of the prime minister, and his mind was already concocting countermeasures. "Better safe than sorry" had always been his mantra.

Above all, he would shield his charge from that piece of information and all it portended. If he had his druthers, he would shut down the whole operation and spirit Mr. Churchill home to Chartwell posthaste.

"Beastly grub, Thompson. And I slept like a top, spinning all night, wrestling with my black dog."

"Keep him at bay, sir. You have better things to think about today."

"Do I? What about? The disintegration of the peace? About the threat from our wartime allies?" He grunted his contempt. "Can you hear the waves, Thompson, the red tide rolls?"

He was sitting up in bed. The train would be in St. Louis shortly. Truman was to appear on the observation platform before the crowds that were assembling and make a brief speech. Then they would move on to Jefferson City, where they would debark and drive in a caravan the twenty miles to Fulton. The president and Churchill would be driven in an open car passing through the streets of Fulton, which were going to be lined with cheering people.

"You must be at your best, Sir," Thompson said.

Churchill wore his green, dragon-pattern silk robe. He picked up his unlit cigar from the breakfast tray, and Thompson was quick to light it. A few puffs seemed to alter his mood.

"There is something, sir, that cannot wait . . . " Thompson began.

He had made his decision. Whatever Churchill's mood, he had to raise the issue of Maclean. It was too important a matter to postpone. He was conscious of Churchill observing him with sudden intensity.

"Your look is ominous, Thompson."

Thompson had rehearsed his opening gambit.

"The Russians already have your speech, sir. Stalin is probably having it for breakfast."

Although Churchill was always quick with a response, but when the matter was particularly grave, he seemed to look inward first before offering a riposte.

"How is it possible?"

His eyes narrowed as he waited for an explanation. Thompson did not hesitate. Churchill listened patiently, his expression growing grim as the report progressed.

In thorough detail, he revealed everything he had heard from Victoria, leaving out only the references to Maclean's "death warrant" remark. He would have to deal with that himself. He had checked his Wembley and, even at this moment, was prepared to act at the slightest hint of danger. He was not happy about the open cars they would ride in, but he dared not suggest a change or his reasons for making the argument. Besides, he would sit directly in front of Mr. Churchill in the car, which would be surrounded by Secret Service agents. He gave them high marks for presidential security, and he hoped that would extend their zeal to Mr. Churchill's safety.

"She witnessed the exchange?" Churchill said, when he had finished. "Is she certain it was a Russian?"

It was exactly the question he had posed to Victoria the night before.

"She had no doubt. She followed the man to the Soviet embassy. I believe her implicitly."

"Even though she willingly betrayed our confidence?"

"Yes. But she had been so ordered."

Churchill's face had flushed, always a sign that he was trying to control his anger.

"Don't be too harsh on her, sir. She merely obeyed her superior."

"Am I not the superior to her superior?"

He shook his head angrily, grunting his disgust.

"Not officially, Sir," Thompson said, gently.

Churchill was not to be dissuaded.

"How dare she? She should be cashiered immediately.

264

She is not trustworthy. I want her to be sent back immediately to Washington."

"On what grounds, Prime Minister?"

"She is a traitor."

"That's exactly the point, Prime Minister."

"What is?"

"Someone *is* a traitor, but it is not her. She is an innocent victim. Her boss, I feel certain, is a Russian agent."

Churchill pondered the accusation, chewing the tip of his cigar and then shaking his head.

"That is a hard leap of faith, Thompson. We are talking of the first secretary of the British embassy. It is beyond belief. Maclean is a longtime member of the foreign service, a Cambridge man, and an English gentleman. It is utterly impossible. How could he possibly be working for the Russians? It is unthinkable."

Thompson let him rant. There was no point in interrupting his tirade. It was one of his great weaknesses, a partiality to the Victorian concept of the educated English gentleman as the pinnacle of civilized manhood. During the war, he had often been disabused of the notion. Still, it stuck to him like glue.

"You don't reach the rank of first secretary without distinguishing yourself as a loyal British subject. You are jumping to conclusions instigated by a foolish young woman."

He pursed his lips and repeatedly shook his head in the negative, his expression a remarkable likeness to a bulldog. Thompson waited until the denial tantrum subsided somewhat.

"My God, Thompson, if this is true, he is privy to all of the embassy's communications. He can roam freely, perhaps even into atomic facilities. No! Too bizarre, Thompson, too far-fetched—the woman is fantasizing. You are being naïve. Besides, how do you know the Russians have the speech? And if they have, so what? Let Uncle Joe choke on it if he is having it for breakfast."

He made grunting sounds as if talking to himself, then, after a long pause, addressed Thompson again.

"The woman has cast a spell, my good man," he whispered, gently.

"I don't think so, sir. I am not easily fooled. You forget I was a detective at Special Branch."

Churchill waved his cigar in front of him.

"No, no, no, Thompson, I have cast no aspersions on your insight. Allow me to vent my rage."

"I have, sir."

Churchill puffed on his cigar. Thompson could see that the revelation had the effect of energizing his thoughts and stimulating his thirst for action, always a remedy to chase away his black dog.

"How can you be so certain that this Benson fellow will pursue the suggestion?"

"He is a friend of Maclean. Besides, he will be bribed by an advance copy of your speech."

"So much for the secrecy of my immortal words," Churchill mused, obviously unhappy with the revelation.

"Miss Stewart assures me he took the bait."

"You are a scheming jackal, Thompson."

"Yes, sir."

"Directly under the nose of Halifax! How could this happen?" Resignation had finally overcome the shock. "If they can burrow into the embassy in Washington, they are not only ubiquitous, but outperform us in cunning." He smiled. "Although I must say, Thompson, your maneuver with our Miss Stewart is quite brilliant. Our official counterspy operations are in need of a wakeup call."

"Thank you, sir."

Thompson felt a strong sense of vindication for his action.

"As you stated in your speech, sir, we are dealing with a 'fifth column.'"

"And apparently deeply embedded." Churchill shook his head in a gesture of sadness. "There is nothing more contemptible than a traitor." He exchanged glances with Thompson. "Do you think he'll panic and run?"

"Perhaps. My guess is he will try to divert suspicion. He might be too arrogant to run and, if he is really a spy, the Russians will not want to lose such an important asset. He is obviously an expert. Undoubtedly, he has been at this game a long time."

Churchill nodded, lost in thought. He took a deep puff on his cigar, the smoke expelled in a series of rings.

"I detest people of that class and education for betraying their country. Such a presumption of superiority! As if their embrace of the Communist ideology will offer a better world while we lesser minds adhere to archaic principles." He looked at Thompson. "I do sound a bit like a British imperialist Tory snob, don't I, Thompson? But then, that's what I am, especially to my enemies."

Sensitive to his own antecedents, Thompson's silence, as always when such matters were broached, was designed to indicate his reaction. He was, after all, a former policeman. In his retirement, he had become a grocer. Churchill was born to the silk, an aristocrat. The class distance between them was a reality.

"I will have to inform Attlee," Churchill mused. "Maclean will have to be dealt with one way or another." Again Churchill's expression registered disgust. "I am not without blame here, Thompson. The man was operating on my watch as well. Also, the circumstances of the revelation seem so bizarre. After all, the handing over of my speech in advance is not exactly giving away state secrets. Whatever his reaction, I must do my duty. The man must be stopped."

"In this case, sir, it's not the sensitivity of the information, it's his access that is dangerous."

Churchill nodded.

The reference to danger reignited Thompson's worry and the sense of guilt for bending the truth, however slightly. In his mind, the dots were being connected and the picture was emerging. Perhaps his logic was based on the romantic notion that the pen was mightier than the sword. If so, the speech was the drawn sword and the wielder of the sword, like all enemies, was to be vanquished.

Maclean, by giving the speech to the enemy, was the middleman in the transaction, a traitor, and a spy. Perhaps he was bending logic as well, but it was not Thompson's job to assess motives, only to prevent a violent action against his charge.

"If it were my decision to make," Churchill said, recalling Thompson to the conversation. "I would leave the bird in the cage. If he doesn't fly away, he could be far more valuable to us than he is to the Russians."

"I thought that would be your inclination, sir, hence my little caper with Miss Stewart. She is quite contrite and would like to make amends. Despite what she saw, she believes the man is a loyal subject and, if the man decides he is safe enough and stays on the job, our little plan might validate her opinion. As for me, I have no second thoughts. Clearly, Donald Maclean is a Russian spy."

"You've become quite devious in these matters, Thompson."

"I've learned that, sir, at my master's knee."

Churchill smiled his impish smile, which assured Thompson that he was in the process of beating away his black dog.

"It is intolerable, of course. I will recommend that Clement follow my suggestion. Of course, it could be a matter of letting the horse out after the barn door is closed. God knows what he's already passed along to the Russians. One hopes that our people have a similar foothold in Stalin's lair. During the war, I was probably a lot more virtuous than I might have been. I am partly to blame for what is happening. Perhaps, if we had been more diligent, we would not be in the situation we are in now."

Thompson was satisfied with Churchill's reaction to the revelation. But it did not give him peace of mind. Like the hint of the sea as one gets closer to the coast, Thompson could catch the scent of impending danger.

Churchill pushed away his breakfast tray. He appeared indignant and pugnacious about Thompson's revelation.

"When will this iron horse reach its destination?" he asked testily.

"Shortly. I think you had better get dressed, sir."

"And face that confounded shower?"

He got out of bed and opened the curtain to look at the passing landscape. Then he turned suddenly, grew quietly thoughtful, nodded as if in consent to some inner question and smiled. In that brief moment, his entire mood transformed.

"Of course," he said, obviously addressing his inner self.

"What, sir?"

"By God, Thompson, it's not an iron *fence* at all; it's an iron *curtain*, of course, an iron curtain. Yes, iron curtain. We must make that change."

"The speech is mimeographed and ready for distribution shortly, sir."

Churchill shrugged.

"Never mind, I have found the perfect metaphor: iron curtain. Yes, iron curtain." He reached for his atlas and opened it to the map of Europe. "Of course," he muttered. "Of course."

Beside his bed was the speech. He picked it up, flipped through the pages, and asked Thompson for a fountain pen. Sitting on the bed, he wrote furiously in the margins for ten minutes referring from time to time to the map in the atlas.

"Perfect," he said, reading his handwritten paragraph. "Listen, Thompson."

Churchill cleared his throat.

"From Stettin in the Baltic to Trieste in the Adriatic, an iron curtain has descended across the Continent. Behind that line, lie all the capitals of the ancient states of Central and Eastern Europe: Warsaw, Berlin, Prague, Vienna, Budapest, Belgrade, Bucharest, and Sofia. All these famous cities and the populations around them lie in what I must call the Soviet sphere, and all are subject in one form or other not only to Soviet influence but to a very high and, in many cases, increasing measure of control from Moscow."

"Brilliant, Sir," Thompson said, when he had finished.

"Toady," Churchill said. "But by God, old man, you've got it right!"

269

He practically danced to the shower as he shed his dressing gown. Thompson could hear the words of Noel Coward's "Mad Dogs and Englishman" emanating off-key from beyond the shower door.

***

Thompson sat in the front seat of the open car containing Truman and Churchill as it made its way, part of a caravan, through the streets of Fulton. Secret Service men formed their usual pattern of protection at various points in the front and rear of the automobile carrying the two leaders.

The cars moved slowly along through the streets. Churchill and Truman acknowledged with waves the good-natured cheers of the crowd, which roared approval whenever Churchill gave his two-fingered victory salute. Thompson's head swiveled from side to side as he nervously scanned the faces in the crowd.

The excited atmosphere of adulation and goodwill struck Thompson, as cries of "Winnie!" and "Harry!" rang through the air.

"Quite a crowd for a small town," Churchill commented to Truman, who waved to the cheering people lining the streets.

Occasionally someone would break through the human barrier and insist on shaking Churchill's or the president's hand. Both obliged readily. Thompson would have preferred tighter security.

"These people are the salt of the earth," Truman said. "I have many friends here."

As if to emphasize the point, he would occasionally call out to people who lined the route by their first name.

Thompson had delivered copies of the speech to the temporary Presidential Press Office prior to their boarding the cars, with the proviso that it be released to the press one hour before the speech was to be delivered. Victoria had been assigned to help supervise the distribution.

She would then join the press in the gymnasium to watch Churchill deliver the speech. The plan called for Truman and

270

Churchill to lunch with the president of the college at his residence adjacent to the college and, at the appointed time, repair to the site of the speech. After the speech, the official party would return to the president's home for a reception and then be driven the twenty miles back to Jefferson City and board the train for the homeward journey.

Thompson noted that Victoria looked tired and drawn and had expressed deep concerns about facing her boss again. She confessed that her sense of betrayal of Maclean was profound, although she continued to believe implicitly in his innocence.

Thompson did not argue the point and remained noncommittal. He felt profoundly sorry for the young woman. She had blundered into a situation for which she was totally unprepared. He dreaded the prospect of her future. If it was determined that Maclean stay on the job, she could be in an awkward—perhaps dangerous—spot herself, an unwitting secretary to a Soviet spy, an expendable pawn in the game of espionage. He was not happy with this thought.

Thompson had determined that once Churchill had been ensconced at the luncheon, he would visit the gymnasium where the event was to be held and check out the security precautions.

Although he was satisfied that President Truman's security detail was efficient and dedicated, he was determined to make his own assessment, as he had done numerous times before at such events. In making a speech to a large crowd, the speaker was always a vulnerable and tempting target. Unfortunately, the "death warrant" remark reported by Victoria had heightened his anxiety and was sending ominous signals to his vaunted antenna for danger. Churchill, if he knew the situation, would have called him an old worrywart, as he had done many times in the past.

Thompson's response was unchanging: "I'm just doing my job, sir."

They reached the home of President McCluer, who made the introductions of the various local officials, and the group sat down to lunch. Thompson arranged for Churchill to have a bedroom available for his usual nap after lunch then went off to inspect the site of the speech.

Crowds had already begun to assemble outside the gymnasium, and many people milled around the campus. The weather was sunny and mild. There were numerous uniformed policemen brought from the surrounding towns, some armed National Guardsman, and the men from the Secret Service checking out the security arrangements.

Properly identified by his credentials, he entered the gymnasium by the front door and surveyed the rows of seats. He knew how many the gym would hold. Rows upon rows of metal chairs faced a platform from which Churchill and Truman would speak. Along the sides of the gym were wooden bleacher seats. The interior was festooned with bunting in the colors of the two national flags.

Behind the two-tiered rostrum were a number of rows of metal chairs reserved for distinguished guests. Thompson walked around the entire perimeter of the gymnasium, trying to discern any place that might offer a special vantage for an armed assassin. Almost everywhere he looked suggested vulnerability. A wooden platform to the rear of the gym was obviously reserved for the press, still cameramen, and a newsreel camera operator.

"Tight as a drum," said one of the Secret Service men in the president's detail who recognized Thompson. "We've covered it all. Your man should be quite safe."

"I appreciate that," he replied, politely.

"Should go off without a hitch."

"I'm sure," replied Thompson, wondering if any death threats had been received regarding Truman.

They were, he knew from their previous meetings, a common occurrence, especially during the war. This situation was different. He was dealing with speculation and instinct triggered by an overheard remark reported secondhand. In wartime, the enemy was far more clearly defined.

He continued his surveillance tour, checking all possible entrances and exits. He made note of the scorecard openings above the gym and found their entrances in the boys' and girls' locker rooms.

A bank of lockers pushed against the door, obviously impossible to penetrate, sealed the door in the girls' locker room. There was no way for anyone to get at it. He tested the weight of the lockers. They were sturdy, impossible to move.

The boys' locker room had been designated as a first aid station, and he noted that a few nurses and doctors were already on duty and two ambulances were parked outside. He was satisfied that that contingency had been met. The attack of angina that Churchill had experienced during a visit to the White House a couple of years before was a worry, although it was apparently under medical control. His bad health habits, his weight, his drinking, his smoking ten cigars a day, his rich diet, his lack of a rigid exercise program, were a perpetual source of friction between Churchill, and his family and doctor. The presence of a medical team was reassuring.

He sought out the doctor in charge, introduced himself, and learned that there was a well-equipped hospital nearby.

"We are ready for all contingencies," the doctor assured him.

Thompson noted that two policemen manned the exit to the locker room—all seemed in order. He explored the area further.

The door to the scorecard area in the boys' locker room was accessible. The banks of lockers were not jammed against the wall as in the girls' locker room. The door was secured with a lock that joined a chain that passed through prongs on either side of the narrow door. Satisfied that the door was locked, he continued to inspect the area and found that all logical security needs had been met.

Then why, he wondered, did he continue to feel a premonition of danger? Perhaps he was exaggerating his own prescience.

After he had completed his inspection, he stood on the platform behind the rostrum, at the exact place Churchill would stand to make his speech. He bent his knees to approximate Churchill's five-foot-six height and surveyed the area. A keen shot could easily find its mark if an assassin were so motivated.

He closed his eyes for a moment, as if he were attempting to divine the scenario of an attempt on Churchill's life. He tried to put his own mind into that of a potential assassin's. Why here? What would be gained if such an attempt would occur in the midst of Churchill's speech? To whom would Churchill's blunt warning offer the greatest threat? The answer seemed obvious. Again he determined that, although a motive might have relevance after the fact, it had little importance to the victim before the fact.

Again, he surveyed the gymnasium. The press people were beginning to gather. A newsreel crew was assembling on the press platform. Churchill had barred television cameras, fearing that the hot lights would inhibit his speech. Some reporters were slowly moving through the entrance. Volunteer ushers were being instructed on procedures. A beat of expectation was beginning to take hold.

He was certain that the Secret Service would keep the president well guarded on the platform. But as his eyes roamed the area, he realized that the only real vantage point for a sniper assassination was in the openings near the manual scoreboard, and he was currently satisfied that they had been secured.

He left the rostrum and picked the spot where he would sit during the speech. He asked one of the Secret Service men who had been observing him to please reserve him the chair he had chosen. It afforded the most complete view of the area available.

Finally, he ended his inspection. He had gone over in his mind all dire possibilities. Still he dismissed them as inadequate.

He was sure he had missed something.

Chapter 24

Dimitrov was exhausted. He had barely slept during the past three days. He had been transported by air to and from the United States not only on Russian aircraft but also by American military transport, a profound irony.

Now he was back in Beria's office, reporting on his interview with his activated mole. Churchill would be speaking in a few hours. Dimitrov reported in depth on his conversation with Mueller.

"Are you satisfied that your man is up to the assignment?"

"Absolutely."

"What was his reaction?"

"Exhilaration, comrade. He is enormously motivated. He hates Churchill with a passion. I stoked his fires. The man is a Nazi through and through. Hate runs in his blood, exactly as I had expected. I promised him a reprieve if the job goes well. He is skeptical of that and, of course, he is correct."

"Stalin will be pleased. He would like to see our adventure succeed. In my opinion, if we miss this moment, we will not try again. It will be too late."

"Then let us pray we do not miss the moment," Dimitrov said, flattered to be in Beria's confidence.

He felt certain that for his efforts, his friend and mentor, Lavrentiy Pavlovich, would reward him handsomely, especially if the Churchill assassination was successful. He was hoping that he might be made his deputy, now that Beria was deep into the mission of securing the atomic bomb for the Soviet Union.

Although that mission was top secret, Beria had confided that the operation was proceeding better than expected and had held open the hope that one day Dimitrov would join him. This was Dimitrov's most fervent wish.

Beria had hinted that certain scientists in Great Britain and the United States were being highly cooperative and that the means to create the bomb were now in the hands of Soviet scientists.

"We will have the bomb," Beria told him. "That I can guarantee."

"I am sure we will, Lavrentiy Pavlovich."

"It will be a triumph." He paused and smiled. "Perhaps you will be at my side when we announce it to the world."

Dimitrov's heart quickened.

"Ivan Vasilyevich, you are a genius. Stalin will be quite pleased and, of course, I will mention you for high honors."

Dimitrov was elated.

"Let us hope your man is resourceful enough to carry out the assignment."

"That will be good news for the world," Dimitrov said.

At that moment, a telephone rang in Beria's office, and he picked up the phone and listened. Dimitrov saw his complexion, which a few moments ago had turned beet red, become ashen.

"Are you certain?" Beria asked sharply, listening as the voice on the other end offered what seemed like a long narration. "How could this happen?"

He listened again, nodding, his anger obvious.

"Do you think he is compromised?" he snapped.

Again Beria listened. His color changed to beet red again. Beria snarled into the phone, listening, his eyes narrowing, his thin lips pursed.

"Homer is our most important asset. How could it happen? A reporter? Not reveal his source? Are they crazy? Their free press will do them in."

But as he listened to the voice at the other end, he seemed to calm, nodding.

"He has called a meeting of the entire embassy, you say. He'll shake up the embassy. You think it will deflect suspicion. Good, good, very smart."

He listened again.

Beria nodded, calming now, apparently satisfied.

"It could be a bluff, a rumor, a reporter fishing. Perhaps MI6 is trolling; I wouldn't put it past them. You think this ploy will work? I agree. Homer is very clever. He will know when it's time to close up shop. If he says he's not compromised, we must listen to him. If he is, it could close down the others in the group."

Dimitrov felt uncomfortable. Apparently, Beria had forgotten his presence. But it was quite clear from listening to only Beria's side of the conversation that an attempt had been made to compromise an important agent in America.

Dimitrov knew, of course, that he was one important cog in the vast intelligence apparatus and that he was not privy to every secret, despite his friendship with Beria. Nor, for that matter, was Beria privy to all of his secrets. Only Dimitrov knew what Mueller looked like, and in the event he escaped, his picture and dossier would be passed to all those in pursuit of him.

Again, Beria listened, nodding, his eyes narrowing behind his pince-nez. The normal color had returned to his complexion.

"He must be informed. No contacts. Do you understand? For how long? Until I say—is that clear?"

Beria nodded and slammed the receiver back in its cradle. He remained for a long time with his back to Dimitrov, and when he turned again, he was apparently startled to see that he was still present. Quickly, Dimitrov noted, he masked his surprise. Beria got up from his desk and approached him.

"You have done well, comrade. In a few hours, the results of your efforts could be realized."

He enveloped Dimitrov in a bear hug.

"You are my trusted friend, comrade. We will go far together."

Dimitrov was ecstatic. The gesture augured well for the future.

"Thank you, Lavrentiy Pavlovich."

Outside the building, where he had left his driver and car to await his return from his meeting with Beria, he was surprised that they were not in sight. He had barely arrived when two cars came up beside him, tires squealing. A number of men rushed out and strong-armed him into one of the cars.

Instantly, he knew what had happened and why.

Beria had been subtle, but his message was now delivered: No witnesses to the plot would be left alive. Now, there would be only Beria and Stalin.

Dimitrov barely had time to contemplate the situation before he was bludgeoned to death.

Chapter 25

The lunch over, Churchill was given an upstairs bedroom for a short nap. Afterward, he dressed and joined Truman in the study, where he was engaged in quietly reading a mimeographed copy of Churchill's speech. Truman acknowledged Churchill's presence with a nod and continued reading. In a short while, they would be summoned to leave for the site of the event. Churchill lit a cigar and watched the president as he continued to read.

He weighed showing the president his scrawled marginal paragraph about the "iron curtain" reference, but decided against it. He would hear it soon enough.

Instead, he patiently awaited the outcome, well aware that his remarks might be judged inflammatory in the current political climate, especially in the United States. Truman's face revealed nothing of what he might be thinking. Churchill knew his speech was breaking new ground in postwar thinking, but he was determined to express what he believed was an accurate cautionary portrayal of the truth.

Hadn't he done the same in warning the British about Hitler's designs years before the monster had thrown down the gauntlet. Indeed, he was not modest about referring to those gadfly years in the speech. People castigated him for his views then, especially after Chamberlain came back from his conference with Hitler and told the nation he had negotiated a pact that would give the British peace in our time. Poor Neville, he thought, a sad figure who chose the wrong side of history. Peace in our time had been an illusion. He was very much afraid that such a wish in the case of the Russians was just as illusory.

"These are harsh accusations, Winston," Truman said.

Apparently, the president had finished his reading. His expression revealed that he was none too happy.

"Harsh, yes, Harry," Winston replied. "But remember these are my words, my analysis, not yours."

Truman took off his glasses, wiped them, and held them up to the light.

"Of course, I will entertain any suggestions you might have to alter the speech, Harry."

Truman nodded and rubbed his chin. Churchill knew that his offer was merely protocol. He was certain that Truman would honor his views, which he might privately agree with. Nevertheless, he was quite prepared for criticism from the president after the speech. The important thing for Churchill was to get the message out, whatever the reaction.

"I wouldn't think of asking you to change a word of it, Winston. Besides, you may be ahead of us on your theory. I'm afraid, though, the United States isn't there yet. And there is always the hope that the Russians might be more forthcoming, especially with the United Nations now a reality."

"I would like nothing better, Harry. Perhaps I have a jaundiced view of their intentions. In my opinion, these people want hegemony. They want their ideology to prevail. We of the West are seen as yesterday's dishwater, failed nations, adhering to a rotten capitalistic system. They see themselves as the future . . . " Churchill shook his head " . . . a future without freedom, a future without democracy, a future without any possibility of dissent. Note, Harry, I was quite circumspect. I did not attack their ideology per se, only their tactics in dealing with the rest of the world."

Truman nodded then smiled thinly. He looked at the text and read from it.

"Who can argue with a man who writes this? 'The Americans

and the British must never cease to proclaim in fearless tones the great principles of freedom and the rights of man, which are the joint inheritance of the English-speaking world and which through the Magna Carta, the Bill of Rights, habeas corpus, trial by jury, and the English common law find their most famous expression in the American Declaration of Independence.'"

A long silence ensued as Truman looked directly into Churchill's eyes.

"That statement forgives just about anything," Truman said. "I wish I had speech writers that could write as well as you, Winston."

"I offer my services then. I assure you, Harry, I am a better speech writer than a poker player." Truman laughed and shook his head.

"Aside from Stalin, who will be flummoxed, there'll be lots of people pissed at me, Winston, for arranging the speech. But after they hear the speech and absorb all the gloom and doom, they'll agree it does end on a note of optimism, Winston. I'll give you that."

"How do think the audience will react?"

"Respectfully, Winston. This is more like a lecture than a political stump speech, and obviously, you're not just speaking to a tiny audience in a small Midwestern town. People here are restrained. Don't expect any rousing reaction from the crowd other than appreciation and polite acceptance. But to the outside world, I think you're setting off the opening gun of a new kind of conflict. Apparently, judging from the enormous interest of the press, there is much more here than I might have expected."

"It is your presence, Harry that makes this an event."

"It could indicate my endorsement of your views, Winston," Truman said, with an air of concern.

"Granted, Harry. But it will, in my opinion, further separate your own views from Mr. Roosevelt's. But then, poor man, he did not live long enough to play the rejected suitor."

He rebuked himself for the remark. It was unseemly and indicated his edginess. He adored Franklin, despite their differences, and wished never to besmirch his memory. Truman seemed to turn reflective. Perhaps his remark was offensive to the president, who had to live under the enormous weight of Roosevelt's shadow.

"I must confess, Winston, that I still weigh my actions against his, always wondering how he would react. I regret I didn't know him as well as you. I barely got to spend time with him."

Churchill caught the resentment and realized he had foolishly opened up a raw wound and was instantly contrite.

"You need no more proof of your leadership, Harry, and I am honored by your willingness to make the introduction of this former prime minister. I would not have missed it for the world, and I pray that my words will not cause you grief."

He was, at this moment, grateful for Sarah's insistence that he accept the invitation. Little Sarah, he thought, with some emotion. Of his five children, he was more emotionally attached to his rebellious child than the others, although he loved them all equally. At odd moments of uncertainty like this, he would dwell on his family and what they meant to him.

He missed Clemmie above all, missed her wise counsel. Was he having second thoughts about his speech? Was he going too far? Was there an element of bitterness in it since he had got the boot as prime minister at a most critical time in world history? Had he the right to make such accusations? Was he upstaging his successor? Although he knew his outward appearance radiated confidence, he was subject to these occasional bouts of ambivalence. Had he stepped too far over the precipice? Was his timing right? Or was he to be characterized, as he had often been, as the bull in the china shop? There goes old Winnie again!

But then his thoughts lit upon Thompson's revelations that morning about Maclean. Indeed, if Maclean was a planted Russian agent in the most sensitive overseas post of the British foreign office, one might speculate that there were others equally concealed. Here was a blatant example of Soviet fifth column intrigue. His speech had it dead right on that score.

He must inform Attlee of this as soon as this day was over. He was certain his successor would be appalled by his bizarre accidental discovery, although the information would probably raise serious doubts among those charged with such security. Nevertheless, he knew that Clement trusted his judgment in security matters and would act accordingly in the national interest. He hoped his advice would be taken on keeping Maclean in place to monitor his activity. It would give them a window on Soviet chicanery.

At that moment, he was tempted to tell the American president what he had discovered, but he desisted. It was not his place nor in his authority. Besides, he was certain that the British side would act properly and hopefully share the information. The self-restriction was not without resentment. He was not at all happy with being out of power, despite his gentlemanly façade of acceptance.

"Well then, Harry, I hope my words won't put you in political danger."

"Hell, Winston. If you can't take the heat, get the hell out of the kitchen."

Churchill was grateful for the vote of confidence.

"'Though it be honest, it is never good to bring bad news,'" he quoted.

"*Antony and Cleopatra*," Truman said chuckling. "Don't be impressed, Winston, I've used that one often."

"I, as well. The Bard has provided me with much to plagiarize."

At that moment, one of the president's aides came into the living room and announced that they were ready to start for the gymnasium.

"Well then, Mr. President," Churchill said, "the fat is in the fire."

Thompson, who had just come back into the house, heard Churchill's closing remark. It did not put his mind at ease. He continued to be bothered by the nagging sense that he might have missed something. He moved close to Churchill.

283

An aide arrived to announce that the cars were loading for the short ride to the gymnasium. As they reached the car, Thompson requested that he be allowed to stand on the running board as the car moved toward the gymnasium. With the president of the college between Truman and Churchill and the Secret Service man sitting next to the driver, there was no room to shoehorn him into the car.

"Sorry, Sir. Can't allow that," the Secret Service man had responded to his request.

"Really, Sir, I do have my duty," Thompson protested.

"We have the matter well in hand," the Secret Service man replied, politely.

"I do insist," Thompson said.

Churchill overheard the remark.

"It's all right, Thompson. No need to hover."

Churchill had often rebuked Thompson for what he called "excessive hovering."

"With respect, Sir . . ."

"Desist, Thompson. You are making a scene."

"Sorry, Sir," Thompson said, surrendering, unable to chase his discomfort.

Chapter 26

Shaken by the thumping upbeat music of the band, Miller awoke from a troubled sleep, sweating profusely and in pain. His leg was swollen and pulsating. He reached for the bottle of aspirin in his pocket and opened the cap. His hands shook, and upending the bottle, the aspirin tablets spilled out, dropped, and scattered down the stairs. He tried to retrieve some of them, but they had dropped too far down, and the pain foreclosed on his leaving his post.

Peering out into the gymnasium, he observed the crowds, who were moving into their seats. The band played stirring Sousa marches. He tried to will himself to transcend the pain but he was having less and less results. He had begun to perspire profusely.

The rifle was beside him, the note nearby. He estimated that he had less than an hour before the arrival of Churchill and Truman.

He had adjusted Stephanie's nurse's uniform during the long wait and had removed the wig and hat and rolled down the stockings. The uniform was too tight and he had to keep the top buttons open to leave his arms free enough to hold the rifle.

Planning a quick getaway, he slipped on the wig and put the nurse's hat over it. Using the hand mirror, he put on lipstick and surveyed his handiwork, judging it barely acceptable. Although he had dry-shaved earlier in the day, it had not been very effective and his beard was returning.

Stephanie's uniform was closer fitting than he had expected, but he felt certain that in the resultant confusion, he would manage to get through the locker room to the rear entrance without discovery.

Hopefully, he would quickly get to his car and find a safe refuge until the smoke cleared and he was able to move on. Beyond that, he would have to depend on his instincts. What worried him most was the increasing problem with his leg. At some point, he knew, he would have to get treatment.

The pain was a grim reminder of Stephanie Brown. The Jewess had duped him. She deserved her fate, as did all her deceitful tribe. The memory energized him, and the stab of anger took his mind off the pain.

Picking up the rifle, he mounted it in the crook of his arm and checked the telescopic sight. He was concerned about the tremor in his hands, although mounting the rifle against the lip of the scorecard container steadied the barrel enough to take accurate aim through the telescopic sight. Timing would be crucial.

The most critical problem was to wait for enough loud applause to mask the sound of the shot and give him his chance to escape. Unfortunately, there was no way of knowing when this would occur. It stood to reason that if these Americans loved the fat pig so much, their applause was sure to be prolonged and loud. He felt certain that luck would carry him through and that, in the end, he would be preserved to carry on the war.

Except for the annoyance of the pain, he felt surprisingly calm. He had his battle plan. All he needed now was the appearance of his target and the right moment. Below, the rows and rows of seats were being filled with an eager, expectant audience. Various dignitaries were beginning to take their seats on the platform. The band continued to play rousing patriotic music.

He remarked to himself on the puny audience compared to the great rallies he had attended in Germany, where Hitler strode down the center of the vast stadium lined with a sea of raised hands and a thundering cry of thousands of voices: "Sieg Heil! Sieg Heil!" The cry reverberated in his memory. His eyes filled with tears.

At last, the waiting was over. From the entrance of the girls' locker room, he saw Truman and Churchill emerge. Churchill was wearing a resplendent scarlet robe, and Truman was turned out in a black one. They were wearing robes denoting academic distinction. Churchill was to receive an honorary doctorate, a fact conveyed by the newspaper story.

Through his telescopic lens, he could see his target: a stocky, balding man with a round, pink face, who followed Truman to the platform. The audience rose, and the band played "Rule, Britannia!" and "The Star Spangled Banner." Through the sight, he visually roamed through the faces of the dignitaries then tested his aim on the speaker's rostrum, which was festooned with a number of microphones and an arrangement of ivy for decoration.

At this moment, he could easily pull the trigger and kill Churchill and, for good measure, Truman. He resisted the temptation. For some reason—perhaps the sense of honor and obedience drummed into him by his SS training—he was determined to follow Dimitrov's order.

From his own perspective, he had come to believe in his unique destiny, that fate had chosen him to avenge his führer by killing Winston Churchill, the devil incarnate who had done the Jews' bidding, their puppet on a string. He appreciated the irony of the Russians' desire to kill Churchill for their own reasons. They had their agenda; he had his. The convergence was just another example of his extraordinary luck.

He watched the ceremonial proceedings: The crowd stood, the national anthems were played, and then came the Pledge of Allegiance. A minister rose and offered the invocation, and the audience settled down.

A dignitary in a robe, probably the president of the college, made a short speech, then another man conferred upon Churchill the honorary degree. When that was done, Truman took the rostrum and introduced Churchill; his introduction seemed oddly flat and very brief.

"Mr. Churchill and I," the president said," believe in freedom of speech. I understand Mr. Churchill might have something useful and constructive to say."

The pain made his leg twitch. Perspiration rolled down his forehead, pooling in his eyes and clouding his sight. Truman's introduction did not rouse the audience to cheers as Miller had expected. He had taken aim, his finger tightening on the trigger, but the moment passed too quickly. Churchill stood and walked the short distance to the rostrum. Churchill began to speak.

"I am glad I have come to Westminster. The name Westminster is somehow familiar. I seem to have heard it before. Indeed, it was at Westminster that I received a large part of my education."

The audience chuckled politely, but there was little applause. With rising tension, Miller waited for a burst of applause. The pain in his leg was excruciating. It was no longer a match for his mental discipline. His heartbeat accelerated. With the sleeve of the nurse's uniform, he wiped away the sweat that had dripped into his eyes causing a burning sensation.

The action caused the rifle to swerve from its target. Through the sight, he observed the dignitaries on the platform. Although most of them had their eyes on Churchill, one man, sitting just to the side of the rostrum, was paying no attention to the speaker. Like a moving searchlight, his eyes were scoping the area in a persistent arc, looking upward briefly to the spot where he was perched. Instinctively, he lurched backwards, further obscuring the barrel of his rifle from the man's prying eyes.

By pulling the rifle back, he had lost his position and had to make a painful correction, shifting his weight and losing the rifle's perch on the lip of the scoreboard, forcing him into a position that was much harder to maintain. For the moment, he lost his concentration, and when he had regained it and fully positioned himself again, Churchill was deep into his speech. The audience sat in rapt attention. Without the metal lip for support of the rifle barrel, he needed all his will power to keep his arm steady. Finally, he felt ready again, his finger on the trigger, his eye focusing through the scope as he waited for the masking burst of applause to begin. So far, the reaction of the audience had been tepid.

The speech confused his expectations. Although he paid little attention to content, the speech was measured but not rousing. The applause was sporadic but not as spirited as either he or the Russians had contemplated. He felt seriously handicapped by not being able to judge the length and loudness of the applause.

He forced himself to be alert to the content and instinctive about the moment of greatest applause. It was a gamble he had to take or abandon the mission completely. Then suddenly, he heard a beginning hesitant wave of applause.

Churchill was saying something about the atomic bomb, then the words: "It would be criminal madness to cast it adrift in this still agitated and un-united world."

The applause held briefly then quickly subsided. He had expected it to be sustained. What was going on here? Why were these people merely polite? Why were they not enthusiastic with excitement as the crowd was with Hitler? He was baffled.

Beads of sweat burned into his eyes. Pain shot up his leg. He had to move the barrel farther forward to keep the target in his sights. He was having difficulty keeping the rifle in position. His arm had begun to shake. Looking through the scope as he sighted again, he saw the man who had caught his attention before. The man looked up, his eyes squinting. In the magnification of the telescopic vision, the man was looking directly at him. Could he be seen from that distance?

Again, he was forced to retract the rifle barrel. Waiting a moment, breathing deeply, slowly expelling his breath to calm himself, he repeated the difficult maneuver of sighting on his target. In the process, he noted that the man who had been looking upward had disappeared. Churchill's voice boomed on into the silence.

What was wrong with these people? Had they no respect for this leader? Were his words so lifeless and hollow? Hitler had brought the house down at the end of every sentence.

***

Thompson's nerves were on edge. It had taken all of his powers of persuasion to get the Secret Service to allow him to take the seat he had chosen directly to the side of the rostrum. His discomfort level had risen as the group entered.

He had long trusted his sixth sense and the agitation it generated. At times, he had attributed it to supersensory perception, but only after the fact, when its danger signals had been validated. When it was not accurate, he dismissed the feeling as a kind of false positive, meaning that the danger had passed on its own, without his intervention.

As his eyes surveyed the gymnasium, something had caught his attention, but so briefly, he could not trust it as valid information. At first, he dismissed it as merely a manifestation of his paranoia. A glint, a tiny movement emanating from the opening near the scoreboard had arrested his interest, but only for a mini-second.

Yet the more he fixated on the area, the more he was troubled by what he had imagined he had seen. Earlier, he had checked the entrances to both scoreboards. One had been inaccessible. The other was locked, secured by a chain. Had he missed something?

He kept his eyes glued to the spot, concentrating his gaze, frustrated by the limitations of sight, wishing he had a pair of binoculars.

Churchill's words set off a modest round of scattered applause. At that moment, he saw the glint of what he had only imagined before. His mind would not allow further speculation. He had to act, see for himself.

Rising from his seat, he moved quickly off the platform. People looked at him with raised eyebrows. The ever-alert Secret Service people look puzzled. He offered a smile to reassure them that nothing was amiss, hoping he was suggesting a common personal emergency.

As soon as he had moved through the boys' locker room entrance, he went swiftly to the chained door behind the bank of lockers. Grabbing the chain, he pulled hard, expecting resistance.

Unanticipated, the metal loop slipped out effortlessly, the chain dropping to the floor. In a split second, the ruse became clear.

Cautiously, he opened the door and moved up the metal staircase. From the gym floor, he heard fragments of Churchill's voice . . . the words, "their most famous expression in the American Declaration of Independence."

The applause began like a rolling clap of thunder. He drew his pistol and moved up the steps.

The applause swelled. Miller aimed, his finger on the trigger. Then suddenly, a clatter behind him disrupted his concentration, and he turned to see dark movement behind him. He quickly shifted the position of the rifle to the danger coming from behind him. A man was ascending the steps. He shifted the position of the rifle and aimed it squarely at the man climbing toward him.

In the semidarkness, he could make out the man's features, recognizing him at once as the man who had been looking upward from the platform.

"Stop," he said, his voice masked by the applause.

In the shifting of his position, he had been forced to put pressure on his bad ankle. A stab of pain shot through him, but he retained enough of a grip on the rifle to continue to aim it at the intruder's midsection. Then he saw the pistol in the man's hand.

"The pistol," he hissed. "Drop it."

He heard the sharp sound of the pistol as it clattered down the stairs.

Thompson froze, forcing calmness, looking upward. He was no more than ten steps from the person and was shocked to see that it was a woman. The woman was youngish, obviously determined, not panicked, wary, her expression pained but not by anguish. She was wearing white. The barrel of the rifle, he noted, was unsteady, and the woman's balance seemed precarious. In the background, he continued to hear Churchill's resonant voice, like a clarion in the wilderness, the only sound emanating from the gym.

His mind quickly assessed the situation, the reality of the

assassin's predicament and his own, the sense of waiting, both of them, ears cocked, listening for the obliterating sound of mass applause.

Thompson stared at the woman and moved slowly upward one step, then another.

"Stop," the woman ordered. "I'll shoot."

A *man's* voice! Thompson instantly understood the plan, the escape route, the disguise, the medical team below, and the exit to the rear. This was someone who wanted to preserve his life, had planned carefully.

"Go on then," Thompson said, taking another step.

"I will," the man threatened.

"Not yet," Thompson said, rising again to the next level.

As he moved, Thompson listened to Churchill's words, calculating the moment when the applause might break out again, his muscles taut, ready to spring and, if necessary, take the bullet, forcing the man off-balance, inhibiting his positioning. That was his hope. He had read the speech and heard it rehearsed, knowing by the rise and fall of Churchill's cadence when applause was to be expected.

"Who sent you?" Thompson asked, moving upward yet another step.

"None of your fucking business, Jew."

Thompson smiled at what seemed like the obvious clue, perhaps too obvious.

Disgruntled Nazi, he thought.

"It's over, lad. You've lost."

"We've just begun," said the man with the gun, with obviously false bravado.

His accent struck Thompson as American.

Keeping his eyes on the barrel of the rifle, Thompson took another step.

"One more and it's over," the man with the gun said.

"I doubt that," Thompson said, still separated by two steps.

He searched for the man's eyes. They stared back at him with cold contempt.

Suddenly, Thompson stiffened and raised his arm.

"Heil Hitler!"

The response was immediate, a reflex. The man raised his arm, loosening his grip on the rifle. At that moment, Thompson heard the words, "a special relationship between the British Commonwealth and Empire and the United States."

Thompson heard the swell begin and moved upwards swiftly, elbow raised, as he struck out with his left hand against the barrel, the grip weakened, too late to prevent the discharge. He heard the sharp popping sound of the shot, then felt a searing pain in his upper arm. For a moment, he was thrown back but managed to stop his downward motion by grabbing the handrail, which bent under him but held his body weight.

Thinking that the bullet had found its mark in the intruder, Miller had turned quickly to point the barrel toward the man on the rostrum. There seemed a momentary restlessness in the audience, which appeared to have quickly dismissed the popping sound, the report muffled by the downward direction of the bullet into the stairwell. Churchill did not miss a beat in his speech and the audience settled. But before Miller could aim, a hand had grasped his bad leg and pulled on it. The pain seemed to explode in his head. The man grasped the barrel of the rifle and wrestled it forward. Miller struggled to retain it but could not hold his position on the stairway, and he began to topple. The rifle slipped out of his hands. Instinctively, he reached for his pistol, but strong hands had pinned his arms.

He kicked himself free with his uninjured leg taking the bulk of the pressure. The man began to fall, slipping partway down the winding staircase. Miller tried to regain his balance but his leg collapsed under him, and his downward motioned continued until the body of the man who held fast to the handrail halted it abruptly.

Miller reached out and grasped the man's throat. The man struggled, letting go of the handrail and grabbing Miller's wrists in an attempt to pry them loose from their death grip. The man grunted, gasping for air.

"Nothing will stop me. Churchill is a dead man," Miller hissed into the man's ear.

The words seemed to give the choking man renewed strength. He pushed upward, and Miller's grasp loosened. Then his leg gave way, and he began a freefall, careening downward headfirst.

It took Thompson a few moments to regain his sense of awareness. The applause had ended. He could hear Churchill's voice in the background but could not understand what he was saying. His breath came in gasps as he tried to ascertain the full extent of what had transpired. He felt shaky, obviously too old for such physical challenges. Quickly, he appraised his wound. Blood was flowing, but the bullet had merely grazed his forearm.

Below he could see the crumpled body of the assassin. The nurse's uniform was ripped open by the force of the fall, and the wig had slipped off from the man's head. A pistol lay intact in his belt. Thompson made his way down to where the body lay.

The person's face was visible, the eyes open, empty of recognition. Thompson, who had seen such scenes many times before, reached out and felt the body's neck pulse. He couldn't find it. Clearly, the man was dead. He contemplated the body, inspecting it further. It was that of a blond male, the Aryan model. He looked foolish in his nurse's uniform, torn apart now, the white stockings ripped. He noted that the man's left ankle and calf were swollen, an obvious clue to a previous trauma.

Going through the man's pockets, he found what he recognized as car keys. They were attached to a leather holder stamped with the logo of what he knew to be Chevrolet. It gave him yet another clue to what was being contemplated as an escape option.

This was a well-planned operation. The man had worked out his exit strategy with care and foreknowledge. Such planning hinted at a lone gunman. This was not a suicide mission. The man had carefully prepared for his own survival. A car, he deduced, was parked somewhere nearby, surely close to the exit from the locker room.

Leaving the body, Thompson moved up the stairs. He looked across at the other scoreboard. It was clearly unoccupied, confirming his first assessment.

Churchill was continuing to deliver his speech without incident. Occasionally, there was applause.

Thompson found the rifle, inspected it, and from his knowledge of weapons, noted that it was SS issue PPC 7.92 Mauser, which seemed another obvious clue to the origins of the perpetrator, too obvious. His eyes scanned the perch the assassin had chosen. He found the remnants of sandwiches, an empty milk bottle, and a note with its blatant words of vengeance. Overkill, he decided. Someone was working overtime to pin this on disgruntled Nazis. He put the note in his pocket.

As always, he had trusted his sixth sense, and yet again, this had saved Churchill's life. He was suddenly aware of the origin of this subliminal activity and the idea that had triggered it.

He has signed his death warrant. The words that Victoria had heard Maclean utter echoed in his mind. That was the trigger to his intuition.

As he pondered the fortunate and somewhat miraculous outcome and how much he and Churchill owed to Victoria's confession, he was aware of the dilemma he now faced.

During the war years, the Russians had always chosen the path of suppression, preventing public knowledge of such attempts, as if such a revelation would have a self-perpetuating power. At this moment in time, to reveal a Russian connection, of which he was now certain, would only further inflame an already gravely unsettling situation.

He debated informing Churchill of what he had discovered. That too, he rejected, knowing that such a revelation would greatly inhibit Churchill's future action and spur his family and friends to urge him to keep a lower profile. Their persistence was not to

295

be discounted. Worse, if he revealed this assassination attempt, Churchill's leadership might be foreclosed forever. No, he decided, the world needed this man.

While it would be impossible to validate the truth of his deduction that this was most likely a Russian operation, rather than a Nazi revenge killing, he stuck with the theory that the speech and the assassination were intricately connected. *Would this be a final attempt?* The question brought him to the outer limits of his logic. When they returned to Britain, he would go back to his grocer's business and Churchill would return to a life of creative retirement in Chartwell. It was best, he concluded, to let sleeping dogs lie. Out of respect, fear, and loyalty, he felt in his bones that his decision was correct.

His mind groped with a scenario that would remove all traces of the assassination attempt, meaning removing the body and all the so-called clues that were meant to deflect the truth and inspire the idea that was designed to pin the crime on a disgruntled Nazi determined to avenge the death of his führer and the defeat of his party. If the assassin's bullet had found its mark, he mused, the ploy might have worked, and the "blameless" Russians' most formidable enemy would be gone. The death of Trotsky came to mind. And yet, the man had reacted by rote to his "Heil Hitler" salute, a sure sign of Nazi indoctrination.

They had found the perfect assassin, a genuine Nazi who spoke English with an American accent. Clever buggers, he thought.

He inspected the wound in his arm, which had ripped a hole in his jacket and stained his shirtsleeve with blood. The pain had subsided. Bending over the body, he tore off a strip of material from the lower part of the white skirt and fashioned a makeshift bandage, which he wrapped around his upper arm.

Moving down the staircase, he stepped over the body, went through the door, and reattached the chain. Revealing his credentials to the guards at the door, he stepped outside to where the ambulances were parked near a line of cars. He went down the line searching for Chevrolets, found a number of them, and tried the keys.

On the tenth try, he found his objective. He turned over the motor; it kicked in and caught. Then he shut off the ignition again, walked to the rear of the car, and raised the trunk. It was empty, except for a spade—a miraculous find, which partially settled the matter of disposal. The issue now was to get the man's body and weapons out of the area without being observed and to find a final resting place.

Making his way back to the gymnasium, he stood near the platform and observed Churchill's speech. It was unusually long, spoken in Churchill's carefully cadenced manner and conviction. He surveyed the audience who were listening intently but not reacting with the expected enthusiasm that one might have wished for. For Churchill, the speech was more professorial than political, and he was deliberately speaking over the heads of the audience in the gymnasium to the world at large.

Finally, the speech was over. The audience rose as one and gave the former prime minister a standing ovation. Indeed, this was the moment the assassin might have chosen for the masked shot of death.

Plans called for the president's party and Churchill to spend an hour or so at a reception at McCluer's home then to head back to Jefferson City for the return trip. Thompson followed the group through the girls' locker room, which exited to the parking lot from which he had just returned. The caravan of cars began moving into the parking lot. As Churchill waited, he whispered to Thompson.

"Did I make a botch of it, Thompson?" Churchill asked.

"Not at all, sir. It was quite compelling."

"The audience seemed bored."

"Not at all, sir. *Reserved* would be a better word."

"The applause was not exactly deafening," Churchill mused, his voice tired.

"Thank God," Thompson mumbled.

Churchill, thankfully, did not hear the comment.

"I have been told the newsreel camera broke down in the middle of the first iron curtain statement."

"Attentive reporters will carry it, sir, despite it's not being in the text."

"Are there still attentive reporters? I wonder."

Thompson knew the signs of a new wave of approaching depression.

"Better to have gotten the message across in your own way. This was a fine speech, sir, one of your best. Your view needed to be articulated."

"And so it was," Churchill snickered. "And an egg was laid."

The cars moved forward and Churchill and Truman settled themselves in the backseat of theirs along with the college president.

Thompson held back deliberately, as the caravan moved on toward the president's house. Now he was faced with the dilemma of body disposal and getting back to the train before it departed.

Standing in the lengthening shadows as darkness descended, Thompson watched as the ambulances and the medical personnel moved out of the locker room with their equipment. Although his course of action was clear, there were no guarantees he could accomplish it without incident. In such matters, many things could go wrong. If observed, the embarrassment to Churchill would be profound. Few, if any, would understand Thompson's motives. The chances were that, if discovered, he would be detained and forced to reveal the facts of the attempted assassination.

It was of some small comfort to know that he did not kill this man. Of course, the evidence of the weapon and the vantage the man had chosen would prove his point that the man was bent on killing. But who? Truman? Unfortunately, the intended victim could never be validated. Only Thompson knew the truth. *Churchill is a dead man.* The words reverberated in his mind.

Would he be believed? He doubted it. Conspiracy theories would abound. If he was caught trying to dispose of this body, God

298

knows what a Pandora's box would be opened. In his heart, he both detested and feared what he must do. The risk was enormous and his justification could easily brand him as a fool. Aside from the humiliation it would engender, what he was doing was clearly illegal and subject to punishment. Perhaps, too, he might be charged with murder. The thought was chilling, and he put it out of his mind. He knew what he had to do.

He moved quickly to the Chevrolet and drove adjacent to the locker room exit, then opened the trunk. Seeing the spade again, he saw its presence as an act of providence. The method of burial had been chosen for him.

The crowds were dispersing rapidly and he could see the line of lighted headlights as people headed away from the college. The police were no longer guarding the exits; apparently, they shifted their presence to the front of the gymnasium to supervise the departure of the crowds.

He moved through the exit door and found that it could be left open securely with a hook attachment and a metal eye drilled into the floor. The locker room was deserted now. He found the light switch and plunged the room into darkness. Moving inside, he looked into the gymnasium. People had begun folding and carting away the metal chairs. The cleanup work had begun in earnest. The photographers and reporters had moved out in buses.

Closing the door that led to the gymnasium, he quickly ducked behind the bank of lockers, pushed opened the door that led to the metal stairs, and dragged out the man's body, setting it up at the edge of the lockers. Peeking out behind the bank of lockers, he noted that the area continued to be deserted.

Quickly he kneeled and, using the fireman's technique, lifted the body and draped it over his shoulder, securing it by holding on to its wrist. His arm wound pained him and complicated the chore. He staggered with the effort for a moment but managed to raise himself upright. Suddenly, he was startled by the sound of metal crashing to the floor. It was a Luger pistol. He'd have to make another trip.

Again he looked around the bank of lockers. Suddenly, the door to the gymnasium opened and a man looked inside.

"Somebody shut the lights," the man said.

"Never mind," another man said, and the door closed once again.

Carrying his burden, sweating profusely, Thompson moved through the exit door and threw his burden into the trunk and closed the lid. It took him a moment to catch his breath, and then he opened the car door on the driver's side, abruptly closing it again when he remembered the Luger on the locker room floor and the assassin's Mauser still in the stairwell.

Rushing back into the locker room, he picked up the Luger, put it in his belt, and then he entered the stairwell once again and moved up the stairs looking for the rifle. He found it quickly where it had fallen, removed the ammunition clip, and hunted around for the spent bullet and shell. He found the shell but could not find where the bullet that had grazed him had lodged. Finally, he gave up, calculating that even if it were found one day, people would not connect it to the event.

Then he remembered that he had dropped his Wembley, which was also difficult to find. He had to move up the stairs to where he had been when he had dropped the weapon, and then moved down again. Still he could not find it.

He decided to remove the rifle first and come back again. The locker room was still in darkness, and he was able to get the rifle through the exit and into the backseat of the car. Then he returned to the stairwell to look for his Wembley. As he moved from stair to stair, he heard movement in the locker room.

Although disconcerting, he continued to search for the weapon, finding it finally and returning it to his holster. When he came out the door to the stairwell, the locker room was a blaze of light and people were using it once again as a smoking lounge. With an air of nonchalance, he moved to the exit, which someone had closed.

"Speech was a little dry," someone said, a man's voice.

"Said a lot, though," an older man answered. "Can't trust those Russkies? What do you think, bud?"

Thompson turned. The question was obviously addressed to him.

"Good show," Thompson said, facing the men.

"He's a Brit," one of the men said.

"Figures."

Thompson smiled and went out the exit door, got into the car, and began to drive out of the lot. His heart continued to pound, and sweat was pouring out of his body, dampening his clothes.

At the exit to the parking area, a policeman suddenly moved into view, waving a searchlight. Thompson braked the car, fearful that the policeman would ask for credentials to prove the ownership of the car.

"Where are you going, buddy?" the policeman asked politely.

Thompson flashed his identification as a member of the official party.

"I work for Mr. Churchill. Just had to pick up some material left by him inside the gymnasium."

The policeman looked at the credentials and flashed the searchlight into Thompson's face. If the man had been thorough, Thompson thought, using his policeman's logic and training, he would have asked far more questions. Thankfully, he missed seeing the rifle that Thompson had thrown on the backseat.

Easy now, he admonished himself, realizing that the effort had tired him and he was beginning to make mistakes. It occurred to him suddenly that this mission required the incompetence of others to succeed.

The policeman waved him ahead.

He now had to work by instinct alone. He calculated that the reception at the president's home would last no more than an hour, and the official party would make the twenty-mile drive to Jefferson City in about forty minutes. He estimated perhaps another

301

half hour or so before the train left the station. This left him little time to dispose of the body. Thankfully, the gas tank was almost full. The assassin had obviously planned well on that score.

He managed to follow the signs that pointed in the direction of Jefferson City. As he drove into increasingly rural areas, he searched for some side roads that might lead him into some deserted spot that could give him the cover he needed to accomplish his purpose.

After twenty minutes of driving, he took a chance and moved into a dirt road that ran parallel to a creek. He braked the car at a place that looked deserted enough for his purposes, took out the spade, and began testing the soil for the softest spot he could find. Then he began to dig. The pain in his arm was intense and his back was beginning to hurt. Using all the strength and endurance he could muster, he managed to dig a hole deep enough to serve as the final resting place for the body in the trunk.

He stripped the body, put it into the hole, and filled it up, patting it down carefully. The whole aspect of what he was doing disgusted him. As if to assuage these feelings, he said a prayer over the body, a catechism he remembered from boyhood, ending with "Forgive me, Father." For some reason, he also remembered the last words of Sydney Carton from *A Tale of Two Cities* and recited them aloud.

"It is a far, far better thing that I do than I have ever done; it is a far, far better rest that I go to than I have ever known."

Not to know the true identity of the body struck him as un-Christian. With a heavy heart, he got into the car, drove another few miles, found another deserted spot, and again dug a hole in which he threw the weapons, the clothing he had stripped from the assassin, and other items he had found in the car, including what looked like a packet filled with U.S. dollars. *Blood money,* he thought as he threw the packet in with the rest and covered everything up.

By the time he was finished, he was exhausted. His arm was killing him, and his back pain had gotten worse. For the first time in years, he started to sob.

Had he done the right thing? Would the body remain hidden for years? In his early police training, he had been told that the earth held many secrets and bodies were often discovered during construction projects, many of them impossible to identify. He wondered if forensic science in the future would improve the process and make it possible for identification in all circumstances. He tried to wish it from his mind but knew he would have to develop some mental strategy to cope with the memory. His own death would take care of that, he thought bitterly.

Checking the time, he knew he was cutting it close. According to his calculations, the train would be leaving in less than a half hour. Reaching Jefferson City, he found an open pharmacy, bought bandages and antiseptic, and received directions to the station. It was impossible now to abandon the car anyplace but close to the station. At this point, he was too exhausted to speculate what would happen when the stray car was discovered. He parked the car within a short walk from the station, removed the spade and put it in a nearby garbage bin, and then walked to the station.

Thankfully, the train was still there, but he could tell by the steam rising from the engine that it would embark shortly. He nodded to the Secret Service men posted at the entrance to the car that contained Churchill's suite and his adjoining compartment. He stripped, attended to his wound, which although painful did not look serious. Then he showered, slipped into clean slacks, shirt, and sweater, and knocked on Churchill's compartment door just as the train began to clang forward out of the station.

He found Churchill had changed into his blue siren suit, preparing to leave.

"Thompson," Churchill remarked, taking a lit cigar out of his mouth. "I thought you had been hijacked."

"I was in one of the last cars in the caravan, sir. I was certain you were secure. The Secret Service has provided excellent security."

Churchill inspected him but showed no sign of exceptional curiosity, for which he was thankful.

303

"I'm off for an informal supper and another round of poker with Truman and the boys," he said. "I am geared for revenge, although I believe Truman and his minions will not be so merciful this time around."

"I gather their reaction was less than enthusiastic."

"I'm afraid so, Thompson. I expect brutality to reign. The press has been hounding Truman for his comments. So far he has been tight-lipped, but he did remark to me that he would try to make it right with Uncle Joe, a futile exercise I'm afraid. But then, I had no illusions that I would come out of this unscathed."

Churchill smiled and took a deep puff on his cigar.

"But you have, sir," Thompson said.

Despite his exhaustion, he enjoyed the irony.

"Not quite, Thompson," Churchill said, moving toward the door. "The poker gallows await."

Chapter 27

Maclean chuckled as he read the story Benson had written in the *Washington Star.* Hardly a scoop, it hadn't even made it into the larger story above the fold. But then, as news stories went, it was already three days after the event—meaning, old news.

He read it over again and then aloud to himself:

"It has been rumored that the Russians had somehow obtained a copy of Churchill's speech in advance. This came as a surprise to most reporters following the story, who had not received the speech until a short time before Mr. Churchill delivered it. Officials at the British embassy, where Mr. Churchill had been staying prior to leaving for Fulton, were somewhat surprised.

The incident did prompt First Secretary Donald Maclean to take the matter seriously and call together senior staff to find ways to tighten security procedures, indicating that the relationship between Russia, Britain, and America had taken on a new dimension."

"'This is Washington, a city of busybodies,' a British embassy source commented. 'But considering that the speech was being delivered by the eloquent former Prime Minister, the Russians were wise to find a way to secure it in advance and prepare themselves for the consequences, if any.'"

The aftermath was now in play, and from Maclean's perspective, it was delicious. He looked at the mimeographed sheet, which he had had the information people at the embassy prepare. It contained many of the choice comments in the press, almost all negative.

Among the postings were what Maclean considered "juicy

little facts," which he had encouraged to be included. Items such as the information that sometime after the speech, Truman had telegraphed Premier Stalin and invited him to come to America and deliver his side of the story to the same forum at Westminster College.

Truman had even offered the battleship *Missouri* to bring him to America. Maclean and Boris had had a good laugh over that one. Of course, Stalin had refused, and he was quoted in *Pravda* as saying "the speech was a pack of lies."

In New York, the widow of President Franklin Roosevelt denounced Churchill as a "warmonger" and in the nation's capital, three senators, including Claude Pepper, termed the Fulton address "shocking."

The *New York Times* had questioned Churchill's "dangerous lack of judgment." In Britain, the *London Times* criticized Churchill's harsh description of the Communist governments, saying "the Western democracies have much to learn from Communism in the working of political institutions and the establishment of individual rights and in the development of economic and social planning."

Pearl Buck, one of America's most important writers and a Nobel laureate, told an audience that the world was "nearer war tonight than we were last night."

To add insult to injury for Churchill, the "iron curtain" reference was not in the advanced text and many newspapers did not carry it. Nevertheless, an alert reporter from *The Washington Post* had caught the reference, and it became a sidebar to the story. The most dramatic mention was not even preserved for posterity as a filmed image. The only newsreel camera failed at exactly the moment it was first mentioned.

Maclean reveled in the criticism and mishaps. Although there was some praise for the speech in very conservative circles, the overwhelming opinion of it was negative. A dark thought intruded: If his speculation had been correct and Churchill was harmed in any way, the results for his side would be decidedly negative. The speech had inflicted far more harm on Churchill's position than on Maclean's own.

The outcome was surely a debacle for the former prime minister. The Allies were weary of war and the timing and content of Churchill's speech was, in his opinion, merely an exercise in pique, ego, and narcissism.

He kept a particularly amusing cartoon in his top desk drawer. Opening it, he looked at it again. It featured a tired "John Q. Public" sitting on a curbstone in Fulton amid the swirl of abandoned decorations and pennants. Underneath was the caption borrowed from a Kipling poem: "The Captains and the Kings departed."

He was relieved. Everything was going swimmingly. Before the speech, Maclean had been quite worried that the Russians might overreact to Churchill's potential remarks and take drastic action. In his meeting with Boris, he had urged him to press his superiors to stay calm. Churchill was Churchill, a born gadfly, a Cassandra with a cigar, out of office and powerless, which did not mean they could cavalierly shirk off his words of warning, but any punitive action against him would be counterproductive at this juncture.

True, he was able to cut a wide swath with his raging about so-called Russian duplicity and danger. Giving the devil his due, he had the ability to gain worldwide attention for his views. Unfortunately, he was on the wrong side of history.

Iron curtain, Maclean mused. *He must have put that in as an afterthought. Great image, but then Churchill was the consummate wordsmith.*

He was ready to put aside the incident of the so-called security breach. The source of Benson's inquiry about the speech would remain a mystery. Perhaps, as Boris had suggested, he was merely fishing, using the age-old journalist's ploy. Thankfully, the issue had blown over. Another potential disaster had been diverted. Nothing was perfect in this business. It would not be amiss to speculate that others might have their eyes and ears trained on the Russians. Perhaps their communications systems were not totally secure. For Maclean, the important issue was to deflect any suspicion from him. Indeed, he decided, his handling of this situation was brilliant and well worth a self-congratulatory pat on the back.

Churchill had finally left the embassy—much to the relief of the ambassador—and was heading up to Hyde Park to pay his respects at the grave of Franklin Roosevelt. He had not attended Roosevelt's funeral, an act that Maclean had suggested to the Russians was an indication that the wartime friendship between Roosevelt and Churchill had hit rocky times.

Victoria had returned to work after a few days' rest. She was oddly muted, perhaps still tired, which might have explained her standoffish attitude. Nevertheless, he respected her feelings and desisted from any overt sexual moves. He could not imagine her as the source of Benson's alleged information.

"I missed you awfully, darling," he told her.

"And I missed you."

They had embraced and he did detect an odd coldness. He did not pry. By the time her first day back was over, he knew she was privy to the various security stirrings that he had set in motion. Secretaries reveled in gossip. At the end of the day, they sat together in his office, drinks in hand.

"It was a fascinating experience," she told him. "One I will treasure all of my life. Mr. Churchill is a most amazing man. His speech was beautifully delivered."

"I thought so, too, darling."

He paused and smiled.

"Apparently, the Russians had an advance copy, not exactly worth a big security brouhaha, but worrisome."

"Yes, I heard the secretaries talking," Victoria acknowledged, turning her eyes away.

"In an odd way, I'm glad they did. What Churchill had to say did not come as a surprise to them. In my opinion, if there was a security breach, it was at their end, not ours. What I mean to say is," Maclean continued, "I wouldn't call their getting the speech much of a security breach. I'd say it was an excellent idea, a diplomatic courtesy. The problem for me was they quite obviously couldn't be trusted."

Observing her, he noted a sudden flush on her cheeks, and she broke out in a broad smile.

"Wonderful," she blurted.

Her comment confused him.

"Wonderful?"

She was flustered.

"What I meant was that his speech was very courageous. Considering it was against the tide . . . you know what I mean."

She put her drink down and moved closer to him. Her sense of psychic distance seemed to be disappearing.

"I think I do," he replied.

"What I mean, darling, is that his speech took great courage, considering the present climate."

"Yes, it did."

"Do you think he was right? About the Russians, the iron curtain, the fifth column?"

He was baffled. She had not shown much keen interest in such matters before her Churchill assignment.

"He was indeed, despite the negative reaction," he said gravely. "But in one way, it was salutary."

"I don't understand."

"The assignment has inspired your interest in world affairs."

She nodded and laughed.

"It is not my principal interest, my darling."

She moved closer, and he enveloped his arms around her.

"I did miss this," he said, kissing her hard on the mouth and cupping her breasts.

"I am so happy," she whispered.

He noted that her eyes welled up.

Chapter 28

Wearing a paint-stained blue siren suit, a cigar stuck in his mouth, Churchill put a layer of cement on a brick he was holding, set it carefully on the garden wall he was building at Chartwell, and pressured it skillfully into place. He was so absorbed in his work that he did not see Thompson come up the path until he was almost in front of him on the other side of the wall.

"Well, sir, I'm afraid I must be off. Just came to say good-bye," Thompson said. "I've paid my respects to Mrs. Churchill."

Churchill continued his work. His cigar, which he held in his mouth, had gone out and Thompson leaned over to light it.

"Whatever will I do without you, Thompson?" Churchill said, sucking in the smoke.

"I'm sure you'll find someone else to light your cigars, Prime Minister. It's time I stayed put in my other life."

Churchill took another deep puff, and after assuring himself that the brick was plumb, straightened and contemplated his old comrade. Their eyes met and held. It was, Churchill knew, an emotional moment for both of them. Over the years, they had bonded and enjoyed an intimacy that few men ever experienced.

"La commedia è finita" Churchill said, "Now why did I quote that language?"

"Because it is quite true. For me, the play is over. I must say, Sir, I enjoyed every minute of our association."

"And here I am, Thompson, still vertical. I suppose that can be attributed to your service as my keeper and shadow."

"And hoverer, sir."

"I must say, Thompson, that with you around, my intrepid hovering shadow, I felt always safe from harm. Our recent American foray, I owe to Clementine, who harbored visions of the Wild West and dangers from vicious outlaws and hostile Indians. Thankfully, we have come through the trek all wagons intact and all personnel accounted for."

"We can be thankful for that, sir."

Thompson paused and turned his eyes away. Churchill knew Thompson's usually repressed emotions had risen to the surface. He was having similar difficulties. His eyes welled with tears. Then both men seemed to recover simultaneously. Churchill cleared his throat.

"I wonder, Thompson, if the trip was worth the candle."

"You said what had to be said, sir. They will understand soon enough."

"Do you think so, Thompson? I am being pilloried by friends and enemies alike." He lowered his voice. "Mr. Attlee, I'm afraid received a bit of a shock preview of what I was trying to say. I informed him about Maclean. I must confess that I enjoyed his reaction."

"Did he have his doubts about the information?"

"I must tell you, Thompson," Churchill chuckled. "He did not. And it didn't surprise me. He has come to believe that the upper classes are the ruination of our country, forgetting that despite his Labor credentials he is one of its members."

"Do you think he will shut Maclean down?"

Churchill smiled.

"He did understand the benefits of keeping the man in our sights for the time being. I did not have to suggest it. He may be dull, but he is not stupid."

"So Maclean will stay at his post?"

"I believe so. As long as he is useful to us."

"I'm sure Miss Stewart will be relieved."

"Ah, yes, Thompson," Churchill remembered. "I did receive

a letter from her a few days ago. She sends her regards to you, Thompson, and calls her experience one of the most memorable in her life. Poor child. She wrote she had not a shadow of doubt about the first secretary's devotion to Great Britain."

"Poor child, indeed," Thompson said. "I'm afraid she will one day learn the truth the hard way."

"They will all have to learn the truth the hard way."

Churchill reached across the garden wall and grasped Thompson's hand. The wall separating them foreclosed on the possibility of an embrace, which would have been out of character for both men.

"Good-bye, old friend," Churchill said, eyes moistening, his voice cracking.

Thompson nodded and swallowed hard.

"Do you remember, sir, what President Roosevelt said to me when you introduced me to him at your first meeting at sea?"

"I do."

"With respect, sir, it bears repeating at this moment. I shall always cherish the words until the end of my days. He said: 'Take care of the prime minister. He is the greatest man in the world.'"

Churchill's eyes could not contain his tears, which trickled down his pink cheeks. For the first time in his life, he felt unable to find words. All he could do was nod.

"God keep you . . . " Thompson paused and cleared his throat, ". . . Prime Minister."

Through blurred vision, Churchill watched him turn and disappear down the garden path.

Epilogue

Winston Churchill became Prime Minister again in 1951. He served until 1955. He won the Nobel Prize for Literature, accepted the Order of the Garter, and became an Honorary Citizen of the United States. He died on January 24, 1965, at the age of ninety-one, the same day and time as his father, as he had predicted.

Lavrentiy Pavlovich Beria was arrested while Khrushchev was premier of the Soviet Union. He was executed in December 1953 for crimes against the state.

Josef Stalin, who has been blamed for the death of millions, died on March 5, 1953, exactly seven years after the date of the Fulton speech. He is buried in the Kremlin.

Donald Maclean escaped to the Soviet Union from London in the spring of 1955. His wife, Melinda, and their children joined him two years later. He learned Russian, worked in a Soviet foreign policy think tank, and died in Moscow at the age of sixty-nine. His escape was shrouded in mystery, and in the opinion of many, could not have happened without the tacit consent of MI6.

Harry Truman died in his hometown of Independence, Missouri, in 1972 at the age of eighty-eight. Although he left office as an unpopular president, he is now one of the most revered presidents of the twentieth century.

W. H. Thompson died in the seventies. He wrote a book entitled *I Was Churchill's Shadow*. The last words in his book stated: "I acknowledge Winston Spencer Churchill as the greatest man I have ever known, and no words can express adequately my pride to have been some service to him."

The so-called Iron Curtain Speech grew in influence as time went by. It became the clarion call of the Western democracies and made it easier for the Truman Doctrine to succeed and save Europe from further Communist incursions.

Victoria Stewart returned to England, founded a secretarial school in Hampshire, using the fact that she had taken dictation from Winston Churchill as her principal marketing tool. She married an accountant, had two children, and died in 2001.

Franz Mueller's body was never found, although in 2002, a construction crew building a shopping mall near Jefferson City uncovered a World War II German PPC 7.92 Mauser and a Luger pistol of the same vintage. Some small traces of clothing and paper currency were found nearby. The currency was too damaged to determine the denominations and, therefore, was presumed counterfeit.

Stephanie Brown's disappearance remained on the books of the D.C. Metropolitan Police Department for ten years. Her parents offered a reward of $10,000 for information about her whereabouts, later raising it to $25,000. Both parents died in the eighties, broken-hearted and still believing that their daughter was alive. The area in which she was buried became a national park. She was never found.

The Soviet Union collapsed in 1992.

* * * *

About the Authors

Warren Adler: Acclaimed author and playwright Warren Adler is best known for *The War of the Roses*, his masterpiece fictionalization of a macabre divorce adapted first, into the Golden Globe and BAFTA nominated blockbuster hit film starring Danny DeVito, Michael Douglas and Kathleen Turner, and later into the staged version based on the original novel.

Shortly following the success of *The War of the Roses*, Adler fueled an unprecedented bidding war in a Hollywood commission for his then unpublished novel *Private Lies*. He went on to option or sell several of his works to film and television including his Fiona Fitzgerald mystery series, *Random Hearts* starring Harrison Ford and Kristin Scott Thomas, *Trans-Siberian Express, Funny Boys, Madeline's Miracles* and *The Sunset Gang*, which was adapted into a trilogy for PBS' American Playhouse Series starring Uta Hagen, Harold Gould, Jerry Stiller and Doris Roberts who earned an Emmy nomination for her role in the "Best Supporting Actress in a Mini Series" category.

An **essayist, short-story writer and poet,** Adler's works have been translated into 25 languages, including his staged version of *The War of the Roses*, which has opened to spectacular reviews worldwide. Adler has taught novel writing seminars at New York University, and has lectured on creative writing, motion picture adaptation and the future of e-books. He lives with his wife Sunny, a former magazine editor, in Manhattan.

James C. Humes: Pulitzer Prize nominated author of *Churchill: Speaker of the Century,* James C. Humes is a former presidential

speechwriter who worked for Ronald Reagan, George H.W. Bush, Gerald Ford and Dwight Eisenhower. Before his speechwriting career, he represented the U.S. State Department in lectures on American government all over the world. He has served as a communications advisor to major U.S. corporations, including IBM and DuPont. He is the author of more than 30 books, and one of the few Americans alive today to have met Churchill who told him at age 18, "Young man, study history. In history lie all the secrets of statecraft." A widely sought speaker across the country, Humes lives in Pueblo, Colorado and is Visiting Historian at the University of Colorado at Colorado Springs.

More Political Thrillers from Warren Adler: For complete catalogue including novels, plays and short stories visit: www.warrenadler.com

 Join the discussion about this book on **Goodreads**

Connect with Warren Adler on:

Facebook – www.facebook.com/warrenadler
Twitter – www.twitter.com/warrenadler

CPSIA information can be obtained
at www.ICGtesting.com
Printed in the USA
FSOW02n1157260517
34707FS